ROARING

PRODIGIUM ACADEMY BOOK TWO

KATIE MAY

EXPRESSO PUBLISHING, LLC

To the hot Amazon driver who witnessed me licking chocolate from my phone like a lollipop and didn't run screaming. You the real MVP

CONTENTS

FOREWORD

This is a paranormal academy reverse harem romance and is not suitable for anyone under the age of 18. There is strong language and sexual situations. Like, a lot of sex. Do not read this book if that offends you. Seriously, don't. Stop right here. You have been warned.

Vanessa - Vin's twin sister and a fellow hunter. Violet declares her as her designated best friend soon after meeting.

Cynthia - Violet's roommate who is a banshee and the Woman in White. Their friendship falls apart when Violet accuses her of murder.

Mikey - Merlin's son who created sex dolls of Violet. He is killed by Diedre.

Headmaster Lupine - the previous headmaster who blamed Violet for the murders. Now dead.

Diedre Stevens - a vampire teacher at the school who committed the murders in order to frame Violet. Revealed herself to be Violet's "sister." Now dead.

Dracula - Violet's father and the leader of the vampires. He is the most hated and feared monster in the entire world.

Previously on Prodigium Academy…

Violet Dracula, the daughter of Vladimir Dracula, is sent to Prodigium Academy to learn how to be a perfect monster. She's extremely clumsy and kind-hearted, all of the qualities that others look down upon in the monster world.

While at the academy, she meets Frankie, the son of Frankenstein, who is a mad scientist with a lab beneath the school.

Mason, the son of Medusa and a known drug-addict.

Jack and Hux, two men forced to share the same body and the son (sons?) of Jekyll and Hyde.

Finally, Vin, a Van Helsing and her sworn enemy.

She also develops an attraction to Dimitri Gray, son of Dorian Gray, who is a teacher at the academy and a trained assassin.

When dead bodies show up on campus, each with bite marks on their necks, the vampires are the prime suspects in their murders, Violet especially.

During a trip to detention, Violet meets Cal and Barret, who are the Cupid and Boogeyman, respectively. Both men

CHAPTER 1

VIOLET

Have you ever been kicked in the dick before?

Well, if you answered no…same.

I've cut off dicks on more than one occasion, but I can't say I've ever been kicked there before. Granted, I don't *have* a penis, but I imagine it'd be pretty damn painful. Movies show men keeling over in pain, anguished gasps escaping their lips. Is it the equivalent of a boob punch? I *have* been punched there before…and then the girl died choking on cock. Not my cock—we've already established that I don't have one—but the cock of Cupid.

Long story.

Discovering that my dad may not be my dad and that I might not even be a vampire is my boob-punch-slash-dick-kick.

Dracula isn't the stereotypical, warm and fuzzy type of parent. He's more likely to stab me in the chest and snap my neck than give me a hug. He's a monster through and through. But he's *my* monster. He's the man who raised me, cared for me in a way only he's capable of. The thought that he may have lied to me my entire life is shocking, unnerving, but not at all surprising. It's sort of like I've been treading water for hours on end and a particularly ferocious wave pulls me under. I'm not expecting or wanting death, but I can't say I'm too surprised.

I glare at the laminated menu, thousands of thoughts clamoring for attention in my mind. It becomes increasingly difficult for me to pick and focus on only one.

The restaurant Dad has chosen for dinner is an elegant steakhouse a few miles from the Academy. Flames from hanging chandeliers illuminate the room in a soft, golden glow. Each of the waitstaff is bedecked in black pressed pants and button-up shirts.

"Are we still waiting for one more?" a soft voice inquires, and I lift my head to gaze at the waiter. He's a handsome man with dark skin and even darker hair, plush red lips, and broad shoulders. The uniform sticks to his broad chest, accentuating his lean muscles. Two black earrings are plugged in his right ear, and tattoos line his muscular arms where the sleeves are pushed up.

"He should be here," I insist...for the fifteenth time in the last two hours. Dad is running...errr...a little late.

The handsome waiter—Morgan, his name tag reads— smiles sympathetically.

"Another round of bread?" He nods to the empty plate in front of me.

"And a little more of the good stuff..." I wiggle my empty wine glass. "And I don't mean cum. I swore off cock on Halloween."

Morgan sputters, cheeks tinting pink, but nods quickly and takes my glass and empty bread bowl. I can't technically get drunk. The perks of being a vampire, I suppose. Well... not a vampire.

I don't know if I believe my sadistic, murderous teacher and half-sister. Diedre Stevens attempted to kill me in a futile attempt to create discord between the vampires and other species. Honestly? It worked. Most of the monsters at the Academy haven't been able to make eye contact with me, the disdain thickening the air like syrup. Two vampires have already transferred schools due to the bullying and murder attempts.

It's a real problem, guys.

It's been a week since Halloween, and things have been… weird. I've been able to avoid my new guy friends for now, but I know my luck is going to run out. Hux, for one, is getting agitated, and Jack is anxious. Mason is confused, and I'm pretty sure Vin is annoyed.

And Frankie…

I brush his name beneath the proverbial rug, knowing that I don't have the mental or emotional strength to think about him and his confession. Nope. Not today, Satan.

Today, I'm going to enjoy a nice dinner with my invisible, absentee father.

Winning.

Morgan returns with my now full wine glass and another loaf of bread. At first, he was surprised by how much I could eat. Namely, three loaves. I think by this point, he has just accepted me, flaws and all.

As I trace the rim of my cup, I ask absently, "Why do men suck?"

"Excuse me?" He lifts a pierced brow.

"And not the normal type of suck. Honestly, you don't even understand the comedic timing of that sentence. I can assure you, it's funny. But yeah, men suck. Dads suck. Guy friends suck. Boyfriends suck. And I, unfortunately, am unable to suck. I'm talking about cocks."

With a heavy exhale, I run the pad of my thumb over the nameplate stitched to the wall.

Violet Dracula.

The second one—the one that had previously read Cynthia Clit—is now gone. My old roommate, also known as the Woman in White, left after we got into a fight. Long story short—I accused her of buying my sex doll and, in a round-about way, of murdering our fellow classmates.

Not my finest moment.

She retaliated by hanging my sex doll at the school's Halloween party like a piñata and allowing students to whack it with baseball bats.

Not her finest moment.

Honestly, despite our tenuous relationship, I hadn't actually expected her to *leave*.

It…stings, rotting away what little cheer remains like a caustic acid. I can feel it like a physical ache, like a wound that is only just beginning to fester.

I don't like this feeling. At all. I don't like the pressure on my chest that restricts my blood flow. I don't like the loneliness that presses in on all sides of me, like a steadily shrinking vise. It feels as if I'm being displayed in a glass case. I can see the world, see the people, but I'm unable to interact with any of it. Instead, I'm gawked and laughed at like some sort of fucked up novelty show.

See Dracula's infamous daughter. A vampire who isn't a vampire.

A monster who isn't a monster.

My hands clench into and out of fists as I work to control my ragged breathing. I don't like the turbulent directions my thoughts have headed down. At all.

I'm a monster, dammit! I need to start acting like one.

With shaky hands, I push open the already unlocked door —Dracula failed to procure me a key on my first day of school. All I want to do is collapse on my uncomfortable bed and sleep the day away. Forget the last few weeks.

Diedre's words.

Dracula's no-show.

Frankie's confession.

Lock all of it in a cement box and bury it thousands of miles below the earth. No amount of digging could uncover all of its secrets.

I've just tossed my bag onto my nightstand when I spot the silhouette on my bed.

"Mother shitter!" I scream, immediately throwing a right hook at the intruder's face. I miss—of course—and accidentally trip over the edge of the faded, red rug in the center of the room. Before I can face-plant, a muscular arm wraps around my waist and pulls me upright.

"Careful, my precious treasure," a rough voice cautions. I detect a hint of an orgasm-inducing British accent, sending fireworks shooting through my bloodstream.

"Hux," I breathe as I spin towards my savior with a soft smile curling up the corners of my lips. For a brief moment, I forget my promise to swear off cock.

Hux is…

Well, he's Hux.

His elegant, masculine face is framed by thick black hair pushed behind his ears. With his strong nose, chiseled jawline, and tan skin, he embodies an effortless, primal type of beauty. The type of beauty that could ask you out for dinner one day and gut you the next. A wicked scar curves down his cheek, somehow accentuating his harsh features even more.

"You've been ignoring me, my precious treasure," he continues, his voice and words curling around me like a bittersweet perfume. Fuck, I've missed him. Both of hims. Or…them. Hux takes an intimidating step closer until I'm forced to tilt my head back to maintain eye contact. "I don't like being ignored."

"And I don't like people attempting to kill me twice in one day." I shrug my shoulders nonchalantly, ignoring the way his face tightens dangerously. "But we don't always get what we want, do we?"

With a vigorous head shake—as if I could somehow clear my cluttered thoughts—I push away from Hux and turn towards my wardrobe. At one point, I had hidden a body in here. My body. Well, my sex doll's body.

Long story.

"I got you a gift," Hux states, shoving his hand in his back pocket. With an elaborate flourish, he holds out a crushed, melted chocolate bar.

Um...?

"You don't have to fight this battle alone," he vows seriously, lowering his head and extending his hand like some sort of offering.

"This battle?"

What the ever loving fuck is he going on about?

"The Great Period," he continues solemnly. "Chocolate is the elixir, yes?" When I gape at him wordlessly, his brows scrunch together. "I can give you a body, if you'd like. I heard that bloodshed is also necessary to appease the monster that emerges on your Great Period." He bows his head once more subserviently.

"You'll get a body for me?" I ask breathlessly. Emotions assault me from all directions, smothering me under their intense weight.

"Anything for you, my precious treasure," he vows.

"A live one?"

"Of course."

I have to take bug spray to the surge of butterflies that flutter around in my stomach. Fucking feelings.

And fucking perfect men who offer to collect me still-breathing bodies.

"My brother would like to speak to you," Hux continues, and I detect a hint of annoyance in his tone. I, on the other hand, smile eagerly and bounce from foot to foot.

Fucking hell, it's been less than a week, and I'm already rethinking the whole "cocks-be-gone" promise I made myself.

Hux's face twists and distorts, a grimace of pain tightening his features, before his brows smooth over and a blush darkens his skin. Quickly, he pushes his hair forward until it's obscuring both his cheeks. And his scar.

Fumbling in his pocket, he procures a pair of glasses and slides them up his nose with the pad of his middle finger.

"Violet," Jack says, a smile illuminating his handsome face.

I will remain mad.

I will remain mad.

I will remain—

"I missed you so fucking much!" I squeal, practically throwing myself at him. I wrap my arms around his neck, reveling in the feel of his silky black hair beneath my fingers. He stiffens instinctually underneath me before gradually allowing his taut body to relax.

Jack? He's a damn good hugger. My body molds against his, his hard angles contrasting with my soft curves. The feel of him momentarily soothes my ravaged emotions.

"I thought you were mad at us," Jack whispers, pulling me away so he can stare intently into my eyes. Those butterflies I previously mentioned? They return with a vengeance. I can feel their wings flapping erratically each second I remain in this timid man's presence.

It's not logical that two entirely different men could make me feel so much, so quickly. I've known them for less than two months, and already, I can't remember my life before them. They have embedded themselves so deeply in my soul that I'm beginning to think they're a part of my genetic makeup.

As a descendant of Jekyll and Hyde, Jack and Hux have the same quirk as their father—fathers? Both brothers inhabit the same body, but only one is allowed to emerge at a time. I have no idea what happens to the other. Does he simply disappear, reverted to a splotch of darkness in the deepest abyss of their mind? Or is he a passenger in a car he can't get out of? Do they have one mind, or two? One heart, or two?

But it would be rude as fuck to ask any of those questions.

"So, why were you mad at us?" Jack questions, and I note a flash of vulnerability and pain before he quickly tries to mask it.

I blow out a breath, detangling myself from his arms so I can flop on the bed. My blonde hair cascades around me in messy ringlets. Jack sits patiently on the edge, giving me a moment to collect my thoughts.

"I wasn't mad at *you* specifically," I settle on at last, steepling my fingers together on my chest.

"So you're mad at Hux?" Jack surmises, quirking a dark brow. Instantly, he winces, rubbing at his forehead as if he's attempting to fight off a headache.

Or a Hux.

"No, I'm not mad at either of you," I say quickly, pushing myself onto my elbows. "I'm mad at…everything. The world, for one."

"I will destroy the world," Hux growls sharply, eyes flashing in the dimly lit room as he makes an appearance. Jack wrestles for control against his more…um…psychotic brother and flashes me a sheepish smile.

"Sorry about him," he says, his tone reproachful. "He can be a little…"

"Adorable?" I fill in, warmth seeping into my bloodstream.

"I suppose you can say that." Completely back in control, Jack places his hand on top of mine, the edge of his thumb brushing against my breast. "Tell me what's wrong." He smells like pine and cinnamon, the fragrance curling around me addictively. It settles something inside of me, soothes my monster.

"You sure?"

"Positive." His tone brooks no room for argument.

Taking a fortifying breath, I admit, "I don't know what's wrong with me. I've never been a normal monster, but something has changed in the last month." I push myself up all the way until I'm sitting cross-legged across from him. His hand is still on mine, warmth suffusing me in a delicious, golden glow. "I think I'm scared."

What is more pathetic than that? A monster being scared.

If my dad could see me now…

"Scared?" Jack winces, rubbing at his forehead. "Hux demands to know who you're scared of. He offered to…" He pauses briefly as he listens to Hux's message before relaying it. "He offered to find the…errr…perpetrator, hang them by their toenails, and gut their innards. Then, you'll dance together in their blood beneath a full moon."

I practically fucking swoon.

Bloody moonlit dances? I need to take a fan to my overheated ovaries.

"It's not a person," I assure my psychopathic monster, and the fire in Jack's eyes dims to embers. "It's…it's you!" Yup. Real smooth, Violet. Real fucking smooth. "That's not what I meant!" I make a move to facepalm myself only to remember my hand is still connected with Jack's. Our combined hands end up awkwardly touching my forehead before I drop them both to my lap. "Look, I don't know how to explain this. I have feelings for…people. Lots of feelings. Feelings I haven't ever felt before. And…and I'm scared because I have all of these feelings and I don't know how to deal with them." My words leave me in a burst of air. Immediately, I want to capture them all and shove them back into my mouth. Embarrassment floods me as I stare intently on a sliver of bamboo flooring visible through the torn carpeting.

"Violet…" Jack begins in a soft voice. It wraps around me like a tightening leash, threatening to propel me straight into his arms. Once I'm there, I'm not sure I'll ever be able to leave again.

"Look at that spider web!" I deflect quickly, pointing to a spider web in the corner of the room. "That's one sexy-ass spider, if I do say so myself."

"Violet—"

"Oh, look. There's a bloodstain on the wall. I never noticed it before. I wonder who was killed here."

"Violet…"

"And there's a—" Before I can finish my next observation, Jack breaches the distance between us and kisses me.

Kisses me.

Internally, I'm screaming like a fucking tween holding the hand of her crush. His lips are soft against my own, and licks of fire erupt on my skin.

I hesitantly tangle my fingers in his thick black hair as he kisses me faster and faster, nails pressing into my waist.

You shouldn't be doing this, a voice whispers in the back of my head. Darkness nips at my heels as Jack's tongue prods the seam of my lips, demanding entrance. *Frankie just confessed that he is your mate. Isn't this…cheating?*

Then why does it feel so right?

I shove those thoughts away—fucking annihilate them—and focus on kissing Jack back with reckless abandon.

For a brief moment, I think that Jack has transitioned into Hux without my knowledge. The kisses are harsh and brutal. He bites down hard on my lower lip, drawing blood, before licking it up. When I meet his hooded eyes framed by glasses, I know that it's still Jack kissing me, still Jack gripping my waist with a bruising intensity.

I tilt my head to the side, giving him access to my neck. He kisses down the column of my throat, his breathing just as ragged as mine.

I did that. Me. I caused this collected man to unravel in my arms with lust.

Jack stops abruptly, his lips hovering over my fully covered breasts, and wrenches himself away from me. His cheeks are flushed, and his hair is wildly tousled from my hands. The sight of him sends a pang of primal satisfaction and possessiveness through me.

"Hux is so freaking pissed at me," Jack murmurs, gripping his head. His glasses begin to slide down his nose, but before they can fall off completely, I crawl forward and push them back into place. His eyes flicker up towards mine, a myriad of emotions lurking in those fathomless depths. I could drown in them.

Which would be a pretty shitty way to die, if I'm being completely honest. I met a ghost once who died by drowning, and the girl is still bitter about it to this day. Though I can't decide if it's because of how she died or *because* she died. Semantics.

"These feelings are new to all of us," Jack begins in a hushed voice. His eyes caress my face, lingering a moment longer on my lips, before he meets my gaze once more. "But you can't just ignore us, Violet. You can't shut us out."

"I…" I don't know what to say, so instead, I clamp my lips together.

Score one for Violet!

"Please don't shut us out," Jack continues, planting a tender kiss to my forehead.

I want to tell him that I'm scared—fucking terrified— that my "feelings" are going to get these men killed. I want to tell him that my heart is a fucking minefield, and no matter how carefully I tread, it always ends up blowing back up in my face.

I don't.

Instead, I blurt out, "I'm naming the spider Jerry!"

Fuck me.

"How many times do I have to tell you?" I seethe, lowering my face to her level. I want her to see the determined set of my jaw, the sincerity in my eyes. I want her to know that whatever relationship we once had is over. "I am—"

Before I can finish my sentence, she pushes up onto her tiptoes and kisses me. Shock and disgust make me momentarily immobile. I just lift my arms to push the bitch away when she steps back with a satisfied smirk.

What the…?

"See you around, Vinny Poo." She wiggles her fingers and sashays down the hall as my mind struggles to catch up with what just happened. It feels as if there's slime on my lips, and I have the irresistible urge to stick my face in a pot of acid.

I've turned to do just that when I spot a familiar shock of blonde hair framing a cherubic, almost elfin, face. Her eyes are wide with hurt and disbelief, and her lips are popped open. Betrayal contorts her beautiful features, and that one look stabs me, flaying me open, until I'm standing before her damaged and unloved.

Fuck!

"Violet!" I plead, wondering what the hell she saw. If the pain emanating from her eyes is any indication, she saw more than I would've liked. When she looks at me like that, like I shattered her heart in my hands, I feel abhorrent and disgusting…like a monster.

The darkness that is always percolating just under the surface, waiting for me to unleash it, returns with a vengeance.

"Violet!" I begin stalking towards her, determined to take her in my arms and…

And what?

Shake her until she sees reason? Until she knows that Cheryl means nothing to me and she's my fated mate?

Kiss the daylights out of her?

Before I can do any of that, she turns on her heel and, with a burst of vampiric speed, races away.

When her golden mane disappears around the corner, I feel my heart splinter down the center. One section remains with me, but the other...

The other leaves with her.

Violet: you talking about your dick?

Mason sends me back a dozen eggplant emojis and heart-eyes.

Mason: I'll be there

Still smiling, I slip my phone back into my pocket. That smile abruptly fades when I spot Vin and Gills—aka Cheryl —together on the other side of the hall. As I watch, she takes a step closer to him, and he bends his head down. I can't hear what is being said, but her face puckers in annoyance and something akin to hurt.

He's not your boyfriend, Violet. He can do whatever he wants when he wants with whomever he wants.

Then why does the sight of them together kill me?

Before I can make my hasty retreat, Gills's eyes flicker towards mine, and the hurt in them quickly transforms into avarice. She turns back to Vin, pushes herself onto her tiptoes, and kisses him.

The room begins to spin rapidly like I've been caught in a whirlpool. I place a hand against the wall to steady myself, remind myself where I am. Conversations from passing students enter one ear and then immediately exit out the other. My heart hiccups once before stilling as pain bombards me. It's like he tied a rope around my neck and hanged me from the gallows.

Gills sashays away with an exaggerated sway to her hips, but I barely notice her. I barely notice anything, actually.

Don't care. Don't care. Don't care.

You are a strong and mighty warrior, Violet. You will cut off his penis and give him a severed cock blowjob as his tears bleed life into you.

Vin finally turns in my direction, and the anguished expression marring his face claws at the black hole where my heart should be.

"Violet," he pleads, but I'm already backing away.

laments, dramatically fanning his face. I can't help but snort at Cal's petty-ass attitude.

Not that he's wrong. The man *is* gorgeous.

The world depicts Cupid as being a pudgy baby wearing a diaper. The reality? Cupid is a sexy hunk of man meat. His light pink hair is rumpled, and I can't tell if I find it endearing or concerning. Cal is obsessed with his appearance, so I'm going to go with the latter. His skin is lightly tanned, devoid of any blemishes, and his broad shoulders narrow down to a tapered waist. Brilliant red wings sprout from his back, swaying with each movement he makes.

"I'm pretty," Mason retorts, dropping his own container of ice cream onto the dusty counter. "You're...well, you're not hideous."

Cal ruffles his feathers, eyes narrowing into slits, as Mason flashes a shit-eating grin.

"He's Cupid," Barret mutters. "Of course he's not hideous."

The Boogeyman? Sweet as can be, but not the sharpest tool in the shed. He doesn't really understand sarcasm.

"Enough!" I step in between Medusa's son and Cupid, placing a hand on both of their chests. I push Cal backwards, planting myself firmly in front of him as I face Mason. As always, he is bedecked in a purple flannel shirt unbuttoned over a simple gray one. His signature beanie rests snugly on his head, magicked by Frankie to remain on him no matter the situation. When I turn back towards Cal, he flicks his eyes downwards and offers me a wry grin.

"What were my two favorite people doing before I arrived? You weren't having fun without me, were you?" Though his tone is teasing, I detect jealousy lingering just beneath the surface.

I've always known that Cal has a serious case of FOMO—

CHAPTER 6

MASON

"What the fuck did you do?" I roar as I storm into Vin's room in our shared house. The man himself is sitting at his desk, absently twirling a blade between his fingers.

He doesn't look up when I enter, and that pisses me off more than anything else.

"Answer me, dammit!" I explode, lunging forward and turning his chair to face me. My breath rushes out of my lungs when I note his despondent, agonized expression. The dude looks like someone ate his puppy.

My anger diminishes as I release his shoulders and collapse onto the floor in front of him. I'm a monster, but even I'm not heartless enough to kick an already fallen man.

In a softer tone, I ask, "What the fuck did you do?"

Reaching into my shirt pocket, I grab a lighter and a joint of Fairy Blossom. When I offer a second one to Vin, he surprises the shit out of me by accepting it. In all the years I've known him, Vin has never partaken in drugs, except for a few times at parties. But depression smoking? Hell no. He must be more upset than I initially suspected.

"I fucked up, Mase," he whispers brokenly, scrubbing a calloused hand down his face. I spread my legs out in front of me and rest back on my palms. My joint dangles precariously from my lips as I inhale sharply. Immediately, tingles race up and down my spine as the drug's magic cocoons me.

"Tell your old friend Mason all about it," I say, patting my lap. "Come here. Let me cuddle you."

His disgusted look? Fucking hilarious.

"I keep screwing things up with Violet," he admits at last, taking a long drag of Fairy Blossom. When he blows, purple smoke suffuses the room in a light sheen. "I've never had a girl I actually cared about before, you know?" He leans back in his desk chair and closes his eyes. "She's my mate, man. My fucking mate."

I freeze, shock making me momentarily immobile. I stare up at my best friend, my brother, and confusion and anger war for dominance within me.

"But...but you're a Van Helsing," I protest feebly, dropping my joint onto the ground with shaky fingers. "You can't have a mate."

"Don't you think I know that?" He scoffs, shifting uncomfortably in his leather chair. "But she... I don't know how to explain it. I just know, okay? I just fucking know."

Is that why I don't feel jealous or possessive when Violet's around Vin and the other guys? Because they're her mates too?

There must be something in my expression, something hinting at my rapidly percolating thoughts, because Vin quirks one dark brow at me. "What's up with you?"

"Nothing," I blurt instantly. When Vin continues watching me with shrewd eyes, I ramble, "So what the fuck did you do that hurt her so badly?"

Because friend or not, brother or not, I will not hesitate to rip out his spine and gift it to Violet as a macabre necklace.

Sort of like a macaroni necklace but with…bones.

"She saw Cheryl kissing me," he responds pensively.

Like a dam with too much pressure applied, I fucking crack. In the next moment, I'm on my feet and barreling down on the dumbass hunter, dropping my joint in my haste. He doesn't lift a hand to stop me, despite easily being able to. I've just punched him a second time when I feel hands on my shoulders, pulling me backwards.

"What the hell?" I seethe, facing the intruder. Frankie holds his hands up placatingly and takes an automatic step backwards.

"I heard fighting," he deadpans, flickering his gaze from a bloody Vin to a livid me. "I needed to make sure I didn't need to hide a body." He uses his middle finger to push up his thick glasses. "Now, what the bloody hell is going on?"

"Bloody hell," Vin mocks, staggering to his feet. He wipes at a blob of blood that has formed on the corner of his lips. "You're not even British."

"This *asshole*," I hiss, seriously wishing I had Violet's skill at coming up with creative insults and nicknames, "kissed Cheryl in front of Violet."

The change that comes over Frankie's face is drastic. Before, it had been merely impassive, almost bored with the conversation at large, but at my words, his eyes flash coldly and his lips curl into a hideous sneer. He looks seconds away from pouncing on Vin and finishing what I'd started.

"*She* kissed *me*," Vin protests immediately. Now at his full, impressive height, he towers over both me and Frankie. The intricate pattern of tattoos on his skin undulate, ripple, as he flexes. "The last thing I wanted was that viper putting her lips on me."

CHAPTER 7

VIOLET

"Hey, this is Vlad. I can't get to the phone right now, but your call is very important to—shut the fuck up, back there! Can't you see I'm on the phone? Please leave a message." I listen to the high-pitched beep and grind my teeth together.

"Hey, Dad. It's me. Again. Call me back, please. I need to talk to you. It's important." With a disgruntled sigh, I end the call and shove my phone into my backpack. Facing my reflection in the mirror, I purse my lips and cock my hip to the side.

A new me.

An unbroken me.

Today, I am wearing a black jacket over a thin white shirt that stops just above my belly button. My jeans are skintight, conforming to my thighs like a second skin. I've left my blonde hair down, but I've added a few streaks of white to the unruly locks. The change is small—hardly noticeable—but I feel more empowered than ever before.

My reflection offers me a sardonic smirk as I take a deep, fortifying breath.

"Make this day your bitch, Violet," I tell myself curtly. "And give that bitch a spanking."

With that pep talk, I hurry down the staircase—managing to only trip once—and wave at the phantom manning the receptionist desk.

I've just left my dorm building when I'm bombarded by two unfamiliar men. My back straightens as if someone stuck an electrical rod up my asshole.

They encircle me, their keen gazes flaying me open and stripping me bare.

"Can I help you, gentlemen?" I ask, lifting a brow. One of the men is tall and willowy, a white business suit hanging off his lean muscles, as if he accidentally got a size too large. The other is wearing a gray suit that accentuates his over-whelming amount of muscle. Both have snow-white hair, icy blue eyes, and the remnants of frostbite on their fingers. They must be descendants of the Yeti or the Abominable Snowman.

"I'm Charles the Third," the first one announces, his stuffy, nasally voice immediately grating on my nerves.

Though...I'm pretty sure you're supposed to give a last name before you can call yourself the third. Unless his last name is literally Thethird. Huh.

The larger man simply grunts, bobbing his head up and down jerkily.

"We're recruiters for the Roaring," Charles Thethird continues, puffing out his chest. "Have you heard of it?"

"Of course," I say, mimicking his haughty tone. Truth be told, I only just learned about it a month ago. Dad kept me fairly secluded in our Romanian home before my arrival at Monster Academy.

The Roaring is a game—or, a set of games. It pits the most

dangerous and intelligent monsters against each other. There are battles of wits, but also battles of strength and physicality. Students from across the world come to Prodigium to participate in the Roaring. Hell, it's not even just students. Some of the more seasoned monsters play as well.

"We don't see your name on the list of competing monsters," Charles Thethird says, crinkling his nose as if he has gotten a waft of a particularly pungent smell.

Me. I'm the smell.

"Um…" How do I kindly say that me and athletic events don't mix well? Unless it's a competition to see who can fall the most times in a ten-minute time frame. Then, I'm your girl.

A part of me—a part that I don't dare to acknowledge—is terrified. The games are immensely dangerous, and more people die than survive. I'm not sure I'm ready for death yet.

But this is a new me, a better me. I came to Prodigium Academy in order to make myself a better monster. All I have ever wanted is to make my dad proud. And winning the Roaring? There's no way he won't be proud of me. I will train diligently, find my limit, and break through it.

I'll prove Dracula, Vin, and all of the other monsters wrong.

"You know what," I begin, flashing a cocksure smile I don't actually feel. But you know what they say—fake it until you make it. "Sign me up. Violet Dracula. With a D."

Charles glances up from his clipboard with piercing eyes. "We know how to spell Dracula."

"Well, pleasure doing business with you all." I smile first at Charles and then at his terrifying brother before skipping away, a bounce to my step that hadn't been there prior.

Look out, world. Violet Dracula is back.

~

I'm writing notes to Jack in Proper Ways to Dispose of a Body—a class once taught by my very own psychopathic murderous sister, Ms. Stevens, and now by pudgy Mr. Skeletal—when a classroom attendant rushes in. He pants, offering a slip of a paper to the monotone professor, who I'm pretty sure, before teaching, worked at a gas station. He uses *a lot* of gas analogies in his speeches.

Don't ask.

"Violet Dracula," Mr. Skeletal says, clearing his throat. "You are requested in the headmaster's office."

I still, my movements in direct contrast to my rapidly pounding heart. I haven't met the new headmaster yet, but the old one...

He sort of tried to kill me.

The whole situation put a sour taste in my mouth.

Jack stiffens, his narrowed eyes the only indication that he has transformed into Hux.

"I will be going with my precious treasure," he bites out, moving to follow me.

"You will not!" Mr. Skeletal's voice turns shrill, as if he truly believes that the louder he screams, the more commanding he sounds. "The headmaster only requested a meeting with Ms. Dracula."

"I wouldn't do that if I were you," I warn my teacher with a pointed look in Hux's direction. He's either oblivious or stupid...or both. The verdict's still out on that one.

Instead of taking my advice, Mr. Skeletal moves around his desk until he's toe to toe with my glowering monster.

"You will sit back down instantly—" Before he can finish his command, Hux's hand is around his throat and he's pinning him to the wall. The class immediately breaks into anxious whispers. Gills—overdramatic bitch—begins to scream bloody murder. The noise makes me want to scratch my own ears off…if that's even possible. As my dad always says, if there's a murderous will, there's a way.

"You will not keep me from my precious treasure, do you understand?" Hux thunders darkly, and I swear my vagina jumps for joy at having him threaten a teacher for me. Heat suffuses me, migrating from my stomach to my core.

Mr. Skeletal attempts to speak, legs kicking as his face turns a hideous shade of blue.

"Do. You. Understand?"

"Umm…he can't answer you, Chocolate Bar," I say, tapping Hux on the shoulder. When he turns towards me, I pantomime choking with both my hands wrapped around my throat. Understanding flares in his eyes, and he drops our teacher unceremoniously to the ground.

"You are lucky, Mr. Skeletal Dick, that my mate has offered to show leniency." Hux's face could've been hewn from stone, slashing eyebrows pulled low over glowering eyes. "Kiss her feet."

"We really don't have to do all of this," I begin half-heart-edly, but Hux has already grabbed Mr. Skeletal by the scruff of his neck and has lowered his face to the ground.

"Kiss her feet," he demands.

Immediately, Mr. Skeletal begins peppering kisses to my Mary Jane shoes. It's awkward as fuck, if I'm being completely honest with myself. What the hell am I supposed to do? I can't very well make eye contact, now can I?

Finally, our teacher ambles back to his feet, body physically shaking, and writes two hall passes for me and Hux.

"Let's go, my precious treasure," Hux breathes, wrapping his arm around my shoulders and pulling me into his side.

The halls are vacant as we exit the classroom, the rest of the students either in their classes or at their dorms.

"I'm sorry if I scared you," Hux begins in a soft, demure

voice. His ebony lashes feather against his chiseled cheekbones as he blinks at me. "That was never my intention."

"Scare me?" I release a bark of laughter. Before I can stop myself—before I can even wrap my head around my actions —I turn us both so Hux's back is to the wall. "That was the sexiest thing I've ever seen in my life."

I've kissed Jack before, but never Hux. Would he taste the same? Feel the same?

Without giving myself a moment to reconsider, I press my lips to his. At first, he stiffens underneath me, as if my touch, my kiss, has set off a thousand internal alarms. And then, his lips move under mine in the sweetest, most innocent of kisses imaginable. He growls against my lips, but doesn't make any effort to deepen it.

It's almost as if he's unsure, hesitant, allowing me to take the reins and control the pace.

Fuck, that's sexy.

I grab his hands and place them on my breasts. My nipples are already beaded diamonds, desperate for his touch. He begins to knead my fleshy globes as my tongue enters his mouth, tangling with his own. It's a dance, a battle, reminiscent of swords clashing against shields. Surprisingly enough, he tastes different from Jack. It's barely perceptible —something I wouldn't even notice if I wasn't searching for it specifically. While Jack tastes like spearmint, Hux has a distinct peppermint flavor that assaults my taste buds in the most delicious way possible.

I trail my hand down his sculpted chest until I reach the waistband of his jeans. I pause there, caressing the sliver of skin exposed, before lowering my hand. I cup his erect cock through his jeans and begin to rub in tandem to our heated kisses.

Hux makes a noise in the back of his throat—a combination between a pleading mewl and a groan—and begins to kiss me harder.

"It was so fucking sexy when you choked that teacher," I pant as his finger caresses the seam of my jeans. Fuck, why didn't I wear a skirt today? Of all the days…

He begins to rub me as I rub him, our breathing turning ragged. He's not even touching my fucking skin, and I'm seconds from exploding.

"Fuck," I murmur against his lips as his palm cups my wet pussy through my jeans. The friction—combined with his kisses and whispered praises—sends me tumbling over that steep edge.

But I'll be damned if I don't take him with me.

As my orgasm shakes my legs, I begin to rub Hux even harder, bordering that precarious line between pleasure and pain. When I squeeze tightly, Hux releases a hiss of pleasure. Spurred on by his inarticulate praises, I bite down on his bottom lip, and he roars as he comes, his cock twitching beneath my hand.

We're both breathing heavily by the time we're finished, and Hux reverently leans his forehead against my own.

"That was…amazing. Thank you for sharing that with me, my precious treasure," he whispers, lowering his lips to my own in a tender kiss.

"I'm glad you liked it," I reply, and for some undefinable reason, my cheeks darken in color. I almost feel embarrassed, which is ridiculous. I have made more men orgasm than I care to admit.

Then why does it feel so different with Hux?

My stomach is a tumultuous mixture of happiness and fear, but I can't decipher where the latter emotion stems from. Still, I can't stop the blissful smile from curling up the corners of my lips.

"I'm sorry you'll have to walk around with cum in your

pants," I say, mentally high-fiving myself. The same thing happened once before with Vin—excuse me, he-who-shall-not-be-named—and it fills me with a primitive, savage sense of satisfaction.

You see those hunky men, bitches? Well, back off. That's my cum in their pants. Well, his cum. But he only came because of me. So, ha.

"We should go see what the new headmaster wants," I say at last, reluctantly stepping away from Hux. His eyes are glazed, as if he's high off of lust, and a dopey grin lights up his face. Honestly? I can't remember the last time I've ever seen Hux smile. Hell, I'm pretty sure I have *never* seen him smile before.

"I will wear my cum for the rest of my days, Precious Treasure," Hux vows. "Or perhaps, I will bottle it up and serve it to you on our wedding day."

I totally would've face-planted if Hux hadn't been there to catch me.

"Wedding day?" I stutter out. My mind immediately conjures up images of me walking down the aisle dressed in a midnight black gown with a matching veil.

Hux smiles unrepentantly. "Of course. You are to be my wife. I wouldn't have it any other way."

CHAPTER 8

Hux's dogmatic statement is still echoing in my mind as we step into the main office.

The lobby is sparsely furnished with a dozen or so plastic chairs arranged against the wall and a single receptionist desk.

Bird Lady—with webbed fingers and feathers on her neck and cheeks—smiles at us before nodding towards one of the chairs.

"He'll be with you in a second," she assures us, just as the headmaster's door swings open and Dimitri Gray steps out. My eyes practically bug out of my head and my brain momentarily stalls as I stare up at the dangerous assassin.

I haven't seen him since he rescued me from Bloody Mary's son, and my eyes immediately travel over him as thoroughly as his do me. Seemingly satisfied that I haven't been injured since he last saw me, he nods towards the office.

"Come along, Ms. Dracula," he instructs in a curt, no-

nonsense voice. When Hux—wait, Jack—makes a move to follow us, Dimitri holds up one hand. "Please wait out here."

Jack hesitates, shuffling from foot to foot, as he argues with his alter ego. After a moment, he sighs reluctantly and sits back in the uncomfortable plastic chair.

"We'll be right out here," he promises me. He eyes Dimitri warily before leaning even closer, his arms resting on his thighs. "We don't sense any threat from him."

"Is that something your monster can do?" I question. "Sense threats?"

Because that would be fucking sweet.

Fire creeps up his neck and cheeks as he ducks his head sheepishly. Dimitri, behind me, releases a cold guffaw, as if both men are privy to a joke I'm not a part of. My eyes narrow, but I turn on my heel without another word.

If Jack's keeping secrets from me, I'll carve my initials into his ass. Wait, no. That's fucked up, even for me.

And I happen to like his butt.

Though my initials would be a good way to claim him…

I enter "Dimitri's" office with a mutinous tilt to my chin.

Please, please don't tell me that Dimitri is the new headmaster.

The first thing I notice is how different the office is from Lupine's. While his had been elegant and stuffy, Dimitri's has a modern flair. The mahogany table has been swapped out for a sleek black desk with silver legs. The bookshelf and suit of armor have been removed entirely, replaced by decorative plants. There are no personal pictures or memorabilia that I can see. It feels…cold. Empty. The bleak white walls paint the room in a harsh light.

I move to sit in the leather chair opposite the desk, and Dimitri surprises the shit out of me by perching on the edge of the table. His long legs extend until they're nearly touching mine, and damn if goosebumps don't pebble across my body.

"So…" I begin awkwardly, forking my fingers through my blonde curls.

Dimitri crosses his arms over his chest and glares at me, his slashing eyebrows pulled low over hard eyes.

It's the sort of look that makes you want to piss your pants.

And have his babies.

"You're the new headmaster," I blurt out. "That's cool. Is it because you like giving *head*?" I ask, emphasizing the sexual innuendo with a wiggle of my eyebrows.

Once, when I was younger, my father sewed my lips together as punishment for telling a skeleton he had a boner. I never really understood why…until now.

Thou shall not ever speak. I'm pretty sure it's a commandment.

Dimitri continues to regard me coldly, his frigid stare having the opposite reaction than he probably hoped for. Warmth travels up the tips of my fingers, down my spine, and to the soles of my feet.

"I was told that you joined the Roaring today," he begins curtly. His face remains carefully impassive, so I can't tell how he feels about this development. If the icicles forming in his eyes are any indication, he hates it.

"I thought it would be fun." I shrug casually, and a muscle in Dimitri's jaw twitches.

"Fun," he scoffs, pushing himself off the desk and standing. He takes a step closer until he towers over me, hooded eyes carving out a piece of my heart and soul. "Did you know that thirty-nine percent of all competitors die every year in the Roaring?"

I anxiously chew on my thumbnail. "That's an interesting statistic. Did you get that off the internet? You know you can't always trust that. Now, a book…a book is where the truth is at."

I swear he looks seconds away from throttling me.

"Drop out of the competition," he says immediately, his tone brooking no room for argument. I hiss out a breath through clenched teeth, my good mood from earlier rapidly fading.

I *hate* when people try to tell me what to do. Who the fuck does Dimitri Gray think he is?

"No," I say with a smug smirk.

His eyes narrow. "No?"

"You heard me. N. O. That spells *no*, if you're wondering." I cross my arms over my chest, mimicking his pose, and I swear his eyes hurl metaphorical daggers at me.

"Why do you have to be so fucking stubborn?" He shakes his head ruefully, finally pulling his eyes away from mine. Thank fuck. I had to blink for a good minute now, but I was determined not to lose the unofficial staring contest.

"Why do you have to be a stone-cold asshole?" I retort back. "Speaking of... How did you become headmaster, anyway? Isn't it kind of taboo to take the job of the man you killed?" When his gaze flickers back up to mine, holding me hostage, I bring my hands up placatingly. "No judgment. You do what you need to do to get that promotion."

"The monster world considers me a hero," he says, face devoid of expression. He could've been reciting passages from a cookbook with all the excitement he's emanating. "I stopped the string of murders by killing the evil headmaster who was determined to frame the vampires...and Dracula's daughter. But alas, I couldn't get to him before he murdered poor Ms. Stevens." At the latter statement, he levels me with a pointed look, and I pantomime zipping my lips shut and throwing away the key.

Because Ms. Stevens? Your homegirl stabbed that ho.

"Good for you," I say, ambling to my feet. "Seriously, good. For. You. Maybe I'll come visit and give you a congrat-

There's also the fact that he put my life on the line in order to play hero. He could've told me ahead of time about Headmaster Lupine's wicked scheme. Instead, he bottled it all up inside of him, hoping that the inevitable eruption would spare the two of us. I still remember the knife entering Frankie's heart. The pain, the horror, the shock… They all battled for dominance as I watched him fall to the ground.

That image assaults me whenever I close my eyes.

"Violet," Frankie whispers. Out of the corner of my eye, I see Jack casting furtive, albeit confused, glances at the two of us.

"Frankie."

"Can we…?" He scrubs at his jaw, eyes anguished. "Can we talk?"

I mentally inventory myself, ensuring there are no cracks in my armor, before turning towards Jack.

"Can you give us a moment?" I question. He hesitates, no doubt arguing with a protective and possessive Hux, before nodding and walking farther down the hall.

Taking a fortifying breath, I focus my attention once more on Frankie. "Okay, let's talk."

CHAPTER 9

I fix things. It's what I do, who I am. If I see a problem, I work tirelessly until I'm able to uncover a solution. My father covets my analytical brain and dispassionate exterior. In his mind, caring makes you weak. *Emotions* make you weak.

It's why he created a monster like me in the first place.

I've never dealt with emotions before. Not soul-crushing heartbreak. Not lust. Not love.

But science? I understand science. Molecules and atoms and corrosive solutions. It's the rest of the world I don't get.

I'm capable of creating a drug that can make you laugh nonstop, but apparently, I can't find the words to speak to my mate.

Mate.

Pain ricochets through my body. Is it wrong that I assumed she would be overjoyed by the news? When I first understood the reasons for my feelings—that she was made specifically for me—I wanted to sing it from the rooftops.

Confess my feelings to the sun and moon. Violet? She had run.

Taking my entire heart with her.

Focusing on her now, I study the minuscule changes that have occurred in the last week. Same pert nose and luscious lips. Same glimmering eyes, as if she is in the know of a secret. Same petite body with surprisingly generous curves. But…

"You have highlights in your hair," I note abruptly. I have the irrational urge to grab one of the silky strands and inhale her fruity scent.

A pleased smile blossoms on Violet's face as she grabs one of the white curls and inspects it in the hallway lighting.

"You're the first to have noticed."

I shove my hands into my back pockets and rock back and forth. Silence stretches between us, so fragile I don't dare attempt to break it. The tension in the room is so thick, I'm practically gagging on it.

It's Violet who speaks first. "Frankie…" She blows out a breath, hands bunching into white-knuckled fists. Like me, she appears to be at a loss for words.

Which proves how royally I fucked up. Dracula's crazy, eccentric daughter is *never* quiet.

"I screwed up," I admit at last, forking my fingers through my too-long hair. It's in desperate need of a trim, the errant strands brushing my eyes. "I should've never kept the truth from you about Headmaster Lupine. And I definitely shouldn't have put your life on the line in order to prove myself to you." My mistakes and transgressions are piling up on me, like dirt burying a steel coffin. The thing I regret the most? Hurting the woman standing before me. Heart palpitating, I drop to my knees before the golden-haired goddess. "I refused to get on my knees for my father. He wanted to use me—to mold me into his perfect monster. He taught me that love was a weakness that should be eradicated like a disease, and I think a part of me believed that. That's no excuse for my behavior." I scrub at my jawline, muscles clenching as I prepare myself for her inevitable rejection.

Why would she want to be with a monster like me? A creature built in a lab instead of a womb? A man who isn't truly a man, but a beast?

"We can take things slow," I plead, staring up into her hooded eyes. "Learn about each other. And I won't begrudge you if you choose to pursue a relationship with the other guys."

Please give me a chance. Let me prove myself to you. Prove that I can be a mate worthy of your love and affection.

When Violet doesn't immediately answer, her face drawn tight, my heart plummets, bottoming through my stomach. I've prepared myself for her rejection—had even thought myself strong enough to endure it—but the full force of my emotions takes me by surprise. Disappointment, pain, and yearning.

Crippling anguish washes over me, and I climb to my feet, lowering my head like a kicked puppy. Fuck, why did I think she would forgive me? All I want to do is eat my bodyweight in chocolate and lick my wounds in private. I've just turned to retreat when Violet grabs my hand, halting my progress. I can't stop the embers of hope flickering to life in my stomach.

"Where are you going?" she huffs, releasing my arm to put her hands on her hips. "Aren't you going to ask me?"

"Ask you?" I furrow my brows in confusion.

"On a date." She rolls her eyes, as if that should've been obvious.

A date.

With Violet.

My metaphorical heart kickstarts as a slow smile curls up

my lips. I quickly try to mask it—a product of my father's cruel lessons—before stifling that impulse. This is Violet, not my father. I'm allowed to smile in front of her. I'm allowed to show emotion.

"Oh, what the hell," Violet murmurs, more to herself than to me. "I am a fierce, independent woman. And this is the twenty-first century. I can ask a guy on a date if I want."

Is she expecting a response?

Before I can formulate something moderately intelligent, she places a manicured hand on my chest. "Frankie?" She peers up at me through her fringe of fluttery lashes. My breath hitches in my throat at the sheer perfection of the woman before me... But that awe quickly turns into worry as her eyes continue to blink rapidly.

"Violet, are you having a seizure?" I ask anxiously, hovering my hands just above her shoulders but not daring to touch.

Her eyes narrow dangerously at my question, and her lips purse. "I'm attempting to be coy, dammit."

"Oh, um, good job?" When she continues to glare up at me, I finally give in to my baser impulse and place my hands on her shoulders. "Carry on."

"Frankie, will you go on a date with me?" she asks at last, and it feels as if I can finally breathe. Before, the room had been devoid of oxygen, as if a vacuum had sucked it all out. In her presence, my lungs are finally able to take in that precious air.

"Yes," I whisper as something akin to giddiness courses through me.

When the fuck have I ever been giddy before?

Violet smiles, leaning forward to peck me on the cheek. My skin tingles from the connection, and I can't stop the dopey grin from appearing on my face.

"I need to get to my next class, but I'll see you at lunch,

okay?" With another smile aimed at me, she skips down the hall towards where Hux is waiting for her. At least, I assume it's him and not his kinder alter ego. Only Hux is capable of looking like he wants to write "H hearts V" on the wall with my blood.

He casts me a skeptical glance, but I don't bother to acknowledge him.

Violet has asked me on a date.

Me.

Only when she's out of sight do I hurry to my lab in the basement of the academic building. What type of perfume would a psychopathic vampire want as a gift?

Oh! Nothing's more enticing to Violet than the sweat and blood of her enemies.

Ideas run rampant through my brain in tandem to my rapidly beating heart.

Violet has given me the opportunity to prove myself, and I'll be damned if I mess it up again. I'll never be a hunter or a fighter, but I'll set the world on fire if that was what she needed.

She didn't know what she agreed to when she said yes to my monster.

Hopefully, she's okay with a little murder and mayhem.

CHAPTER 10

VIOLET

I'm walking to the cafeteria the next morning—mouth already watering at the prospect of sticking my fangs into Jack's neck—when my phone releases an ear-piercing ring. I pull it out of my jacket pocket, nose scrunching, until I see who is calling me.

"Dad?" I say eagerly, placing the phone to my ear. I pause in the middle of the forested pathway. A few goblins cast me evil side-eyes as they brush past me, and I respond by baring my fangs. Probably not the smartest move when vampire hate acts are so high on campus, but what can I say? I'm a petty bitch.

I step a little ways off the trail, leaves and twigs snapping beneath my feet.

"Hey, homegirl," Dad replies. "What's baking in the oven?"

"Oh my god." I pinch the bridge of my nose. "Are you going through a phase again?"

My dad and his fucking phases…

"Just keeping it kewl and on the downlow, homie. Now, waz shaking?"

This is Dracula, my friends. The most feared monster in the entire world.

"Why haven't you been returning my calls?" I demand, leaning against a tree. The rough bark scrapes against my skin where my shirt has ridden up, but I relish the tiny licks of pain.

"Been busy taking names and fucking them."

For the love of…

"I need to talk to you," I blurt abruptly. "About Diedre Stevens."

There's a prolonged pause on the other end of the line. For a moment, I believe he has hung up on me. I glance at the screen bemusedly, just as his slightly shrill voice echoes from the phone.

"I don't know what you're talking about."

"Dad," I begin, bringing the phone back up to my ear. "You're acting suspicious as fuck right now. She said—"

"Not now," he cuts in, tone scathing. "We'll meet Friday night. I'll text you the address."

With that ominous statement, he hangs up on me. I stare at the now dark screen of my phone with growing confusion and horror.

One thing is for certain—Vladimir Dracula is hiding something from me.

My confusion doesn't abate by the time I enter the cafeteria. If anything, it grows like a seed finding soil and taking root in my stomach.

The inside is exactly how I would imagine a human cafeteria to look like. Of course, there are *small* variations—like the buffet of human body parts run by monsters with spiders for hair. A few human donors sit on uncomfortable plastic chairs against the far wall. Opposite them is a separate hallway that leads to the private feeding rooms.

It's the latter location I head to, my mind consumed with Dracula's curt tone. He almost sounded…afraid. What the fuck does he have to be afraid of? He is the apex predator; the monster that other monsters are wary of.

I've just reached the private feeding rooms when I notice Jennifer pacing just outside. She's a vampire like me, with an hourglass figure and pitch-black hair. Her smoky eyes turn in my direction, and I'm struck by the pure, undiluted *hatred* there. Like, damn, girl, did I pee in your Cheerios or something?

"They're not letting us fucking feed," she hisses, baring her fangs.

"Huh?" I turn towards my usual room. Jack is scheduled to meet me in the next five minutes, after he finishes class.

"The fucking vampire haters," Jennifer seethes. "They're not letting us feed."

My brows furrowing, I push open the first door.

Only to vomit in my throat when I catch a glimpse of Cheryl's tits as she rides Fish Boy.

Have you ever seen tits made of gills before? Have you? Because let me just say, they're a sight to behold. Every time they bounce, the blue gills sparkle in the artificial lighting. I'm pretty sure her nipples are a shade of blue as well.

And…

I really should stop staring at my nemesis's nipples.

The boy she's riding like a fucking pogo-stick is the same asshole who attacked me the first day of school. His girlfriend, Ali, was murdered only a few weeks earlier.

Just proves my point. No men are loyal.

His cock—lined with gills—thrusts in and out of a moaning Cheryl.

For the longest time, I sorta assumed they were related.

Cue—actual, honest-to-god vomit.

Cheryl meets my eyes as she continues to ride Fish Boy. Pure malice flashes in her gaze as she throws her head back, thrusting her blue tits further in my direction. She begins to knead the heavy globe as her other hand plucks at her clit.

"Oh, Vin!" she screams as Fish Boy's hips begin to move erratically.

"You know, I can literally see that the man you're fucking is not, in fact, Vin," I point out.

"Harder, Vin! Harder!" She leans forward, tits swaying, and Fish Boy places a hand on the back of her head to hold her steady.

"Still not Vin," I murmur.

Her voice is a gasp when she speaks next. "I'm just remembering the way he used to fuck me. Or wait…maybe I'm thinking about Mason." She twists her head to smile up at me, tweaking her own nipples. "Actually, I'm most definitely thinking of Vin."

Of course, that immediately makes me think of what I'd witnessed in the hallway, and my vision becomes coated with a red sheen. Jealousy pulsates through me in tandem to my repeatedly beating heart. I clench and unclench my hands as I stare Cheryl down.

Vin's not with her. If he was with her, she would be rubbing that in my face. Don't let her win, Violet. Don't let the bitch fucking win.

I take a deep, calming breath just as Cheryl begins screaming louder, her voice overshadowing Fish Boy's own inarticulate phrases.

This is so fucking weird.

"I'm just going to…um…leave." Slowly, I back out of the

room, just as Fish Boy grabs his gilled-dick, pulls it out of Cheryl's cunt, and spins her around to spill his seed onto her breasts. It's…blue. And sparkly. Using his dick, he begins to rub it into her nipples, which I swear are turning into seashells. No fucking joke. You can't make this shit up.

The door closes silently behind me as I step back into the hall. Jennifer leans against the wall, arms crossed over her chest and one eyebrow raised.

"See what I mean?"

"Are all the rooms like that?" I gesticulate towards the room of horror. I'm pretty sure I need to bleach my eyes out after that scene.

"Some people are fucking. Some are just sitting and refusing to leave." With an irritated huff, Jennifer turns on her heel and stalks away, no doubt to feed on the public donors stationed in the cafeteria.

I open doors at random, my agitation growing by the second. In one, there's a full-blown orgy occurring. A male is fucking another male against a table as he sucks on a girl's pussy. In front of them, two girls are rubbing their nipples together while two men fuck them from behind.

And…

Now I'm thinking of orgies.

With my guys.

Well, not *my* guys, but my guy friends who are guys.

The third room proves to be the same—a big, giant clusterfuck. Literally. It's the fourth room that gives me a pause.

A single man is leaning against the table, his arms crossed over his chest and a scowl firmly fixed on his face. He has hair so dark it's almost the color of pitch, and he wears a form-fitting black t-shirt that clings to his pectorals. Tattoos run up his arms from the tips of his fingers, a myriad of colors and symbols. He looks extremely badass and extremely scary.

"Hey," I begin awkwardly, lifting my hand and wiggling my fingers. "Um…I was wondering if I could use this room to drink."

Kill 'em with kindness is what my dad always tells me. Well, at least the first part. Kill 'em.

He doesn't answer, eyes narrowed intently on me.

"Is that a yes?" I tentatively ask, quirking a brow. I swear I see his scowl deepen, as if my voice alone irritates the shit out of him. "A maybe?"

"Vampire scum don't deserve to eat," he bites out at last. I'm shocked by the aversion in his tone. It goes beyond petty squabble. It's absolute hatred and loathing.

My temper flares immediately as I stalk up to the cumquat.

"Because I'm a vampire? Because you're afraid I'm stronger than you? Faster than you?" His eyes narrow dangerously the closer I get, but it only fuels my hate fire. "Who the fuck are you? Do you even go here?" I shake my head vigorously.

Focus, Violet.

"Zombies need human brains to eat. Ghouls need live body flesh. Witches require human body parts for their spells. What makes us so fucking different? Is it because we're more durable? Because we're more powerful?"

His nostrils flare as I take another step closer. Before I can continue my amazing rant—if I do say so myself—my back is pressed against the wall and his hand is around my throat.

"You're all disgusting vermin," he hisses, spittle flying in my face. "None of you deserve to live. Watch out, little vampire. You're soon going to find out that you have more enemies than friends at this Academy." Abruptly, he releases me, nodding towards a fridge in the far corner of the room. "You can have one bag. That's all we're going to allow."

"We?" I want to fight back—push my luck—but there's something dangerous lurking in his dark eyes. Something that makes me tremble with barely veiled fear.

"The Anti-Vampire Resistance." His lips curl into an evil smirk. "You're lucky Dimitri Gray is headmaster, or else I'd stick a stake into your heart."

Yeah, let's not and say we did.

"Nice talking to you," I murmur, quickly grabbing the blood bag and using my vampiric speed to exit the room.

What the ever-loving fuck is happening?

I nearly trip over my own two feet when I enter the cafeteria and see the public donors. Or, lack thereof.

Every single human donor is dead, their lifeless, glazed eyes staring up at the ceiling. I can't tell who—or what—killed them. I recognize a few of them—a man named Jerry, a woman named Sarah, a woman named Alixandra, and a man called Harry. A few vampires hover on the outskirts, faces etched in horror.

Anxious murmuring erupts across the cafeteria. I watch as Vin removes himself from the Van Helsing table and inches a step closer to me. He doesn't speak to me or even acknowledge me, but I know he's as aware of my presence as I am of his.

"Pinkie!" Mason hurries through the throng of whispering monsters until he's able to pull me into his arms. His gaze narrows on the sea of dead donors. "What the fuck happened?"

Did that guy do this? The Anti-Vampire Resistance guy?

The doors to the cafeteria fly open as a group of professors hurry inside. At the front, leading the charge, is Dimitri himself. He looks like darkness personified, his all black clothes juxtaposed by his pure white hair. His eyes search the crowd before stopping on me. He surveys me from head to toe, inspecting for injuries, before he turns away to face the dead donors.

"Somebody better start talking." He doesn't yell—doesn't even raise his voice—but the entire cafeteria stills, knowing danger when they sense it.

Hands shaking, I rip open my blood bag and suck it dry. I'll ask one of the guys to come to my room tonight so I can feed, but for now, I'm going to rely on stale bagged blood. It tastes almost sour, as if it's been sitting out for a while. It's nothing compared to the raw power in Vin's and Jack's blood.

"What happened?" Dimitri spins in a circle before leveling his gaze on a trembling werewolf. "You. My office. Now."

The wolf looks as if he's seconds from peeing his pants, but he complies with a jerky bob of his head. Only when he scurries away does Dimitri focus once more on the assembled students.

"Vampire hate acts will *not* be tolerated in my school. Anyone who participates will immediately be sent to detention...or worse." He allows his threat to linger in the air, hovering precariously like the blade of a guillotine seconds before it drops. "Until I get to the bottom of this horrendous act, I will be calling students to my office every hour. Is that understood?"

No one is moving. Hell, I'm pretty sure no one is even breathing.

I want to tell Dimitri about Cheryl and Fish Boy. The scary man from the private feeding room.

But if there's one thing monsters hate, it's snitches. In this world, they don't just get fucking stitches. They get buried... ten feet under, and the majority of the time, still alive.

My stomach gurgles suddenly, capturing the attention of the entire cafeteria.

"Is there something you'd like to add, Ms. Dracula?"

Dimitri asks coyly. I spot Cynthia—my old roommate—sitting at a table across the cafeteria, her eyes concerned. When she spots me looking, she blanks her expression and focuses on her human liver.

"I'm…" I trail off as my stomach rumbles a second time. "Oh shit!"

Literally.

Before I can even take a step, my stomach bottoms out, and I literally shit my pants.

"Come on," Mason says gently as the cafeteria breaks into laughter. Jack, who has just entered the building, immediately hurries towards me, face drawn in confusion. Vin follows from behind.

"Having a shitty day?" Cheryl—now fully dressed—jests snidely, too low for Dimitri to hear. Mason snarls at her, removing his plaid shirt to wrap it around my waist.

Ignoring the bitch, I whisper, "Mase, I don't feel so—" My stomach twists once more, and I release a pained whimper.

"Everyone, quiet down!" Dimitri says from behind us, his voice cutting through the laughter and amused whispers like the crack of a whip. When I glance over my shoulder, his face is utterly impassive, except for the slightest downwards tilt to his lips.

My eyes are drawn to a figure standing directly behind Dimitri, a large smile on his face. No Name Asshole. His tattoos ripple as he crosses his muscular arms over his chest. When he meets my gaze, he nods once in acknowledgment.

Motherfucker!

Oh, it's on.

Let the games begin, asshole.

CHAPTER 11

VIOLET

Fortunately—or perhaps unfortunately, depending on how you look at it—my shitting incident is overshadowed by the deaths of the donors. Seven. Seven innocent men and women were slaughtered

Anger rages to life in my stomach, swirling with the intensity of a whirlpool.

It's not as if I'm unfamiliar with death. Hell, I have killed a few people myself. I am, however, against killing people who don't deserve it. And those donors? They did nothing except offer their blood to starving vampires.

I toss and turn all night but am unable to comprehend the point of killing the donors. Just to fuck with the vampires? Or is it for something more sinister?

The next morning, the first official Roaring practice takes place over by the cemetery. I wake up early and don a pair of gray sweatpants and the customary red t-shirt bearing the Academy's crest. I brush my blonde curls back into a disheveled ponytail, a few disobedient strands tumbling down my cheeks.

"You rang, Pinkie?" Mason uses his hip to push open my bedroom door. Like me, he's wearing the Academy-issued red shirt with the hideous golden crest. A pair of low-slung basketball shorts complete the ensemble. As always, his beanie rests snugly on his head, concealing his snakes.

I turn away from my reflection and stick my hands on my hips. "I need you," I say without preamble, eyeing the throbbing vein in his neck. Jack hadn't answered my call, and I'm still pissed at Vin. The only other options were either Frankie or Mason, and since I'm pretty sure Frankie doesn't have blood...

"Thank, fuck," Mason murmurs. "I've been needing you so fucking long that my Little Mason is beginning to ache." Before I can ask what the hell he's talking about, he whips off his shirt, baring his chiseled stomach and chest to me.

Dude has a six-pack. And good lordy, I have the irresistible urge to get on my hands and knees and lick down the trail of hair to his prominent V. Then, I'll grab his cock and whisper, "Come to mommy," before sucking him dry.

Focus, you thirsty bitch, I chastise myself, wrenching my gaze away from his mouth-watering body.

"I'll even let you ride me," Mason continues, untying his shorts and shrugging them down. Once they're around his ankles, he sticks his thumbs into his boxer briefs, pushing them down just enough for me to catch a glimpse of his pubic hairs. I'd half expected them to be dozens of tiny snakes, but instead, they're dark and curly. "Why the fuck are you still dressed? Get naked, dammit."

"Um...Mase?" I lift one brow at him, my gaze still fixed on the outline of his erection. "I meant I need to drink from you. And no, not drink your cum. I meant your blood."

The expression on his face? Priceless.

He glances down at his scantily-clad body and then back up to me.

"Well…" He crosses his arms over his chest, as if attempting to cover his nipples. "This is awkward."

"Get over here and let me drink," I say, moving to perch on the edge of my bed. "Maybe I'll give Little Mason a present afterwards as a reward."

He practically sprints over to me—well, waddling would be a more accurate description given his shorts are still around his ankles.

"I can get dressed if you want me to," he says, completely unashamed with his semi-naked body. Not that the man has anything to be ashamed over—he looks like a god personified. With heated eyes, he sits beside me on the bed.

"Nah." Grinning wickedly, I place my nails in the center of his stomach, just above his belly button, and slowly drag them upwards. They graze his peaked nipple, and he shudders delicately, his cocksure smile fading to be replaced by lust.

"I've never done this before," he breathes as my fingers trail lightly over his neck. "How do we…?"

Without answering, I throw my leg over his thighs until I'm straddling him. His hands instinctively settle on my ass, holding me in place.

"Be a good boy for me, and stay still," I purr, licking his pulsing neck. I hear him audibly gulp seconds before my fangs descend.

It's a fucking explosion. Stars burst behind my closed eyelids like errant fireworks. Lust ricochets through my body. It feels as if someone has pumped gasoline into my veins and then dropped a flame.

Mason's hips begin to buck against me as I continue to feed, his blood warming my body and amping up my own desire.

With a burst of speed, I push Mason on the bed and hover over top of him. With one hand, I grip his jaw, tilting his head to the side, and the other travels down his washboard abs and to his underwear, fingering the hem.

"Oh, fuck," he groans, as I stick one finger inside and caress his shaft. Pulling my fangs away from his neck, I grin at him, using my tongue to collect the remaining droplets of blood from my lips. His eyes follow the movement before fluttering closed, a pained groan escaping him.

"Does Little Mason need some attention too?" I tease, kissing down his chest. I run my tongue over one nipple and then the other as his chest rumbles with laughter.

"Fuck yes. He misses you."

"He's never met me before," I counter, finally reaching that happy trail I noticed earlier. I alternate between long, taunting licks and tantalizingly soft kisses.

"We think about you a lot," he protests, the noise nothing more than a breath of air. "Especially when he's getting rubbed by Mr. Hand."

"You're such a weirdo." Using my fangs, I bite through his boxer briefs and toss them aside, baring his long, hard shaft.

"Oh, fuck. That was hot," he moans, his dick twitching. Ignoring Little Mason, I begin planting teasing kisses on his thighs—first one and then the other. "Don't be mean to me like that, Vi," he pleads.

"Mean?" I gasp in mock horror. "I'd never!"

Before he can protest, I sink my teeth into his thigh.

"Fuck!" he bellows as I consume his blood. When I pull away seconds later, his thigh is still dripping that enticing red liquid. Instead of using my venom to heal it, I rub my hand through the rapidly growing puddle and then wrap it around his dick, using the blood as lube. "Fuck, fuck, fuck!" He drops his head back to the bed, eyes closing, as I lick the tip of his throbbing cock.

The taste of his pre-cum combined with his blood nearly sends me spiraling over the edge. I can tell it does the same to him. He's gripping the blankets in an effort not to come too soon.

"Let's play a game," I taunt, running my tongue down the side of his thick shaft. When I reach his balls, I take one into my mouth and suck gently before releasing it to speak. "I bet I can make you come in less than thirty seconds."

"Oh, please," he huffs, his breathing uneven. "What do I get when *I* win?"

I smirk, leaning forward until I'm staring into his hooded eyes glazed with lust. "I'll let you eat me out."

"And if you win?" he breathes, gaze flickering from my bloody lips to my heaving chest and then back up to my eyes.

Smiling deviously, I position myself back over his dick. "You'll see. Start the timer."

His hand shaking, he reaches for my phone on the edge of my bed and switches it to the clock setting.

"On your mark. Get set. Go." He pushes the start button just as I swallow his cock. I work on relaxing my jaw in order to swallow him further. I'm a pro, for fuck's sake. And proud of it. Still, Mason's long—longer than any other man I ever blew before—and I'm forced to wrap my right hand around the girth I can't quite swallow. My other hand fondles and plucks at his balls.

I begin to hum low in my throat, my fangs grazing the skin of his dick. I know this combination will send him straight over the edge.

He curses, gripping my hair as he begins fucking my mouth in earnest.

"Fuck, fuck, fuck, fuck!" he screams as his cock twitches once before exploding in my mouth. I swallow up every last drop like a champ before releasing him with a satisfied smirk.

He's breathing heavy, sweat coating his bare chest and forehead. His eyes practically rolled into the back of his head when he orgasmed, and I'm slightly concerned they'll remain there.

"Where the fuck did you learn how to do that?" he pants before his face tightens. "Actually, don't answer that, or else I'll go on a murder spree."

When he continues to lie on my bed, utterly sated, I amble to my feet and straighten my clothes.

"Wait, baby..." He grabs at my hand, attempting to tug me back to the bed. "You didn't get off. Let me take care of you."

"The great Mason wants to give me an orgasm?" I say in mock surprise. "I thought that was beneath you."

At least, that's the rumor that has been floating around the Academy. He uses girls for pleasure, but doesn't care enough to get them off himself. Selfish prick, if you ask me.

His eyes narrow as he gives my hand another tug.

"Come here," he demands.

"Nah..." I dance towards my duffle bag and throw in a change of clothes. After practice for the Roaring, I have to head straight to my first class of the day. "You'll have your chance." I smile down at the indolent male, ignoring the butterflies that have taken up residence in my stomach. "Besides, I won the bet."

"What do you want me to do? Pound into your sweet pussy? Lick you dry? Finger you to heaven?" He winks seductively at me, and I swear my vagina winks back. Shameless hussy.

"You'll see," I say lightly. "Now get your ass up and dressed. It's time to train."

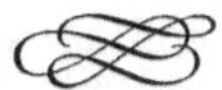

CHAPTER 12

VIOLET

At some point during the night, it must've rained. Pregnant gray storm clouds can still be seen hovering over the horizon. A frigid wind blows at the back of my neck as I step into the cemetery bogged down with weeds. My eyes automatically flicker to the large oak tree planted right in the midst of all the gravestones. It feels like it's been years since I first met Jack and Hux, but I know it can't have been more than a few weeks.

Mason sulks beside me, still peeved that I hadn't allowed him to give me an orgasm. And, friends, my vagina is livid with me as well.

Later, I tell her seriously. It's important to have a good relationship with your furburger—to nurture it and feed it. If you don't, it'll wither up and die a slow and painful death.

Near the largest tomb at the edge of the cemetery, over fifty students stand in a single-file line as Mummy—aka, King Tut—paces before them. When he catches sight of

Mason and me, his eyes narrow into slits through the pale bandages on his face.

"You're late!" he bellows, his voice echoing through the silent graveyard. Even the dead are still sleeping at this hour.

I exchange a wide-eyed glance with Mason before breaking into a run and joining the end of the line.

I spot Vin and Jack standing together, identical expressions of concern marring their handsome faces. Before I can lift my hand up to wave, Cheryl sticks her head out from the opposite side of Vin and smiles smugly at me. Disgust swirls in my gut like a live nest of snakes as she loops her arm with Vin's. I can't help the pang of jealousy and rage that explode within me like errant fireworks, despite the fact he shoves her away with a sneer of disgust.

Surprisingly enough, I see Frankie standing farther down the line, his back ramrod straight. Frankie? Competing in the Roaring? The man sells drugs in exchange for getting out of gym class. Exercise and him is the equivalent to...exercise and me. Let's be honest—why run a mile, when you can stay at home, curled beneath a blanket, while binge-watching Netflix and eating ice cream from the tub? Some people need to get their priorities in order.

"This year alone, there are over three hundred monsters registered to compete in the Roaring," Mummy begins in a curt voice. His hands are clasped behind his back as he paces, giving him a regal, imperious demeanor. Even in the full-body wrappings, he looks every inch the Egyptian king.

"Three hundred," a girl squeaks, and Mummy whips his head in her direction, leveling her with a glare that reminds me distinctly of a frosted-over sword.

"Are you scared?" he whispers menacingly, taking a step closer until he's towering over the slip of a girl. When she defiantly shakes her head, lower lip trembling, Mummy releases a harsh bark of laughter. "Well, you should be. The Roaring is immensely dangerous. Last year, we had one hundred and fifty-seven deaths. Do you know how many people competed last year?" He doesn't wait for an answer, spinning on his heel until he has resumed his eccentric pacing once more. "Two hundred. One hundred and fifty-seven monsters died out of the two hundred competitors. Does anyone know that percentage?"

Don't pick me. Don't pick me. Don't pick me.

"Violet?" Mummy stares at me intently.

"Um…"

Mental math. The bane of my existence. Give me a cadaver, and I can tell you how to remove the heart with minimal damage to the other organs, but ask me to solve a math problem without a calculator, and my brain turns to mush. That's third grade shit right there. Fourth grade, they teach you the good stuff—like how to use a fucking calculator.

I pretend to think about it for a long moment. "…you carry the eight and move the four to the right."

"That's seventy-eight point five percent," Gills, of all fucking people, says helpfully. She throws a pointed look in my direction, her lips curling in a hideous sneer. I half want to warn her that her face will stick like that…if it wasn't already ugly as sin. The obstetrician probably took one look at her face, one look at her butt, and told her mother that she had birthed a set of twins. "I wonder how many vampire deaths there were?"

Mason tenses beside me, and I notice Vin giving Cheryl a scathing glare. She merely fluffs up her orange hair with a roll of her eyes.

"Are we late?" a familiar voice inquires. "Please tell me we're not late. I *told* you that we should've left earlier."

"No fucking way," I breathe as Cal and Barret saunter

through the gravestones, Cal's magnificent wings on full display for the world to see. "Cal? Barret?"

Before my brain can even catch up to what is happening, I'm racing towards them, my hands outstretched. One of my arms links around Cal's neck while the other encompasses Barret.

"What are you doing here?" I pull back to stare into each of their faces. Due to their past transgressions, Cal and Barret are forced to remain in the upper levels of the Academy. I'm not exactly sure what they did that was deemed horrific enough to be locked away, and I haven't dared to ask. They have only been allowed outside a few times before—every Halloween night. Even then, they had a chip in their necks that would explode if they didn't return to their prison by midnight.

"We're competing," Barret replies with an easy smile, ruffling my blonde curls. "Are you happy to see us, Cheese Curd?"

Someone begins laughing behind me, but she quickly smothers the noise when Barret swivels his head in her direction. I place my hand on his arm to reclaim his attention.

"Of course," I reply earnestly. When Cal's feathers begin to ruffle—quite literally—I place a hand on his arm as well. We all have our vices, and Cal's makes him a drama queen.

"She *would* be friends with the psycho monsters," a cold voice retorts from behind me, and I spin on my heel, unsurprised to see the shit head from yesterday standing in line with the rest of us monsters. He's wearing the customary red shirt, but it does little to dissipate the darkness that seems to cling to him like a second skin. With his tousled black hair, numerous piercings, and the tattoos that cover every available swath of skin, he's a sight to behold. I might've even considered him sexy, if he wasn't such a pompous jackass.

"What's your problem?" I hiss, baring my fangs. When I take a step closer, all of my men spring into action. Vin and Mason step up to either side of me, while Jack and Frankie take up the rear. Even Cal and Barret look as if they're charging into battle, fierce scowls on their faces.

The man continues to look at me, anger and rage simmering in his fathomless black eyes. They're like twin abysses—one wrong move, and you could get lost in them forever.

"Don't talk to me," he says through gritted teeth. He clenches his jaw and stares pointedly over my head, almost as if my face physically pains him.

"Alex, leave the vampire whore alone," Cheryl whines, slithering up to him like the lizard she is. She places her hand on his arm—as she just did with Vin—and like with him, Alex levels her with a frosty glare before storming away.

Silence engulfs the cemetery as I realize I've garnered the attention of the entire student body present.

"That was fun," Mummy says dryly. "May I please proceed? I feel like I need to ask for your permission now, Violet. You have a tendency to disrupt me a lot."

"Oh." My cheeks aflame, I reach behind me to grab Cal's and Barret's hands, pulling them into line with me. "Carry on."

Mummy's eyes flash dangerously, but he turns back towards the assembled monsters with a haughty set to his chin.

"This morning, we're going to play a game in preparation for the physical side of the Roaring." He pauses, allowing his words to sink in and the excited murmurs to begin. Monster games? There's nothing better. Except for maybe sex games. "Capture the Flag."

Everyone begins to talk over each other, the anticipatory energy almost infectious. To Frankie, who is now standing on the opposite side of Cal, I ask, "Is it like the game we played before?"

"No. In this game, there are only two flags and two teams. Your goal is to guard your team's flag as well as capture the other team's."

I focus on Mummy just as he begins describing the boundaries. "The Blue Team will have to protect the area from the academic hall to the houses. The Red Team will be hiding their flag from the academic hall, past the dorms, to the cafeteria. Are there any questions?"

When I raise my hand in the air timidly, he gives me a long, hard look that would make a lesser monster shit her pants. After a moment, he shakes his head with a scoff and focuses once more on the line of students.

"Since there are no questions..." *Asshole.* "Teams will be broken down the middle...here." He pushes one werewolf to one side and her shifter friend to the other. Fortunately, this arrangement allows me to be on a team with all of my guys... and to have Cheryl and Alex on the team opposite me. I'm all for teamwork and everything, but not if it involves me making deals with the devil himself. Or herself, in this case.

"Blue Team!" He throws a bunch of hideous blue jerseys at us, and I awkwardly slip it over my head. It's two sizes too large and smells like sweat and piss. What did the person do? Roll around in it while helicoptering his penis?

Mummy turns towards Cheryl and her bitch crew. "Red Team!"

"What are the rules?" a girl standing beside Cheryl inquires in faux innocence.

"No killing," Mummy says bluntly. "Anything else is fair game. If it gets cut off, chances are, it'll grow back."

Cheryl tosses me a smug smile, as if she's already envisioning all of the malevolent things she plans to do to me.

Note to self—stay far, far away from the she-bitch.

My eyes latch on Alex, who is rooted to the spot, eyes surveying me with an unwavering intensity. In those obsidian depths, I can see a banked fire just beneath the surface.

Also note to self—stay away from Shit Face.

Mummy hands the red flag to Cheryl and the blue flag to me.

Motherfucker. I imagine this is what it feels like to be a mother, to be forced to care about someone's life more than your own.

Because I'll be damned if I let Cheryl have my mother-fucking flag baby.

"Cheryl will be the captain of the Red Team," Mummy announces, and Cheryl practically preens, winking first at Vin and then Alex. It's like she can't decide what dick she wants, so she's attempting to sample them all. "And Violet will be the captain of the Blue Team."

Instead of the cheers I expected, my team immediately breaks into disheartened grumbles. Mason can't help but shake his head in amusement.

"Everybody!" I motion for my team to gather around me. Half of the people I don't recognize, but I can only pray they're not anti-vampire fanatics. The last thing I need to be is stabbed in the back by my own teammates. "We need a team chant."

"A team...chant?" one of the girls asks, quirking a brow. The guy beside her covers his mouth to keep from laughing.

"Yes." I narrow my eyes at her before turning towards the rest of the group. "How about... Blue Team, Blue Team, don't be shy, stand right up and stick your foot up Cheryl's ass until she's coughing up blood and shoelaces." I eagerly place my hand in the center of the makeshift huddle.

Only Cal, Barret, and Mason join me in my chant.

"For fuck's sake, Violet," Vin grumbles, pinching the

bridge of his nose. I swear the man always does that around me—as if my stupidity is capable of oozing up his nostrils. Well…who's the stupid one now?

Stupidity is not contagious. Idiot.

"I'm sorry," I say with an over-exaggerated pout. "Did you not want me talking about murdering your girlfriend?"

"She's not my girlfriend," he hisses, glaring at me.

I place my hands on my waist and raise my chin. "Do you want her to be?"

"Fuck, no. There's only one person I want—"

Before he can finish whatever he was going to say, Mummy lifts his whistle to his lips, and a shrill sound pierces the air.

"Let the games begin!" he roars.

Immediately, my teammates disband, leaving me standing there awkwardly with Mason, Frankie, Vin, Jack, Barret, and Cal. I stare into each of their handsome faces before sheepishly holding up the flag.

"What am I supposed to do with this?" I question. On the other side of the unofficial line marking each territory, Cheryl and Alex watch me closely. Have you ever been stripped naked and jabbed in the stomach with a hot poker? If you answered yes, then that is what this feels like. I'm on display for them to see, with the sole goal of inflicting as much pain as possible.

"You protect it," Mason says casually, reaching into his flannel pocket to grab a joint. I eye it—and him—distastefully, but choose not to comment. He knows how I feel about that shit. According to Dracula, my mom died of some hardcore fairy weed when I was just a child. I don't remember much about her, except for the color of her eyes…and even that is fading with time.

"And we protect you," Vin adds curtly. He crosses his burly arms over his chest and lowers his face so he can make and maintain eye contact. "I'll always protect you, Violet. Even when you hate me."

I roll my eyes in exasperation. This man can be so fucking confusing. One second, he's saying sweet shit like that, and the next, he's sucking faces with my moral enemy. And yes, I meant moral, not mortal. I am virtuous; she's sin personified. I have morals; she takes those morals and shoves them up her petite ass.

Thus, she's my moral enemy.

"So…shouldn't we, like, run and hide?" I ask warily, eyeing the collection of monsters lining up at the barrier. I notice that Cheryl and Alex have already disappeared, no doubt to hide their own flag. What I wouldn't give to pry that flag from their cold, dead fingers…

Instead of responding, Jack grabs my hand and pulls me out of the cemetery, through the woods, and up the steep staircase leading to the academic building. It's an old structure, its bricks bleached from sunlight and vandalism, with ivy crawling up and down its sides. At this early in the morning, the building is empty, the silence almost deafening in a macabre sense of irony.

"So this is where the other half lives," Cal murmurs lazily, shoving his hands into his pockets and meandering farther down the hall. Despite his nonchalant tone, I catch a flicker of pain in his eyes, one he quickly tries to hide.

"Actually," Mason drawls, taking another long drag. "It's where we have our classes. There are dorms for the underclassmen, like Violet, to live in. We live in a house."

Cal and Barret exchange an unreadable look.

"A house," Barret repeats wistfully, and my mind flashes back to their abandoned floor at the top of this building. There are a dozen classrooms lining the walls and a dusty teacher's lounge, but there're no bedrooms. No beds. No television and no couch.

My heart breaks for these men, and I make a vow that after the Roaring is over, I'll find a way to free them. No monster should be locked away.

Well, except the ones who murder small children.

And the ones who decimate entire cities.

And the ones who hang their enemies by their fingernails in the rafters of a gymnasium.

And the ones who—

You get the idea.

But Barret and Cal? Boogeyman and Cupid? They don't deserve the shit hand they've been dealt. If I can do something about it, I will in a heartbeat. Hell, I'll even seduce and sleep with Dimitri Gray if it's required of me.

The things I do for my friends.

"So, we just sit here and wait for someone to try and steal the flag?" I inquire, stepping into an empty classroom and pulling myself onto the teacher's desk. I recognize the room as Dimitri's old one, before he became the headmaster.

"Yes, ma'am." Mason climbs onto the desk beside me and places his head on my shoulder. "Until then, we can finish what we started..." He trails off suggestively, his fingers walking down my stomach until it reaches the apex of my thighs.

"Don't be a turd," I hiss, shoving his hand away. I know my face is flushed, and I can literally see my chest heaving as desire courses through me. All I can picture is Mason finger fucking me while the rest of the guys watch.

Fortunately, all of the guys—sans Cal—remain oblivious as they attempt to fortify the classroom. The cupid is staring at my legs intently, pink brows furrowed. When I clear my throat pointedly, his head whips up, and he flashes me a sheepish smile.

"We have to hope that the rest of our teammates find the

other team's flag," Vin mutters, shoving a desk in front of the door.

"What happens if none of the flags are found?" I question, swinging my legs.

"Then we all lose," Jack replies gently.

Frankie drops to the ground and removes his backpack—I swear he even showers with that damn thing.

And…

Now I'm thinking of Frankie showering, the soapy suds cascading down his body. His hand wrapping around his cock. Sweat and shower water beading on his forehead.

Down, girl, I tell my libido seriously.

Using my fang, I pierce my bottom lip until blood is drawn. The stab of pain helps ground me to the present, to the here and now. It helps remind me that I'm alive and breathing, and that I can't get on my hands and knees and start licking Frankie's cock like a lollipop. You know, normal things.

"I have something in here that might be able to help…" Frankie mutters, removing first a bowl, then a slimy eyeball, and then a six-foot liver. Keep in mind, Frankie's backpack is two feet long, max. I swear it must be spelled.

I wonder if you can spell a vagina to fit more cocks in it at the same time.

Focus!

"People are going to be searching for me, correct?" I ask, running a finger across the distressed wood.

"Of course," Vin murmurs curtly. "You have the flag."

"No, she doesn't." Barret glances first at me and then at the flag I placed on the desk beside me. "She's not even touching it."

Cal and I exchange a look of camaraderie before shaking our heads and pasting on smiles. "You're right, Barret," I say.

"But it's just a figure of speech. What Vin meant was everyone knows I have the flag with me."

Here's the thing about Barret. He's not stupid. Honestly, he's not. He just processes things differently than other people. Sometimes, that means he takes things too literally, and other times, he becomes bored with the conversation, zones out, and misses all of what was being said.

"Wait!" I say suddenly, jumping to my feet.

"Uh oh." Mason grimaces. "I don't like that expression on your face. It means you're up to something."

My smile widens as wariness flitters across each of the men's faces.

"I have an idea."

CHAPTER 13

VIOLET

"This is fucking stupid," Vin grumbles as we stand in the foyer of their shared house.

"Trust me." Ignoring his muttered curses, I sashay to the supply closet immediately opposite the kitchen. I spot a vacuum, a broom, a duster, and my sex doll.

Yup. Apparently, it's a thing.

Fake Violet is hunched over currently, dressed in only a revealing bra and thong. Her blonde tangles obscure her face from view. I can't help but note the lacerations on her arms and legs as well as the wires visible on her stomach. This Fake Violet? She endured a pretty severe beating at the hands of my classmates, and her body still bears the marks.

"This is never going to work," Vin—the Debbie Downer—laments as I haul the life-sized doll from the closet. Mason quickly moves forward to help me, his hand accidentally grazing her plump breast. Color rises to his cheeks as he lowers it to her distorted stomach.

"Sorry," he mouths as we maneuver her onto a kitchen chair.

At first, I wonder why none of the guys bothered to help me, but when I catch a glimpse of their faces, I see why.

They're positively livid. Cal's wings are flapping erratically as angry red splotches erupt on his cheeks. Barret, my gentle giant, is spewing vitriol with his eyes. Jack appears concerned, and Vin looks as if he wants to rip the limbs off of every person who'd attended that party. Frankie's face is devoid of any emotion, except for his eyes. A banked fire percolates just beneath the surface, demanding an outlet.

"I can't believe they did that," Cal hisses, running a hand through his light pink hair. Suddenly, he whirls on Vin, who is standing closest to him. "How could you have let this happen?"

"Me?" Vin comically points to his chest before taking a step closer. "Why the fuck are you blaming me?"

"Maybe because you're always breaking her heart," Cal refutes instantly, and Vin blanches as if he has been physically struck. Only his eyes move to focus on me, and in them, I see a decade worth of yearning and pain.

"I didn't..."

"You guys are supposed to protect Cheese Curd," Barret adds in a low, dangerous tone. His untamed green hair stands on end, almost as if his agitation is physically manifesting itself.

"What did you just say?" I know, without even having to look, that Jack has transformed into Hux. His hands ball into fists as he slowly, mechanically, turns towards the mammoth monster.

Hux is significantly shorter than Barret, but I have no doubt they'll be evenly matched in a fight. What Hux lacks in body mass, he makes up for in pure stealth. And insanity.

Insanity...passion...

Is there really a difference?

"Do not talk to me about how I protect my precious treasure," Hux hisses through gritted teeth. His eyes spew an almost incandescent fury, capable of lighting this entire room on fire. "Who the hell even are you?"

Cal moves to stand protectively in front of Barret, his chest puffed out. "Your mom's secret lover," he sneers.

Hux's face creases adorably.

"My mom's dead."

Barret pushes up onto his tiptoes to whisper conspiratorially in Cal's ear, "How can you fuck his mom when she's dead?"

For the love of…

"I'm going upstairs!" I announce suddenly. Without waiting for them to respond, I spin on my heel and hurry to the second level.

Each of the doors are closed, so I choose a room at random and let myself inside. It's surprisingly sparse, with a single queen-sized bed in the center of the room flanked by two nightstands. A desk sits against the far wall with a laptop closed overtop of it. Clothes are haphazardly strewn across the floor. And when I see the black tee-shirt, I realize the room I have wandered into is Vin's.

"There are much easier ways to get into my bed," the man himself murmurs from behind me. When I turn, I see his lips quirked upwards into his customary smirk. That smirk fades when he catches sight of the expression on my face. "We need to talk."

"What we need is to protect the flag," I counter, opening up his first drawer and grabbing a pair of tight boxer briefs. Fire races through my veins, but I try to smother my reaction before Vin notices.

"No, Violet."

"I'll just grab what I need and—"

"No." Vin drops his hand onto the top of the dresser, effectively caging me in. I can feel his chest touch my back with each of his exhales. "I'm not doing this with you."

"I don't know what you mean," I answer stiffly, my back ramrod straight. My traitorous body wants to lean against his and consume his warmth, but I shut that shit down fast. I won't give him the satisfaction.

"I'm not allowing it this time," he continues, his breath tickling my ear. Goosebumps pebble on my skin at his close proximity, and I pray that he doesn't notice. "I'm not allowing you to shut me out and ignore me again."

I spin on my heel so fast that he staggers back a step, his arms dropping to his sides.

"You don't get to decide that," I hiss, jamming a finger against his sculpted chest. "You don't get to hurt me and then act pissed when I hurt you."

"That's just the thing!" he shouts, hitting my finger away. Once more, he cages me against his hard, muscular body. My nipples pebble through the thin material of my shirt as he leans over me. "We're in this cycle, Violet, and I want us to get out. I can't *stand* not having you in my life. I don't want to hurt you again. I never wanted to hurt you. All I have ever wanted was to be by your side, and you're not *fucking letting me.*"

"I saw you," I point out, unwilling to let this argument go. Jealousy seeps through my pores when I remember Cheryl's lips on his. "I saw you with that…with that snake."

"*She* kissed *me*," he snaps, taking another step closer until his chest touches my own. "I didn't kiss her back. I don't want her lips anywhere near me."

"Am I really what you want, Vin?" I question, tilting my head back. "Because I'm pretty damn confused right now. Sometimes, you act like you hate my guts, and other times, you act like—"

Before I can finish my rant, he presses his lips to mine.

Like you want to kiss the shit out of me.

Vin kisses me with a bruising intensity, as if he wants to claim and possess me. It's hard and rough and dirty. His tongue tangles with mine as we fight each other for control. Instead of roses and rainbows, it's swords and shields. Our kiss is an atomic explosion, decimating everything in the general vicinity but leaving behind new life.

He glides his hand under my shirt, pulling down my sports bra so he can palm my breast. His thumb flicks over my pert nipple, and I moan into his mouth. His lips leave my own to travel across my cheek and to my ear.

"You drive me fucking insane," he whispers hoarsely.

I lower my hands from his waist and to his ass, giving it a tight squeeze. "Right back at ya."

With a moan, he begins to kiss me once more, his cock hitting my pussy with each thrust of his hips. I continue to knead his ass cheeks before a wicked idea occurs to me.

Without breaking the kiss, I pull down his gym shorts and boxers until I'm touching bare flesh. His cock springs free, already dripping with pre-cum, but I pay it no mind. At least for now.

I pull my lips away briefly to spit on my hand, and Vin watches me in confusion.

"What are you—?"

His question turns into a hiss of air as I stick one of my fingers into his tight asshole.

"Fuck!" he curses, hips jerking.

"You hurt me, Vin," I whisper, smattering angry kisses down his neck. When I reach the juncture between his neck and shoulder, I bite down. I don't use my fangs—that's not the point—but the low moan he releases tells me that he knows who the predator is in this scenario.

Spoiler alert—it's not him.

I add a second finger to the first, breaching the tight ring of muscles.

"I don't like you with other girls," I continue, scissoring my fingers in his anus. "Even if they instigate it."

"I'll kill them all," he moans, dropping his forehead to my shoulder. And I have to admit, the idea has merit. But alas, we can't go murdering every female who looks at him funny. That's a little too crazy, even for me.

"I love it when you get all psycho on me," I purr, removing my fingers from his puckered hole. Before he can complain, I slap first one asscheek and then the other. His cock bobs, pre-cum dripping onto the ground, and I realize the kinky shit likes it. Smiling at my newfound knowledge, I spank him again, harder, and his eyes roll back into his head.

"Violet…"

"Say you're sorry," I hiss as he begins to paw at me. When I don't move away, he eagerly pulls off my shirt and rearranges my sports bra so my boobs spring free. My nipples are beaded nubs, and he wastes no time in running his thumbs over them both.

"I'm so sorry," he whispers, lowering his head to flick his tongue over my nipple. "I'm so fucking sorry. It'll never happen again."

"It better fucking not," I hiss, grabbing his cock and giving it a quick, sure stroke. "I don't know how many more chances I can give you, Vin. You hurt me twice already."

"I'll never hurt you again," he vows as I press down on his balls. He hisses through clenched teeth. "I fucking promise."

I let go of his cock and move my hand back to his ass. I spank him again, *hard,* and his cock jerks before his cum spills over the floor. He curses, eyes rolling to the back of his head in bliss, as my smile turns…pretty damn evil, if the reflection in the mirror is any indication.

"Fucking hell!" he curses as I press a tender, chaste kiss to the corner of his mouth.

"You're mine now, Vin," I both promise and warn. "And I'm a pretty damn selfish monster. Now that I have you, I'm never letting you go."

~

Like with Mason, Vin is pissed as fuck that I won't allow him to get me off.

Sigh. The troubles of being a female, am I right?

I give him a small, sultry smirk and pat his cheek. "You'll just owe me one later," I tell him with a wink, my mind already running rampant with the possibilities.

I know Vin and Mason are both as straight as can be, but I can't ignore the throb in my pussy at the thought of the two of them taking me together.

Biting my lip to contain my lust-filled moan, I quickly change into a pair of Vin's boxer briefs and one of his black tee-shirts. We have been up here for almost twenty minutes. No doubt, the others will be wondering what we have been doing for so long. I'm surprised Hux hasn't raided the room already.

"Will this work?" Vin asks gruffly as I grab my discarded clothes. I flash him a smile, but internally, I'm envisioning his face as I finger his asshole. What can I say? I'm insatiable.

"Of course. I'm a genius—"

I tumble to the ground as my foot catches on the edge of his desk chair.

Fucking hell.

"Okay, *genius*," Vin says sarcastically, leaning against the wall with his arms crossed over his chest.

"Aren't you going to be a gentleman and help me up?" I extend a hand, and he rolls his eyes.

"Haven't you realized? I'm an asshole." He shrugs unre-pentantly, but helps me to my feet anyway.

"You sure do like things in your asshole," I tease. When his eyes flare with heat, I'm very, very tempted to forget about this whole stupid game, tie him to the bed, and ride his cock until we either pass out from pleasure or pain. But alas, I'm too competitive to let Cheryl win.

I'm the team fucking captain, and I'll make Cheryl my bitch by the end of the day.

Speaking of...

"Did you know that Cheryl's nipples turn into seashells when she's aroused?" I mention casually as we exit Vin's room. The hunter staggers over his own two feet, nearly faceplanting before he rights himself. And he calls *me* clumsy.

"Why the hell are you staring at Cheryl's nipples?" he snaps. "When she's aroused?" He tries to hide his reaction—he honestly does—but it slips through before he can mask it. Instead of aroused at the prospect of two girls having sex together or even confused, he's jealous.

Oh, the irony.

"What would you say if I told you that I fucked her?" I ask nonchalantly, and his nostrils flare. Now, he doesn't even bother to contain his jealousy—it radiates from him in tangible waves. "That I kissed those perky breasts of hers and licked her seashells. What if I said I buried my face in her pussy while she played with my nipples? Or that our slick pussies rubbed against each other? That our nipples brushed as she swirled her tongue around first one and then the other?"

Vin releases an enraged roar, lunging forward until he's pressing me against the wall. I'm so startled I drop my spare clothes onto the ground. He places his palms on either side of my head and rubs his nose against my own. His breathing is labored as he struggles to gain control of himself.

I wonder…

"And what if I told you that Fish Boy was there as well?" I quirk a single eyebrow as pure madness reflects back at me in his brown gaze. "That I played with his cock while he—"

He slams his lips to mine in another claiming, possessive kiss. When he pulls away, his eyes are wild, crazed, and refuse to focus on any one thing.

"Don't talk about shit like that, okay?" he snaps, lowering his face to my neck. I run my fingers through his short dark hair.

"But what if I told you that just today, I gave Mason a blowjob?" I place my hands on either side of his face, forcing him to look at me. "What if I said that *he* licked my nipples. What if I told you that I ran my tongue down his cock?"

The madness gradually recedes, replaced by…lust. Pure, unfiltered lust.

Interesting.

"What about Hux and Jack?" I continue, gauging his reaction. "I kissed both of them. I rubbed my pussy against Hux's cock until we both orgasmed."

His pupils become dilated, and his breathing shutters in and out. His now erect cock touches my thigh as he crowds even closer.

"And what about Frankie?" I lick my lips, and his eyes follow that movement. "What if I want to grip his cock in one hand while I jerk off Mason in the other? What if I want to run my tongue down the vein in Jack's cock?"

He closes his eyes, as if my fantasies physically pain him, before reopening them and focusing on me.

"That is so fucking hot," he breathes, devouring my lips once more. He sucks sharply on my bottom lip, pulling it between his teeth, before releasing it with another pained groan. "I don't know how to fucking explain it. I'm not into guys or anything, but the thought of you with my friends makes me so fucking hard. I want to *watch* you run your tongue over Mason's cock. I want Jack and Hux to play with those perfect breasts and nipples of yours. I want Frankie to pound into your sweet pussy lips." He presses his forehead to mine, squeezing his eyes shut once more. "But the thought of you with anyone else..." A low growl reverberates through his body. "I'll tear them limb from limb."

"Even if it's a girl? Isn't that, like, a guy's fantasy?" I question seriously, but Vin releases another snarl in answer.

"No. No one else." He lowers his hands to squeeze my ass, just as I did to his.

"Well, hot fucking damn," Mason breathes from the end of the hallway. I jump at the intrusion, but Vin merely holds me tighter, glaring at his best friend. Even from this distance, I can see the outline of Mason's cock in his loose shorts. "I have to agree with Vin, here. The thought of you jerking him off makes me hard as hell. But the thought of you sucking Cheryl's tits makes me want to murder the bitch. And that's coming from a man who watched lesbian porn." He shakes his head once as if attempting to clear his muddled thoughts. "But, Pinkie, you should get down there before the guys blow a gasket. Thanks to Cal, we know exactly what you've been up to, and I'm pretty sure Barret is explaining what a boner is to a very confused Hux."

Heat swarms low in my stomach at the thought of all of them waiting downstairs for me, knowing that I just made Vin come. There's something empowering about that sensation, something I can't put into words.

"Let's win this game," I tell them firmly, shoving Vin away from me. "And then I'll take a bath in Cheryl's tears."

CHAPTER 14

VIOLET

I glare at the disgusting green slime Frankie coated me in. According to him, it's designed to dampen my scent against strong shifters and werewolves. It also makes me impossible for witches to track.

"I feel like ET's love baby," I murmur to Barret, who is crouching beside me. The green sludge sticks to my fingers like some sort of fucked up super glue.

"You're still cute though," Barret assures me, and I can't help but flash him a happy smile. Ladies and gentlemen, get yourself a boogeyman in your life. Even when you're covered in green slime, he'll make you feel beautiful and treasured.

"Thanks, Boo Bear," I say, leaning forward to peck him on the cheek. Immediately, crimson rushes to his face, and he ducks his head with a chagrined, almost bashful, smile. Turning away from him, I focus on the cemetery in the distance, the dark slabs of cement shrouded in a light, gray mist.

The rest of my guys surround a very lifeless looking

Violet. I dressed her in my Academy-issued red shirt and shorts and tied a fake flag around her left wrist. From this distance, I can't see her dazed eyes or the numerous scars marring her porcelain skin. Hopefully, that means Cheryl won't be able to see them either.

"Let's finish this," I whisper darkly as the group steps over the unofficial line marking the end of our barrier. On cue, Cheryl, Alex, and a dozen other monsters crowd around us, hideous sneers distorting their features.

"Well, well, well, what do we have here?" Cheryl's shrill voice carries in the wind, reaching me where I huddle behind an overgrown bush. "The little slut and her merry gang of fuck-ups."

"I'll show you 'little slut,'" I mutter beneath my breath, bracing myself for a fight. Barret places a calming hand on my shoulder and gives it a reassuring squeeze.

Taking a deep, fortifying breath—rebuilding my previously shattered defenses—I focus once more on Cheryl with a clinical detachment. I can't think about her as the bitch who banged my men or the girl who kissed Vin. I can't think about her as anything other than my enemy. With a clear head, I allow my gaze to wander over her, stopping briefly on the flag tied around her ankle. It almost appears to be a sock —which was no doubt her intention.

"Give us the flag, Vinny Poo," Cheryl cajoles, sauntering a step closer. My men close around Fake Violet, obscuring her from view.

"Choke on dick," Vin responds tersely, and he better not mean his dick, or else I'm going to stab a ho.

She pauses abruptly a few feet away, eyes narrowing into thin, unforgiving slits. "Why are you protecting her?" she hisses.

Before Vin can respond—and hopefully, declare his undying devotion for me—Alex removes himself from the throng of students, head canted to the side. He closes his eyes briefly before reopening them and focusing on my hiding place.

"It's a diversion," he snaps, grabbing Cheryl's arm to pull her backwards. "That's not Violet."

Before their group can make it more than four steps, the ground rumbles and then the graveyard explodes with a bang. Monsters sail through the air in every direction at the intensity of the detonation.

"Hell, yes!" I jump to my feet and fist-pump the air. Frankie offers me a cheeky wink from where he still stands with the others, and a burst of laughter escapes me unbidden.

I spot Cheryl up ahead, groaning, and I skip forward feeling significantly lighter than ever before.

"Violet, let me do it, dammit!" Vin protests when I stop above the simpering redhead.

"It's the twenty-first century, baby." I wink at the glowering hunter before bending down and untying the flag from her ankle. "The ladies are leading."

Before I can celebrate my win, a leg kicks out and knocks me onto my ass. I blink rapidly, attempting to orient myself, as Cheryl throws a punch at my jaw. My head reels to the side as she straddles me, her knees on either side of my hips.

"I'll take that," she says cheerfully as she grabs first her flag and then my flag I had wrapped around my ponytail.

With a grace and agility fitting her dainty size, she jumps to her feet and saunters over to where Alex is now standing. All they need to do is bring the two flags to Mummy and they'll win the game.

I cannot let that fucking happen.

"...shove my fist right up her Egg McMuffin," I murmur darkly, eyes spewing vitriol.

"Violet, please stop talking about fisting my ex." Vin

moves to stand beside me and places a restraining hand on my shoulder. I don't know if he's attempting to pull me towards him or keep me from lunging after Cheryl fucking Ness, and frankly, I don't care.

"I'm gonna Happy Meal that bitch," I announce snidely, shrugging off Vin's arm and charging forward. There's nothing more dangerous than a girl on a mission.

There's nothing more dangerous than a vampire out for blood.

With a burst of vampire speed, I ram my shoulder into Cheryl's legs, knocking her off her feet. She lands on her ass with an audible thump, and I can't help my grin of satisfaction. That smugness turns into annoyance when Alex touches my shoulder, prepared to spin me around.

"Dude, you're going to leave a mark, and I don't like them in any non-sexual context," I hiss, kicking my left heel back and jamming it into his kneecap. He releases me with a pained groan, and I take advantage of his momentary lapse of concentration to reach down and grab both flags. "Poor little Alex," I taunt as I begin to walk backwards.

He's still keeled over, but his eyes are fixed firmly on me, watching my retreat. Pure hatred emanates back at me, barraging my senses. It hangs like a palpable entity over both of our heads, reminding me eerily of a guillotine. You lie there awaiting your inevitable fate, unable to see anything but the blade glinting overhead. All you can do is wait for it to fall.

The wind stirs his pitch-black hair as his eyes cloud over. It's like a cauldron of ink being spilled. Slowly, painstakingly slow, the black devours the whites around his eyes until I'm staring into pure darkness. He lifts his hand, and the mist gliding over the gravestones gradually recedes.

"Oh, shit," I murmur, peering over my shoulder at the other guys. They're far enough away to be unaware of my predicament, busy fighting off the remaining monsters who weren't rendered unconscious by the blast.

A crackling sound has my attention diverting to one of the graves. As I watch, horrified, a pale, gnarled hand breaches the freshly strewn dirt, followed immediately by a second. I spin in a circle, terror raging through me, as more and more hands appear. Those hands are followed by skeletal heads and lean bodies.

Necromancer.

Alex is a fucking necromancer.

One of the skeletons grabs my ankles, and another wraps his bony arms around my stomach. One, I could take out. Maybe even five. But two dozen? All grabbing at me and pulling me to the ground? Fuck, no.

"Poor little vampire," Alex tuts, leaning over me with a malicious smirk.

"Let me go and fight me yourself, you coward," I hiss as a rough hand grabs at my blonde ponytail, yanking it backwards. "Don't be a cock. I would've said pussy, but let's be honest… Which one is actually stronger?"

Alex continues to smile, unperturbed by my taunts.

The knobbly hands continue to paw at me, pulling me towards a fresh patch of dirt near the opposite end of the cemetery.

This fucker is trying to bury me alive! Not cool.

I try another tactic, wrenching my face away from one of the hands attempting to cover my mouth. "Wait! Please, wait! You don't have to do this. I know you hate Dracula and everything—"

"Dracula?" Alex raises a pierced eyebrow. "I don't have a problem with him." He takes a step closer until his silhouette blocks out the steadily rising sun. He's all I see, all I hear. He consumes the entirety of my senses. "It's *you* I hate."

"Me?" My words become garbled as one of the skeletons

places his hand over my mouth. I attempt to bite down with my fangs, but release a pained cry when I hear a snap. Blood drizzles down my chin from my broken fang, and I try my damn hardest to hold back my tears.

As abruptly as the skeletons converged on me, they release me and crawl back towards their respective graves.

Alex stands over me, panting, his eyes fixed on the lick of blood from my broken fang. His expression shutters as he bends down and grabs the two flags. Without a word, he strides across the cemetery to where Mummy is waiting.

"Violet!" Hux roars, and I turn my head just as he tosses a partially shifted mermaid into a gravestone in his effort to reach me. In quick strides, he hurries towards my side and tenderly cups my jaw. "Whom do I have to kill?"

"We lost," I lament as somewhere in the distance, I hear Cheryl's squeal of victory.

Vin and Mason join the huddle next, each covered in a layer of blood with their shirts ripped. Behind them, Frankie stands with an impassive expression on his face, his cold eyes flicking across my body until it rests on my bloody mouth.

"What happened?" Cal demands, stalking towards my other side with Barret hot on his heels. When he sees me, his face scrunches together in sympathy. "Ouch. That looks like it hurts like a bitch. At least you're still cute."

"Very cute," Barret agrees, and I roll my eyes at their attempt to humor me.

"We lost," I repeat again. That realization settles in my chest like a heavy ball of lead, intermingling with the tangle of nerves already present. "We lost, and Cheryl won." I clench my hands into fists before slowly, carefully, raising myself to a sitting position. An idea occurs to me as I turn towards the gathered men. "It's the universe deep-dicking us. If you can't stop it, enjoy it. At least if the universe makes you preggo, you'll get child-support from that bitch."

Just because they won the battle, doesn't mean they won the war.

I have one goal in life, and one goal only—destroy Alex and Cheryl, no matter the cost.

THE IDEA OCCURS TO ME WHEN WE'RE ALL GATHERED AROUND Mummy, after the first official training session for the Roaring has commenced.

Alex sits across the circle, sipping from a water bottle, and I nudge Barret inconspicuously with my elbow.

"Think you can do me a favor?" I ask, batting my lashes up at the tall, imposing man. Barret's brows furrow in confusion before he follows the direction of my gaze. Understanding dawns as a mischievous grin—reminiscent of Mason's—lights up his handsome face. "Maybe, instead of water, Alex can be drinking dead bugs?"

"I can do something even better," he whispers, closing his eyes. I whip my head in Alex's direction just as he begins to choke. His eyes widen in horror as his hands reach up to grab at his neck. To my macabre fascination, dozens of beetles crawl out of his mouth. The girl beside him screams and scatters, and the male on the other side vomits. A centipede slides out of first his left ear and then his right, followed immediately by a swarm of gnats. Dark liquid seeps from his eyes like tears of tar, solidifying into a collection of stink bugs, millipedes, and worms.

"You're right," I say to Barret, canting my head to the side as panic flitters across Alex's handsome face. "This is better."

As if he's heard my words, Alex's head snaps in my direction, eyes hurling vitriol and pure hatred. He looks seconds away from launching himself at me and wringing my neck. With a sly smile, I give him a finger wave that quickly transitions into me flipping him off. Maybe it's stupid to poke the beast, but I'm done being bullied by this asshat.

I stare at Barret first, his face scrunched in concentration, before focusing on Cal, who is deep in conversation with Mason and Vin, one hand absently rubbing up and down Barret's thigh. Hux sits on the other side beside Frankie. Alex may have the powers of the undead, but me? I have an army.

And I might not win the battles, but I always win the war.

Always.

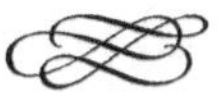

CHAPTER 15

MASON

With a heavy sigh, I toss the joint on the ground and stomp on it.

She's late.

A-fucking-gain.

Honestly, at this point, I should stop acting surprised. Mother dearest only cares about two things—her image and Zeus's cock. She wouldn't know love if it bitch-slapped her in the face.

In the distance, cresting the boughs of trees, is Prodigium Academy. It's been my home for the better part of three years—my one escape from this hell I have found myself in. Behind those brick walls, I have made friends and created my own makeshift family. And I met Violet.

I chuckle darkly as I remember Butt Wipe's face completely consumed by slimy bugs. The asshole deserved it for what he did to Violet. Fortunately, her fang grew back in less than an hour, but it still hurt her like a bitch. Any man who hurts Violet deserves that...and more. Alex is lucky she didn't tell Hux the truth about her chipped fang. He would be six feet under with nails beneath each of his fingernails by now.

"It has been a long fucking day," my mother exclaims as she materializes behind me, stalking forward. Her snakes cascade around her shoulders in a myriad of colors—red, orange, green, and even a few yellow. They slither and hiss as they set their eyes upon me, but fortunately, I don't turn to stone. That would be a pain in my ass if I froze up every time I came into contact with my mother. She stops before me and air-kisses both of my cheeks. "Did you get my present?"

I clench my hands into fists and take another haggard breath. Externally, I'm calm and collected. Internally, my stomach is a tangled nest of nerves and anger, each strand more vicious than the snakes on my head.

"I did," I say, moving to sit beside her on the stone bench. She smooths out her silver gown, glimmering like starlit silk, before sighing heavily.

"A mother only wants what's best for her son—"

"I'm not severing the mate bond," I cut in resolutely. I still remember the fury that pulsated through me when I'd entered my bedroom the day before Halloween to find that spellbook on my desk. It had been an ancient tome about mate bonds. More importantly, how to destroy one. The thought of purposefully doing that to Violet...

Revulsion courses through me, causing my body to shiver.

Yup, no thanks. Not happening.

"But the prophecy..." Mom pleads, and for a moment—for a painful, fucking moment—I think that her anguish is sincere. I think that she actually cares about what happens to me. But Mom? She has never cared about me. I'm the bastard child she never wanted, a reminder that she wasn't good enough to be Zeus's wife. I don't know who my father is, and I don't give a damn. I don't really care about Medusa, either.

I care about Violet, and that's it. She's my mate, my other half, a puzzle piece that was created in the heavens to fill the emptiness constantly plaguing me. I know innately that Violet will never hurt me. The prophecy about Dracula's daughter being my murderer is a hoax. There's no way that crazy, eccentric girl will do anything to harm me. The only pain she's capable of is of the broken-heart variety. She can completely destroy me, if she ever desires to. She holds my heart—or what remains of the tarnished organ—in her hands, and can either squeeze blood back into my system or crush it completely. The choice is hers.

"I'm done talking to you about this," I say, getting to my feet and brushing off my slacks.

"We're done when I say we're done!" Mom hisses, eyes narrowed into slits.

"I'm curious…" As I speak, I begin to walk backwards. "What do you get out of my death? Why do you care so much?"

"I'm your mother—"

"You've never cared about that title before," I point out, ignoring the rage that appears in my mother's eyes. I hold up my fingers in a peace sign before swiveling on my heel and walking back in the direction of the school.

Mom's voice stops me like an ice cube being rubbed up and down the nape of my neck. The hairs on my arms stand on end at her words. "I'll do whatever it takes to protect my son. Remember that."

Before I can demand answers, she disappears in a flash of emerald green light.

～

I'M EXHAUSTED BY THE TIME I FINALLY MAKE IT TO THE cafeteria for breakfast. Mom's warning plays on a continuous loop in my head. Was she…was she threatening Violet? My mate?

I shake my head vigorously at the preposterous notion. Surely, she meant something else entirely, right? She loves me enough not to hurt my kind-of-girlfriend.

Even I struggle to believe that.

Violet's already at the table with Vin when I arrive. My heart warms at seeing the two of them together. I'm grateful they were able to work out their issues. Hopefully, their rekindling relationship means Vin will stop being an egotistical asshole.

One can only hope.

"Hey!" Violet enthuses when she sees me. Her smile disappears when she catches sight of my expression. "What's wrong? Do I have to maim or kill anyone? Or both? Give me a name. I'm pretty adept at hiding a body."

"Don't be ridiculous," Vin scoffs, wrapping an arm around her shoulders. It's a surprisingly…intimate move, as if he's laying his claim on her for the entire world to see. "You don't need to do that by yourself. I'll help."

"You'll help me murder and hide a body?" Violet breathes, staring up at him with fuck-me eyes. My cock twitches in my pants, and I have the irresistible urge to lay her over the table and pound into her slick heat. There's something about my girl talking about murder that drives me crazy.

"Of course." Vin shrugs nonchalantly, and I swear Violet nearly faints from ecstasy.

"Slut," Cheryl fake coughs from a few tables over. I notice that Alex sits beside her, though his attention is fixated on Violet, expression unreadable. I really need to figure out what that guy's problem is. Or kill him.

Either option is appealing.

Violet turns towards Cheryl lazily, a hint of mischief in her smile. She grabs Vin's shirt collar and pulls him towards her, kissing him fiercely. Vin doesn't hesitate to kiss her back, wrapping one arm around her waist while the other tangles in her blonde curls. She pulls away from him seconds later, lips already swollen, and turns towards me. Smirking at the little temptress, I close the distance between us and kiss her as desperately as Vin just had. I still taste the fucker's saliva on her lips, but for some reason, that only amplifies my lust. When she finally releases my lips, she turns back towards Cheryl with a smug smile and offers her a middle finger.

Cheryl, I notice, isn't smiling. Her eyes are narrowed in pure rage. With a flick of her orange hair, she turns towards Alex, effectively dismissing us.

But Alex is still focused intently on Violet. I could be mistaken—I usually am, especially when I'm high—but he almost appears…jealous. His dark eyes flare with a banked fire before he purposefully wrenches his gaze off of Violet and focuses on whatever Cheryl is saying.

Remembering the embarrassment in Violet's eyes when the asshole made her shit her pants, I grip Violet's hips and pull her towards me once more. She moans against my lips instantly, her soft fingers kneading my neck.

I reach up to cup her breast through her pink shirt, loving the way she mewls into my mouth. Fuck, I want her. I want her so badly, I can barely think straight. Thoughts of my mom and Alex dissipate as I continue to kiss this goddess in my arms. Before I can proposition her, I hear the sound of glass shattering.

We jump apart, startled, to see Alex stomping away, his plate having been thrown against the cafeteria wall.

"What the fuck?" Violet murmurs, staring after him in confusion.

"Fuck…" I repeat with a wink. "I like that word."

"So do I." Vin attempts to shift himself on the bench to hide the evidence of his arousal.

"You know what I like?" Violet whispers, a teasing lilt to her voice. Vin and I both lean forward expectantly as she trails fingers down both of our chests to the outline of our cocks. "I like—"

"Violet Dracula, please report to the headmaster's office!" a voice declares over the speakers.

Violet doesn't immediately drop her hands from our crotches as she strokes us through our pants.

"What do you like?" Vin begs, closing his eyes.

We lean in even closer, until all of our lips are a centimeter from touching. Her eyes dance with humor as she stares first into my eyes and then Vin's. All I can focus on, however, is her intoxicating scent that curls around me. All I can picture is a naked Violet as I thrust in and out of her ass while Vin destroys her pussy. The image makes me so fucking hard, I'm in physical pain.

"What the hell do you like?" I gasp as she continues to stroke us.

"Ice cream," she whispers at last, and I blink at her.

"Huh?"

Without bothering to respond, Violet removes herself from between us and leans down to grab her backpack. "I need to get going." She bites down on her lower lip with a sultry smirk. "But you two can feel free to jerk each other off while I'm gone…as long as you film it."

It's only then I realize how fucking close I still am to my best friend. If I were to lean any closer, we would be kissing and our cocks would be touching.

We jump away in tandem, both of us offering Violet identical glares.

"Not happening," the Van Helsing says curtly, rolling his eyes.

"I'd rather cut my own dick off than suck his." To Vin, I add, "No offense. I'm sure it's delicious."

"None taken."

Violet huffs once before sighing. "A girl can dream."

"Never going to happen," I say as she leans forward to peck me on the lips. Fuck, what is this? What are we doing? Is she my girlfriend? Am I her boyfriend? What does this mean?

When she pulls away, it's only to give Vin the same kiss she gave me.

"I'll see you losers later," she declares, turning on her heel and racing away. I stare at her ass before it disappears around a corner.

"Fuck," Vin murmurs, dropping his forehead onto the cafeteria table.

"Fuck her," I say. In the mouth, in the vagina, in the asshole. I'm open to just about anything.

Vin snorts at my crude comment before his eyes abruptly narrow. I follow the direction of his gaze to see Cheryl fucking Ness sashaying over to us. Can't she take the hint? We want nothing to do with her.

"Go away, Cheryl," Vin snaps without pretense. Cheryl merely fluffs up her hair and flashes him a smirk, sitting in the chair opposite him at the table.

"Oh, please. As if I want your micro-penis anymore. I found myself a new man. A better one." She lifts her chin up haughtily, eyes carefully gauging Vin's reaction. If she expects him to be jealous or even remotely upset, she's sorely mistaken.

"You mean Alex?" I laugh darkly, and she whips her head in my direction, eyes narrowing even further. "The man who can't stop staring at my girl? Be careful, Cheryl, or else you're going to run into the same situation all over again."

I know I'm being mean and heartless, but I no longer give a damn. Cheryl's torment has extended from emotional trauma to physical. She'd *hurt* Violet, and that's not something I can forgive.

"I was going to give you a warning, but now I'm not sure I want to," she says flippantly, inspecting her sea blue nails.

"Cheryl…" Vin hisses.

"I was *trying* to be a nice person, especially when I heard what they planned to do to Violet…" She trails off, attempting to appear forlorn. Instead, she looks even more like a shark than ever before. And sharks? They attack at the first hint of blood.

"What do you want?" I languidly lean back in my chair, attempting to adapt a nonchalant front. I don't trust Cheryl further than I can throw her, but if she does have information about Violet, I can't afford to take any chances.

Ignoring me completely, Cheryl focuses her gaze on Vin. "We were good together, weren't we? The two of us…against the world." She moves to take his hand where it rests on the table, but he pulls it back quickly. She takes a deep breath, shoulders heaving, before blurting, "Kiss me. Kiss me, and I'll tell you what you want to know. If you don't, something terrible will happen to Violet, something you could've prevented. All I want is one kiss, Vin. One kiss. And then I'll leave you alone."

For a moment, I think Vin is actually considering her offer. His hands steeple together underneath his chin as he stares down at her pleading face. Abruptly, he throws back his head and releases a torrent of laughter.

When he finally calms down, the amusement fades from his face as quickly as it appeared. "No."

"No?" she screeches, garnering the attention of the next table over.

"No. I won't betray Violet like that. Ever. Cheryl? Me and you? We were over long before Violet came into the picture. I never loved you, and you never loved me. We were toxic for each other. Don't think I'm oblivious to all the men you fucked when we were together. And I know you know about all the times I cheated on you." Vin relaxes back in his chair, his arms folded over his chest.

"But I love you," she whines, extending her hand once more. Before she can make contact, her head is slammed into the table with a sickening crack.

Vanessa stands over the trembling girl, her face a mask of raw fury.

"I always knew you were pathetic," she hisses as Cheryl begins to sob. "Extorting my brother to get him to kiss you?" She snorts, ramming Cheryl's face once more into the distressed wood. Blood oozes from the blue girl's nose as tears flood her eyes. I feel a pang of sympathy, mainly because I hate seeing any female in distress. But that sympathy quickly transforms into white-hot rage when I think about all she has done—and all she will continue to do —to Violet. "You're vulgar and a bully, but that doesn't give you the right to take what doesn't belong to you."

"I was handling that," Vin says dryly, leveling Vanessa with an unreadable look. His twin merely smiles, wrapping Cheryl's curly hair around her fist.

"And I'm ending it," she declares. "Why don't you two get to class? I'll figure out what Cheryl knows."

There's a reason I've always been terrified of Vanessa Van Helsing, Vin's twin sister and Violet's designated best friend. And this right here? This is the reason why.

No wonder Violet claimed her. Better to have her as a friend than an enemy.

CHAPTER 16

VIOLET

I'm ushered into the headmaster's office as soon as I arrive in the sparsely furnished lobby, bypassing one of the instructors and a young monster nursing a bruised scalp. Preferential treatment for the win, yay!

Dimitri Gray sits behind his desk, hands clasped together in a picture of faux superiority. He's the epitome of calm and collected, his face devoid of any emotion and his eyes glacial.

"How's my favorite sociopath doing?" I ask lightly as I slide into the seat opposite him. "Planned any assassinations lately? Is that taboo to ask about?"

Dimitri continues to stare at me impassively. "I am not a sociopath."

"No?" I quirk a single blonde brow at him as he finally allows himself to relax.

"Sociopaths are much more erratic and prone to violent outbursts. As such, they're unable to live a normal life. Psychopaths, on the other hand, can be quite charming."

Well, slap me with a flaccid dick. I think Dimitri Gray just confessed to being a psychopath.

Why does my vagina instantly burst into flames, in desperate need of being squirted and put out with psychopath cum? Pretty gross analogy, but you get the idea.

"Have you reconsidered what we talked about before?" Dimitri crosses his muscular arms over his chest and leans even further back in his seat. I attempt to adopt his nonchalant pose... Unfortunately, that leads to me falling off the chair and landing on my ass with an "oomph."

"About me joining the Roaring?" I ask from where I still sit on the ground. "Nope. Haven't changed my mind. Still competing."

"Violet..."

"Don't you *Violet* me!" I lunge to my feet in a surprisingly graceful move and point a finger in Dimitri's direction. "This has nothing to do with you."

His teeth grind together as he stands to his full, impressive height, towering over me and making me feel unbelievably small and dainty. And...safe. The man is a glorified serial killer, yet I have never felt more protected than I do in his daunting shadow. "You'll die," he hisses, the sound eerily similar to the snakes on Mason's head.

"Why do you care?" I counter immediately, and I have the pleasure of seeing a crack in Dimitri's apathetic exterior. I can't put my finger on the emotion in his ice-blue eyes, but it's enough to stop me from mounting another argument. My tongue feels like cotton, and I open and close my mouth repeatedly, unable to conjure up another word.

As quickly as it appears, that flicker of life dissipates, leaving his face expressionless once more. "You're right. I don't care. Die for all the fucks I give."

He briskly steps away from me, moving to sit once more

behind his desk. My lungs struggle to replenish their air supply, as if when he left, he took all of the oxygen with him.

"Don't be an ass," I snap, dropping myself back into the leather, high-back chair.

"Don't be an idiot," he retorts immediately. Silence ensues as we both glare at each other, each of us demanding compliance. I want him to tell me what the fuck is going on, and he demands I listen to him without questions. Frankly? That's not going to work for me. I'm a stab first, ask questions later kind of girl, except for when it's my own freedom on the line.

If Dimitri expects me to listen, I'll need answers.

Like, why? Why is he so insistent I quit the Roaring before it has even begun? Why does he express such a keen interest in me, of all people? Is it because of who my father is?

Dimitri tilts his head to the side as he examines me as thoroughly as I examine him. Finally, he reaches into his desk and procures a heavy textbook. "There's a new class starting tomorrow at nine in the morning. It's designed to focus on the analytical side of the Roaring. I, of course, will be teaching it, and I expect you to attend." His tone brooks no room for argument, but of course, being the smartass I am, I can't help but complain a teensy tiny bit.

"I have class that hour," I say immediately, attempting to hand him back the textbook. "I can't just skip—"

"You can and you will." He levels me with a no-nonsense glare, the message clear enough.

He will not put up with my shit.

"Fine," I concede at last, shoving the book into my backpack. "Is that all?"

The smirk on his face bodes trouble for me. "Remember, Violet, that there *is* a difference between a sociopath and a psychopath. The one similarity?" His smile grows until twin dimples appear on both his cheeks. "You can't trust either."

~

I STARE AT MY REFLECTION IN THE FULL-LENGTH MIRROR AS I dab blush onto my cheeks. Hopefully, I don't look like a fucking clown. My eyes automatically flicker to Cynthia's deserted bed, as they always do when I have a joke I want to say. My stomach tightens into knots when I see that it's, once again, empty.

Dammit, I actually miss the girl. A lot. Who knew I would grow so attached to a female with a retractable vagina and five sets of tits?

Shaking my head vehemently, I turn towards the dress I have draped over the bed. It's a tiny black number with spaghetti straps and a belt cinched around the waist. On me, the hem ends just above my knees, still modest, but show-casing my long legs.

I slip it on, loving how soft it feels against my skin. I have forgone a bra, but decided underwear was necessary, given how short it is.

I complete the ensemble with a silver bat necklace I got from Dracula himself. My blonde curls tumble around my shoulders, the white highlights heightening the golden locks. I feel beautiful. Sexy, even.

Confident.

I can't help but smile at my reflection and see her smile back at me. Her eyes are alight with happiness. The shadows that once plagued her are nowhere to be seen. Sure, they still make a periodic appearance like pesky weeds, but they're no longer completely consuming me.

A knock on the door startles me, and I grab my clutch off my bedside table.

"Coming! I hope you're—"

My words trail off when, instead of Frankie at the door as I expected, I see Cynthia. The Woman in White has her dark hair loose today, cascading around her shoulders in snarly waves. She wears a flowy white dress that tightens around her breasts before sweeping outwards at her waist. Her pale skin has undertones of yellow and dusky brown, a common trait in all banshees.

"Violet," she says stiffly.

"Cynthia." I fold my arms over my chest and step away to let her inside. Despite not sleeping in here the last few days, it's still her room. She hasn't officially made a request with the registrar's office to switch roommates.

"I'm just picking up a few of my things," she declares as she stalks to her closet, ripping it open and grabbing a white dress off its hanger. It's the exact same color and style of the dress she has on. Pretty sure it's the only thing she owns. She haphazardly tosses the dress over her arm and turns to stare at me. Her eyes give me an assessing once-over before she nods sharply. "You look cute."

"Thanks," I say sincerely, shocking even myself. Shouldn't I be more pissed at her? She gave the assholes at school my sex doll in order to create a life-sized Violet piñata. At the same time, I hurt her initially by accusing her of murder and being obsessed with me. The entire thing is fucked up, yes, but I do believe she feels guilty for the part played at the Halloween party. I have caught her looking at me a few times, concern emanating from her eyes.

"Don't mention it." She waves my praise away dismissively before nibbling on her lower lip. "Do you have a...a date?"

I smile softly, smoothing down the skirt of the dress. "Yes."

"Is it Mason?" She tries to sound nonchalant, but her voice tightens marginally at the question. According to Dimitri Gray—stalker extraordinaire—Cynthia is in love with my snake-headed boyfriend—maybe boyfriend? She hasn't said anything to me about it, and I haven't pressed, but the heartache in her eyes is clear enough to see. Shit on a stick.

"With Frankie," I say, and her shoulders instantly sag in relief.

"That's good," she blurts out. "I mean, I think you'll be good for him."

"But…" I rock back on my heels, debating what I'm going to say. On one hand, I don't want to hurt Cynthia, despite our rocky past. But on the other… "I'm sort of seeing Mason, Vin, Jack, and Hux as well." When she merely stares at me, mouth agape, I take a tentative step forward. "It's still new and very, very complicated. And the last thing I ever wanted was to hurt you—"

"I see," Cynthia says stiffly. Movements robotic, she turns on her heel and makes a beeline for the still open door.

"Cynthia!" I plead.

"You don't have to explain yourself to me." She pauses in the doorway, but she doesn't make a move to turn back towards me. "It's what I expected anyway."

"What you expected…?" Before she can leave completely —and, consequently, leave my life completely—I grab her arm and wrench her to an abrupt halt. At least, that's what I attempt to do. Instead, I pull her arm straight out of its socket and awkwardly hold it before me, eyes wide with horror.

Still, it has the desired effect. Cynthia stops moving and reluctantly turns to face me.

"Can I please have my arm back?"

"No," I say stubbornly, coming quickly to a decision. I hide the arm behind my back and take a step away. "Not until you tell me what you meant."

"It doesn't fucking matter—"

"It does so matter. *You* matter. And I won't have you

placing your worth on any guy's affection. Cynthia, you're so much more than one guy's opinion of you. You're funny, sweet, and have an amazing set of tits." Her lips twitch at my poor attempt at a joke, but she keeps her face blank. "Mason and I…we're complicated, but I care about him. A lot. I care about all of them."

"Why do you get one hundred guys pining after you while I get none?" Cynthia explodes, throwing her hand up in the air. I wince at the venom in her voice before forcing myself to relax. It's what I wanted, after all. A conversation.

"That's not true," I begin helplessly, but she whirls on me, eyes spewing anger.

"Don't play dumb, Violet, because I know you're not. You're beautiful and funny and smart, and you have half the guys at this school eating out of your hand. Even that cupid and boogeyman are in love with you, but you're too dumb to see it." She takes a step closer until we're nose-to-nose. Hers is bent at an unnatural angle, and I wonder if it's possible for me to buy her a new one. I'm pretty sure it's not a gift I can get off of Amazon.

"What about you?" I ask just as viciously. "What about Pete?"

"Who the fuck is Pete?" she sputters.

"Pete the Pumpkin? Sits at your lunch table? The man can't stop fucking staring at you! Don't you see?" I grab her hand—the opposite of the one I literally still hold—with mine and give it a squeeze. I can't make her more confident, I can't make her fall in love with Pete, but I can give her the push necessary. "You're such an amazing person, Cynthia, and I'm sorry I screwed our friendship up. I wouldn't blame you if you never forgive me. But just know, I'm here for you. Always. I'm sorry Mason doesn't love you back… Actually? I'm not sorry. Maybe it makes me a selfish monster, but I can't imagine my life without him in it. I can't imagine my life without any of them in it. So go ahead, call me a slut or a whore. Tell me I'm a bitch. It doesn't change the fact that I'm happy with my guys, and I just want you to be happy too. Maybe it works out with Pete…maybe it doesn't. Maybe you'll find yourself a nice hairy werewolf dick to trampoline on. All I know is that you won't know unless you try. I never intended to hurt you, but you're only hurting yourself by falling for a man who will never love you back."

By the time I finish my speech, I'm breathing heavily, my chest heaving. Cynthia stares down at me with an unreadable expression before she turns on her heel and stalks out the door.

Leaving me with a severed arm that I awkwardly drop on her bed.

Fuck! Did I just make this worse? I think the problem with friendships and relationships is that we always have an unrealistic expectation of the other person. When they don't meet those standards, we deem them failed. It's a never-ending, vicious cycle that ruins more relationships than it saves.

"Are you ready?" a quiet voice inquires from the doorway, and I quickly compose myself.

"Let's do this."

CHAPTER 17

My hands are sweaty, despite repeatedly rubbing them against my khaki pants. I'm…nervous. It's not an emotion I'm used to dealing with.

Actually, I'm not used to feeling *any* of these emotions. The sweating hands and rapidly thudding heart. The erratic breathing. The skitter of my pulse whenever she looks at me. I'm a monster—an experiment—and I was designed by Frankenstein himself not to develop emotional attachments. Quite literally, it's not in my DNA. I'm created to do two things—experiment and be experimented *on*. You can imagine my surprise when I discovered Violet was my fated mate.

I've read about it in books. Who hasn't? The stars have chosen her, chosen her soul, to match perfectly with my own. Where I'm jagged, she's smooth. Where I'm hard, she's soft. We're nothing but contradictions that somehow irrevocably belong together. I don't know if I even believe in karma and all of that shit. Sure, I've sinned in the past, but I truly believe

I have done good things as well. And though there's darkness inside of me, it's interwoven with swatches of light—a light that only Violet seems capable of evoking.

"You look…stunning," I say to her now as I pull the car into the crowded parking lot. She glances coyly at me out of the corner of her eye, but I notice a slight blush to her cheeks that hadn't been there earlier.

"You said that eleven times already," she points out, swatting at my chest.

"Then I'll say it twelve times. You look beautiful."

And she does. Violet? If I didn't know she was a vampire, I would believe her to be an angel. It's not just her soft curves, accentuated in the skintight dress, and golden hair tumbling down her shoulders. It's *her*. She embodies an inner light and warmth that surrounds me and steadily melts the ice around my heart. It sounds like a cliché, but it's true. Before I knew her, I thought she was a witch sent to torment me. I'd never experienced such a strong reaction as I did when I first spotted Violet Dracula.

But if she is a witch, I'll willingly allow myself to be pulled under her thrall.

"What are we doing here?" Violet asks curiously as she stares at the modernistic, four-story building directly in front of us. Flashing, colorful lights are visible through the numerous windows lining the length of the wall. At the front entrance, a long line of monsters and humans alike snake around the building, disappearing from view.

"I thought you would want to go out," I say sheepishly. I scrub a hand through my messy brown curls as panic vibrates through me.

Oh, god. I fucked up, didn't I? I should've stayed at home. I should've taken her to my lab and gifted her the perfume of Cheryl's tears I made earlier today. I should've—

"I do," she declares, cutting off my internal rambling.

"Thank you, Frankie. I appreciate this. A lot. It's been...a stressful few weeks." She laughs half-heartedly, but her gaze goes hazy and distant. No doubt, she's thinking about her crazy half-sister, Ms. Stevens, who attempted to murder her. I don't know what exactly transpired during those few minutes before Dimitri and I were able to reach her, and I don't dare ask. I only know the truth about Ms. Stevens because Dimitri told me...and I have no fucking idea how *he* knows about that. Violet is surprisingly fragile for a monster. Vulnerable, almost. She wears her heart on her sleeve, which for most people, isn't a bad thing. But for Dracula's daughter? It can prove to be fatal.

"I've never done this before," I admit as I hurry around the car to open her door. When I spot the goosebumps on her arms, I make quick work of removing my tweed suit jacket and draping it over her frail shoulders.

"Gone to a club?" she asks as we cross the busy street, her arm brushing my own.

"Gone on a date," I blurt out before I can lose my nerve. When she glances at me out of the corner of her eye, my cheeks heat. "I've never...been attracted to anyone like this before. I thought there was something wrong with me—"

"There is nothing wrong with you," Violet cuts in adamantly. She pauses in the middle of the congested street and takes my hand in hers. Mine are so much bigger than her dainty ones. It makes me feel even more protective of her. "You're Frankie—*my* Frankie—and you're amazing."

Heat blazes through my body at the compliment. More than that, at the sincerity *behind* the compliment. I sometimes think Violet is too pure for this world, too pure for me.

"Let's get inside," I say at last, instead of blurting out all of the things I *actually* want to say.

A crease appears in the skin between Violet's brows as I guide her towards the front of the line. Someone behind us begins to scream obscenities, but I merely cast him a look capable of withering flowers. He shuts the hell up immediately.

"Shouldn't we wait in line?" Violet whispers, her smoky voice curling around me and settling at my dick.

"Not if you're me," I retort cockily, stalking up to the bouncer. Pablo and I? We go way back.

As in, I enhanced his dick by five inches.

"Pablo," I greet as soon as we are at the front entrance.

"Paul," he corrects, his bald head glinting in the strobe lighting. "Do you want to come in?" He doesn't spare Violet a glance.

At my look of annoyance, he steps away from the door—ignoring the mutterings of the other patrons—and allows me to pass. Before Violet can step through as well, he steps back in front, muscular arms folded over his chest.

"She's with me," I say bluntly, glaring at the imbecile. He almost appears…disappointed? What the hell?

Very reluctantly, Pablo—Paul—steps back and allows Violet to enter. Immediately, she intertwines her fingers with mine in a surprisingly possessive move.

Paul brushes his fingers across my shoulders, a wistful expression on his face. "Do you think we can meet up later?"

"I don't take clients on weeknights," I dismiss, pulling Violet in after me.

Immediately, the scent of sweat and alcohol barrages my senses. Flashing strobe lights illuminate the concrete dance floor in hues of pink, blue, and green. Music blares from the speakers, almost obnoxiously loud.

Shit, this was a bad idea. A very bad idea.

"What the hell was that about?" Violet screams in my ear. Even this close, she has to raise her voice in order for me to hear her.

"What?" I turn towards her in confusion, surprised to see jealousy swarming in her gaze.

"Did you fuck that guy?" she queries, and my eyes widen comically.

"Huh?"

"Paul? Did you fuck him?"

I think back to the earlier days of school. My numb days. For the longest time, I thought there was something wrong with me. I would seek out "pleasure" any way I knew how, but nothing worked. Girls, boys…it was all the same to me. I couldn't get hard to save my fucking life. I even went so far as to ask Mikey, Merlin's son, for solutions. I've never actually *fucked* a person, but I have engaged in sexual activities with members of both sexes. I wouldn't be able to tell you what they looked like, let alone what their names were. So Paul? There's a very real possibility I gave him a hand job and he attempted to give me one.

"Are you…jealous?" I ask in amazement, staring at the tiny blonde temptress before me. What in the world does she have to be jealous over? Does she not know yet that she's my stars and my moon? My sun? My entire world?

"It's stupid." Flames engulf both of her cheeks as she ducks her head. "Come on. Let's get something to drink."

"Wait…" I pull at her arm gently, and she immediately spins until she's back in my embrace. I settle my hands on her thin waist as she wraps her arms around my neck. "Talk to me."

"It's just that…" She leans forward until her lips are against my throat. My breath hitches at her close proximity. All I can smell is her; all I can feel is her. In that moment, the rest of the world doesn't exist, my entire focus centered solely on the blonde vampire in my arms. "I thought you were a virgin. I thought I could be… Fuck, it's really stupid. Don't listen to me. I think it's the whole 'mate' talk thing."

My heart skips a beat at hearing her so candidly address the mate bond. For the last few weeks, she has regarded it like an elusive entity. A ghost, almost. In her mind, if she doesn't acknowledge it, then it doesn't exist. She failed to realize that it's constantly lurking just above her shoulder, waiting for the correct time to pounce.

"I am." I press my face to the top of her head and inhale her spicy scent. She must be wearing a new perfume. It reminds me vaguely of rose gardens and cinnamon. "A virgin, I mean. I am one." My arms tighten imperceptibly around her as I lower my lips to her ear. "And I am your mate. You might not want to admit it yet, but I know it as surely as I know I'm a monster, an experiment. And, yours." Her breath catches as I begin to sway us back and forth, right there in the middle of the walkway. "I don't have a heart. Not technically." I grip her hand and place it between our bodies, directly over my chest. "The thing you feel...the thing that beats...it's not real. It's an illusion, a machine. Something Frankenstein put inside of me to make me feel more... human. But if you rip it out of me, it won't kill me, as you have seen firsthand." She shudders delicately at the memory before tilting her head back up. "But losing you *would* kill me, because in the short time I have known you, you have become my heart." I take another deep breath as we continue to sway.

"I'm nothing but an illusion, Violet. I'm nothing but parts and wires and spells. I don't technically have a heart, but that's only proof that the heart doesn't dictate who you can and can't love. That responsibility is for the brain alone. That was the one thing my bastard father actually gave me. It's yours, if you want it. I can't give you the world like the others. I can't lasso the moon for you. But I can give you the one thing I once treasured above all else—my mind. It's the only real thing inside of me, and it tells me repeatedly that I was made for you. I can't give you every-thing, but I can give you that. It's the only true thing I have."

Her lips hover over mine as her pupils dilate. All I would need to do is lean forward an inch…

A body jostles me from behind, effectively breaking the moment. Violet takes a step away from me, focusing intently on a button on my dress shirt. Fuck, I almost thought…

Would it be crazy to say I almost thought she was going to kiss me?

"Come on!" I yell into her ear, guiding her towards the bar. "Let me get you something to drink."

I don't come here often—read as, at all—but the bartender is an old client of mine. I'd concocted a potion designed to make people fall out of love. He was still hung up on his ex, but she was engaged to marry a different guy. Normally, I don't create potions that impact emotions, but he was a special case.

"Frankie, my man!" he says enthusiastically as soon as I step up to the counter. He slaps me on the shoulder as I awkwardly stand there, shuffling from side to side.

"Um…"

Fuck, what is his name again?

Before I can make an ass of myself, Violet sidles up beside me and smiles at the bartender.

"Hi, I'm Violet, Frankie's date. And you are…?"

Thank the lord.

"Benji," he introduces, extending a hand. I can't help but notice the way his eyes light up when he stares at her, as if she's a tasty morsel he wants to devour. I suddenly under-stand Violet's reaction with the bouncer.

Because, fuck, I'm jealous. I don't like the way he looks at her one fucking bit. The acid in my stomach churns like lava as I level a penetrating glare in Benji's direction. I stop myself before I go all caveman and carry Violet over my shoulder, away from the handsome man's intense, piercing gaze.

Instead, I tangle our fingers together and bring our conjoined hands to my lips, kissing her knuckles affectionately.

Benji's eyes widen in understanding and something akin to awe. He knows that I don't date, so I imagine this is freaky as fuck for him.

"What can I get you two?"

"Um…whatever she's having!" Violet points towards a giggling female carrying a bright red drink with an umbrella inside of it.

"Coming right up. And you?" He turns towards me expectantly.

"I'll have the same."

Alcohol and me? We don't mix well. As in, it does nothing for me. I don't experience the same high as other monsters do when they consume the heavy-duty fairy shit.

Benji returns with our drinks a few minutes later, and I lead Violet to a somewhat secluded booth in the corner. She slides in, her dress riding up her thighs, but before I can make a move to sit opposite her, she grabs my hand and pulls me into the seat directly beside her. I stumble, nearly spilling the fruity drink on her lap, before I right myself and cast her a glare.

"Violet…"

"What?" she asks innocently, batting her lashes at me. Her lips part around the straw of her drink, and my cock twitches in my pants. I can't help but imagine her lips wrapped around *me* instead. "This is nice," she admits after a moment, placing her drink on the table. "I can't remember the last time I've been out and had fun."

"Me either," I confess. I'm pretty sure I've *never* been out before with the sole purpose of having fun. My "fun" consisted of a clean laboratory and a dozen patients demanding my services. Clearing my throat, I rub the pad of my thumb down the sides of my sticky glass. "I really like you, Violet."

"I really like you too." She turns to face me fully, eyes twinkling. "More than I want to admit."

"Why?" I place my hand on top of hers where it rests on her thigh. My pinkie brushes her silky-smooth skin, and I swear my eyes just about roll into the back of my head. Fuck.

"Why what?" She stares at our joined hands with rapt fascination.

"Why don't you want to admit you have feelings for me?" I can't ignore the pang of self-consciousness. Does she believe I'm not good enough for her? Does she wish I was thinner or more muscular? Does she want me to be a vampire? I try to hide my hurt behind a reinforced steel barricade, but it slips out unbidden. Her eyes immediately flicker back up to my face, wide with horror.

"No! It's not that." She blows out a breath and squeezes her eyes shut. "It's just weird, okay? To have strong feelings for more than one man."

"You have feelings for...the others?" I'm not surprised. I see the way she looks at them, and they, her. I imagine it's similar to the way I do. "Violet, I told you before... I don't care. And I'm pretty sure they don't either. I don't know how to explain it..."

"But the thought of them touching me turns you on?" she fills in with a quirked brow. "And the thought of anyone else touching me makes you furious?"

"How did you know?" She slips her hand out from underneath mine to cup my face. My own remains on her soft thigh, rubbing soothing circles into the skin there.

"Because the other guys said the same," she confesses with a shrug. "It doesn't make any sense—"

"Unless they're your mates too," I cut in, and the more I think about it, the more it makes sense.

"You can't have more than one mate," she insists, but I'm already shaking my head vigorously.

"Not normally, no. But when have you ever been normal?" Violet's face instantly falls, and I mentally chastise my dumb self. Fuck. "What did I say?"

"It's not you. It was just something Ms. Stevens said…" She rolls her eyes and offers me a tentative smile. "Actually, it doesn't matter. This is our date, and I'm determined to have a damn good time."

"Do you want to dance?" I nod in the direction of writhing bodies, but one glance in Violet's direction shows she has something else in mind.

She leans forward, her movements almost cautious, as if she's gauging my reaction, and presses her lips to mine. It's a soft kiss—innocent, by normal standards—but licks of fire dance through my veins. I'm getting burned, but it's so fucking worth it.

"Frankie," she murmurs against my lips as I return her kiss with vigor. Instead of chaste and sweet, it becomes feverish. Needy. Desperate. It's as if we want to consume each other.

I've never felt anything like this before.

Her hand wraps around my wrist on her thigh, and at first, I think she's trying to make me remove it. Instead, she glides it up the inside of her thigh until it reaches the thin material of her panties. My balls ache as I moan into her mouth.

"Violet…?" I trail off, a question in that one word.

"You can touch me. If you want." She almost appears sheepish, embarrassed, and her cheeks are crimson. Hoping to put her at ease, I brush one finger down her panty line before moving the material to the side. From this angle, my body covers her from view, and I intended to keep it that way. No one is allowed to see her like this.

I sheath one digit inside of her already wet pussy, basking in her moan of pleasure.

"Fuck, Frankie!"

"Do you like that?" I whisper, planting kisses up and down the column of her neck.

"Yes." It's a cry and a plea combined. The message is clear —keep moving your finger.

Without delay, I add another to the first and begin to rub them back and forth, collecting her juices. She mewls softly, clawing at my back as my thumb brushes her clit, the touch tantalizing.

Violet suddenly freezes, her grip on my shoulders tightening, and I remove my hand from her pussy.

"What's wrong?" I ask instantly. Have I unintentionally hurt her? When she continues to stare at something over my shoulder, I follow the direction of her gaze to see none other than Dimitri Gray himself sitting at the bar, drink in hand. His eyes are fixed on Violet, despite Benji attempting to engage him in conversation. The thought of him watching her doesn't bother me. If anything, it makes me feel even better. Dimitri is a scary motherfucker, and I know that he'll protect her no matter what.

"Shall we continue?" I whisper in Violet's ear, and her breath hitches sharply.

"In front of...?"

"Only if you want to."

It's her choice. It'll always be her choice.

With a sly, mischievous smile, Violet opens her legs, giving me a clear view of her wet thong and the outline of her pussy lips. I make quick work of sliding the panties off her legs and sticking them in my jacket pocket. Then, I position myself so I'm to the side of her instead of directly in front of her. This new angle still allows me to see her pussy folds…but it also allows Dimitri to see them too. And the other dancers, but most of them are too preoccupied with each other to pay attention to the booth in the corner. Besides, it's secluded enough to only have a handful of people gathered in front of it, dancing to the thrumming music.

Dimitri's eyes widen comically as I gently caress her pussy. I don't enter her—not yet—but continually move my finger up and down her lips. Her eyes close as she rolls her head back, lips parted slightly. Flicking my gaze to Dimitri, I slip two fingers into her wet heat and begin to scissor them.

The headmaster's pupils dilate, and his hand instinctively goes to his pants, palming himself through the material.

"Fuck," I hear Violet murmur, and I see that her gaze isn't on me, but on Dimitri.

"Do you like that, pretty girl?" I whisper in her ear. "Do you like me playing with your pussy as he watches? Do you like knowing anyone can look over at any time and see us?"

She cries out, the noise nearly making me shoot my load, but I force myself to remain patient. This isn't about me.

I use my free hand to push down her dress straps until her tits pop free, nipples already beaded. I roll one between my fingers as I continue to thrust my fingers inside of her.

"You're so beautiful, Violet," I whisper as I lean forward to kiss up her boob until I reach her peaked nipple. I outline it with my tongue before pulling it into my mouth. With a whimper, she tangles her fingers in my hair as I allow the bud to slip through my teeth. "So fucking beautiful."

I've never been overly interested in a woman's breasts before, but hers? I could play with them all day. They're quite easily a handful, and I find that I like touching them. When she moves, her tits jiggle, and I've never seen anything more beautiful.

I clamp down on her clit, and she comes with a scream I quickly capture with my lips.

"Fucking hell," she breathes, her words barely audible over the roaring music. She pulls back just enough to stare into my eyes. "And now..." Before I can stop her—not that I even want to—she unzips my pants and pulls out my rock-hard cock. It twitches in her hand as she rubs her thumb over the slit. With another smirk, she slides down to the floor, nipping and kissing at each inch of exposed flesh. She slides my pants even further down and runs her tongue along a raised vein down my inner thigh.

"Violet," I warn darkly as she continues to kiss and suckle at my skin, never touching me where I so desperately need her to.

"Fine, fine, fine. I swear you guys are no fun." She runs her tongue down the length of my cock before sucking the head fully in her mouth. Groaning, my eyelids droop closed at the onslaught of pleasure. Pure, indescribable pleasure.

I watch Violet's head bob up and down, sucking and licking as she goes. She hollows her cheeks as she feeds my cock even further into her mouth.

"Fuck!" I squeeze the table, curbing the desperate need I have to fist my hand in her hair and fuck her mouth.

She uses her hand to wrap around the part of my shaft her mouth can't take. Her other hand teases and fondles my balls.

Pleasure blooms inside of me, zipping through my veins with each and every swirl of her tongue and graze of her teeth. She stares up at me with wicked eyes and begins to increase her pace. I'm putty in her hands—hers to do with whatever she pleases. The feel of her throat constricting around me feels fucking amazing. I can only imagine what her pussy would feel like.

I'm so close to coming—so fucking close—that when she

presses down on my balls, skating that precarious edge between pleasure and pain, I explode inside of her mouth. Some of my cum dribbles down her chin, but for the most part, she drinks it all, bright eyes dancing.

"Violet… Oh my fucking god." I pull her towards me and kiss her feverishly, still able to taste myself on her glistening lips.

"Do you think Headmaster Gray enjoyed the show?" she teases, turning towards the bar. I had completely forgotten about our little voyeur.

But the bar stool Dimitri was sitting on is now vacant.

CHAPTER 18

DIMITRI

Violet *fucking* Dracula.

The bane of my existence.

I squeeze the bathroom countertop so tightly, my knuckles turn white. My cock is so fucking hard that it's almost painful.

Why does she do this to me?

How does she do this to me?

"Can I give you a hand with that?" a coy voice says from behind me. Someone must've followed me into the bathroom.

I lift my head marginally to meet the pair of bright green eyes staring back at me. She's pretty, I suppose, with large tits clearly visible through her skin-tight shirt. Hourglass figure. Mane of curly orange hair. The old me would've fucked her against the grime-coated bathroom stall and then sent her on her merry way. The new me…

I'm almost tempted to fuck her anyway, just to stop the incessant babbling in my head. It's like there's an angel on one shoulder and a devil on the other, both demanding I listen to them. The devil wants me to forget about Violet, forget about her doe-like eyes and mischievous smirk. Forget about her peaked nipples as Frankie plucked them between his fingers. He wants me to fuck this red-headed woman until we're both screaming our release, her too-large tits bouncing in my face.

But the angel? He's revolted. Instead of seeing a beautiful woman, he sees a complication that will stop us from getting what we so desperately desire.

"Get the fuck out," I hiss at the woman, and she scatters like her life depends on it. In all actuality, it probably does.

Without bothering to lock the bathroom door, I pull my throbbing cock free from the confines of my pants. My eyes roll back into my head as I begin to stroke myself from base to tip. Violet's hooded gaze flashes through my head. The lust emitting from her bright eyes. The sultry tilt to her lips.

And her pussy glistening with the evidence of her arousal.

I begin to stroke myself faster and faster as the image changes. Now, she's leaned over Frankie, her cheeks hollowed as she sucks him. Her glorious breasts brush against his knees with each bob of her head, her nipples beaded diamonds.

Just before I reach the impending explosion, I press down on my balls in the way I saw Violet do to Frankie. Pleasure courses through me, momentarily stealing the breath from my lungs. My vision turns hazy as I press my free hand to the sink to steady myself.

Fucking hell.

Fucking Violet.

With a growl, I shove my dick back into my pants, not bothering to clean myself up. It'll feel like a win for Violet if I do that—though I don't understand my own logic.

Believe it or not, I don't stalk Violet all the time. I actually wasn't at the club to see her.

I have a job to do, and her fucking show almost caused me to fail at it.

Heart hammering, I wash my hands, refusing to stare at my reflection in the mirror. The rumors are true about me and my family—the mirror shows the truth about our monsters, the truth about us. And the last thing I want to be reminded of is the darkness polluting my soul, distorting me into a monster completely unrecognizable.

Fuck me.

Fuck my monster.

And fuck Violet Dracula.

Only when I feel like myself again do I emerge from the bathroom.

My eyes immediately want to latch on to the booth I had last seen Violet and Frankie at, but I will myself to look away. My control is tenuous at best, and I don't trust myself around her. When I'm in Violet's presence, I'm not Dimitri Gray the headmaster, Dimitri Gray the assassin, or Dimitri Gray the monster.

I'm hers. And I hate it.

Instead of entering the main dance floor, I turn towards the steep staircase leading to the upper levels. The second floor is for the VIP members only, but it's the third and fourth floor that capture my interest. Only the true monsters party up there.

I find my victim on the third floor, a cigarette in one hand and a glass of whiskey in the other. An unfamiliar female sits at his feet, sucking his dick, and his four business associates spread out in a semi-circle around him, each with a female of their own. Fortunately for them, my client only hired me to take out Matthew Peder. He owns a winery a few miles away from here, but that's only a front. According to my source, he also traffics females.

Particularly, vampire females.

Since I took the job at the Academy, I've been extremely selective over which cases I take. And since I met Violet, I haven't taken any that would force me to leave the city.

This man? This chupacabra?

He'll pay for all he has done.

I remain in the shadows as I watch him converse with the other men. At one point, the female finishes her blowjob and moves to perch on the arm of his chair. When he begins to finger her pussy, I look away with annoyance.

Finally, Matthew excuses himself from his companions to refill his glass. Using the shadows as coverage, I follow him to the purple-lit bar.

"...take it for what it is," a very drunk Matthew slurs to the impassive bartender. "And what it is, is a pain in my ass." He guffaws as if he just told the most hilarious joke before taking the proffered bottle. Over his shoulder, the bartender —a man named Bernie—meets my gaze and dips his head slightly in acknowledgement. I have been around enough for Bernie to know not to question me. If there's one thing monsters covet above all else, it's self-preservation.

Before Matthew can turn around, I grab his shoulder and tug him a short distance away, towards a mirror I had installed years ago.

There are numerous purposes for mirrors. They show you your true self, the darkness you attempt to hide behind a teasing smile and a beautiful face. But they're also a pathway, a portal, if you will. You just need to know how to use them.

Matthew lets out a strangled cry, attempting to scream for his friends, but I have already pulled us both through the mirror.

It's a sickening sensation, like wading through knee-deep

tar. It clings to my body and makes movement nearly impossible. Still, I trudge forward, darkness closing in on all sides of me like a steadily shrinking room. I have entered this realm enough times to know how to maneuver through it, how to contort it for my own gain. A moment later, a speckle of light breaks apart the monotony of darkness. I drag a whimpering Matthew towards that light and step through.

We enter a sparsely furnished room with pure white walls and white tiled flooring. It's caved inwards, leading towards a simple drain in the direct center of the room. There are no windows or doors; in every direction, all you can see is glossy white paint. A simple chair rests a few inches away from the drain, and a table sits opposite it.

It's the chair I lead a struggling Matthew to, shoving him down and using the installed cuffs to restrain him. Fat, ugly tears roll down his chubby cheeks as he stares up at me.

"Please, I have a family. I have a wife and kid at home."

I just barely hold in my snort. According to my extensive research, his wife left him years ago after she found him balls deep in a hooker, and he has no kids. Hell, he doesn't even have a pet.

There are two things I hate more than anything in this world—crying and lying. And Matthew? He has just done both.

"Please," he sobs, violent tremors jerking his body forward. "Please. I need to get home to my family. Please. My wife…she'll be lost without me. She loves me, and I love her. Haven't you ever been in love before?"

For the first time in the many years I have done this, I pause. My hand lingers over the second restraint. It lasts only a second—hell, a millisecond—but it's enough for Matthew to notice.

"What's her name? Or his name? What if this was her you were doing this to? What if this—"

I shove a gag into his mouth before he can say another word.

Keeping my face blank, I move towards the table in his direct line of view, caressing each blade with a calculated tilt to my head. Shall I use the knife this time? The dagger? My contractor didn't specify how he wanted the kill to go. He trusts my judgement. I suppose I should make it as quick as possible to get it over with and head back to the club.

Though torture does sound enticing…

Matthew spits out his gag and levels me with a fury-filled glare.

"I'm going to find your whore and fuck her senseless. I'm going to wrap my hands around her neck and give it a twist until she's nothing but a sack of meat. Then, I'm going to fuck her again while I make you watch."

Cold fury radiates through me as I move my attention away from the table to the man held hostage before me. Well, that settles it.

The bastard is going to suffer for hours, maybe even days, until he's screaming for death. No one can threaten Violet.

With a cruel smirk, I grab a set of pliers from the table and take a step closer to him.

"Let's play a game," I say as I kneel down before him. The vitriol in his eyes is quickly replaced by terror. Good. He should be scared. He has unleashed a beast inside of me, a beast I hadn't even realized existed. "My bet is I can make you beg for death in less than five minutes." With quick fingers, I unzip his pants and grab his disgusting dick, holding my pliers just above it. "Prove me wrong."

CHAPTER 19

The music courses through me as I spin around in a circle before coming back to Frankie's embrace. We sway together, our hips gyrating, as the DJ weaves together an intoxicating beat.

Frankie keeps his hands firmly on my waist as we twist and turn—even when I move away, I know I'll always come back to him.

I wrap my arms around his neck and play with the curly hairs resting at his nape. His hair is smooth to the touch, almost unnaturally so, and slips through my fingers like silk.

I never would've expected in a billion years that I would be able to touch Frankie like this without fear of repercussion. For the first few months I knew him, he'd been so reclusive and indifferent. I wasn't even positive he liked me, let alone *liked* liked me. Being with him is as natural as breathing. I know that if I were to fall, he would always catch me.

His words before penetrate the lust-filled fog in my mind.

Could it be possible? Could I be mates to the others as well? A tiny voice in my head can't deny the rightness of such a thing, but I shove that voice beneath the proverbial rug.

No, it's impossible. It's nothing but a foolish fantasy. Every girl hopes to be loved and worshiped by a harem of sexy men, but the truth is much more bleak.

You have to choose one.

Isn't that the way the world works? Two people fall in love, and it's like an explosion of fireworks. You know inevitably that you were made to find this person, made to love them. There has never been a case of a mating bond with more than one person.

What would it even mean? Would the guys have other female mates as well? I don't know if I would be able to live with that, as selfish as it makes me. I want them all to myself. Just the thought of them with another woman has me seeing red.

"Do you need something to drink?" Frankie yells into my ear, and I nod eagerly, pushing my previous thoughts aside. I'll focus on them at a later time.

"Yes, please, with a sparkly dildo on top," I reply back, nipping his earlobe. He smiles at me—none of his usual aloofness remaining—and gives my arms a squeeze.

"I'll be right back. Stay where I can see you."

I wave away his over-protectiveness and shoo him towards the bar. As he leans forward to talk with his friend, the bartender, I can't help but wonder where Dimitri disappeared to. And…if he liked the show.

My feelings for Jack, Hux, Frankie, Mason, and Vin are already complicated enough. I don't even want to think about Dimitri Gray with his icy blue eyes and snow-white hair. Shouldn't Frankie have been jealous of what Dimitri witnessed? Unless…

Nope, not going there. Not today. Not ever, if I have my

say. There's only so much a girl can take before she finds herself a nice corner to rock back and forth in.

I continue to sway to the music, lifting my hands in the air, when I feel a sharp pang in the center of my chest. I don't know how to explain it, but I know innately that something is wrong. My gaze flickers to the bar, but Frankie is nowhere to be seen. All around me, I see sweaty faces and ecstatic grins as the patrons dance and grind against each other.

But no Frankie.

I push aside a particularly disgusting couple until I reach the booth we abandoned.

"Frankie?" Before I can get out another word, a rough hand grabs my shoulder and spins me around to face him.

He's tall, almost two feet larger than me, with pasty white skin and sunken eyeballs. A ghoul.

"Don't scream if you want your experiment to live," he warns, his rancid breath making me want to gag. Still, I don't fight him as we move briskly through the club and out a back door.

Only when we're away from the thrashing bodies do I wrench away from him. "Where the fuck is Frankie?" I demand.

The ghoul nods behind him, and it's only then that I realize we're in an alleyway of sorts. A lone dumpster rests against the graffiti-covered wall. In the distance, I can hear the honk of cars and screech of tires, but we're far enough away from the street that we're obscured from view.

A moment later, Frankie is wrenched from around the corner, his head lolling against his chest and his arms captured by two unfamiliar monsters. One has both gills and feathers clamoring up the sides of his neck, while the other has icicles for hair.

They unceremoniously toss Frankie forward, and he rolls a few times before stopping at my feet.

"Frankie!" I cry, but before I can go to him, the ghoul grabs my hand and yanks me to a stop.

"We're going to have some fun with you, vampire bitch," he hisses, flashing a smile that showcases yellow teeth. Like all ghouls, they're cut into keen points that look capable of tearing the skin off my bones with minimal effort.

"Go to hell," I hiss, attempting to shake him off of me. I need to go to Frankie. I need to—

I let out a startled yelp when I'm suddenly pulled into a strong set of arms. When I attempt to fight, he merely applies a slight amount of pressure, his strength surpassing even my own. This newcomer must be a giant of some sort, if his hulking muscles are any indication.

The ghoul meanders in front of me, a hideous curl to his lips.

"Have you seen this?" he demands, thrusting his phone in front of my face. I stubbornly look away, refusing to give in to their twisted games, but the giant behind me grabs my chin and forces me to face the phone screen.

It appears to be a video of the Monster Capital, located in Romania. Vampires of all ages are gathered in front of the wrought iron fence, hurling obscenities at the stone-faced guards. Their words are garbled and indistinct, but their message is clear—stop treating us like secondhand citizens. As I watch, horrified, one of the vampires grabs a were-wolf's neck and snaps it, releasing a guttural roar of victory. He proceeds to lick the blood off his fingers with a fanged grin.

The ghoul stops the video on the vampire's sneering face and puts it back in his pocket.

"Do you know what this is?" he hisses, lowering his head and peering deeply into my eyes.

"It looks like a protest," I whisper. I can't help but flick my gaze down to Frankie. He looks so still. Too still. Is he faking, as he did before with the headmaster? Or has something terrible actually happened to him?

"Your kind is an abomination," he spits, and I absently wipe the liquid off my cheek. "You guys are already immortal. Why do you demand more? Why do you kill to get what you want?"

"I had nothing to do with that protest," I say, my voice shaky.

"So you don't believe vampires should get more rights?" He cants his head to the side, his milky white eyeballs sending pinpricks of terror racing down my spine. His question feels like a test, one that I don't know how to answer.

"I believe vampires should have equal rights," I try at last. His fist connects with the side of my face, and I stumble in the giant's arms.

"They should have *no* rights!" he screams, looming over me. "Did you know that a vampire murdered my sister? Huh? Did you know that?"

For the first time in forever, terror rushes through me, rendering me immobile. I don't think I could fight back, even without the giant's arms around me. There's something dangerous in the ghoul's face, something unhinged. He won't just bully me or taunt me like some of my classmates; he'll kill me.

"There are thousands and thousands of vampires in the world—" I begin as he steps forward and grabs my arm, twisting it slightly.

"You're all the same." He reaches into his pocket and procures a copper-handled dagger. The blade glints menacingly in the tiny swath of moonlight visible. "You think you're so much better than us, huh?" With his free hand, he reaches underneath my dress and cups my still bare pussy. I sob, twisting my head so I don't have to see the malevolent sneer on his face. "Do you know what this is?" He brandishes the knife in front of my face.

I squeeze my eyelids shut, trying to imagine I'm anywhere else. With anyone else. Isn't this the part of the story where a handsome prince comes and saves me?

Well, my friends, fairy tales aren't real. Knights in shining armor aren't real. If you want to survive, you have to save yourself. You have to embrace your inner monster and be the beast you hate.

"Leave me the fuck alone," I growl, still keeping my eyes shut.

"This is a god-blessed blade," the ghoul continues, voice awed. "One of the only things capable of killing a vampire. And…scarring one."

He removes his hand from beneath my dress and grabs hold of my arm once more. Finally, I risk opening one eye to see him staring at my flesh intently, as if it's a canvas and he's a starving artist.

"Fuck you," I say through gritted teeth.

His smile is slow, predatory almost, and causes my hackles to rise. "If you're offering."

Before I can gather my wits, he presses down on the inside of my arm with the blade. Pain—excruciating pain—explodes in my veins at the first stab of the dagger. I press my elongated fangs into my bottom lip in a desperate attempt to stop my sudden need to scream. But when he presses down again, a cruel laugh reverberating through him, I can't contain the anguished cry.

"Violet…?" a drowsy voice murmurs. And then, more alert, he repeats, "Violet!"

I turn tear-filled eyes to see Frankie now standing, struggling between the two monsters that hold him. "Violet!" he screams again, the agonized noise somehow soothing my ravaged soul. Even amidst the pain, it's comforting to know he cares.

Fuck, I'm screwed up, aren't I?

"Please, stop! Do you want money? I'll give you money! Fuck!" Frankie attempts to headbutt the icicle man, but the second monster quickly wraps an arm around his neck, cutting off his air supply.

The pain is lessening, replaced by a growing numbness. I don't know if it's the adrenaline disrupting my nerves or something else entirely, but I feel nothing. Absolutely nothing. Each swipe of the blade against my skin is nothing more than a tickle.

My head is spinning wildly, and I can feel my vision begin to go dark.

"Violet!" Frankie screams again, face pale. The monster on his left backhands him across the face.

"Shut the fuck up, you fat freak."

Blinding, incandescent fury rushes through me at his words, settling in my stomach like a ball of light. I want to grip it with both hands and give it a pull, but I don't. I can't.

After what feels like an eternity, the giant releases me and pushes me onto the ground. The ghoul stands over me, a cocky smile dancing on his lips. He leans forward to spit on me before straightening, scrubbing a hand down his chest.

"Remember this moment, vampire scum. Remember how hated you are. Of how hated you all are. Do us all a favor and go fall on a wooden stake." He kicks at my stomach before nodding towards his friends, who reluctantly release Frankie. He wastes no time crawling towards me, tears blurring his eyes. His hand hovers above me, as if he wants to touch me but isn't sure where.

"Violet! Fuck, Violet. We need to get you home, okay? You'll be okay."

Almost mechanically, I nod my head, but my eyes are fixated on the once-smooth skin of my arm.

My head swarms with indignation as I read the words now carved into my porcelain skin.

Vampire Whore

WE'RE BOTH SILENT AS WE WALK BACK TO MY DORM, FRANKIE'S coat once more draped over my shoulders. I'm trembling erratically, and my hand fumbles as I attempt to open the door.

"Let me," Frankie murmurs, pushing it open and helping me inside.

My room looks the exact fucking same, so why does everything feel so...different? Maybe the room hasn't changed, but I have. In a matter of minutes, I have grown years in age. Centuries, even. I'm no longer that scared little girl who wandered through life carelessly.

What I've been through…

That changes people inherently. It warps their very genetic makeup.

I drop Frankie's jacket onto the ground, immediately staring down at my distorted skin. Those words glare back at me like an ominous promise and a reminder. It was so easy to forget that I was the most hated monster in the universe. That my father had a thousand more enemies than friends. Now, it all comes rushing back to me, like a bomb that has just been detonated.

I don't cry. I think I used up all my tears in that alleyway, when a little sliver of my innocence was shattered into unfixable pieces. I feel like a ghost gliding through life, never being able to actually stop and smell the roses. Instead, I'm an apparition. A presence that lurks and never participates. I'm…nothing.

Well, nothing but a vampire whore.

"I have a potion that can make this disappear," Frankie whispers hoarsely. He hasn't moved from the doorframe, his eyes glassy with unshed tears. "I'll start on it tonight, and it should be ready in the next few days."

"No." I shake my head once, and then again, more vehemently. "Not tonight."

Still wearing my short black dress, I crawl onto the bed and underneath the covers.

"Violet?" Frankie takes one step closer as I extend a hand, pulling back the blankets.

"Stay with me?" My voice is a plea, nothing but a hushed murmur.

Without hesitation, Frankie crawls beneath the covers beside me and spoons me from behind. His scent surrounds me, comforts me, and somehow, tames the monsters in my head.

Still in his arms, I turn on the bed until I'm facing him, our noses touching.

"I'm so sorry, Vi," he murmurs brokenly. It's almost as if he can't bring himself to speak above a whisper. As if the silence is a fine slate of glass already cracked and moments away from shattering. There's something tranquil and serene about silence, though. It's the secrets we carry, the demons we banish, the fears we hide. But it's also the joy of a first love and the long nights buried beneath the covers, wrapped in someone's arms.

"It's not your fault," I promise, lifting my hand to comb back his tangled curls. I haven't even realized I've used my scarred arm until he pulls it towards his lips and kisses a path down the words. It stopped bleeding back in the alleyway—due to my vampire healing—but the scar will remain. Even if

Frankie can make something to erase it, it can't rectify the pain inflicted on my very soul.

"I promise you, Violet, that no one will ever harm you again," he murmurs as his lips touch the final "e" of "vampire."

I want to tell him not to make promises he can't keep. I want to reassure him that I'm stronger than he believes.

But I don't say any of that. Instead, I nuzzle his neck with my nose and whisper, "Hold me."

Maybe with Frankie by my side, the nightmares will be kept at bay.

CHAPTER 20

JACK

I peer through Hux's—my—eyes as he moves swiftly through the grocery store. He's humming beneath his breath as he pushes the metal cart down the various aisleways.

This is so stupid, I deadpan as my rather cheerful brother stops in front of a chocolate display. He begins to grab items at random, dumping them into his already overflowing cart.

"The Google says this is the key to a girl's heart," he replies out loud, garnering the attention of a couple standing nearby.

Last night, Hux discovered that Violet was going on a date with Frankie, and now, he's insistent he needs to go on his own date with the blonde bombshell. He did extensive research on—what he likes to call—"the Google" on how to ask a girl out. The website suggested flowers and chocolates.

Thus, we now have over fifty-five boxes of chocolates and three-hundred flowers of all types and colors in our shopping cart.

Dude, that's enough! I exclaim as he adds another box of chocolate to the cart.

"We never know when my precious treasure is going to experience her Great Period and require chocolate for survival," he dismisses. "Unless you want me to start cutting up body parts…"

No! We talked about this. No body parts. No maiming. No murder in the name of love.

"A little murder in the name of love is okay," Hux murmurs absently as he continues to pore over the shelves.

We talked about this…

"No murder," he sighs disappointedly. When he spins on his heel, I see an older woman staring at us with wide eyes, one hand clutching her cross necklace and the other raised to defend herself.

Hux smiles disarmingly at her before nodding his head subserviently.

"The great and powerful Google told me that chocolate and flowers were the key to a woman's heart. Would you agree?" he asks, his smoky accent curling around her. She backs away a step, looking rightfully shell-shocked, before turning on her heel and waddling away. "That was rude," Hux tells me. "The Google told me that it's polite to say thank you for starting a conversation."

For the love of…

It's Google, not "the Google," I correct, mentally face-palming myself. *And you can't just talk to humans like you would a monster. They're far more…delicate than us. They require easing into.*

"Excuse me!" Hux waves his hand erratically in the air, capturing the attention of a heavily-tattooed, muscular human. The man saunters forward with his hands in his pockets and a curious expression on his face. "Do you, my new human friend, require easing into?"

Jesus, no.

"Excuse me?" The man quirks one eyebrow, the curiosity on his face dissipating to be replaced by a dark expression.

"You're delicate," Hux states matter-of-factly. "And you'll require me easing into you."

"You motherfucker!" the man hisses, taking a lumbering step forward. I quickly wrestle with Hux for control of his mind. Not because I'm scared for my brother, but because I don't want to be arrested for first-degree murder this early in the school year.

Hux puts up a fight, but soon, I have him shoved in the passenger seat while I take the wheel.

"What the fuck did you say to me?" The stench of body odor and sweat saturates the air, so intensely that I can taste it.

"I'm sorry," I apologize sincerely. "I thought you were my old buddy from college." I rake my fingers over my scalp as I flash a sheepish smile. "You look exactly like him. It was an inside joke between us."

The man continues to stare at me for a long moment, eyes hard, before he releases me with a disgruntled huff.

"Fag," he seethes before continuing down the aisle.

Let me kill him, Hux asserts in my head. *He's a... What word did the Google say? A cumstain? He's a cumstain.*

Ignoring him, I push the cart to the checkout lane and quickly pay for the three hundred dollars' worth of flowers and chocolates. My left eye is practically twitching when I procure my credit card and hand it to the older lady behind the register.

Only when we're in the car, driving back to campus, do I dare speak out loud.

"You can't keep doing this," I tell Hux sternly.

Doing what? If he was here, I have no doubt he would be batting his eyelashes innocently.

"Hijacking my body," I state firmly. "The last thing I remember is waking up in the morning..."

Hux is silent for a moment, too silent, before his timid voice reverberates in my head. *You don't remember us leaving the school?*

"No." I drum my fingers against the steering wheel. "I don't remember anything."

I have lived with Hux for the last few hundred years. For the majority of that time, I have taken control. The few times I allowed Hux free rein, I remained relegated in a tiny sliver of darkness in the recesses of our shared brain. I was still aware of my surroundings and time passing, but I couldn't interact with anything or anyone. I wasn't even capable of using my senses. We have never actually met before Violet—never had a true conversation. We would leave notes for each other to read whenever we swapped. Only with Violet's appearance have we been able to communicate telepathically.

But this new development? Disappearing for hours on end? It's terrifying. Will one of us simply cease to exist? Is that the curse of being two souls trapped in one body?

Quit overthinking it, Hux hisses vehemently. *You know I'll never let anything happen to you.*

"I know," I whisper, but that's exactly what I'm afraid of.

We're both silent as I pull into the school parking lot and grab my bag from the backseat. I imagine Hux's thoughts are a reflection of my own—if only one of us can live, how would we choose which one? Would we force Violet to choose between us?

I scrub a hand down my face as my thoughts begin to run rampant.

What class do we have right now? Hux queries as we step into the academic building. I leave the chocolates and flowers in the backseat of my car for Hux to grab later.

"Roaring with Dimitri. Which we're late for," I grumble, hurrying my pace.

Can you tell my precious treasure I miss her? And that I bought her roses and chocolates? Or should I just throw them at her like they do in the movies?

And…now I picture Hux throwing chocolate bars at Violet's head while he stares at her with dopey, lovesick eyes.

I roll my eyes at his antics as I slip through the classroom door. Dimitri Gray is already perched on his desk, his long legs extended in front of him. I spot Alex and Cheryl sitting in the front row, Cheryl purposefully leaning forward to show a hint of cleavage. Violet sits in the back with Frankie, Mason, and Vin. I notice the latter two are joking amongst themselves, but Violet is uncharacteristically silent. Frankie has one hand on her knee, almost as if he's offering comfort.

Precious Treasure! Hux screams in my head, causing me to wince. Instantly, I'm bombarded with images of me pulling Violet onto my lap and pushing aside her skirt to make love to her. Thank you, Hux. Because I really wanted to start my day with a boner.

Her golden curls are piled haphazardly into a bun at the top of her head. She wears a pink dress with a black leather jacket over it. She looks completely normal, except for her eyes. They're…haunted almost. Shadowed with pain I can't even begin to comprehend.

I move to sit at the desk on the other side of her, directly behind Mason.

"Are you okay?" I whisper softly, and her eyes flicker to me in alarm. She quickly tries to smooth over her expression before I can notice.

"Of course." She forces a smile. "How are my two favorite men doing?"

"Hey, I heard that!" Mason exclaims, spinning around to

face us. Violet sticks her tongue out at him, and Mason grabs his heart in mock pain. "You wound me, oh beautiful one."

"We all know I'm the favorite," Vin states with a derisive snort.

"I don't know, man," Mason teases. "Frankie and Violet are looking quite chummy over there." He winks conspiratorially at the two, and I can't help but note how Violet's face pales and Frankie's hand tightens on her leg.

Something's wrong, I murmur to Hux.

With my precious treasure? he demands instantly. *Did Frankie hurt her?*

I honestly don't know.

Before I can press Violet for information, Dimitri clears his throat at the front of the classroom.

"As a lot of you already know, this is a new class designed specifically to navigate the analytical portion of the Roaring." He clasps his hands behind his back and begins to pace. "One of the main games is a test of sorts. But not a written one. You will be put in a situation with a small group of fellow competitors, and you'll have to work as a team to figure out how to escape with your life."

How does he know all of this? Hux asks in annoyance. Already, he's itching for me to turn away from the stoic teacher and focus on Violet beside us. I'm pretty sure the man doesn't know how to function when he's not staring at her.

Didn't you know? Dimitri won the Roaring a few years ago. They called it the Blood Bath. Every other monster died...except for him and one other.

Who was the other survivor? Hux inquires, only half listening.

Dracula himself.

I watched the games on television with my father, appalled by how gruesome they were. I had competed twenty or thirty years ago, but never again. I didn't want to risk my life for a stupid title and trophy.

But Dimitri Gray and Vladimir Dracula? They won the games...and killed everyone else in the process.

"What if we get paired up with vampire scum?" Cheryl asks innocently, waving her hand in the air to capture Dimitri's attention. He pauses mid-lecture, the full force of his icy blue gaze barreling down on her.

"Then you better hope your partner is a better person than you, Cheryl Ness," Dimitri lectures. "Or else you'll both be dead."

She huffs, clearly not having expected that answer, before crossing her arms over her chest and leaning back in her seat.

"Today, we'll start with something simple," Dimitri declares. "Everyone pair up and—"

"I call Pinkie!" Mason jumps to his feet and grabs Violet's arm. Immediately, she releases a pained whimper, wrenching her arm free from Mason and rubbing it inconspicuously.

What the heck...?

Hux notices it at the same time I do and roars in my head, demanding to be released. I turn towards Frankie, who looks pale and sick, as if he's seconds from expelling the contents of his breakfast across his desk.

"What the fuck did you do?" Vin rises to his feet, every inch the dangerous predator. There's a reason the other monsters fear the Van Helsings. They're hunters, through and through. When they smell blood, they'll latch on to it with all of their teeth and bite down.

Mason is slower to understand what is happening, eyes darting between all of us, before understanding dawns in his eyes. He moves swiftly to his feet as well, standing shoulder to shoulder with Vin, an impenetrable wall of muscle.

Hux has gone quiet in my own mind, but it's not because

he has disappeared. It's because he's filled to the brim with a blistering rage, one that surpasses anything I have ever felt before. It's the calm before a storm. The eye of a hurricane, where you can look in every direction and see rapid winds and piercing rain. It's a subtle type of anger, but one that's capable of igniting an inferno.

"Knock it off," Violet hisses softly. She intertwines her fingers with Frankie's and gives him a reassuring squeeze.

"Did he hurt you?" Vin asks dangerously, already taking a threatening step forward. I can see the violence in his eyes, teetering on the brink of absolute destruction, like a tornado rapidly approaching an unsuspecting town.

"What the bloody hell is going on over here?" Dimitri steps forward, eyes spewing frost, before focusing intently on Violet. "I'm in the middle of a class, Ms. Dracula. If you would like to have a conversation, please do that on your own time."

"You're right." Violet folds her hands on her desk, flashing an innocent smile. "Please proceed."

"Not until you tell us why you flinched!" Vin demands.

Dimitri cocks an eyebrow, eyes narrowing even further.

"What is he talking about, Violet?"

She fidgets under our combined stares, reaching for Frankie's hand as if she's drifting away at sea and he's the only one who can steady her.

"Oh for fuck's sake…" Cheryl sashays forward with a wicked grin, Alex following closely on her heel. Before we can do anything, she grabs Violet's arm and pushes up the loose sleeve.

"Holy shit!" Vin curses, eyes widening in horror. Cheryl releases Violet's arm as if she has been stung by a wasp, mouth agape. She looks physically sick as she reads the words etched into Violet's pasty skin. Only one weapon would cause the scars not to heal.

A god-blessed blade.

A myriad of emotions flicker across Dimitri's face—a storm brewing and gathering speed—before he turns on his heel with a brisk "class dismissed" and exits the room.

"Violet?" I ask gently, grabbing her scarred arm. I rub the pad of my thumb gently over the crude words, anger vibrating through me. My anger, though? It's nothing compared to Hux's. "What happened?"

"It doesn't matter," she says scathingly. She pulls her arm free and bends down to grab her backpack.

"Violet…" I say gently, ignoring Vin's curses and Mason's death threats.

"Seriously, Jack, drop it, okay? I don't want to talk about it." I've never heard Violet sound so choked up before. Usually, she acts as if she's grabbing life by the balls and making it her bitch. This is a shell of the woman I know and love. Whatever those assholes did broke a fundamental piece of her.

On her way out the door, she shoulders past a still silent and gaping Cheryl and a pale-faced Alex. Before I can follow her, I'm pushed to the side by the force of Vin's assault on Frankie. He grabs the man by his shirt collar and pushes him against the wall.

"Why the hell didn't you stop it?" he screams, spittle flying from his lips. Frankie allows the hunter to manhandle him, not even lifting a finger to stop the barrage of fists. I recognize the look in his eyes too well—self-loathing. His dark eyes are rife with frustration and anger.

"Vin, that's enough," I say tiredly, grabbing my friend's shoulder to pull him back. He shoves at me, causing me to lose my footing before I quickly right myself.

"Don't tell me what's enough! Did you see her fucking arm?" he roars, pounding another fist into Frankie's face.

"Of course I did! We all did! But this isn't the correct way to handle it. We should save our anger for the assholes who hurt her."

I want nothing more than to follow Violet and comfort her, but I know that if I leave the room, Vin might actually kill Frankie.

"Did you see them?" Mason whispers, shaking himself out of whatever daze Violet's scarring put him in. "The assholes who did that to her?"

At Frankie's barely perceptible nod, Vin drops him to the ground.

"Then we find them," he snaps, tone laced with acrimony. "And we kill them."

"Wait!" We all turn at the same time to see an ashen Alex standing in the doorframe. His dark eyes swirl like a bottomless black pit. "I want to help."

"Fuck you!" Mason hisses, storming forward and pressing his arm to the man's throat. "It's people like you—"

"People like me?" Alex scoffs once, the sound pained due to his obstructed airway. "What those monsters did is sickening."

"And making her shit her pants wasn't?" I ask softly, and his head swivels in my direction. For a brief moment, I see guilt in his eyes, but it's there and gone too fast for me to comment on.

With one last glare directed our way, Alex storms out of the room, slamming the door shut behind him.

"I'll stay with Violet," Mason whispers, for once forgoing his usual nickname for her. "She might not know it yet, but she shouldn't be alone."

Frankie nods once in understanding, his face already beginning to bruise in some areas from Vin's fists. "I need to finish the potion in my lab," he explains. "It's designed to help with the scarring."

"Good. That's good—" Before I can say another word, I'm shoved to the back of my own mind with a ferocious roar.

"Hux." Vin nods once in greeting, but my brother is too far gone to acknowledge him. His mind is focused on one thing and one thing only—revenge.

"Let's go kill a little piggy, shall we?" he questions darkly.

CHAPTER 21

"Violet, wait!" a familiar voice calls from behind me. I decrease my pace, more in curiosity than anything else.

A second later, Cheryl stops beside me, panting heavily.

"Damn, girl. You're fast."

I shrug nonchalantly. "One of the only perks of being a vampire, I guess."

We're both silent for a moment as we stare at one another. Cheryl rocks back and forth on her heels, anxiously nipping at her lower lip. She forks her fingers through her mane of hair before dropping her arm back to her side.

"Did you kill them?" she asks abruptly, crossing and then uncrossing her arms.

"Who?"

"The guys who did that to you." She nods to my abused flesh. "Did you kill them?"

My heart seems to be growing in a steadily shrinking vise.

"No," I whisper at last, dropping my gaze to focus on my combat boots. "I didn't."

"What they did was fucked up," Cheryl continues, a hint of anger in her voice. "And that's coming from me. And…and I'm sorry. About outing you like that. It was a real bitch move, and again, that's coming from me."

I can't help the tentative smile that curls up my lips, but I still stubbornly keep my gaze lowered. "What can I say? You *are* a bitch."

She snorts. "Can you blame me? My boyfriend left me for you. I think I deserve to be a little bitchy." An awkward silence ensues once more as we both struggle to think of something to say. Finally, I lift my head and meet her piercing blue eyes. "If you find the assholes who did that to you, I'll help you hide the bodies. But, like, don't go thinking this makes us friends or anything like that. I still hate your guts, but just not enough to want you to physically die." With that ominous statement, she flips back her flaming hair and hurries down the hall.

"What the fuck?" I murmur, more to myself than anyone else. Shaking my head at the sheer bizarreness of that entire conversation, I hurry out of the academic building and into the frigid air. Winter is fast approaching, and the bitter winds and deteriorating leaves are evidence enough. As I walk down the familiar pathway to my dorm building, I allow the biting cold to soothe my ravaged emotions.

"Pinkie! Pinkie! Pinkie! Wait up!" This time, I don't bother to slow down as I hear the crackle of leaves and foliage. Mason materializes out of the trees a moment later and jogs towards me, stopping when he's able to match my pace.

"I'm not going to be good company, Mase," I warn him stoutly as we step in front of the ancient dormitory.

He shrugs. "We could be sitting in absolute silence,

making faces at each other across the room, and I'd still want to be with you."

Knowing that nothing I say will deter him, I nod for him to head in first. "Lead the way, Snake Man."

"Snake Man… Are you thinking of nicknames for my cock?" he teases as we pass the front desk and walk to the staircase. "I've always called it Little Mason, but I'm open to suggestions."

"Sorry. I'm pretty sure Tic Tac is already trademarked somewhere."

"Ouch, Vi. You wound me." We finally stop in front of my door on the second floor, and I push it open quickly, determined to hide beneath my covers and forget this shit day ever happened. It's only when the lights are on that I get a good look at the once pristine—if a bit dusty—dorm room.

It's as if someone ransacked everything. Tables and nightstands are overturned, and my blankets have been cut to shreds. All of my textbooks are dripping with an undefinable green liquid. One glance in my closet confirms that my clothes have also been altered beyond recognition, the shirts having more holes than fabric and the skirts cut into thin strands.

"Fucking hell!" Mason breathes as he surveys the destruction of my room. I know I should feel horrified or upset about the damage inflicted, but instead, I just feel numb. It's a similar sensation to how I felt in the alleyway last night, when those monsters carved hurtful words into my skin. There's only so much shit I can endure before it becomes too much. I'm getting buried beneath six feet of pure concrete, and no matter how loud I scream, no one can hear me.

"It's fine." I drop my bag onto the precariously standing desk, two of the legs bent at odd angles.

"It's not fine!" he seethes, chest heaving. "It's not fucking fine!"

"So, what can we do about it?" I eye my bed wistfully before grabbing one of my shredded blankets and pulling it around my shoulders. Once I'm safely cocooned, I sit on the ground with my back against the wall. Mason hesitates only a second before moving to sit directly beside me. "People fear things they don't understand, and vampires? We're the epitome of that. We're stronger, faster, and more durable than any other monster."

"People are dumbasses," Mason protests venomously. "They have no idea what the fuck they're talking about."

"They hate me," I continue, ignoring his outburst. "And they don't even know me." Squeezing my eyelids shut, I release a bark of humorless laughter. "Ironically enough, I might not even be a vampire."

Mason tenses beside me, only his head moving to stare at me attentively. "What do you mean?"

With a sigh, I rest my head on his shoulder. His arm automatically comes up to wrap around me, hugging me to him.

"Ms. Stevens…" I begin, confessing a secret I should've told them weeks ago. "She mentioned something. Something strange."

He doesn't interrupt, doesn't demand me to hurry up. Instead, he's content with allowing me to process the information at my own pace.

"She said Dracula wasn't my father. That I was found by him when I was just a baby. She also said that I'm not even a vampire." The words tumble out of me in a rush, but it's a relief to get that weight off my chest. Since I heard that information, it's been a constant pressure cutting off my air supply. Only now does it feel like I can finally breathe again.

"She's a lying, psychotic bitch who tried to kill you," Mason protests adamantly. "You can't believe a word she says."

"It's not just her." Absently, I draw circles into his chest over his shirt. "My dad acted really weird when I mentioned Ms. Stevens the other day. He told me to meet him in person to discuss it further."

"When?"

"Tonight," I say. "He's supposed to text me a location."

"Do you want me to come with?" Mason peers down at me, nothing but worry in his gaze. He doesn't demand to come with me like some of the others might. He trusts my judgement—sometimes even more than I trust it.

"Yes, please," I whisper, stretching my neck to kiss the stubble on his jaw. "I don't know if I can handle this alone."

"You're Violet Dracula," he says immediately. "You can do anything."

I press my face to his shirt to hide my smile, his faith in me staggering and quite humbling.

"I was also thinking..." Mason trails off, and I can't help but glance up at him, surprised to see his cheeks crimson. When he catches me staring, his blush deepens.

"Yeah?"

"With everything that just happened...and now someone breaking into your room..."

"Mason, spit it out." I poke his bicep, only to have my finger swatted away and then grabbed and nibbled on. With my free hand, I aim a punch at his chest, but he captures my fist and kisses the corner of my lips. Relationship bliss, I tell ya.

"There's an extra room at our house..." Once more, he trails off with a sheepish smile.

"Mason." I sit upright, instantly alert. "Are you asking me to move in with you guys?"

"Only if you want to!" he assures me quickly. When he holds open his arms, I immediately lie against him once more, basking in his warmth. He always makes me feel so safe and cherished, as if his body will protect me from the world's anger and bigotry.

"I don't know," I begin timidly. "Do the others even want me there?"

Mason snorts once, amusement in his voice. "I'm pretty sure Hux already designed a bedroom for you in shades of pink and black."

"Well, if you all agree…" I twist my face until my smile is hidden by his flannel shirt. "Then, yes."

"Really? You'll move in with us?" He's practically thrumming with excitement, his knees bouncing with barely-contained energy. I press a tender kiss to the top of his chest.

"God, this is so weird. It feels as if I just met you, but at the same time—"

"It feels as if you've known us forever," he finishes, brushing back a strand of my unruly blonde hair. "Obviously, we will all be on our best behavior. Even Hux. You don't have to see us if you don't want to."

"Of course I'll want to see you." I roll my eyes at him. "You guys are my boyfriends."

"Boyfriends?" His lips tentatively touch my scalp before lowering to my forehead, leaving a trail of fire in their wake. "Is that what we are?"

"Is that what you want to be?" I fire back, heat suffusing my cheeks. Fuck, why did I just use the b-word? They're my friends with sexy benefits. We never talked about partaking in an actual relationship.

"Violet Dracula." Mason grips my chin to stare intently into my eyes. "I would be honored to call you my girlfriend."

Our lips meet in a soft kiss. It's innocent and pure, but it causes lightning to zip through my veins and fireworks to explode behind my eyes.

I don't know what the future will hold, but I know that with these men by my side, I can accomplish anything.

We pull up in front of a corrugated iron warehouse. There are at least a dozen others sprouting in all directions like the spindly branches of a tree. They seem to stem from an unassuming building directly in the center, with a large, tin roof and a long row of dirty windows. All of the warehouses are spread intermittently down a curving dirt road, some mere feet away from each other, others spanning the length of a football field.

"Are you sure this is the place?" Mason asks anxiously as he peers in both directions.

"This is the address Dad gave me," I answer, though I'm confused by this location as well.

My dad…

He prefers the finer things in life. Elegant restaurants, gothic mansions, five-tiered cakes. He would never be caught dead at a location such as this. Even standing in front of Mason's car, my gorgon boyfriend beside me, unease skates down my spine like an ice cube.

Instead of disclosing to Mason my fears, I lean against the side of his car and cross my arms over my chest. The air is frigid, and in the nearby distance, a forest sweeps up and away, canvasing the hills in skeletal trees.

"Your father is a strange man," Mason muses, removing a joint from his pocket and lighting up. I eye the fairy weed with utter distaste but choose to remain silent. It's his choice; if he wants to destroy his lungs, so be it. Though a part of me is tempted to sneak into his room and flush his entire stash.

Noticing my look, Mason smiles sheepishly, puts it out, and immediately shoves the joint back into his shirt pocket.

"My dad is pretty weird," I concede. "He once hid underneath my bed for ten days to try and scare me."

Mason snorts, flashing me a coy smile. "Pinkie, you know

you just ruined the horrifying image I once had of Dracula, right?"

I pull my jacket tighter around me in an attempt to curb the growing chill. Mason immediately pulls me underneath his arm, holding me to him. "He's my dad. I'm the one person he doesn't have to hide his true self from. And honestly? Dracula's a scary motherfucker and a hard-ass, but he's also funny. And witty. And he always wants the best for me. Sure, he's a stone-cold murderer, but what parent isn't?" I shrug once before turning my face and nuzzling Mason's neck. "He's my dad."

We're both silent for a long moment, lost in an embrace capable of melting glaciers, when Mason removes his arm and rests it above my head. This new position has his lean, muscular body towering over mine, making me feel dainty and small. Vulnerable.

"Pinkie…"

I turn my head away instantly, careful to keep my face bereft of emotion.

"I don't want to talk about it. I told you."

"I know you don't, baby girl. But I just want you to be okay."

Those words…

They tumble around in my brain and rattle my skull. Those seemingly innocent words are like the slash of a whip against my back, each consecutive hit drawing more and more blood.

"How the fuck can I be okay, Mason?" I ask, mouth twisting in a rictus sneer. "You don't know what it's like to be hated." My hands tremble by my sides, and I ball them into fists to hide it. The pain is painted on my heart like a mural I can never scrub clean. It's a tattoo, etched across the surface forever. "Everyone hates me, and not just my classmates. The entire *world* hates me. Everybody keeps asking me if I'm okay, but honestly? I'm a fucking mess. I was just violated, Mason. They touched me. They carved words into my skin. How the fuck am I supposed to look at myself in the mirror anymore? All I see is a trembling, broken girl who cried when she was confronted. I'm not a monster, and I don't know how to be one. I'm weak and pathetic, and maybe I deserve what those assholes did—"

"Don't fucking say that!" Mason cuts in, his face contorted in rage. "What those pieces of shit did to you was not your fault." His eyes soften exponentially as he leans forward, cupping my chin with a tenderness contradicting the feral rage in his eyes. "It's okay to cry. Hell, I would still be crying if that was me. But you don't have to fight this battle alone anymore. There are haters in this world, sure, but there are also people who care about you immensely. People who will lay down their lives for you." Eyes still ensnaring mine, he rests his forehead against my own. "I promise you, Violet, that I won't let them hurt you again. I would rather stab my own eyes out than watch you go through this pain a second time."

I sniffle, the enormity of my emotions for this man taking me by surprise. My throat closes, and I have to swallow multiple times—almost as if I'm swallowing the words that want to spring free. Instead of divulging my soul, I whisper, "When did you become so romantic?"

A wry grin curls up his lush lips. "When a beautiful vampire tripped into my life."

Snorting, I push at his shoulder until he reluctantly parts from me. "I did *not* trip."

"You were on the floor when I saw you," he points out.

"Because Vin shoved me," I counter.

His eyes darken momentarily. "And I still need to beat the shit out of him for that."

"I already did. With a slimy green arm. We're good now."

Mason snorts and wraps his arm once more around me. "You're such a freak, Violet. But you're my freak. My beautiful, perfect freak."

"We're only freaks because society doesn't understand normal," I point out helpfully, pressing up onto my tiptoes to kiss his cheek. My smile fades, tightening into a grim line. "Mason, I'm going to take this seriously."

"Huh?" He lifts a brow, twisting his head to stare down at me.

"The Roaring. I'm going to train, and I'm going to win. I'm not going to allow fear to dictate what I do anymore." The strength of my resolve startles even me. I'm tired of hiding in the shadows when my body craves the light. What those monsters did to me bent me irrevocably, but I'm still standing. Maybe I no longer have as many pieces, but that doesn't mean I'm broken. The fire lingering just beneath my surface is still raging, strengthening to become an inferno.

"I'll help in whatever way I can," Mason vows immediately. He doesn't tell me it's stupid or dangerous. He doesn't try to placate me. He knows that this is what I need to do to overcome my trauma. I need to stare in the mirror and be proud of the monster looking back at me, not hiding away in fear. Winning the Roaring? There's no greater accomplishment than that in the monster world.

It's time to grow some fucking ovaries and let the world know what I'm made of.

A ping from my phone interrupts my internal monologue. Frowning, I pull out my device and stare at the blinking text message on the screen.

Dad (Dracula) (Papa Bear) (Psychotic Murderer): I have to cancel. Sorry.

"Fuck," I curse, staring intently at the words and willing them to change. Canceling once, I understand, but canceling twice? Something doesn't add up.

"What's wrong?" Mason asks, instantly on alert.

"My dad." I hold up my phone so he can read the text. "He canceled."

"He canceled before," Mason points out. "Why is this any different?"

"I don't know."

Maybe I'm wrong, maybe this is just my dad being his normal, flaky self, but I can't ignore the sliver of unease that embeds itself in my heart.

"Let's just go home," I tell Mason at last, unable to tear my gaze away from the words on the screen. They rub me the wrong way, but I can't put my finger on what it is exactly. With a sigh, I toss my phone into the backseat of the car and enter through the passenger door. I'll call my dad tomorrow, and then the next day, and then the next day, and then the next day. I'll call until my fingers bleed and my voice goes hoarse.

He'll give me answers, dammit. I won't accept anything else.

CHAPTER 22

VIOLET

I spend the next week extensively training for the Roaring. Kernels of excitement appear in my stomach, intermingled with the dread and worry already there. I can't ignore how excited I actually am for the games to begin.

"You need to be careful, Violet," Vin hisses in the early morning sunlight as I drop down to do another set of twenty push-ups. My arms are shaking, and sweat coats my body like a second skin. "You don't want to hurt yourself trying to keep up with us."

He's on one side of me with Jack on the other. Both men move fluidly as they do push-up after push-up with the other fifty competitors.

"I'll have you know I'm super athletic," I huff out between pants. "I do all my own stunts…never intentionally. But still, I do them. So, *ha*."

On the twentieth push-up, my arms give out and my face collides with the grass, wet with morning dew. Laughter rings out from farther down the line of students, and I don't have to look to know it'll be Gills and Alex.

Mummy releases us for the day, and my men immediately jump to their feet, prepared to shower away today's sweat and dirt. I remain on the ground, attempting to do a few more push-ups. Every muscle aches, though I don't know if it's from the push-ups today or the five-mile run we did yesterday.

"Violet," Jack says gently. "Vi."

"Just a few more," I pant.

"Vi…"

"A couple more."

Abruptly, a hand grabs the back of my shirt and drags me to my feet. My legs wobble, threatening to give out, but the hand holds me steady, pulling me against a sculpted chest.

"You're working yourself too hard," Vin grumbles in my ear. "I don't want you to get sick or hurt yourself."

"News flash, I hurt myself all the time. Just last night, I hurt myself after I tripped down the staircase in my dorm and face-planted into a potted plant," I point out. Despite the guys' protest, I'm still living in my dorm room. For now. I have every intention of moving out…*after* the Roaring is completed. I can't afford to be distracted, and these men? They're the biggest kind.

"Be sensible," Vin hisses. "You can't win the competition if you're dead." He gives me a long, eloquent look that says more than a thousand words, but I merely roll my eyes.

"I also can't win if I choose donuts over running every day…which I still do, make no mistake. But a push-up and salad usually evens it out." I shoulder away from the men and bend down to grab my water bottle, topped full with Jack's blood. The assholes at school are still refusing to allow us to eat in the cafeteria, so I have to be creative.

The warm liquid leaves tingles in its wake, eliciting full-body goosebumps. Fuck, he tastes good.

As I pull the bottle away from my lips, I catch the men staring intently at the words on my arm, still red and ragged from the week earlier. Frankie has been working tirelessly on a balm designed to eliminate the scars, but I'm honestly not sure I want them gone anymore. They're a reminder of what I've endured and what I'm still fighting for. Whenever I see those crude words burned onto my skin, anger swirls low in my stomach like a whirlpool. That anger grows and grows, until it's the size of a tsunami seconds from cresting the shoreline. All this rage needs is an outlet.

I know the guys went searching for the monsters who did this to me, but so far, they're shit out of luck. It's like the ghoul and his friends disappeared into thin air. No one has heard from them since that fateful night, when my life was forever altered.

"Violet," a soft voice inquires from behind me. I turn with a heavy sigh, unsurprised to see Cal. The rest of the guys stand a short distance away, murmuring amongst each other.

Of course, they'd send the one person I can't possibly get mad at. He's too freaking adorable.

"What, Cal? Are you going to tell me that I'm being stupid? That I'm pushing myself too hard? That I should focus my anger on other things?" I bite out, tone scathing. His eyes flash with pain before he quickly masks it.

"Not at all, actually." He takes a step closer until his body blocks out the others. "You might find this hard to believe, but I understand what you're going through."

I snort cynically, giving him a lingering once-over. "You had words carved into your skin as well?"

"No." He shakes his head sadly. "But I know what it's like to be feared and hated because of what type of monster you are."

Guilt instantly suffuses me as I stare into his golden-flecked eyes. A century of sadness peers back at me, swallowing me whole.

"Fuck, I'm sorry," I say instantly, ducking my head.

"I didn't even understand what was happening," he continues. "One second, everything was normal, and the next, I was here. In the upper levels. Unable to interact with the rest of the world." His tone is laced with pain—so much pain, that my heart aches for him. When he moves to sit on the ground, long legs extended, I don't hesitate before sitting next to him, wrapping my pinkie around his.

"You don't have to tell me if you don't want to," I whisper, gauging his reaction carefully. His beautiful face is tightened in pain, the lines around his mouth harsh and unforgiving. When he catches me staring, he flashes me a half-hearted smile that doesn't reach his eyes.

"It's fine," he assures me. "If you're going to be friends with a monster, you might as well know his story." He glances towards the others, who are congregated beside one of the larger tombstones, far enough away where they can't overhear our conversation but still close enough they can keep an eye on me. "I won't tell you Barret's story—that's his choice—but I will tell you mine. If you want to hear it, that is."

"Yes." When he begins to fidget, I brush my pinkie over his lightly, stilling his movements. "But the same goes for you. You don't have to tell me anything, Cal, if you don't want to."

Heaving out a breath, Cal runs his fingers through his wispy pink hair, the strands sticking out in all directions.

"The rumors are true, you know. About Cupid." He snorts once. "Not about being a baby who wears diapers and shoots arrows. As you can see, I'm very much a grown-ass man." With a dramatic flourish, he gestures towards his sculpted body that exudes raw sex. "As an incubus, I need lust to survive, but I'm also part fairy, believe it or not." He gestures towards his red wings sprouting from his back. "Of the Summer Court, actually. And they? They require love."

We're both silent for a minute, listening to the melodic wind rattle the tree branches and caress the gravestones.

"So you're half fairy and half incubus?" I question, staring at Cal in a newfound light. That would explain the wings. The only other incubus I know is Dimitri Gray, and unless I'm missing something, that man doesn't have any on his body.

Not that I've seen his body naked.

Not that I've imagined it naked.

Naked Dimitri. Nope. Not going there.

"Correct." He bites down on his lower lip. "I discovered early on that I could survive on either one—lust or love. I didn't need both." I watch in rapt fascination as he grabs a blade of grass and rubs it between his fingers, the gesture absent-minded.

I don't push him to continue his story. I can see that whatever he's about to tell me is going to be hard on him. These are his demons, his ghosts, coming back to haunt him. They're crawling through the earth and pressing their keen claws into his ankles. He can either fight their hold or allow them to drag him under.

"I also discovered that I can manipulate those two feelings," he continues, voice devoid of any emotion. "I can make people fall in love as well as create immeasurable lust. I thought I was helping people...enhancing what they already felt. It was a win-win, you know? I made them fall helplessly in love with each other, and I used that love to feed myself. I would go through towns and send out waves of love and lust. It made people happy, and I thought I was doing the right thing."

"But…?" I ask softly, and he finally rips his gaze away from the abused grass.

"But the monster world didn't see it like that." He releases a ragged sigh and turns to face me completely, shifting slightly. "Some of the communities I impacted were strictly monster communities. As such, the monsters saw fit to act on their inner desires, despite the fact that mating bonds usually only happen between monsters of the same species. Werewolves would mate with vampires. Ghouls with zombies. Witches with incubi. You get the idea. I didn't know it at the time, but I wasn't just making monsters fall in love. I was finding people's soulmates."

I gasp harshly. "You mean…?"

"Monsters who shouldn't have mates suddenly found theirs," he finishes. "True love and all that shit." Throwing his head back, he releases a self-deprecating laugh, the noise rattling my ribs and my teeth. It's a harsh, cold sound, and such a contrast to the warm man I first befriended back in detention.

"And then you ended up here," I whisper in growing horror, but Cal shakes his head.

"No. First, they murdered my family to ensure this would never happen again. My baby sisters. My mom and dad. Even my aunts and uncles and cousins." Pain emanates from his gaze, and it takes every ounce of willpower not to give him a hug.

Oh, fuck it.

Leaning forward, I wrap my arms around Cal's neck in a desperate embrace, his heart thumping beneath my own.

"Cal, I'm so fucking sorry."

"They saw me as something they could use," he whispers, his arms hanging limply by his sides. After a moment, he timidly hugs me back, hungry for love and affection after years spent in his prison. "So they made me come here, to train me. At first, I was a normal student, just like you, but when I began to fight back, they shoved me in the upper levels." His voice turns choked, as if he's overcome by a strong emotion. "I've been alone for so long."

"You won't be alone anymore, Cal," I promise, pulling back so I can stare into his glimmering eyes. Gently, I brush back strands of his unruly pink hair in desperate need of a trim.

He tries to laugh, but the noise is bitter and angry—a product of all he has endured. "You promise? I'm way too beautiful to be alone."

I snort out a laugh at his attempt at a joke. "You're right, pretty boy. Way too beautiful." Worrying my fleshy bottom lip, I query, "How long have you been up there? In detention, I mean?"

His face hardens, twisting into an unreadable mask hewn from stone.

"Two hundred and fifty-seven years. This is the second time in over one hundred that I have been able to feel the sunlight on my face. Normally, I'm only released every Halloween night." He arches his neck, eyes closed, as he soaks up the blistering rays. "Feel the grass beneath my fingers." He tugs a second strand out of the ground and holds it up for me to see. "Hear laughter and joy." As if on cue, my men break into raucous laughter a short distance away. "Feel the wind on my face." His eyes close once more as pure bliss erupts on his face.

"Cal…"

"Barret and I made a deal with Dimitri and the Monster Council," Cal continues, voice a hushed murmur. "If we win the Roaring, we'll get to go free, be normal students. Normal *monsters*." He swallows suddenly, and I feel my pulse skitter in response.

"And if you lose?" I voice the question I really, really don't want the answer to.

"If we lose…" His Adam's apple bobs. "If we lose, we'll work for the council."

"For how long?" Terror thrums through me, vibrating on its own separate frequency.

Cal's face is grim when he speaks next. "Forever."

CHAPTER 23

VIOLET

The first official ceremony for the Roaring is a grand affair. Monsters come from every country, every ocean, and every cave. Tents have been erected on the far side of campus, each befitting royalty. Though the games don't technically start until tomorrow, the Academy puts on an elaborate ceremony in the graveyard followed immediately by a ball in the cafeteria. Classes are momentarily put on hold until the Roaring ends a week from now.

As an official competitor, my dress has been custom made and paid for by the school. They want their little soldiers to look their best before they're sent to the slaughterhouse. But, unlike the movies and books, we do it willingly.

Of course, I can't fucking get the damn dress on. They expect me to wear a corset, of all things. A *corset*. I stare at the material for so long, I'm afraid I'll go cross-eyed. The black laces are loose currently, wafting in the breeze from my open window in a seemingly mocking display.

"Fuck you, corset," I hiss, offering it my middle finger.

The corset doesn't respond, obviously, but I swear the laces begin to billow faster as if in laughter.

And...

I'm officially losing my mind.

"Do you need help with that? Or do you just want to keep glaring at it as if it'll get legs and arms and spider monkey your boobs," a dry voice says from the doorway. I spin quickly, futilely attempting to cover up my scantily-covered body. I'm dressed in only a pair of lacy pink panties and a matching pink bra dotted with black bats.

Cynthia rolls her eyes at me before gesturing for me to spin around. At my confused expression, she rolls her eyes a second time. It's pretty weird looking, considering her eyes are half out of their sockets, as if she haphazardly shoved them in her eye sockets but didn't bother to secure them.

"I don't have all day," she snipes. Eyeing her as one would a cornered, feral animal, I give her my back and hold up the corset. I quickly slide off my bra and cover my boobs with one hand. I love Cynthia and all, I do, but that girl does not need to see my nips.

She makes quick work of the laces, and I suck in a heavy breath, as it feels as if my soul has left my body. How do people wear these things? After this dance is over, I'm going to walk around shirtless in order to let my boobs breathe.

Once the final lace has been tightened and tied, Cynthia steps away from me, her face bereft of expression. "Do you need help with the dress too?" She nods towards the monstrosity draped over my bed.

"If you have the time..." I trail off sheepishly, and she snorts.

"My only other plan for today was to eat a liver and maybe get high." She stalks forward to grab the dress for me to step into.

After she helps me into my dress, she stays to brush my

hair into an elegant half-up, half-down hairdo. With painstaking delicacy, she applies a light coat of makeup, accentuating my bright eyes and cupid bow lips.

"Do you have a dress to wear?" I question as she dusts a layer of blush over both my cheeks. As a vampire, I'm naturally pasty and fair-skinned, but being an introvert who likes to hide in her room and eat cake doesn't help matters. I distrust all of those people capable of having perfect tans.

"Yeah," she states simply, stepping away to survey her work. "In my room."

"Where have you…?" I trail off before steeling my resolve. "Where have you been staying?"

Am I mistaken, or does Cynthia look embarrassed?

"At first, I was staying with a friend. Loxley. You remember her?" I shrug, vaguely recalling a little ho who sat in front of me in some of my classes. "But now, I'm staying with Pete."

"No fucking way!" I lean forward eagerly, and she ducks her head, thick black waves spilling forward to cover her face in a curtain of ink. "When did this happen?"

"After our talk, I confronted him. He confessed that he's been in love with me for years now." Her voice takes on a wistful, dreamy quality. "We began to date soon after."

"Wow. I mean…wow. I'm so fucking happy for you, girl!" I lean forward to hug her before remembering I'm a fluffy pile of skirts and ruffles. "And you're already living together?"

She glances in both directions anxiously, almost as if she's expecting someone to be hiding beneath my bed. Actually, given what I know about Dimitri, I wouldn't be surprised.

"To be honest, he's my mate." She says the words conspiratorially, as if they're a dirty curse word. Her face is pale, ashen almost, beneath the LED lights of the mirror.

"And that's a bad thing, why?" I query, watching her face

carefully. There's a minuscule tick of her right eyebrow, and her black tongue extends to lick her lower lip.

"Because banshees don't have fated mates," she confesses. "There hasn't been a case recorded yet."

My heart stutters to a stop as I process the full ramifications behind her words. Cal's story from yesterday reverberates through my head, rattling my brain. Is he somehow behind this?

What the hell is going on?

"Are you excited for the Roaring?" I question, attempting to change the subject.

"Fuck, no. I'm not competing. But my family is coming to visit me. My little brother, Justin, will come as well. He's six months old and absolutely adorable!" Her tone takes on the dreamy quality all people seem to have when talking about babies. You know the type—saccharine sweet to the point of sickening. "You'll have to meet him."

"I'd love to," I whisper, but a strange knot enters my stomach. I don't know what exactly this emotion is, so I shove it beneath the proverbial rug before it can take root and grow. Instead, I focus once more on the fact that Cynthia has found her mate.

Cynthia curses abruptly, pulling her phone from her dress pocket. "Shit. I need to go. Pete's waiting for me. You look beautiful, by the way." Before she has even finished speaking, she's halfway out the door. I lift my hand in a timid wave, but I can't stop fixating on what she just confessed.

Cynthia—a banshee—has found her fated mate. I don't know the history of banshees, so I have no way of knowing if there's truly never been another case before, but I *do* know that I'm the first vampire to have found her fated mate...or mates.

The questions are beginning to pile up, forming a

mammoth wall of secrets and deceit. It's surrounding me, trapping me, with little to no hope of escape.

Shaking my head vigorously, I turn towards the mirror once more and study myself. I look...beautiful. It's not a word I use to describe myself often.

The corset emphasizes my hourglass figure—heavy breasts, tapered waist, and generous ass. It also makes my boobs look pretty damn good, if I do say so myself. The dress itself is pale pink interwoven with black lace. It cups my breasts before spilling outwards in three layers of pink skirts. At the hem, the pink swirls into shades of onyx that cascade across the floor with each movement I make. My blonde hair is artfully curled into perfect ringlets, with a small portion tucked away in a golden clip. Two flyaway strands frame my face. The makeup isn't heavy, but it heightens the golden flecks in my eyes and my already lush lips. The blush highlights my prominent cheekbones.

It took some urging, but I eventually used the balm Frankie created on my scars. The words are nothing but smeared pink lines, and even those are beginning to fade. Soon, they'll be nothing but a horrible memory, though the scars on my soul are still as prevalent as ever. Nothing can eradicate that hurt.

I spin once, enjoying the way the fabric glides across the floor, before smiling at my reflection.

It's amazing what a little confidence can do for a girl. Some people think we dress up and wear makeup to impress people, and maybe that's true for some, but not all. Sometimes, we want to look beautiful in order to *feel* beautiful. We have trouble seeing past our flaws and mistakes, our transgressions and sins. By dressing up, we're donning a mask—one we're capable of removing whenever we so feel the need. It's our battle armor and our sword. Our shield and our convoy. It's a way for us to see the beauty the rest of the world already sees.

"Knock knock!" a cheery voice exclaims. "Don't bother responding, because I'm coming in anyway."

Without preamble, Mason pushes open the door, the others at his heels.

I take a moment to survey them all as they do the same for me.

Mason is bedecked in a three-piece suit with a pink tie. He still wears his customary beanie, the exact same shade of gray as his suit.

Vin, behind him, is handsomely dressed as well in a black suit with a white undershirt and white cufflinks. The material conforms to his muscular body, revealing his shapely thighs and toned arms.

Surprisingly, Hux is in control today. His suit is almost identical to Vin's, though he has a pink bow tie completing the ensemble. His thick black hair has been combed back, his wicked scar proudly on display.

Frankie is the only one not wearing a suit. Instead, he has on tan dress pants with a light blue collared shirt tucked in. His normally disheveled curls have been tamed into some semblance of control.

Behind them all, Cal and Barret stand, looking dreadfully out of place and uneasy, as if they're unsure of where they fit in this new dynamic. Frankly, I'm unsure too.

Cal's pink hair is stylishly tousled, sweeping across his forehead and into his eyes. There are slits in his white suit jacket for his red wings to pop through, and if he were to extend those wings, they'd easily encompass the length of my room. Barret is smartly dressed in a black suit with a red undershirt, the exact shade of Cal's wings. With his green hair, he looks like a life-sized Christmas ornament, though I'd never admit that to him.

All of them take my breath away.

For as long as I have been staring at them, they have been staring at me. Their eyes are physical caresses across my suddenly overheated skin. A girl could die from that burn.

Seriously. Look it up. Type in "spontaneous combustion." Do it.

"Pinkie, you look—" Mason begins.

"Like a fucking vision," Frankie cuts in, devouring me from head to toe with his warm gaze. I once thought it was icy and detached, but that's not true anymore. Licks of flame dance on my skin from his stare.

"You look radiant," Hux breathes, stomping forward until he's able to touch my shoulders. "The most gorgeous gem in all the lands."

"So fucking cheesy. If I were to say that, she would laugh in my face," I hear Mason murmur from somewhere over Hux's shoulder, but my attention is consumed by the ruggedly handsome man before me. There's something feral about his beauty—something untamed—like a beast roaming the countryside.

"I will escort my precious treasure to the ceremony," Hux announces abruptly. His words are domineering, bossy in nature, and brooks no room for argument.

Still, the rest of the men begin to grumble as Hux extends his arm for me to take. With a small smile, I place my hand in the crook of his elbow and allow him to pull me out of my room.

"At least we have a nice view," I hear someone—probably Mason or even Vin—whisper to the others. I have no doubt that all eyes are trained intently on my skirt-clad ass.

As we walk through the thick forest interspersed with oaks and maples, I can't help but stare at the other monsters also bedecked in their best dresses and suits. I spot Birdy—the school's secretary—giggling with a group of men who look at least twenty years younger than her. I always suspected she was up to shady shit. She really ruffles my feathers sometimes.

Snort.

Walking up ahead, arms hanging stiffly by their sides, are two monsters with gills clamoring down both of their blue necks. Cheryl's parents. Or at the very least, a relative of my enemy.

Hundreds and hundreds of monsters are in attendance. More than I have ever seen in one setting before. Vampires and werewolves and ghosts and ghouls and a few that belong in the bottom of the ocean. A skeleton skips merrily across the lawn, an eerie sight to behold. And then...

"Holy fucking shit," I breathe as my eyes lock on the huge man lumbering forward.

Big Foot.

The Big Foot. I remember Cynthia's old roommate was his daughter, and she would tell me stories about the monster with feet the length of a twin-sized bed. He's naked, his coarse brown hair on display, and between his legs rests a...a cock.

The size of a twin-sized bed.

Hanging there.

Collecting dirt.

And his balls...

"Stop fucking staring at another's man cock," Hux hisses, hurling daggers at the oblivious man stepping forward to join a group of monsters.

"It's like a monument," I whisper. "A monument for cocks."

"Violet..." he warns. "Unless you want me to go over there and castrate him, I would stop talking."

Reluctantly, I wrench my gaze away from the humongous, almost ethereal, penis. Another thing I'm able to check off my bucket list.

Revel in a monster cock the size of a bed? Check.

"Precious Treasure." Hux clears his throat once, and when I turn to stare at him, he's very purposefully looking away, pink dusting his cheekbones. "I told you this before, and I'll tell you again—you look beautiful. You look like everything I have ever wanted. Like the sun and the moon and the stars. I could live in darkness for all of eternity if you're by my side."

"Hux," I begin, unable to articulate any of my thoughts. "I sort of want to kiss you right now."

Before I can even finish my sentence, he's lunging forward, lips puckered. I laugh and swat at his face half-heartedly, laughing harder at his look of bemusement.

"But I can't. I have makeup on."

"You don't need makeup," Hux insists adamantly. "You're beautiful without it. But you're also beautiful with it. Hell, you'd be beautiful if you were wearing a plastic bag and had a disco ball balancing on your head."

Yup. It's official. I'm putty. I swear I melt with each consecutive word he says.

I'm too busy making googly eyes at him—and him at me —that I don't hear Vin's warning until I collide into some-one's back. I would've fallen to my ass if Vin hadn't lunged forward and caught me.

"Who the fuck dares hurt my precious treasure?" Hux hisses—because he's extra like that. I don't bother to correct him and say *I* ran into *him*. Sometimes you just need to let Hux be.

The man spins around on his heel, nearly pulling the woman he's with off her feet. A third male hovers off to the side, watching the interaction with narrowed, hate-filled eyes.

I stare at the woman first, mainly because something

about her haunted, blood-shot eyes calls to me. Her blonde hair is smoothed into a flawless high ponytail, not a strand out of place. She wears a skintight black dress that one would see at a cocktail bar instead of a ball. Still, she's gorgeous, embodying a feminine beauty and grace. Her eyes are hazel, but laden with such pain and sadness that my heart skips a beat. And though she's smiling, it doesn't meet her pensive gaze.

The man beside her is a giant in comparison. His hair is black as pitch, gelled away from his aristocratic face. With a sharp nose, strong jawline, and high cheekbones, he appears almost too beautiful, too handsome. But the coldness in his eyes makes him appear hideous, at least to me.

Finally, my gaze rests on the third male. On his familiar black hair and obsidian eyes. On the tattoos interspersed across his tan skin. On the bulb in his eyebrow and the earrings in his ears. On the smirk pulling up those delectably wicked lips.

"I'm sorry," I stammer out at last as the man stares down at me. These must be Alex's parents. His facial structure is similar to his mother's, but the jet-black hair and fathomless dark eyes are inherited from his father.

"Don't fucking talk to us, you vampire scum," his father sneers at last. I can't help but notice that the woman blanches at the venom in his tone, shooting me a sympathetic glance before she quickly covers her reaction.

"Do not talk to her like that!" Barret snaps, moving to stand in front of me. As I watch, my friendly giant seems to grow in size until he's towering above us all, his muscles flexing in a rare show of power and dominance.

"Do you know what you cost us?" the man continues, peering around Barret's bulky form to glare at me with incandescent fury. "What you cost my wife?" He tugs on the woman's arm until she tumbles towards him, face twisting in pain. I watch the exchange with growing horror.

The fear and pain cloying her eyes…

Could that be from him?

"I don't even know you," I say simply. The man surprises us all by spitting at my feet, face scrunched in disgust.

"You should do the world a favor and kill yourself. You're not deserving of the air you breathe."

It takes both Mason and Cal to stop Hux from lunging forward and ripping the man's head clean off his neck. Not that I blame him. I'm also feeling quite murdery today, thank you very much.

All of my pain and anger from before comes rushing back with the strength of a hurricane. It whips at my hair and bites at my face. Pain like no other sparks in my heart like errant fireworks.

"What did I ever do to you?" I hiss, baring my fangs.

"Dad," Alex warns, flashing me a glare full of loathing. He looks as if he'd very much enjoy wrapping those tattooed hands of his around my neck and giving it a squeeze. "People are watching."

It's true. Our exchange has garnered a crowd of curious onlookers. No one will step in if this escalates to a fight, but the monster world knows not to mess with Dracula—and by extension, me—with witnesses around. My father's revenge is well-known across the globe. Hell, I'm pretty sure there are still heads spiked on the fence surrounding our summer home in Hawaii from the last monster group who pissed Dad off.

Alex stares at the assembled crowd, still far enough away not to hear our conversation, and releases a belittling laugh. The noise is reminiscent of starless skies and double-edged swords. Of daggers and full moons. There's something dark and sinister about it, something that makes my skin crawl like thousands of fire ants have been set free under my skin.

My heart thunders in my chest as Alex steps around his father and leans forward, under the guise of pushing back a strand of my curly blonde hair, and whispers in my ear, "I'd watch what you say, little vampire. Tonight, not even Dracula can protect you."

When he steps back, the cruel smile is still firmly in place.

"What the hell does that mean?" Mason hisses, still gripping one of Hux's arms. I can see Hux struggling to regain control of his beast, his monster.

"Don't threaten me," I add, lifting my head to meet his crow-black stare.

"Halloween is when we can embrace our inner monsters, but the Roaring? The Roaring is when the monsters actually get to play," Alex tuts, gripping his father's arm and pulling him away. "Let's go, Dad. The bitch isn't worth it." His cold laughter rings out as he drags his father down the path, away from me. His mother remains behind for only a moment, eyes surveying my face with the same intensity I had examined hers.

"Helena!" Alex's father screams, the noise clawing at my skin. She winces, face paling, before leaning in closer to me.

Immediately, Vin and Frankie step up to either side of me. Barret continues to expand until it's almost comical—if he wanted to, he could crush her beneath one foot.

"Take care of my boy," she whispers hoarsely, ignoring the men on either side of me.

"What?" I bite out in disbelief. She couldn't possibly be talking about Alex, could she?

"Please."

"Helena!" Alex's father snarls. I watch as Alex futilely attempts to drag his dad away, but the man stays firm, feet rooted to the ground.

"Please," Helena repeats. With one last beseeching glance at me, she spins on her heel and mechanically walks back towards her husband and son. Once she's in range, her husband grabs at her frail arm, tugging her to him, and I note a muscle in Alex's jaw twitch.

"What the bloody hell was that all about?" Cal hisses, his red feathers ruffling in the early winter air.

"The usual," Mason spits, finally releasing Hux. Cal, after a moment, releases his other arm and takes a tentative step away from the frightening monster. "Vampire haters."

"No, this seemed different," I say, watching the three of them disappear in the foggy graveyard. "Personal, almost. Alex even told me that it wasn't something Dracula did, but something *I* did."

"But what the hell did you do?" Vin asks, throwing his hands into the air. "You have a collection of stuffed unicorns, for fuck's sake."

"Hey." I spin on my heel and level an accusatory finger in his direction. "Those are magical horses with horns. *Not* unicorns."

"They're totally unicorns," Mason throws in.

"I have to agree with them on this one, Cheese Curd," adds Barret.

"Horses. With. Horns."

"Unicorns," all of the men parrot, sans Hux, who is still glaring at a tree trunk as if it has personally offended him. Shit. This isn't good.

Frankie notices Hux's predicament at the same time I do and nods subtly at me.

"I need to talk to you guys about something," he says coldly to the others, shoving his hand into his pants pockets.

When all of them furrow their brows, Frankie inconspicuously nods his head in Hux's direction, teetering the line between insanity and coherence.

"Huh?" Barret murmurs, but Cal grips his hand and tugs him a short distance away.

"Hux?" I whisper once all of the guys are situated in a circle away from us. "Sweetie?"

Yeah, I'm still trying out pet names for him.

Baby Daddy, Cum Buddy, and Chocolate Bar. Chocolate Bar is my personal favorite, but I'm still struggling for it to catch on.

Hux growls low in his throat as I push up onto my tiptoes and place my hands on both of his cheeks. They have a light layer of stubble on them that grazes my palms and fingers, generating goosebumps on my sensitive skin.

"He threatened you," he manages to hiss out at last, voice guttural and nearly unrecognizable.

"But he didn't do anything," I promise, continuing to hold his cheeks and willing his eyes to flick down to mine. "And he won't do anything. You want to know why? Because I have you to protect me."

"I didn't protect you before," Hux seethes, and I detect shame in his tone. Self-loathing.

"You couldn't have," I counter. "You didn't know I needed you."

"But—"

"No buts. What happened wasn't your fault." I hold up my arm, allowing him to see the faded pink words. Already, the letters are indistinguishable and impossible to read. "These scars are already fading thanks to Frankie, and soon, they'll heal completely. And I'm not just talking about the physical ones, but the mental ones too. Because of you, Hux. You and the others. You're healing me each and every day. I wouldn't be standing here if it wasn't for you. Sometimes I wish I was a normal girl with a normal life, but that'll never be me. And that'll never be you. I'm okay with that. I know that my life won't be easy, but you guys make me feel like I can do anything. Like I can *survive* anything."

"What type of mate am I if I can't protect you?" He runs his fingers through his long black hair, and my breath catches on the "mate" word. Instead of diving into all of my muddled feelings, I fasten my hands behind his neck and tug his lips down to mine.

"The best kind."

Aware of the eyes probing into my back, I lean in close, teasing his mouth with my lips. Hux groans low in his throat, slipping his tongue between my lips and cupping the back of my head. I don't even care that with each tug of my curls, he's destroying the immaculate hairdo Cynthia spent an hour on. I don't care that each brush of his lips against my own causes my lipstick to smear. All I care about is calming the storm raging just beneath the surface of my monster.

My fingernails dig into his shoulders as he tilts his head to the side, devouring my lips at a deeper angle until the embers in my belly transform into a flame.

"I can't let anything happen to you," he whispers against my mouth. "I—we—won't be able to survive it."

"I'm always going to be here, Hux, annoying the shit out of you. You can't get rid of me." Our breaths fan together as our lips meet once more. "You too, Jack." There's a pause for a moment, and then the kisses become even faster and more intense, his mouth slanting over mine. I don't have to look to know that Hux has transitioned into Jack.

"He's been like this since we saw those words carved into your skin," Jack admits. "You're the most important thing in the world to him."

His lips touch mine once more, biting sharply on my lip. The aggressive move surprises me—completely unlike both Jack and Hux. It's punishing, almost. Still, I open my mouth and kiss him back with a fervid intensity, promising him the world in our clash of lips.

Somebody clears his throat from behind us.

"Guys, we're going to be late," Mason says, voice heady with amusement and lust.

I don't know what I expect to see when I turn around, but it isn't the flames dancing in all of their eyes. It isn't the pure and unfiltered lust emanating back at me. Even Cal and Barret are staring at me as if they have never seen me before. When they catch me looking, Cal looks away with a frown, but Barret's smile grows. I half expected jealousy and anger—hurt, maybe—but that's not what I see at all.

Oh, the possibilities…

"Let's finish this ceremony," Hux says, straightening out his rumpled suit. I only know it's Hux because his accent becomes more pronounced. Once more, he extends his arm for me to take. "And then, we can pretend to be a normal girl and a normal guy at a ball together. What do you say, my precious treasure?"

I smile softly at him. "We'll never be normal, Hux. How can we be? We're a bunch of monsters."

CHAPTER 24

VIN

The commencement ceremony is a drag. Monster after monster steps up onto a stage and speaks a few words about how excited they are for the Roaring to begin. When Dimitri fucking Gray materializes, I notice every girl in attendance—and a few of the males as well—straighten in anticipation. Out of the corner of my eye, I spot Violet exchange a glance with Frankie. When she faces the front once more, there's a delicate flush to her cheeks that hadn't been there prior.

Great. Even my mate is obsessed with our headmaster.

My mate.

Those two words still cause a torrent of butterflies to be unleashed in my chest. It seems surreal—utterly impossible—that someone like me found the one person I'm fated to be with for the rest of my life. If I wasn't so positive that Violet was perfect for me, I would think it was a cruel twist of fate.

A Dracula and a Van Helsing.

It sounds crazy, even to me, and I'm the asshole living it.

When we're finally dismissed, Violet is swept away by her other...err...boyfriends? Mates? Fuck if I know or even care. All that matters is that they protect and care for her when I can't.

Say, now, for example. Before I can follow after her, a hand clamps down on my shoulder, halting me.

"Vin," my father says shortly, staring at me like I'm a bug he wishes to squish. I imagine it's the same expression he gives the monsters he hunts—like we're nothing. Stefan Van Helsing is a tall and imposing man, well over six feet tall. He would be handsome if his mouth wasn't twisted in a rictus grin and if anger wasn't written into every line of his wicked visage. Vanessa stands on the other side of my father, face pinched tightly. It's the only outward sign of her distress.

"Stefan," I reply just as cooly. We don't use titles, him and me. For as long as I can remember, he has always been Stefan to me. Now, my grandpa, on the other hand...

My heart pinches, as it always does, when I think of him. He was the only person—sans my twin—to have ever truly loved me. All of the other love bestowed upon me was conditional, with heaping layers of expectations I couldn't even begin to meet. Even my mother, with her cherubic face and honey blonde hair, saw me as an object to twist and distort for her schemes. Her angelic face belies a wicked streak a mile long. She and my dad are carved from the same cloth, after all.

I'm a pawn for them to use, nothing more.

Abruptly, Stefan grabs my arm and drags me towards the gray tomb erected in the center of the graveyard. I've never seen it up close before, despite having lived on campus for years now. The dilapidated, seventeenth century chamber curves steeply at the top, the gray stone transitioning to a wooden cross. The name carved above the door has been eradicated with age, the words barely readable.

Where will I go when I die? Will I be buried here, in a graveyard that we use for our enjoyment? Will I be one of the forgotten ghosts, name etched across the stone covered in ivy and grit? Before, I wouldn't have cared. My sole purpose in life is to kill monsters, to be the champion for humanity that's forced to work in the shadows. Maybe that's what makes *us* monsters. We're the silent killers, the assassins who hide in the darkness, never able to show our true selves in the light.

My morbid thoughts are interrupted by a fist connecting with my cheek. My head whips to the side as pain erupts from the point of contact. It feels as if my brain is rattling around in my skull.

"What the fuck?" I hiss, spitting out blood and swiveling to face my father once more.

"You're a disgrace. A disappointment." He spits at my shoes, the gesture reminding me eerily of when Alex's father spat on Violet's. "You've been hanging out with Dracula's daughter? Fucking her?" His face turns red with each sentence, hands fisting by his sides, as if he wants to punch me a second time.

Vanessa pales slightly, eyes widening imperceptibly, as she glances between me and my father. My mother merely crosses her arms over her chest and levels me with a blistering glare.

"Dad…" Vanessa begins. If anyone can talk sense into Stefan, it's her. She's always been his perfect angel.

"Shut the fuck up, Vanessa," Stefan hisses, and my temper flares.

"Don't talk to her like that!"

"Does she have a magical pussy, is that it?" Stefan goads, ignoring my outburst. "Is that vampire bitch good at sucking cock? Maybe I should test her out myself. Before I drive a stake through her heart." His eyes gleam with pure malice, lips pulling away from his teeth. A cold chill chases down my spine.

"She's nothing," I bite out, hating myself a tiny bit for the lie I have to spew. "Just an oblivious whore I like to fuck. Do you really think it would be anything more? That I would betray my family like that? After what her bastard father did to my grandpa…your father?" I stare into his icy brown eyes, rife with anger, and work to keep my own face impassive. "Violet Dracula is just a means to an end. Nothing more."

"We have big plans for her during the games," Stefan replies evenly, eyes cataloging every miniscule twitch on my face. "Big, *big* plans."

Fuck, what exactly does he mean by that?

I want to shake his shoulders and demand answers, but I know that will only make things worse. The only thing that might save Violet is being the perfect son, the perfect hunter, the perfect monster of all monsters.

"That better not be a threat, Stefan Van Helsing," a cold voice says as a lean figure materializes from around the corner. Dimitri's hands are tucked into his pockets as he adopts an insouciant, almost lackadaisical, posture. "My Academy has a zero-tolerance policy for hate crimes. If I discover you or any of your hunters have hurt a monster on this campus, I will not hesitate to invoke the punishment at the highest extent of the law."

Death.

He means death.

Stefan actually pales at his threat. Dimitri's name has been passed from hunter's to hunter's house. A nightmare and a lesson combined.

Don't fuck with bigger monsters than you're capable of taking on.

And Dimitri Gray? He's the biggest one.

Stefan smiles cordially at the expressionless headmaster. "Of course not. We wouldn't think to harm a hair on any student's head. I apologize for the miscommunication." He leans forward, under the guise of giving me a hug, and whispers scathingly in my ear, "Kill the bitch."

Every muscle in my body tightens at his words, but I force myself to remain calm. Hating myself a little more, I nod once, my chin hitting his shoulder.

"Consider it done," I respond stiffly.

Stefan slaps me on the back—much harder than necessary—before stepping away and allowing my mother, Felicia, to step forward. She kisses both of my cheeks, her sugary perfume curling around me and making me gag, before putting her lips to my ear.

"Don't let me down, son."

I'm left trembling as she glides away, my father trailing after her like a besotted puppy. Soon, only Dimitri and Vanessa remain with me.

Dimitri slides cool blue eyes over to my sister, assessing whether she's friend or foe, before turning to me.

"You know I'm not going to allow any harm to come to… the vampires," he says, voice colder than the breeze ruffling my dark hair. I have the distinct feeling he was about to say something else—a specific name—but caught himself at the last second. To be entirely honest, I don't care that the headmaster at my school is obsessed with my sort-of girlfriend. Yeah, I want to stab him and all that, but at least I can be assured that he'll protect her. It's always better to have someone as scary as Dimitri as a friend instead of an enemy. If he's your friend, he'll protect you with every fiber of his dark, soulless being. And if he's your enemy…

There's a reason the monster world fears Dimitri Gray.

"I'll take care of my family," I reply, infusing sincerity in my words, making my statement impossible to deny. Dimitri continues to stare at me oddly, almost judgmentally, before he nods once and stalks away without a backwards glance.

"They won't stop until she's dead," Vanessa points out, but her tone isn't malicious, only matter-of-fact. And I know she's right. Fuck, I know she's right, but what does she expect me to do? Kill my family? Hurt the people who raised me? The mere thought is inconceivable and sends a cold chill sweeping over my arms. I'm at a crossroads, and every direction has a train barreling my way. Try as I might, there's no escape. I'm forced to stand with my feet cemented to the ground and face whatever the universe deems I deserve. In this case, it's blood. Lots and lots of blood. I'm gagging on it, drowning in it, dying with it cascading down my lips.

"I'll figure something out," I reply stiffly, shouldering past her.

"How?" Vanessa screams at my back. "Fuck, Vin, how do you expect to save her? The Van Helsings have an army. Sure, you apparently have Dimitri Gray on your side, but is that enough?"

I freeze, one foot in front of the other, as her words ricochet around in my skull. The mere prospect of failing Violet is horrifying. There can't be a world without her in it, without her spunky attitude, penchant for hot pink and black, and intoxicating laugh.

I'll protect her with every bit of darkness within my body, every light. With the dichotomy that makes up any person.

Is that enough?

"It has to be," I whisper. I refuse to believe any other alternative.

THEY DECORATED THE CAFETERIA WITH STREAMERS AND balloons like it's some sort of child's birthday party instead of a ball for the world's most feared monsters. I would snort at the ridiculousness of it all, if I wasn't in such a dour mood.

Nursing a bottle of beer in the corner of the room, I watch Violet dance between Cal and Barret, her hands waving back and forth in the air. God, that girl is a horrible dancer, but she's just too fucking cute for me not to watch.

My father stands on the opposite side of the room, a glass of champagne in his hand as his eyes remain fixed on Violet with predatory intensity. He looks as if he's seconds away from lunging forward, wrapping his hands around her fragile neck, and ripping her head clean off. It's one of the very few things that can kill a vampire. I should know. I've killed more than I care to admit.

More than I want Violet to know.

If she discovers my atrocious past, will she still look at me with love and happiness? Will she still verbally spar with me, each snarky word heading straight to my cock?

"Why do you look so gloom and doom?" Mason queries, leaning against the wall beside me. He languidly smokes a cigarette with one hand while the other holds a bottle of fairy wine. Not just a glass, but the full bottle. I'm beginning to believe my best friend has a tiny drug and alcohol problem, though I don't have the guts to say anything to his face.

"She's a hot fucking mess." I nod towards Violet, who is currently doing the windmill in the middle of the dance floor. She looks like a princess who has been kept in a gilded cage for her entire life and has finally been allowed to join the real world. There's an innocence to her movements that are entirely unintentional.

How can my parents possibly think that she's capable of hurting anyone? Is it merely their own prejudice against vampires and monsters in general? Is there something I don't know?

Violet once captured a fly and set it free—but not before she named it Buttercup and decided to build it a fly home behind her dorm building. The damn bug died days ago, but us guys constantly switch it out with new ones. I'm pretty sure she thinks the fly is magic at this point.

"She's our hot mess," Mason counters easily, downing his bottle and tossing it to the side. He wobbles slightly on his feet, his words already slurring, as he drapes an arm over my shoulder. "I think I love her, Vin."

His innocuous words cause me to grind my teeth together and fist my hands. Unlike me, he's *allowed* to say that he loves her. He's allowed to say whatever the fuck he wants. I'm the only one leashed by my family's expectations of what is and is not acceptable. And falling in love with Dracula's daughter? That's firmly in the latter category. If I'm not killed for my transgressions, they'll strip me of my title and refuse to allow me to contact anyone in my family ever again, including Vanessa. I'll be nothing more than a bedtime story hunters tell their kids at night, a reminder of what not to do.

Don't fall in love with the enemy.

My anger continues to grow and grow in my stomach. It starts as a diminutive ember, barely flickering with life, before that ember turns into an intense fire that blazes red hot. I can feel it swirling, a tornado of flames, demanding to be set loose.

"How can you love her?" I ask bitterly, taking another sip of my drink. Unlike Mason, I'm not entirely wasted, but a light buzz is coursing through my veins. "I saw the book."

"The book?" Mason steps away from me—practically tripping over his two feet—and raises a single brow. "What the-the hell are you-you talking about?"

"The book about destroying a mate bond, you fucking prick," I seethe, towering over him. Mason isn't short by any means, but compared to me, he's nothing more than an insignificant, pesky bug. "To sever the bond…and kill Violet in the process."

Mason's eyes cloud over in confusion before understanding dawns. That is quickly replaced by anger and hurt. He takes a wobbly step towards me and points a finger at my chest.

"That was a-a gift from my-my mother," he slurs, his rancid breath wafting across my face. I shove at his shoulders to make him take a step back, and he falls on his ass. He continues speaking as if he doesn't notice his new position on the floor. "If you think for one second I would do anything to hurt Violet, then you don't know me at all."

"Guys, what's going on over here?" the vampire in question asks warily. Loose tendrils of golden hair stick to her cheeks as she volleys her wide-eyed stare between Mason and me.

"Nothing," I bite out at the same time Mason says, "Just Vin being a fucking prick."

Violet offers a hand to him, but he ignores it, hobbling to his feet and leveling me with a glare capable of curdling milk.

"Go fuck yourself," he hisses.

"Mase…" Violet pleads, but he's already storming away, surprisingly steady despite how unstable he was just a moment earlier. Turning towards me, Violet places her hands on her hips. "What the fuck was that about?"

"Nothing," I say dismissively. "Go back to the others."

I can see Frankie and Jack eyeing me cautiously. Still on the dance floor, Barret and Cal have stopped dancing and are staring at me just as intently. Testing me, perhaps? Testing my loyalty? Why am I suddenly overthinking this?

Cursing, I pound a fist against my head, and Violet's eyes immediately widen in alarm.

"Vin?" She takes a step towards me, but I automatically step back. She can't touch me, not here, not where my father can see her. The Van Helsings have eyes and ears everywhere. Nowhere is safe from their gossiping maws.

Without bothering to respond—and ignoring the crestfallen expression on her face—I turn on my heel and walk swiftly out of the cafeteria. It's only when I'm outside, eagerly taking in lungfuls of fresh air, do I break into a run.

Faster. Faster. Faster.

"Vin, dammit!" Violet screams. "Get back here! I'm not in the fucking mood to—" There's a loud thump followed by a muffled curse. And then, "I'm okay!"

I make it to my house in record speed, grabbing my key from my pocket and opening the front door. Before I can close it, Violet sticks her foot in the frame, expression positively livid. I can't help but snort at the dirt smeared on her cheeks and the twig in her hair. It looks as if she's partaken in a fierce battle with a fucking forest...and lost.

"You don't get to run from me," she huffs, shoving the door open even further with her vampire strength. "Not again. You fucking promised."

"I promise a lot of things," I murmur, finally stepping away and allowing her entry. I feel unnaturally tired. My eyelids droop as I unknot my tie and allow it to sit over my shoulders. "Just...just go away."

"No," she replies stubbornly. Of fucking course. Because things can't be easy with her, right?

We're gasoline and fire. Every time we clash, an explosion is left in our wake. This type of relationship can't be healthy, but it's the only type I've ever known. It's the only type I want.

If she's fire, I'll happily burn for just a moment in her presence.

"No?" I quirk a brow as I slide off my jacket, draping it over the back of my armchair.

"No," she repeats. Shouldering past me, she sits on the edge of the fading brown leather seat, her hands clasped primly together in her lap. "You're hurting, Vin. I'm not stupid. I know it has something to do with your parents. Did they find out about me and you? Did they threaten you?" Her eyes flash in the ambient silver glow of the moon from the open window. It's the only light currently on in the house, the only light I feel comfortable in.

There's a lot that can happen in the darkness. It's a place where you can strip bare, where no one can judge you or tell you that you're wrong. People crave the darkness because the light is too much for them to handle.

And me?

I only crave one thing, and she's currently sitting in front of me.

"Violet, not now," I sigh, undoing the buttons of my dress shirt.

"I said it before, and I'll say it again—no. We're not doing this today, Vin. Tomorrow, the Roaring is going to start, and we have no idea what will happen to either of us. We could die—"

"Nothing is going to fucking happen to you," I hiss, glaring at the poisonous package wrapped up in beauty and silk. Underneath that immaculate front is a bomb seconds from detonating.

"Tonight, we're not monsters. We're not a Dracula and a Van Helsing. We're just...us, okay?" She bites on her lower lip, and though she doesn't mean for that gesture to be coy, I can't help the heat that flares down below. "And for tonight only, you're going to give up control."

"What?" I bite out as she rises gracefully to her feet and steps forward. One hand rests on my bare chest while the other fingers the sleeves of my shirt.

"Trust me," she whispers breathily, staring into my eyes. I gulp heavily, my pulse skittering the longer I maintain eye contact. But, fuck, I can't look away. "Give me control. Let me take care of you."

"What will you have me do…mistress?"

CHAPTER 25

VIOLET

My panties instantly dampen at hearing that one word leave Vin's wickedly cruel mouth.

Licking my lower lip, I remove my hand from his chest and sit back down in the armchair. I feel like a queen on a throne—powerful and imperious, the world at my fingertips to do with as I please.

"Strip for me," I instruct, greedily lapping up every inch of bare skin already exposed. "Slowly."

Vin swallows once more, a muscle in his jaw working, but he does as I say. He needs this just as much—if not more—than I do.

Keeping his eyes on me, he slowly slides the dress shirt off his shoulders, the fabric pooling around his feet. His skin is heavily tanned, a product, I'm sure, of all the time he spends outside. Tattoos climb down the sides of his chest and cover both his arms. Fuck, he's a work of art.

And he's mine.

I feel selfish and possessive of this beautiful man with the haunted eyes. No one else is allowed to see him. No one else is allowed to set their gaze upon the artwork etched across his skin.

He brings his hands to his dress pants and slowly removes his belt. My eyes latch on where it lands on the ground, a thousand possibilities racing through my head. He hooks his thumbs into the waistband and pushes them down, making quick work of stepping out of them. If it was me, I would be on the ground in a tangle of clothing by now. But, Vin? He looks like sex personified as he flashes me a sultry smile.

The black boxer briefs he wears leave little for the imagination. I can see the outline of his cock—thick and proud—straining against the material. My mouth waters at the sight.

"Wait," I say, before he can push them down as well. "Come to your queen."

Yeah, I'm trying it.

Sue me.

Pleasure blossoms in my belly when Vin obediently steps forward, chest heaving. I flick my chin towards my feet, and he drops to his knees, once more granting me complete and utter control of his body and pleasure. I read an article once that said alpha men often like to give control to their partners during sex—for them to have a safe place where they don't always need to be in charge.

And I'll give him this. I'll grant him a safe space where he's free to do whatever the fuck he wants. To be whoever he wants.

Without speaking, I lift my foot and place it on his shoulder. I don't know what I'm doing—or if I'm even doing this right—but I can't ignore the painful ache in my stomach. I...I *like* being in control. I like seeing a man as proud as Vin on his knees for me. I don't know if I'll be this dominant and confident with any of my other men, but with him? I like holding the leash he has on his tenuous control.

He begins to pepper kisses up my ankle and to my calf, stopping at my knee, and then licking down the same trail his lips just made. He gives the same treatment to my other leg, leaving me a panting, moaning mess.

"Kiss me," I rasp, licking my unbearably dry lips.

"Yes, mistress." He straightens on his knees, his face level with my own, and tenderly, almost reverently, kisses my lips.

"Harder," I beg.

With a groan, he deepens the kiss, his tongue tangling with mine. Fire sparks in my veins as our lips clash and battle. He doesn't just kiss me—he *devours* me. He kisses me like I'm the air he needs to breathe, the food he needs to eat, the water he needs to drink. Each swipe of his tongue against my own tells a story.

I twist my head, and his lips immediately lower to my neck, sucking at the smooth skin there. Tangling my fingers in his short hair, I pull his head back marginally.

"What do you want?" I breathe.

"You," he answers instantly, eyes wild with need.

I release his hair and nod towards his boxers.

"Take them off."

Breathing labored, he stands and slides the boxers down his legs, his cock springing free, already dripping with pre-cum. I lean forward to take his hard length in my hand, tugging twice before releasing him. He groans as if he's in physical pain—pain that can only be alleviated by my touch. A twisted part of me likes having that type of power over him.

Moving to my feet, I turn to give him my back.

"Help me out of this, will you?"

"Yes, mistress." Quickly, he steps forward, hands trembling as he attempts to undo the laces. "How the fuck…?" he mutters beneath his breath as he tugs at them. It takes longer than we both would like, but soon, the dress is in a puddle of pink fluff around my feet. Dressed in only the corset and panties, I face him once more.

"Good boy," I praise, reaching between us to tug on his cock. I rub my fingers over his head before using his own pre-cum as lubrication for the rest of his length. There's something arousing about a man's cock, about the velvety softness over steel. "Get the rest of this off of me."

I once more give him my back as he attempts to remove my corset. If he thought my dress was hard…

After a minute of concentration, Vin stomps away, opens up a drawer in the kitchen, and returns with a knife. In one fatal swoop, he cuts the garment straight from my body. Immediately, my breasts spring free, my nipples already beaded nubs.

I turn towards him once more, and his eyes immediately lower to my aching tits. He's panting, as desperate for a taste of me as I am of him. Soon. We'll do that soon.

For now, the game has only just begun.

"Take my panties off," I command. When his hands immediately drop to the fabric, I click my tongue. "With your teeth."

Eyes radiating heat, Vin drops to his knees before me once more. A wicked smirk pulls up his lips as he captures the waistband of my panties with his teeth, grazing them across my sensitive skin. I moan softly as he lowers the silky material, each tug bringing his face closer to where I so desperately need him.

It's torture, agonizing torture, as I watch his hooded eyes bring the fabric all the way down to my feet. Only then do I step out of them. Vin remains on his knees before me, awaiting my instruction. If his labored breathing and erect cock are any indication, he likes this game just as much as I do.

"Service your queen," I demand, once more sitting back

down on the chair with my legs extended. I know that he has a perfect view of my pussy lips, glistening with the evidence of my arousal.

His lips twitch once at my comment, but he obediently leans forward and swipes his tongue through my wet folds. It's a teasing touch, one that sets off fireworks in my chest. I close my eyes in utter bliss as he brings that delicious tongue of his back to my pussy.

He takes his time, his tongue gliding up and down my slit as he drinks from me. He uses both of his hands to push my legs further apart, resting comfortably between them. I grab the back of Vin's head as he slides one finger into my slick channel.

"Fuck, Vin," I whimper as that finger is soon joined by a second one. His tongue returns to my clit as I buck my hips, demanding more.

"Yes, mistress?" His eyes, hooded with lust, meet my own, and I can't help but growl in frustration.

"More… I need more."

Without preamble, Vin's mouth descends on me with ravenous hunger. Each graze of his teeth and swipe of his tongue sends me closer to that edge. I can hardly breathe, chasing an orgasm that is a hair's breadth away. I need to move; I need to do something. The orgasm builds and builds, until it shoots through me, so fucking intense that I'm blinded by it. Convulsions rack my body as I begin to come back down from my high. My throat is raw from screaming Vin's name.

Through it all, he continues to suck me, lapping up my juices. When he finally lifts his head, his lips are glistening and his smile is smug.

He's not going to be so smug when I'm through with him.

I crook a finger in a come-hither gesture, and he immediately stands. My own legs wobbly, I force myself to my feet and drop down onto my knees before him. His eyes widen slightly as I grip his length.

"Baby girl—" His words cut off in a moan as my tongue darts out to lick the underside of his crown. Keeping my eyes on his blissful face, I draw his swollen head entirely in my mouth, my other hand remaining at the base. His moans amplify my own lust, and I can feel myself getting wet again.

My head bobs as I swallow him, my tongue gliding along the underside of his cock. When he attempts to grab my head and thrust into me, I pull away with a disapproving glare.

"My cock," I warn, tightening my grip on his throbbing length. I wait for him to acknowledge me, to respond, and when he nods once, I lower my lips back to his cock. Instead of taking him in my mouth, I lick up and down the sides like a damn lollipop, reveling in each intake of his breath and hiss through his gritted teeth. I remove my hand from the base to cup his balls, pulling and twisting them.

"Fuck!" Vin curses, body shifting slightly. I grip the head of his cock once more and pull him back into my mouth, bobbing my head as he releases moan after moan. I can feel his cock swell, his release imminent, but I pull away before he can come.

"Fuck me," I breathe, climbing to my feet and kissing his swollen lips. I know he can taste himself on me, and that thought only increases my desire. I'm so wet for him, so ready. "Make love to me."

In the next moment, my back is on the floor with Vin hovering over me. His eyes travel to my heavy breasts and then to where his cock is touching my stomach. He reaches over my head, towards the desk in the living room, and removes a box of condoms. It topples to the floor, nearly hitting my head, as he uses his teeth to open up a wrapper. I watch in fascination as he slides it over his length, his eyes never leaving mine.

"Vin…" I breathe, scraping my fingernails across his back and shoulders. His name on my lips is his undoing.

He slides into me in one long thrust, giving me only a second to adjust, before he begins to move. My eyelids are heavy as I stare into his piercing brown eyes, so dark they're almost black. I feel so incredibly full, the walls of my pussy contracting around his girth.

"You feel so tight, baby girl. So tight. So good."

"Faster," I beg, digging my hands into his sculpted ass. I slap down—hard—and his cock twitches inside of me. Immediately, his hips begin to move, his cock driving in and out of me. He brings his hands to my breasts, kneading the sensitive flesh, as tears blur my vision. It feels good, so fucking good. Things that feel this good shouldn't be real. Is he only a dream? Will he disappear when I wake up in the morning? If my life as a hated vampire taught me one thing, it's that good things never last.

He lowers his lips to my breasts and takes one nipple into his mouth. I begin to cry, desperate for the orgasm only he can bring me. His tongue swipes across the sensitive nub before he brings his mouth to my other, neglected nipple. He immediately bites down, obtaining another moan from me.

"You're so beautiful." He trails his lips up my neck and back to my mouth, pulling me into a heated kiss capable of catching this entire house on fire. "So beautiful."

His thrusts intensify, bringing pleading whimpers from my lips as my fingers continue to dig into his ass. I lower one finger to his asshole and breach the tight ring of muscles.

"Fuck!" he hisses, teeth gritted.

"Yes, just like that." Heat coils between my legs, and I'm pretty sure I'm seeing stars. "I'm so close. So fucking close."

I add a second finger into his asshole, and he immediately picks up speed, each thrust of his hips sending me that much closer towards the impending explosion. The last few flexes of his body send me spiraling over that steep, beautiful edge. My pussy clamps down on his cock as it swells inside of me. He roars out his own release as his teeth bite down on my shoulder.

This time, I'm positive I'm seeing stars as I momentarily lose my capability to speak, hear, or even think.

My body is heavy with fatigue as I finally come down from my high. I'm shaking and crying, repeatedly kissing Vin's sweat-soaked skin.

"Fucking hell," he murmurs, pushing himself onto his elbows and then rolling off of me. Quickly, he removes the condom and tosses it in the garbage. He then grabs at my shoulders until I'm draped over his chest, his arm around me in an iron vise.

"Isn't it nice to let someone else take control for a while?" I whisper, kissing the skin just above his nipple.

He smiles down at me. It's not his usual angry sneer or even his condescending smirk. It's a genuine, honest-to-god smile, one alive with happiness and post-orgasmic bliss.

"Violet?" He kisses the shell of my ear. "I think I'm falling in love with you."

My throat closes as emotions wash over me. They're both intense and refreshing, like a wave of ocean water on a blistering hot day.

"I think I'm falling in love with you too," I whisper. I think I'm falling in love with *all* of these men. It's terrifying and beautiful—a scythe glinting in the moonlight.

I can feel his cock hardening beneath me, spurring on my own arousal.

"Can I give up control some more?" he pants into my ear, his hips already jerking. I reach down to grab his hard length, giving it a stroke. Reaching behind us, I grab a new condom and slide it over his impressive girth.

"Always," I vow, straddling his waist and lining his cock

up with my entrance. I place my hands on his chest and stare into his dark eyes. "In here, with me, I'm in charge. I'm the queen. Do you understand that?" When he doesn't immediately answer, I pinch his nipples.

"Yes, mistress," he breathes.

"Then let's forget the world for another few hours, shall we?"

CHAPTER 26

The sky is a dreary shade of grey, stagnant storm clouds hanging sluggishly over our heads. Fitting, I suppose, for the first round of the Roaring. After all, it isn't just a competition. It's an execution.

I wrap my arms around my waist as I stand alongside the other couple hundred competitors. Normally, I'd be amazed at all of the monsters in one location. Everyone from the original Wolfman to the Mummy from the Egyptian tombs to Cheryl's dad, the Loch Ness Monster. They're all chomping at the chance to taste blood.

Hopefully not my blood. Call me a hypocrite, but I rather like my blood in my body, thank you very much. Ain't nothing sexier than a vampire full of blood.

Pro tip—don't ruin the sexy.

The Academy has decreed we all wear the approved skin-tight red shirts and black shorts. Conformity at its finest. At least the guys look hot in their too-short shorts. I'm pretty sure I can even see some dick if I look hard enough—cough, when I get on my hands and knees and stare up their shorts, cough. Honestly, at this point, I only feel comfortable peeping on Vin. After what we did last night…

My cheeks warm as I chance a glance at my hunter, standing farther down the line beside his father, mother, and sister. He warned me he'll have to play a part until they leave campus, and I can't begrudge him for wanting to protect me. I would do the same thing if Dracula was here.

Which he isn't.

This is the first Roaring in over two hundred years that he chose not to attend. Is he really that afraid to talk to me? The familiar tendrils of hurt unfurl in my chest like a splotch of ink being dropped in water. I honestly can't say why it hurts so much, only that it does. A lot.

Because every little monster wants to be hugged by her daddy and told that everything's okay. That we're both the scariest monsters in the universe and that we're not.

"You okay?" Frankie whispers from the left side of me. Jack is on the right, with Mason directly beside him. I don't see Cal and Barret, only because they were escorted straight from detention to the Roaring and could be anywhere in the line.

"Peachy," I reply, already fixing my gaze on Dimitri stepping up to the raised podium.

"Welcome." There's no microphone, but his voice is easily able to carry. Silence descends as every monster in the vicinity, including the ones in the observation stands, gives him their undivided attention. "As headmaster of Prodigium Academy, it is my sacred duty to run the yearly games," he begins, sweeping his icy blue gaze across the assembled monsters. His eyes stop on me and stay there. "For the first round, each of you will enter the portal."

As he speaks, a vertical pool of light appears in the center of the clearing. It seems to swirl like thousands of stars are residing in its depths. I'm momentarily thunderstruck as I stare at the portal, my tongue turning to cotton.

"Inside, you will find yourself in an arena created by our very own game makers." He nods towards the two men who recruited me. Yet, despite the icicles in their hair and on their faces, they appear warm in comparison to Dimitri Gray. "The rules are simple. You must survive for twenty-four hours. There are traps and creatures beyond your comprehension, all of which have been created by our very own Dr. Frankenstein."

Frankie tenses beside me, face going pale, as we turn to stare at the waving man standing a little bit apart from the crowd. He has pale red hair brushed away from a gaunt, sickly-looking face. His dark eyes gleam with violence and excitement, a combination that makes chills erupt on the back of my neck.

"And as always," Dimitri swivels his gaze back to me, eyes both reproachful and cautionary, "murder is allowed. This is a competition. Only the best of the best monsters are allowed to win. If you can't survive against your fellow competitors, then you don't deserve to be here at all."

Oh, fuck me.

In the monster world, the punishment for killing a fellow monster is immediate death. But in the games? It's a free-for-all.

And you can bet your sweet ass every monster will go after Dracula's daughter.

As you see, I'm fucked, but not in a good way. More in a "stick your cock in my anus without any lube" sort of way.

"Once you're in the arena, there will be a ten second countdown. When the timer gets to zero, all gloves are off. The goal is to not only survive, but to find your way out of the arena before the twenty-four hours are up. If you fail to do so, you will explode with the arena."

Well, fuck me sideways. There are a lot of words in that speech I didn't like. "Death," for one. And "explode."

"We'll stay together," Jack whispers, leaning towards me. "We'll enter the portal as a group. If we stay together, we'll be able to get out of this mess alive."

Logically, I know he's right, but I have the distinct feeling it won't be that easy.

"You may now enter the portal," Dimitri declares, keeping his eyes fixed on me. I can see he's trying to tell me something, but what that something is remains a mystery. Can't he send out smoke signals or something? Maybe do some elaborate charades? I'm not the best at reading people by staring into their eyes.

When it becomes apparent I have no idea what the fuck he's trying to say to me, Dimitri throws his hands in the air.

Awww. Is the scary little assassin scared for me? A girly part of me wants to scrapbook this moment.

"You see here, kids. This was the day your grandpa Dimitri realized he actually liked little ole me. I totally had him wrapped around my pussy lips."

Okay, maybe I would take out the last line. Don't want to traumatize my non-existent grandkids.

The monsters are surprisingly patient as, one by one, they step through the portal, blinking out of existence. Despite having over two hundred monsters competing, it takes less than five minutes for most of the monsters to step through. I lose sight of Vin very quickly, and I still can't see Barret and Cal, but Mason, Frankie, and Jack remain with me as we venture to the starlit-spun opening.

"I would recommend grabbing supplies at the hospital first," Dimitri says dryly just before I step through. At my pause, he levels me with the full force of his penetrating ice-blue gaze. "You're going to need it."

Before I can comment that I'm super awesome and not at all prone to almost dying, a monster shoves me from behind —much to my guys' fury—and I tumble headfirst through the portal.

Have you ever attempted to do a front flip in a swimming pool before? Traveling through a portal reminds me of that sensation. I'm forced to hold my breath as my body twists and turns for what feels like an eternity, but is probably closer to a few seconds.

In the next moment, I am spit out onto the cement, my hands hitting the concrete first.

"Fuck!" I hiss as pain blossoms on my palms where rocks have dug into the sensitive flesh. Fortunately, it takes only a second for my vampire healing to kick in, dispelling the rocks until my hands are as smooth as...butts? Well, Vin's butt. As I spanked it—

Focus!

"Mase? Jack? Frankie?" I spin in a circle, orienting myself as I peer at the arena for the first time.

I half expected the yeti twins to *Hunger Games* this bitch and make it a forest. Instead, I find myself staring at a fleet of skyscrapers. I count at least thirty spread as far as the eye can see. Interspersed with them are small shops and houses. Parks and restaurants.

A city of some sort, though I'm pretty sure no cities I know of are completely abandoned.

There's not a person—or monster—to be seen. The morning sun illuminates the stretch of road I'm standing on. To the right of me is an abandoned grocery store, a few empty cars parked in the lot. Across from me is a second street leading to a downtown area. The traffic lights hanging overhead are currently switched off, the muted hues of green, orange, and red staring back at me.

It's…creepy, to say the least. And that's coming from a girl who drinks blood to survive. Have they decimated an entire fucking city for the games? Honestly, it wouldn't surprise me. Pompei? That was us. Roanoke? Also us. Atlantis? Pretty sure Cheryl's dad was behind that one.

The second thing I note is that I'm completely alone. No Mason. No Jack. No Frankie.

"Fucking hell," I curse again, kicking at a lone shopping cart rolling past. Of course, I misjudge how fast it's sliding and miss it, the forward momentum sending me to the ground in a heap of limbs. "Okay, I deserve that, universe. Now, can you stop deep dicking me and help me survive? Please?"

I peer up into the sky, half expecting the universe to give me a sign that it's listening. Hell, I'd even take a bird shitting on my face.

"Fuck," I repeat when the sky remains birdless. "Fuck! Fuck! Fuck!"

A loud siren echoes overhead, followed by Dimitri's voice. It seems to be coming from all directions—like even the clouds have speakers in them.

"The games will begin in ten. Nine. Eight. Seven. Six."

I glance warily in both directions, ensuring the streets are still empty. We weren't permitted to bring any weapons with us, so that's the first thing I'll need to grab. And then I'll need to find my men.

Fuck, they're probably freaking out right now, especially Hux. I think he's a teeny tiny bit protective of me. Just a little bit.

"Five. Four. Three."

And then, I'll need to find my way out of this arena. Is the exit at the opposite end of the city? Is it in one of the skyscrapers?

I can do this.

I can do this

"Two. One."

Another siren blares, disrupting the previous calm I felt.

"And the first competition of the Roaring has officially commenced!"

CHAPTER 27

VIOLET

I have a rule book I follow when being a badass.

Rule number one: Fake it till you make it. Don't trip or break it. Liberate it.

Rule number two: Everything sounds better as a rap. So go back to rule number one, and rap the shit out of it.

Feel more badass yet?

With a quick glance in both directions, ensuring I'm still alone, I walk towards the parking lot and desolate grocery store. It looks as if the place has been ransacked, graffiti painting the sun-bleached walls and the windows shattered. The few cars littering the parking lot are empty, the doors flung open as if the occupants had been attempting to escape something. Or someone.

Probably the monsters currently roaming these streets.

After confirming the shelves inside the store are empty, I check each glove compartment inside the cars. The first vehicle only carries a handful of napkins and years old bubblegum. The second has a faded photo displaying a smiling couple and a wad of crumpled bills. It's the third car that piques my interest. Nestled between a box of condoms and a fast-food wrapper is a tiny handgun. I'm not skilled enough to tell you the make, brand, or model, but it fits snugly in my hand.

Using what little knowledge I possess, I check to make sure the safety is on before counting the bullets. Seven.

That's good, right?

I check five more fucking times to make sure the safety is on before shoving it in the waistband of my shorts. The last thing I need to do is blow off my vagina. I rather like it, thank you very much.

Now where to?

My feet rooted to the ground, I spin in a circle, surveying my surroundings with a new lens. Buildings extend as far as the eye can see, each one taller and more imposing than the last. Fortunately, I don't see any other monsters.

Unfortunately, I don't see the damn exit.

And as much as I don't want to shoot my vagjay off, I *really* don't want to blow up.

"Eeeny. Meeny. Miney. Mo." I point towards a location at random and squint my eyes against the blinding sun before shrugging and skipping down the path.

Down here, the buildings appear even more dilapidated than before. There's a skyscraper balancing precariously on one side, devoid of any windows. Next to it is what appears to be a once-cozy coffee shop that is now littered with trash and spray paint. The farther I walk, the more my unease ratchets up, strangling my airways.

I can't help but feel as if there are eyes burning into my scalp. That feeling grows with every step I take until I'm physically nauseous. Slowly, as to not alert the monster that I'm on to him, I remove my gun from my waistband and hold it at the ready. There are very few creatures that this weapon will kill, but I don't need to murder the monster in order to win. I just need to get away and survive.

Heart hammering, I peer over my shoulder where I could've sworn I felt the eyes caressing me. But when I look, the street is empty, not even a bird to be seen overhead.

"Fucking hell," I murmur, quickening my pace. I'm becoming paranoid, which will only lead me to make sloppy decisions. All I can do now is put one foot in front of the other and hope I'll make it out of this mess alive.

Something grabs my hair, wrenching my head back, and I let out a startled scream. Wrenching my curls out of the monster's grip, I spin around, gun raised.

No one's behind me.

"What the…?" Before I can articulate my question, I feel a body tackle me from the side, propelling me off my feet. I release an "oomph" as I collapse on the asphalt, grit and pebbles embedding themselves into my skin. Still, when I look, there's no one there.

A fist connects with my cheek, and I finally understand who my attacker is.

The Invisible Man. Or his daughter.

Actually…

A second pair of hands grab my shoulders, holding me steady as the first person continues to rain down his or her assault.

Both of them are here.

Daddy and daughter duo. Killing vamps and taking names. I would actually be kind of jealous of their bonding time if, you know, it didn't include punching my face in.

I buck my hips up while simultaneously jerking my head forward at the person overtop of me. The decidedly feminine scream clues me in that the Invisible Girl is the one destroying my perfect face. Her daddy must be holding me down.

"You bitch," she spits, drops of salvia hitting my face. Focusing on my senses, I wait until I hear the rush of air indicating she's attempting to throw another punch. Before her fist can connect, I grab her hand and twist it, smirking in satisfaction at the audible crack of bones.

Before her dad can retaliate, I jump to my feet and kick out where I suspect him to be. When my foot connects with nothing but air, I duck to the side just in time to avoid his lunge at me.

Okay, you can't see him, Violet, but you have other senses. What do you hear?

Footsteps pounding on the road shake me out of my own head, and, trusting my judgement, I lift my gun and fire two rapid shots into the incoming monster's heart. Behind me, the Invisible Girl releases an agonized shriek of pain and fury as her dad's form begins to flicker, becoming visible once more. His eyes are wide in shock as he stares at the bullet holes in his nether region, blood rapidly gushing from the opened wound.

"Sorry," I mouth, wincing. I never said I had good aim, did I?

Fuck, I'm a penis murderer. The guys will never forgive me for destroying this man's cock. RIP, Little Invisible Man. It was nice knowing you.

Invisible Girl—I really should learn her name—shoulders past me and crouches beside her bleeding father.

"You bitch!" she screams through gritted teeth, hurling daggers at me with her eyes.

Badass rule number three: Run when you accidentally shoot off someone's dick.

Saluting her with my still smoking gun, I race away from her, the wind whipping my golden locks back.

I'm so preoccupied with getting away from the perceived threat that I don't notice the next monster until I'm plowing him over. We land in a tangle of limbs on the cement, my gun slipping from my hand and sliding down the sidewalk.

"Violet?" Cal asks groggily, alerting me to the body I'm still very much pressed up against. Cheeks flushing, I jump to my feet and extend a hand towards the rumpled cupid. He rubs at his head where it bounced against the cement, eyebrows creasing in confusion. "Why the hell did you just tackle me?"

"Long story short," I begin, nibbling on my lower lip as I help him to his feet, "I shot off a cock and now I'm running from Invisible Girl and Daddy."

"Daddy?" he asks in disbelief, eyebrows raising.

"Not my daddy," I say, dismissing his concerns with a wave of my hand. "Her daddy."

"The invisible girl has a daddy?" This time, his eyebrows are practically in his hairline.

"Everyone has a daddy," I counter immediately. "I have a daddy. Barret has a daddy—"

"Did he tell you?" Cal asks abruptly, pink tinging his cheeks. "Because we only did that once."

Okayyyy…

I'm pretty sure we're not talking about the same thing here.

"M-Moving on…" I stammer, raking a hand through my disheveled curls. "Are you alone?"

"I was." He flashes me a devilish grin and bumps his hip against my own. "But now I have a pretty little vampire to keep me company. Fuck, Vi, I'm so happy to see you. I was about to die of loneliness." He throws his arms around me, and I don't hesitate to hug him back. The chiseled planes of his body mold against my soft curves, and I can't help the sliver of desire that courses through me. I shut that shit down before it can completely manifest, though, mentally reprimanding myself.

"I was about to die because I destroyed a cock," I murmur into his neck, my hand smoothing down his feathered wings. I've always wanted to touch these little bastards—to see for myself if they're as soft as they appear. They're not; they're even *softer*.

"Yup. No more of that," Cal exclaims abruptly, pushing himself away from me and placing his hands on my shoulders to keep a respectful distance between us. "We're not at the petting stage of our friendship yet."

"There's a stage for that?" I question, once again ignoring the flutters in my stomach.

"Stage one, we shake hands. Stage two, we hug. Stage three, we heavy pet. Stage four, we fuck," he ticks off, smirking at my expression.

"I'm not heavy petting your ugly ass," I blurt immediately. Flames engulf both of my cheeks, and I quickly change the subject. "Let's go."

Smooth, Violet. Real smooth.

Cal takes my abrupt topic change in stride, walking beside me in amicable silence as I grab the gun and shove it back in my waistband. "Where are we going?" he asks at last after five minutes of aimless walking.

"Didn't really have a destination in mind," I grunt out. "But you're more than welcome to lead if you know a way out of here."

Cal gives me a look out of the corner of his eye before focusing once more on the long stretch of road. "Nah. I'm good with aimless walking."

"We can sing some merry tunes," I tease, nudging his shoulder with my own.

"Merry walking tunes?"

"The only—" Abruptly, I'm pushed around a corner, Cal's lanky but muscular body towering over mine in a protective shield. Eyes intent on my face, he presses one finger to his lips, indicating for me to remain silent. I pantomime zipping my mouth shut as growls reach me from the distance.

Mouth compressed in a grim line, I nudge Cal to the side and peer around the corner of the building.

The seven-foot-long creature crawls across the road, serrated, blood-stained teeth visible as he smiles. The beast has long claws, clearly intended for a quick and ruthless death. One swipe from them will incapacitate any monster in seconds. His form is pitch black, but instead of smooth skin, he has rough scales lining the length of his lean body. As I watch, horrified, he smiles menacingly and slowly licks the blood from his lips with a snake-like tongue. Moss covers the entirety of his body, and when he ventures closer, I notice he leaves a wet trail in its wake, almost like a disgusting snail.

The Bog Monster.

I try to recall the lore on such a creature. It's blind, isn't it? Or maybe deaf? Fuck!

Cal's grip tightens surreptitiously on my shoulder, a warning to remain hidden until the monster passes.

Neck creaking, the monster slowly turns to stare in our general direction. Now, I'm more sure than ever that he's blind. His black eyes, glinting with feral madness, sweep over us without ever sticking. And then, he throws his head back and releases a guttural roar.

The noise courses through me, rendering me momentarily speechless. The allure this monster has is incredibly strong. I ignore the tug in my gut, the craving to surrender, as his scream continues to tighten around me. Only certain creatures have that capability. Vampires, for one. Incubi and sirens. Even some fairies.

Who would've thought the hideous Bog Monster had a power that made you want to rip your panties off? I officially want to vomit.

Cal presses me against his chest, hands almost bruising, as he too fights off the creature's allure.

Finally, the Bog Monster lowers his head and continues his slow, almost lackadaisical, crawl.

Until an unfamiliar female steps out from around the corner opposite us.

Cursing, Cal begins to pull us farther away from the oblivious female—a wraith, maybe—and the Bog Monster who has now honed in on his prey.

The girl's bellow of pain trumpets through the air as Cal breaks into a run, fingers interlocked with my own. We run until we reach the door of a rustic mom and pop diner.

"Fucking hell," Cal breathes, raking his fingers through his pink hair. "That monster had a stronger allure than even me...and I'm fucking Cupid!" I can tell by his face that he's genuinely depressed by this. My poor, over-dramatic man-baby.

"I'm sure riding your cock would be better than riding his," I say soothingly, patting his shoulder. Those vibrant eyes of his blaze brightly as they focus on me.

"You imagined riding my cock?" he asks, voice almost husky. I can feel something shifting between us, something I can't put into words, but like before, I bury it before it can fester.

"Of course not...buddy," I state, punching Cal's shoulder in a totally platonic and friendly move. Because we're friends. Best friends. Only friends. Friends forever. Just friends.

He winces, pulling a face, as he rubs at the spot. "Don't break the pretty."

I pretend to squint my eyes in concentration. "I don't see it."

"See what?"

"The pretty," I deadpan. Cal snorts and tugs at a strand of my hair.

"Bitch," he jests.

"Asshole."

"*Gorgeous* asshole," he corrects, gifting me his back and pointing to his ass. A rather nice ass...

Rolling my eyes at his antics, I survey the building we have found ourselves in. The red vinyl booths and the jukebox in the corner give the restaurant a retro feel. Food in various stages of decay are left on the tables and counter, maggots wiggling and thrashing in more than a few dishes. A fine layer of dust coats every available surface, somehow making this place feel even more ominous and eerie.

"Do you think this is an actual city?" I question, running a finger over the name on the menu. Coffey House. Cute.

"What do you mean?" Cal queries, peeking through the broken blinds at the street.

"This city. Do you think they actually—?"

Murdered everyone who lived here.

The words sit on my tongue, but I don't speak them. I *can't* speak them. It's just too horrible for me to even comprehend—the loss of human life for some sick game.

"No," Cal states firmly, turning to face me completely. "This is an arena, Vi. Nothing more."

I exhale heavily in relief. Most of the monsters consider humans to be a lesser breed, but I happen to like them. Sure, they're stinky and noisy and constantly in need of attention, but they're house and potty trained.

"We need to figure out a way out of here," Cal muses, focusing back on the window. He trails his finger down the dirt-smeared plane almost absent-mindedly. "The other guys are smart. They've probably already found their way out of this hellhole."

"You worried about Barret?" I question, joining him at the

window. He sighs heavily and presses his forehead against the plastic blinds. Cal once told me that while he wasn't in love with Barret—despite their sexual relationship—they were still best friends.

"Of course I am," he answers glumly. "And I'm worried about Tall and Stabby, Beanie, Two-face, and Heartless."

I have a feeling that Tall and Stabby could only mean Vin. Beanie is no doubt Mason, and Two-face is Hux and Jack. Heartless? That's Frankie, though I'll be the first to refute that claim.

"And..." He twists his head so he's facing me. "And I was worried about you. A lot."

My heart thunders to my throat as I manage a wobbly smile. "I'm a badass vampire. You don't need to worry."

"I'll always worry," he declares, eyes ensnaring my own. Both of us—as if following some unspoken consensus—turn away from each other abruptly, clearing our throats.

"We still need to figure out where to go," I say, pushing away from the window and pacing the grime-coated floors. "I think...wait!" I hold a single finger to the air at my unexpected epiphany. "Dimitri mentioned something before I entered the portal. He said...he said I should visit the hospital."

"For, like, a prostate exam...?" Cal asks with a sly grin, winking.

And now, I'm thinking about Cal with his finger up my ass. Thank you, Cupid.

"What if that's our way out of here? Through the hospital?" I'm practically bouncing on the balls of my feet. What if Dimitri wasn't threatening me, but helping me?

"I don't know, Vi," Cal says warily. "A lot of the monsters I've seen are heading in the opposite direction." He gestures towards where we'd been walking before Bog Man's appearance, farther into town. "The only hospital I saw is back the way we came from. Are you sure Dimitri wasn't just fucking with you?"

That's a very real possibility. A *very* real possibility. But just lather my asshole up with lube, bend me over a table, and anal fuck me, because despite Dimitri's glaringly obvious flaws, I trust him. Which is probably—definitely—stupid.

"I mean, I don't—" I break off abruptly as I spot a figure through the window rapidly approaching the diner. "Wait? Is that Jack? Or Hux?" I question, pressing my face to the glass. I can't tell for certain which brother he is. His black hair is messily brushed into a man bun at the top of his head, a few dark strands escaping. The hairstyle doesn't look like something Jack or Hux would wear.

"Wait, I think it is," Cal says, sounding just as eager as I am. All of a sudden, his face pales and he grabs at my arm. "He has a fucking bomb, Vi."

"He wouldn't ever hurt me," I protest immediately, comforted by that fact. They would sooner cut off their own fingers than harm a hair on my head.

"Oh, shit!" Cal curses, pulling me away from the window and racing towards the back door.

I only have a second to see Hux/Jack lift his arm and throw the grenade before I'm pushed into the alley behind the restaurant.

And then, the building explodes.

CHAPTER 28

MASON

I fucking hate clowns.

Ugly bastards, the whole lot of them. White faces. Unruly red hair. Too much makeup.

Stabby the Clown? Fucking terrifying, and that's coming from me.

I'm pretty sure any monster with the name "Stabby" isn't all sunshine and rainbows.

White powder covers his pudgy face, already smearing in some places from excess sweat. Blood has been liberally applied to his cheeks and forehead. The lower half of his face is painted into a demented smile full of serrated teeth. It extends from one ear to the next, completely overshadowing his real mouth. Instead of cheerful, colorful fabrics, he wears what appears to be human skins. A single femur bone is placed in his disheveled red hair.

"Um, Stabby? We don't need to be enemies, my man." I hold up my hands as I slowly step backwards.

Eyes intent on my own, Stabby procures a bouquet of

flowers from his sleeve. Nestled between the tulips is a single blade.

And here I was wondering where he got the nickname from.

Just before he can swipe, Vin appears from around the corner, wraps his hands around Stabby's neck, and snaps it. The clown collapses onto the pavement with a thump.

"Goodbye, Stabby. It was nice knowing you." I give a two-fingered wave as I watch Vin kneel beside his corpse and grab the blade from the bouquet.

"We need to get going," my best friend states, shoving the blade in his pocket.

"Pinkie will be fine," I insist immediately, easily able to read the turmoil in his eyes. Though, despite my words, a tiny trickle of fear cascades down my spine. She will be fine, right? All I know for certain is that the portal threw me on top of an elementary school and I was forced to shimmy down a flagpole. Fortunately, Vin had fallen nearby, and we were able to team up.

But there was no Frankie or Hux/Jack.

No Cal or Barret.

No Violet.

I feel her absence as keenly as Stabby's blade would've felt embedded in my chest. I don't like not knowing where she is or how she's doing. I can already see Vin wrestling with his protective instincts demanding that he upturn this entire fucking town—monsters be damned—until he finds her. I just barely was able to hold him back when I first found him, Dimitri's words to Violet reverberating through my head.

The hospital.

Surely, it was a hint.

I have no doubt Pinkie will be heading in that direction as well.

Hoping to distract Vin so his thoughts won't spiral out of

control, I shove him in the shoulder. "Next time we run into a creepy-ass clown named Stabby, you'll be the bait, okay?"

He snorts, pasting on a smile, but I can tell his mind is still miles and miles away. Probably with a certain dainty vampire with bigger balls than him. I know that he's also worried about Vanessa, but he knows—as well as I do—that she can take care of herself. Violet, on the other hand…

She once knocked herself unconscious trying to chest bump Barret.

We walk in companionable semi-silence, ribbons of red and orange from the proud sun decorating the rickety, decrepit buildings. Semi-silence because, despite our dour situation, I can't stop myself from singing softly beneath my breath.

"Can you shut the fuck up?" Vin gripes, spewing vitriol with his eyes.

"Can you make me?" I taunt. And then, because I'm an egotistical asshole, I wrap my arm around his shoulder and whisper in his ear, *"I'm sexy and I know it."*

"Asshole." Vin shoves at my shoulder, and I release a bark of laughter as I stumble over my own two feet. Despite Vin's normal grumpiness, a wry smile pulls up his lips, and I call that a win. I'm worried about Violet too, but I know we need to remain level-headed.

If anything were to happen to her…

I shake my head quickly as we reach a fork in the road cluttered with abandoned cars.

Vin drops to his knees and tentatively touches a speck of dirt. As a Van Helsing, he's skilled at hunting—almost scarily so. Every trampled blade of grass, every footprint, every overturned rock… He sees them all.

"The monsters were heading this way," he points towards the left road. "Towards the center of the city. That means we need to head this way." He points in the opposite direction, where the road is littered with trash and the cars are scarce.

"If Dimitri was just fucking with us…" I warn tersely. "If we're actually supposed to go downtown like the other monsters…" I once more trail off as a cold chill races down my back. Despite leaving my statement unfinished, the message is clear—we're fucked.

Why do we have to rely on a psychopathic assassin for survival?

"It doesn't matter." Vin spins the dagger between his fingers, eyebrows furrowed in intense concentration. "None of it matters if we don't find Violet."

"Hey," I place my hand on his shoulder, "we'll get her back. She's strong, okay?"

"And she has a tendency to trip over her own two feet and land on a blade," he points out dryly, and my own worry ratchets up another notch. Because, yeah, that totally happened.

"She'll be fine." I don't know if I'm trying to convince him or myself. Maybe a bit of both. Panic claws at my chest at the possibility that she's lying in a ditch somewhere, crying for us. She might not know for certain that we're her fated mates, but I have no doubt she suspects there's something otherworldly and ethereal about our connection.

Abruptly, Vin grabs my arm and pulls me to a stop. His other hand, still holding Stabby's blade, points towards the horizon where the cerulean blue sky is interspersed with fluffy white clouds. Below that, the once tall and imposing skyscrapers give way to family homes with shingle roofs and painted plaster. At first, I have no idea what I'm supposed to be looking at, but then tiny blobs materialize in the distance.

"Is that…?" I recognize the figure in the middle almost instantly. Frankie stands with his lips compressed into a grim line. Streaks of blood run in rivulets from an open wound on his forehead as he stands in the midst of beasts.

Not monsters—I'm a monster, Vin's a monster, Violet's a monster—but grotesque and disfigured creatures that could only be the creations of Dr. Frankenstein.

The one closest to Frankie appears to be a male silhouette with a smooth black face. He almost resembles a shadow, no identifying features in sight. His frame is lean, almost sickly, and he stands perfectly straight with his head cocked to the side. The beast beside him has lips that resemble those of a sea lamprey—circular with row after row of crenulated teeth. His eyes are beady, almost like a spider's, and emit an eerie red glow. His torso is decidedly human, but his body is that of a majestic horse. A centaur, but not like the ones you see in the movies. This fucker is terrifying, exuding danger like it's a palpable entity. The next three monsters have their backs to me, but they appear to be some sort of hound. Their fur is coarse, riddled with rainbow streaks, and their ears are covered in rips and tears.

"Errr, should we help him?" I whisper conspiratorially to Vin, but the hunter merely shushes me, focusing on Frankie with narrowed eyes.

It suddenly occurs to me that the beasts aren't attacking our cold-blooded friend. Instead, they appear to be listening to him, their heads canted to the side in consideration.

Vin nods at me once, and we both immediately move forward to join the huddle. Frankie glances up sharply at our footsteps, but his face slackens with relief when he spots us. Eyes cold, he steps through the throng of beasts.

"It's so good to see you guys," he says—though his tone suggests it's anything *but*. Yeah, our little scientist needs to work on his bedside manner. Sometimes, I have the distinct feeling he's planning on cutting open my chest to experiment on my organs. I think our tentative friendship is the only thing keeping me in one piece.

Abruptly, Frankie's features tighten imperceptibly as he peers around both of our shoulders. "Where's Violet?" Those cold, cold eyes of his land first one me and then on Vin. "Where the fuck is she?"

"We don't know," Vin answers wearily, sounding almost tired. He rakes his fingers through his tousled black hair and heaves out a sigh. "She must've landed somewhere else when the portal spit her out."

Frankie's lips purse, as if he has eaten something sour, but he doesn't answer. Instead, he merely stalks back towards his little beastly friends. I'm going to name them Shadow and Fishy, and the triplets will be Biscuit, Tuna, and Spaghetti.

"What the fuck are they, and why aren't they dead?" Vin snaps, some of his original ire returning as he glares at the disgusting creatures.

Frankie waves a hand at them almost dismissively, as if he can't be bothered to introduce them. "Apparently, I have enough of Frankenstein's blood in me for the monsters to think I'm their daddy." He makes a face before quickly smoothing out his features. "They've been following me around ever since."

"Aren't you a cutie patootie," I coo, crouching down beside one of the mangy mutts. He bares his teeth at me, sharper than those of a shark, and immediately lunges for me. I squeal and run behind Vin, using him for protection.

"Fucking pussy," Vin seethes, shoving me away from him.

"Pussies are stronger than cocks," I point out, eyeing the dog-thing as he drops back to his stomach in front of Frankie. "That's what Violet always says."

The mention of our missing mate immediately cools the light-hearted atmosphere. Vin, if it's even possible, appears even more broody, and Frankie looks as if he wants to cut a bitch. Or a Mason.

"We think she's headed to the hospital," Vin states at last.

"After what Dimitri said, I think you're right." He nods once, already turning on his heel in preparation to leave. "I was headed there myself. Even if for some reason Dimitri was pulling Violet's leg, we'll all be together to travel to the main part of the city. There's too many monsters for us to go on our own." He releases a shrill whistle, and his beasts immediately begin trailing behind him like besotted puppies. To be quite frank, it's weird as fuck to see.

Vin and I exchange a long, commiserating glance.

"We'll get her back," I say for the twentieth time in the last few minutes. His eyes harden with resolve, lips thinning. After a moment, he nods his head in agreement.

"We'll get her back."

CHAPTER 29

VIOLET

Flames immediately engulf the sides of the cozy diner, specks of red and orange and yellow eating away at the siding. Cal's arms are iron vises around me as we both stare at the crumbling building in rapt horror.

"Holy shit balls," I wheeze.

"He must not have known you were inside," Cal murmurs, tone pitched in horror and disbelief. "But fuck, we could've died. I'm too pretty and young to die this early."

All I can do is nod mutely. What if Cal hadn't seen the grenade before Hux/Jack threw it? What if we had still been in the building when it exploded? Fire is one of the few things that can kill a vampire. After all, a body can't put itself back together again when it's decimated into ash. Neither Hux or Jack would ever be able to forgive themselves if they had accidentally murdered me.

"We should see if he's still there," I say, freeing myself from Cal's arms. I don't waste any time racing around the restaurant and towards where I had last seen my lover—

lovers? The street, however, is barren, with no indication that Hux/Jack had ever been here to begin with. I have no doubt that Hux is steadily losing control, his need to find and protect me overriding his logical side. Even Jack won't be able to handle a feral and completely unhinged Hux.

"He left already," I whisper, feeling oddly bereft. All I want is to see one of my men and wrap myself in his arms. I'm driving myself crazy with worry. Are they hurt? Dead? Are they looking for me? Are they heading towards the city or towards the hospital? Question after question continue to bombard me from all sides like a twenty-car pile-up.

"Vi, we need to get moving." Cal's hand rests on my upper arm to guide me away from the roaring flames. "The fire is going to catch a lot of attention."

"You're right." I nod resolutely, peering through the smoke. "We need to head to the hospital. Now."

The next hour is silent as we venture farther away from the main city to an area of town decorated in cozy houses and hipster coffee shops. My anxiety threatens to implode with each step we take. Somehow, the lack of other monsters does little to soothe my jagged and frayed nerves. Shouldn't there be others? Why are we all alone?

"I don't like this," Cal whispers, giving voice to my own thoughts.

"Maybe we should turn around..." I begin hesitantly, peering over my shoulder at the waning sunlight illuminating the numerous skyscrapers. If Dimitri's wrong—or if he's just fucking with me—then I have inevitably led Cal to his own death. "If we make it to the hospital and discover that's not the way out of this hellhole, there's no way we'll be able to make it to the central part of the city before our time is up," I implore. "So we need to make a choice. Trust Dimitri, or follow the rest of the monsters."

We pause in the middle of the street, our chests heaving

as we whip our heads from one direction to the other. This decision feels monumental, like that moment in chess when you have the capability to capture the other player's king. Check-fucking-mate. But in this scenario, I'm unable to see the entire game board and the rules have been written in gibberish. One wrong move, and it'll be game over for all of the players.

"Violet, you know Dimitri better than any of us. Can we trust him?" Cal stares earnestly into my eyes, beseeching me with just his look to trust my instincts.

But…

But what if my instincts are wrong? What if my decision leads to Cal's death? I can feel myself balancing on a scale, one foot on either surface, but try as I might, I can't get it to settle. It keeps tilting precariously in one direction. And I know immediately, unerringly, what we need to do.

"We need to get to the hospital," I tell Cal at last, and I can only pray that my decision isn't my final one. Cal smiles, nodding briskly, before we continue in the direction of the hospital, just barely visible through the smog.

"Cal! Cheese Curd!" a voice screams from behind us. We both turn to see Barret barreling towards us, a wide grin on his handsome face. He captures me first, immediately spinning me in a circle. His strong arms are like bands around my waist, refusing to release me.

"Barret!" I squeal, relieved to see him in relatively one piece. Besides a blood wound curving down his cheek, he appears to be unharmed. His eyes are alive with happiness and joy. "You're okay!"

"Of course I'm okay," he states, confused. "You're looking at me right now."

When he places me on my feet, he turns towards Cal with another beatific grin.

"Come here you, asshole," Cal says, relieved, and Barret

wraps the cupid in his arms, being extra aware of his feathered red wings. Cal gently grabs Barret's chin and guides his lips to his own. The two begin to kiss tentatively at first, almost shyly, before Cal's tongue snakes out and enters the Boogeyman's mouth. It's oddly erotic to watch, and I can feel myself begin to grow wet. When Cal glances at me out of the corner of his eye, I realize the bastard did it on purpose.

"We should get going." I clear my throat around the sudden onslaught of arousal that floods my system.

Cal pulls away, lips wet and swollen from Barret's kisses, and turns towards me slowly. "Did you like watching me kiss him, Vi?"

Barret's eyes immediately smolder, turning heated, as he glances between me and his friend with curiosity.

Honestly, I have no idea how I'm feeling right now. A part of me is jealous…mainly because I want to be in between them while they're kissing. Like the vampire meat in a sexy sandwich. At the same time, those thoughts are dangerous to have. Extremely dangerous. Cal and Barret are two of my closest friends, and the last thing I want or need is my attraction getting in the way of that.

"Let's go," I squeak, flames entering my face. Cal laughs heartily, patting Barret on the shoulder as the gentle giant steps up beside me. Pink dots both his cheeks as he wraps his pinkie around my own.

"You okay, Cheese Curd?" he asks softly, eyes focused straight ahead.

"I'm just peachy." My eyes automatically flicker to his cock, which is still hard from Cal's kisses. "Super duper peachy." Did I sound like a strangled hyena? Fuck me.

"You're prettier than a peach," Barret says, his blush deepening. "Cal is more in the peach category."

"I heard that!" the man in question exclaims immediately. "And I'm offended. What—or who—is prettier than me?"

"Violet," Barret answers automatically, and god help me, but I swear I melt into a puddle of goo right then and there.

"Y'all are good for my ego," I tease, releasing Barret's hand to face them both. Walking backwards—and trusting they would stop me before I tripped over anything—I point first at Barret and then at Cal. "But keep talking. Boost my ego. Make me fly."

"Make you fly?" Cal asks with a snort. "Really, Violet?"

"What? Isn't that a saying?"

"You're saying it, so yes," Barret pipes in helpfully, and when I flash him a grateful smile, he positively preens. Cal merely pinches the bridge of his nose.

"It is *not* a saying. No one says shit like that."

"Violet just did," Barret points out, and I could kiss him. But I don't, of course. Because we're buddies and nothing more. Absolutely nothing. With a capital N. And a capital O. And a capital T. And a capital—

"Violet!" Cal screams abruptly, and I turn just in time to see Alex's father point a dagger at my neck. His black eyes are swimming with pure, unrelenting darkness, like the deepest depths of the ocean. Pure madness and hatred reflect back at me. Alex stands behind his father, looking small and shaken with his pasty skin and tousled black hair. I can't help but note that his mother doesn't appear to be with them, and I feel a pang of sadness for the woman who has no doubt lost her life to these games.

"Hello, vampire bitch." The man smiles, revealing a row of perfectly white teeth.

"Don't touch her." Instead of enraged like I would've expected, Cal's voice is a low and seductive purr, curling around me and dampening my panties. Immediately, I realize that he's fighting Alex's dad in his own way—through pure seduction.

Hunger momentarily blazes in the man's dark gaze before he shakes his head vigorously.

"Your seduction isn't going to work on me," he hisses menacingly, still holding that damn blade to my neck. One look confirms it's a god-blessed dagger. Because why the fuck not? It's been almost an hour since someone tried to kill me. I consider that a pretty good run.

"Let her go," Cal hisses, any and all pretenses diminishing. I can feel his presence behind me, but I don't dare look over my shoulder. I know he won't do anything to put me in danger, including step closer.

Out of my peripheral, I spot Barret standing there with a perplexed expression on his face. He isn't looking at me, however, but at Alex, the skin between his eyes crinkled.

Fuck, I can't let this man hurt Cal or Barret. I need to keep him distracted long enough for them to sneak away—if they can get their heads out of their protective asses for more than a minute and realize that leaving me is their only chance at survival.

"Why do you hate me so much?" I ask bluntly. "And shouldn't I get the name of my potential murderer?"

He laughs humorlessly, the noise scratching at my heart. "You don't deserve my name, pathetic bitch."

Okay, Bitch it is, then.

"Bitch" continues to glare at me with unveiled animosity. He looks as if he wants to shove the dagger into both of my eyes, then up my nostrils, then in my mouth, and finally end the night with some kinky anal knife play.

"You killed my brother," Alex answers when it becomes apparent that Bitch isn't going to.

"What?" I screech. Yeah, I killed a few people throughout my life, but most of them have been hunters sent to kill *me*. Tit for tat, or however that saying goes.

"You didn't even have the decency to bring his body back

to his family," Bitch hisses, spittle flying in my face. "Instead, you kept his head like some demented trophy."

Kept his head…?

Oh, *fuck.*

"Bob?" I squeak, remembering the severed head I preserved and kept in my bedroom. He was the first man I'd ever killed—and for a just reason.

"His name was Patrick," Bitch bites out, his face crumpling with pain. "And you killed him."

"You don't understand," I plead, lifting my hands in surrender. "He tried to *rape* me."

Bitch doesn't stop his relentless pursuit, but I notice Alex's inscrutable expression tense. The hand holding the knife lowers marginally.

"What?" he gasps, staring at me as if he doesn't quite recognize me.

"I was younger, maybe thirteen or fourteen. He cornered me in an alleyway and slapped a hand over my mouth. He began to pull down my pants." I tremble at the memory. I remember how scared I was, how small I felt, as his cock pressed against my ass.

"Don't scream, little one."

And I hadn't. Instead, I had spun around and sank my teeth into his neck, pulling away skin until blood bubbled out. He died instantly.

"My son would never do that, you lying whore!" Bitch screams.

Alex is shaking his head vehemently, denial clear on his face. His eyes harden suddenly as he steps around his father, his blade raised.

"You're going to die for what you did to my family," he growls, pulling his arm back.

"No!" Barret races forward, shoving me away just as Alex plunges his blade into the man's heart. Barret's face creases in confusion as he stares at the dagger protruding from his chest, sickly green blood pooling around him. Genuine fear flashes in his unfathomable eyes as he glances helplessly at me and then Cal before crumpling to the ground.

"No!" Cal screams in anguish, charging towards Alex and his dad. Before he can capture them, they dematerialize in a cloud of black smoke. "No!"

"Barret?" I ask, dropping to my knees beside the giant man. Blood bubbles from his lips as he opens his mouth to say something, his eyes pleading with my own. "Barret?" I whisper again. Tears begin to trail down my cheeks as I stare at my best friend lying in a puddle of his own blood.

"Please, stay with me. Stay with me. You'll be okay," Cal sobs as he drops on his other side, his hands pressing down on Barret's chest. "Violet, do something!" he screams. Refocusing on his best friend, he begins to cry harder. "You're going to be okay, alright? You promised me. Friends forever, remember? You can't leave me alone."

Barret opens his mouth a second time, but only manages to cough up more blood. His eyes turn glazed, the light gradually leaving them, as he stares at the sky.

I'm shaking, my own tears cascading down my cheeks and landing on my slightly parted lips.

Not Barret. Not him. No. No. No. No.

"NO!" Cal screams in a voice rich with denial and agonizing pain. He drops his head to Barret's still chest as a slight green mist begins to excrete from the monster's pores. It cocoons his body in a vibrant glow as thousands and thousands of bugs appear where his body once was.

Barret's dead.

Alex killed him.

My heart stutters to an abrupt halt and then cracks, weeping blood. A strangled sob gets lodged in my throat as I throw my head back and wail my pain for the entire world to hear.

There's no escaping this pain, this heartache. It strangles me like a piece of wire that has been wrapped around my neck.

My wail turns into a scream, a battle cry, demanding blood and vengeance.

Once that fades, I'm left with nothing but a dizzying loneliness and a crippling depression—a Barret-shaped hole in my heart. Trembling, I collapse on the ground beside the collection of bugs and curl into a ball, my tears drying on my cheeks.

Even when I close my eyes, I can still hear Cal's anguished screams.

CHAPTER 30

"We have to go." My voice is soft, quiet even, but it breaks through the anguished cries like a gun being shot.

"No!" Cal screams, pulling at his pink hair while he paces.

Feeling numb, as if I'm no longer in control of my body, I repeat, "We have to go."

Cal whirls on me, eyes burning with pain and fury, but whatever he sees in my expression causes his shoulders to slacken and his face to crumple in defeat.

"You're right," he states, squeezing his eyelids shut. Movements mechanical, he extends a hand to me. "Barret would want me to get you out of here. There's no way in hell I'm losing you too." He stares at me with dead, impassive eyes.

When I remain immobile, staring at the spot I'd last seen Barret, Cal thrusts his hand farther into my face. "Violet," he warns, and I stare at the proffered limb, unable to muster the will to take it. After a moment, I reluctantly interlock our fingers and allow him to pull me to my feet. He releases me immediately, almost as if my touch is toxic, before striding in the direction we were heading before…

Before…

Before "before" became such a horrendous word.

Cal's all business, the lines of his body taut with tension and barely suppressed pain. I know that sooner or later, he's going to fall apart so completely, so *irrevocably*, that he'll barely resemble the man I know and care for. Death has a way of doing that to a person.

Barret's dead. That one thought loops through my head, each time bringing about a blistering stab of pain like a hot poker being shoved through my chest.

Stubbornly, I hold my tears at a bay as we move farther and farther down the road. I can't help but notice that the once-vibrant green grass turns a brittle brown the farther we get from the city. And there, in the distance, is the silhouette of the hospital.

It's an older building that rises majestically over the boughs of trees, ribbons of red and orange from the setting sun illuminating it in a fiery glow. Instead of relief, all I feel is a sense of foreboding as I stare up at the brick structure. Unlike the rest of the buildings in the arena, the windows appear to be intact, if a bit dusty. An abandoned ambulance rests beneath a low-hanging awning, its doors thrown open, as if the humans had been in the midst of an evacuation.

Without trepidation or even fear, Cal stalks up to the glass automatic doors.

"We need to be careful," I caution, peering into the surrounding forest and searching for any threats. The eerie silence makes it feel unnatural—disturbing, even. It makes me itch to run away and hide.

"We need to get inside," Cal counters, voice bereft of any emotion, his grief overshadowing logical thought.

Before I can protest, a figure materializes between two

trees at the edge of the forest, the asphalt shaking with each step he takes.

A cyclops.

He stands over ten feet tall, his single eye a jaundiced yellow color. His greenish skin is tinged with shades of gray and black, almost as if he is ill. When he roars, spittle flying, I see only four teeth in his mouth, each a hideous shade of amber and lengthened into sharp points.

"Oh, fuck." I begin to hesitantly back away, gesticulating wildly for Cal to join me. Instead, he spreads his pink wings and takes to the sky, soaring over the cyclops's head once before landing on its shoulders. He wraps both of his arms around the creature's neck, and I watch the cyclops buck and kick in an attempt to remove the added weight.

"You motherfucker!" Cal barks, his arms tightening around the monster's neck. His hands are just barely able to touch at the center of the cyclops's throat, his muscles straining and rippling. Smoke wafts from Cal's body, and his eyes erode over, the pupils swallowing the irises.

I take another step backwards, but this time, it's not in fear of the cyclops. It's in fear of *Cal*.

There's something primal and otherworldly about him, something that causes every hair on my body to raise. When he bares his teeth, I see sharp incisors that hadn't been there prior.

The cyclops releases another roar, the vibrations threatening to rupture my eardrums.

As they both fall to the ground, Cal still clinging to the monster like some sort of demented spider monkey, I can't help but see the violence in his eyes, teetering on the brink of complete and utter annihilation. He's a tsunami rapidly approaching the shoreline, bringing nothing but death and destruction in its wake.

Cal begins to rain down punches on the cyclops's back,

each blow causing the creature to grunt and hiss in pain. I have no doubt that the cyclops is stronger than Cal, but the cupid's rage is giving him an edge in the fight.

Unable to watch this assault a moment longer, I race forward with my vampire speed, aim my gun, and fire into the cyclops's single eye. Droplets of blood splatter my face and arms, the texture slimy as I vigorously wipe it off.

Still, Cal keeps hitting the dead monster, his knuckles cracked and bruised.

"He's dead," I whisper, unable to raise my voice. "Cal, he's dead."

He doesn't seem to hear me, his movements jerky in his agitation. Tears run in rivulets down his face as his sightless eyes remain focused on the threat.

"Cal!" I lean forward to touch his arm, and he jerks away, falling off of the giant's body. He stares at his hands as if he doesn't recognize them, as if they belong to someone else entirely. His body shakes as he holds up his blood-soaked palm before lifting his eyes to mine.

"What did I just do?" he whispers brokenly, pulling his knees to his chest and wrapping his arms around them. "What did I just do? Did I...? Did I hurt you?" He sounds aghast by the prospect, his lower lip trembling as he fights for control.

"No, you didn't hurt me," I assure, dropping to the ground beside him and wrapping him in my arms. He desperately claws at my skin, as if trying to burrow himself inside of me. His head lands on my shoulder as his body vibrates with silent sobs. I push down his unruly pink hair as I try to comfort him. "I miss him too."

"He was my best friend," he chokes out. "My only friend."

"I'm your friend," I say immediately, the words instinctive. Swallowing, I continue, "I don't know if it's any comfort, but I'm your friend, Cal. I always have been." He pulls his head up to stare at me with glassy eyes. Fuck, seeing him in pain destroys me. Absolutely guts me. His grief combines with my own until I'm suffocating on it. It feels as if there are claws wrapped around my heart, the nails digging into the sensitive organ until it's weeping blood.

"I can't believe he's gone," he laments. "We shouldn't have joined this stupid fucking game."

All I can do is hold him even tighter, hoping some of his pain will transfer into me. Though I'm not sure if I'll survive any more.

"It's getting dark." I press a kiss to his forehead. "We need to find the way out of here."

Cal nods once, jerkily, before stumbling to his feet and pulling me up with him. His hand remains on me for a moment longer, as if assuring himself I'm still here, still alive, before he releases me and steps away.

"We'll have to look through every door," Cal warns as we move to the entrance. The glass doors slide open, and we enter a waiting room with a single receptionist desk, stark white tiles, and a collection of plastic chairs. The entire room gives me the creeps. It was designed, no doubt, to be sterile and clean, but instead, it feels unwelcoming and stuffy.

"I fucking hate hospitals." My lips curl upwards in disgust as I sidestep a fallen wheelchair. "Dad used to make me go and pretend to be a patient so he could steal blood from their blood vaults. He once shoved a hammer into my ear because he thought it'd be hilarious to see the doctors and nurses scream and fret over me. Another time, he told me to tell them to ask for a face transplant. I was six then." I'm babbling, I know it, but the only other alternative is to surrender to my pain. To allow the ice-cold waves to drown me until I'm nothing but withered skin and bones.

"Your dad sounds charming," Cal deadpans, opening up a closet behind the receptionist desk.

"He's an odd man, that's for sure," I agree. I can't help but wrap my arms around myself. There's not a chill or even a breeze, but I can't escape the cold feeling traveling through me. The feeling that we're being watched.

"Barret once hid underneath a desk for an entire day trying to scare someone in detention," Cal muses, his breath hitching. His pain is so raw, so real, that my heart aches for him a little more. I didn't even think it was possible. "But what Barret didn't know was that I had already killed the man." He laughs sharply, humorlessly, the despondent sound tightening the nerves in my stomach. "I miss him so fucking much."

"I do too." I didn't know Barret like Cal did—we had only been friends for a short while—but already, I feel his absence as keenly as if my liver had been removed. In the short time I have known him, he has become a part of me, embossing himself on my skin. He's a tattoo that I don't want to ever remove.

Shuffling captures our attention, and we both turn towards the left hall. I raise my gun, desperately trying to recall how many bullets I have left. Cal bares his fangs and steps in front of me, wings fluffing out around him.

The silence is strained as the footsteps approach. Every muscle in my body is coiled, ready to spring into action. Fear pulses through me, pounding like the beat of a drum, but I ignore it resolutely, prepared to fight.

"A gun?" a familiar, dry voice remarks as Vin steps through the door, Mason and Frankie directly behind him. "Really, Violet?" He scoffs once, but his eyes soften with relief when he sees that I'm unharmed. "Do you really think that would stop me if I wanted to kill you?"

CHAPTER 31

HUX

Darkness.

It's all I know, all I'm aware of. It tightens around me like a steadily shrinking vise as I curl into a tight ball.

"Jack?" I whisper, my pulse skittering as I peer through the inky darkness.

But I can't feel my brother. I can't even sense him.

Instead, I'm shoved into the farthest corner of our shared mind like a piece of scum.

I'm not afraid of the dark. No, after centuries of pure and unrelenting darkness, it's impossible to truly be terrified of it. There are a lot of things that can hide in the darkness, but I much prefer that over the light. There, you can see and experience everything—you're forced to watch the monsters charge at you with their claws extended and fangs bared. At least in the darkness, you can pretend that you're alone.

Unease skates down my spine, as if the Grim Reaper himself is trailing an icy finger across my skin.

I don't like this. I don't like this one fucking bit.

Since we met Violet, we've been able to coexist in relative peace. I can hear all of Jack's thoughts and see through his eyes when he's in control of our body. That differs from before, where only one of us was in charge and the other was relegated to the darkness.

I need to find my way out of here; I need to find my precious treasure.

With a roar, I begin to pound on one of the onyx walls of my makeshift prison. The only reason I know it's there is because my fist meets resistance whenever I throw a punch. My knuckles begin to ache fiercely, but still, I rain down blow after blow.

When it feels as if my body is no longer capable of fighting, as if my knuckles have been scraped of all skin and are red with blood, I collapse back on the ground, one arm curled around my legs. I reach into my pocket and instinctively grab the chocolate bar Violet gave me when I first met her.

It's my first gift. My first present from a person who wants nothing from me except my love and acceptance. For so long, the love bestowed upon me was conditional, and I constantly failed to meet their expectations. Even my own parents referred to me as a monster and beast. Jack may be my brother, but even he never trusted me enough to set me free longer than a month or two at a time. He always wrangled me into the deepest recesses of our shared mind while he once more took the reins.

I understand their trepidation. I'm a monster. I'm the beast that lurks beneath your bed at night, waiting for you to leave the safety of the blankets so I can snatch you up. I've killed people—more people than I care to admit—but I have also saved people.

Shaking my head vigorously, I release a bellow of rage,

rise to my feet once more, and slam my entire body against the wall. Only, instead of a hard surface, my body meets nothing but air. I stumble to the ground, stealthily pushing my hands out to catch myself before I can faceplant.

What the bloody hell?

Directly ahead of me is a thin shaft of brilliant white light, illuminating a few feet in every direction. The light calls to me like a beacon, one I can't possibly resist. One that I don't *want* to resist.

Before I can even take a step closer, muffled cursing captures my attention. I whip my head in the direction of the noise and growl threateningly, preparing to rip the intruder limb from limb. If anyone tries to keep me from my precious treasure, they will pay the price. I will not hesitate to do what needs to be done.

"Who's there?" I bellow, and the footsteps abruptly pause.

A moment later, a timid voice calls, "Hux?"

"Jack?" I stalk forward, my hands extended, until they rest on a pair of shoulders. "What the bloody hell are you doing here?" I demand, my hands tightening on his skin. I just barely resist the urge to shake him.

And then the sheer wonderment and joy of being able to actually see and hold my younger brother bombards me. For so long, he has been nothing but an elusive fantasy. Before Violet, we were forced to write notes back and forth to each other whenever we switched places. While I flourished in the darkness, my little brother thrived in the light. He sought to save the world and the people in it while I sought to destroy it.

"Brother," he whispers, voice choked.

"Where the bloody hell are we?" I demand. "And where's my precious treasure?"

"What do you mean?" Jack questions, sounding genuinely bemused. "Aren't you driving the body?"

I just barely hold in my snort. "I've been in the darkness for the last few hours." Phantom shivers race up and down my arms as I remember the coldness and gripping loneliness. The only thing that made it bearable was the prospect of seeing Violet again. I was nearly driven mad with my fear for her. The last thing I remember was standing beside her as we went to the portal…and then, nothing. I'd assumed Jack was in control of our shared body.

But…

"If we're both here, then what the bloody fuck is happening with our body?" I hiss through gritted teeth, my head whipping towards the sliver of light. As I watch, horrified, it begins to spark and fade, the hole becoming smaller and smaller as the seconds tick by.

"Run!" Jack screams, darting around me and towards the piercing light. I'm right on his heels, finally able to see his silhouette and blurry features the closer we get.

The light is now half as tall as it was initially, significantly dimmer until it's a hue of molten amber instead of silver.

Just as we're about to barrel through the hole, it flickers once and then abruptly dissipates, once more leaving us encased in pure darkness. I can't see my hand in front of my face, let alone Jack.

A roar of pain and fury leaves me as I desperately touch the air where I last saw the light.

No. No. No. No. No.

I can't remain in this place, not after I found my mate. I need to be there for her and protect her.

Who knew how hard it would be to once again live in the darkness after experiencing the light?

"What are we going to do?" Jack whispers, his voice wobbling.

I drop to my knees and pound my fist against the ground. Once. Twice. Three times. Each blow sends pain reverberating up my arm, but I welcome it, allowing it to cool my blistering emotions.

When I don't answer, my free hand clenching around the chocolate bar, Jack continues in a ragged voice, "I think…I think we're not alone. I think there's someone else here with us."

If that's the case, then a stranger is currently in control of our body. A stranger who has the power to get close to my precious treasure…

Rage skitters through my veins as I scream my pain for the world to hear. Hanging my head, I allow my fingers to unclench from the chocolate bar before holding it reverently to my chest.

"Brother," Jack begins softly, placing a hand on my shoulder. When I don't immediately answer, body still trembling with anger, he gives it a squeeze. "We need to find our way out of here."

"Some fucker has taken over our body," I manage to hiss out, still not raising my head. Tension thrums through me, and I can feel my heart racing in tandem to my spiraling thoughts. "What if he hurts Violet? Who the fuck is he?"

"I don't know," Jack says, resignation clear in his voice. "But I swear to you, I'll find a way to get us both out of this alive. We'll find our way back to her."

"We're trapped in here!" I finally lunge to my feet, knocking Jack's hand off my shoulder in the process. I whirl on my brother, lips curling away from my teeth. "You promised me that I wouldn't be trapped in the darkness anymore. You. Promised. Me." My chest heaves with each word as pain flays me open, baring my organs for the entire world to see. I hate being vulnerable, hate showing anyone the person beneath the monster. That person is only reserved for my precious treasure. For my mate.

"There has to be another exit," Jack says resolutely, but I

can't help but notice that his voice shakes. "Once we find our way out, we can overpower the asshole and make him pay."

"I'm going to rip him limb from limb," I warn, tone impassive. "I'll rip his spleen out of his body. I'll gouge out each of his eyeballs and then feed them to him, one at a time. I'll use his heart as a baseball and his head as a basketball. And his tears? I'll lick them from his face as they fall, claiming his pain as my own. And when he tries to run, I'll burn each of his feet until even standing is impossible. Only then will I skin him alive and wear it like a coat of pride. As he bleeds to death, I'll grab his tonsils and tie them into a cute little bow around his face and then gift him to my precious treasure. Do you understand me?"

Jack audibly gulps. "I'll be your moral support."

I nod my head once, accepting that.

"You can hold the body still for me as I enact my revenge," I state seriously.

"Errr…"

"Come." Without a word, I stride in the opposite direction of the light, my hands extended as I feel around in the darkness. "We need to find our way out of here. Now."

CHAPTER 32

VIOLET

I'm in Vin's arms before he can even finish speaking, unable to stop myself from nuzzling against his neck. His body stiffens underneath me, obviously taken by surprise, before he tightens his arms around me and returns my hug.

"What's going on?" Frankie demands immediately, his icy voice curling around me and instantly putting me at ease.

They're safe, and they're here with me. We're safe.

Pesky tears spring to my eyes at the reminder that we're not *all* safe. Not after…

I shove those emotions in a glass bottle and toss it in the churning river. Maybe someone will find them one day and know how to handle them. All I know for certain is that if I allow these thoughts to fester, if I allow them to take root like a carnivorous plant, I'll never be able to claw myself out of the depressive hole I'm already halfway in.

"Pinkie…" Mason steps up behind me, effectively caging

me between the two men. He begins to rub at my tangled curls while Vin buries his face in my neck.

"Barret's dead." It's Cal who answers, his voice carefully blank. When I reluctantly pull back from Vin, it's to see Cal staring blindly ahead with dark, empty eyes. "He's dead."

"Oh, shit," Vin curses, pulling me back towards him. I allow myself to accept his comfort, but only for a moment. A moment of weakness.

Once more, I step away from Vin and press my back against the far wall. Distance. I need distance. If one of them touches me again, I'll fall apart at the seams, losing tiny pieces of myself in the process.

"I see that we all came to the same conclusion," I manage to breathe out, grateful when my voice doesn't wobble. Mason and Vin exchange an anxious, wary glance, but fortunately, they accept my abrupt change of topic. Frankie moves to stand beside me, and though he doesn't touch me, the heat he emits is almost palpable. It seeps through my Academy-issued clothes and sets my skin ablaze.

"If Dimitri was telling the truth, the portal home should be somewhere in here." Vin moves to stand in the center of all of us, once more the unofficial leader. I can't help but find his domineering attitude and no-nonsense tone sexy. Horrible timing? Most definitely.

"What exactly did the scary fucker say?" Mason adds, turning to face me completely. I bite my lip as I try to remember.

Something about…

"Something about bandages, maybe? I don't remember. It all happened so fast."

With a brisk nod at each other, the men fan out, pulling open drawers and doors at random. After a moment of indecision, I hurry to follow.

"So, are we looking for a drawer or closet full of bandages?" I query, wrenching open the drawer behind the nurse's desk. Files. The next drawer proves to be filled with the same.

"Fuck if I know," Vin grumbles. Turning to the others, he says, "I'm going to take the east wing. Mason? Take the west. Frankie, you'll head north, and Cal, you'll head south." The men all nod at his directive, but I wave my hand in the air impatiently. When he doesn't immediately call on me, I speak anyway.

"What about me? Where can I look?"

"You'll stay here." His tone brooks no room for argument. "Continue searching through the lobby, but when you're done, wait for us."

Sit, Violet. Stay. Stay. Good girl. Good girl.

I hate when people treat me like a fucking dog.

When I don't immediately protest, Vin's eyes narrow at my easy capitulation.

"Go." I shoo them away impatiently. "I'll be a good girl and stay here. Cross my heart." To prove my point, I create a makeshift X over my chest and hold my free hand up in the air to prove I'm not crossing my fingers.

Vin continues to eye me suspiciously, warily, before he concedes with a heavy sigh, jerking his chin at the others to split up. Mason skips to me immediately and plants a chaste, tender kiss to my forehead.

"We'll get through this, Pinkie. I promise," he whispers, his breath fanning across my face.

"That's a lie," I protest immediately. "We already lost Barret, and I have no idea where Jack and Hux are."

And I lost a tiny piece of my heart as well, though I don't say that out loud.

Mason's face softens in sympathy before he lifts my knuckles to his lips and kisses them.

"We'll get through this," he repeats. "Even if we're a little broken afterwards."

At my reluctant nod of concession, Mason releases my hand and strides in the direction Vin indicated. It's only then that I realize I'm alone. Completely and utterly alone.

I can't negate the lingering fear that they'll never return, that something will happen to them within the few minutes we're separated. Anxiety is a bitch.

Mumbling beneath my breath, I turn back towards the nurse's station…only to freeze in terror when I spot three dogs circling me, fangs dripping with saliva.

They're hideous creatures with mangy fur riddled with burns and cuts and vibrant red eyes that make me believe I'm staring into hell's bowels. All three of them take a step closer as I instinctively take one backwards.

"Don't hurt the little vampire," I plead. "I promise I'm not as tasty as I look. And I keep razor blades in my skin, so if you try to eat me, you'll get a mouth full of pain."

The beasts continue to stalk forward, their paws thumping against the white tiles.

"If you don't eat me, I'll give you a treat. Do you guys want a treat? Huh? A little doggy treat?" My back hits something solid, and I practically fall on my face in my attempt to spin around. This new creature has an expressionless face—almost like a smooth stone that has been polished over—and a long, slinky body.

Fear cascades through me as the creature tilts his head to the side curiously.

"How about we call a truce, okay? A no-killing-or-maiming truce between friends. We can be friends, right?" I back away from both creatures now, my heart threatening to break free of my chest. "I'm Violet. I'm a vampire. And I love long walks on the beach and giving blowjobs to people. Now it's your turn to introduce yourselves!" I gesture towards the blank-faced man—woman?—who continues to descend on me. "Nope? Don't want to? Okay, I'll tell you more about me. I once stabbed myself with a fork. Accidentally, of course, but that shit hurt like a bitch. It took me an hour to remove it from my neck. Honestly, I have no idea how I missed my mouth that bad. Pure skill, perhaps. Pure fucking skill."

One of the mutts lunges forward suddenly and captures the edge of my shorts with his teeth, tugging.

"I'd like to keep my pants on, please," I say, shaking my leg to dispel the ugly thing. When he whimpers, staring up at me with bright eyes rife with betrayal, I instantly feel like shit. "I suppose I can follow you…" I trail off helplessly, but the mutt lets out an excited yelp and begins running in a circle, chasing its spindly tail. Fuck, it's actually kind of cute in the whole "I'm going to murder and eat your intestines" type of way. Sort of like Hux.

Heaving out another breath, I allow myself to follow the beast down the corridor Cal disappeared down, the other two beasts on either side of me. The final creature remains at my back like a silent sentinel.

Pounding hooves echo behind me, and I turn just in time to see an honest-to-fuck centaur barreling towards us. His lips are pulled into a circular smile, revealing row after row of serrated teeth dripping bright with blood. His beady red eyes remind me eerily of a spider's, and I can't stop the full-body shivers from raking through me.

You know the saying, "Fuck me?" Well, I really, really don't want to be fucked right now.

The only reason I'm not running away like my ass is on fire is because I don't sense any malevolence from the creatures. Instead, they appear nothing but curious, and, in the hounds' cases, playful. It still does little to quell my growing unease as I venture farther and farther down the hallway.

There is no electricity in the building, and, this far down, there are no windows. It isn't too long before the entire hall is submerged in a pool of murky darkness. My footsteps sound ear-rupturing loud as they pound against the smooth tiles. I swear I can hear residual echoes, almost as if someone is walking directly behind me, stalking me. The dogs are quieter, their footsteps muted, while the shadowy figure glides across the floor without actually touching it. The centaur, on the other hand, pounds its hooves against the floor while intermittently releasing a prolonged "neigh."

When the silence becomes too unnerving, too chilling, I begin to sing softly beneath my breath. "Walking down the hall. With my shadow and my dog. A vampire wearing bats… And what the fuck is that?" I pause abruptly, the shadow monster ramming into my back before gracefully sliding through my body.

There, standing in front of a closed door, is a creature plucked straight out of a horror novel. And that's ironic, given that my father is Dracula. He's hideous, with weathered gray skin that appears flaky to the touch. Long lines, reminiscent of black veins, crawl up both his cheeks and bleed into his eyes, turning the whites into a shade of obsidian. His arms are nearly as long as his body, touching the floor, and his fingernails are sharp claws that are twice as long as my hand. Whiskers sprout from around his mouth, the delicate gray at odds with his foreboding appearance. Black cat ears decorate the top of his head, and as I step closer, they twitch. He sniffs the air once before turning back towards his victim, a very unconscious Cal lying in a pool of his own blood.

It's…

It's Cat Man? Nah, I'm pretty sure that's copyrighted somewhere. Maybe Pussy Man?

Pussy Man swings his head in my direction, yellow eyes narrowing into thin slits.

"What do we have here?" he purrs. "A snack?"

"I'm just going to come right out and say 'no.'" I slowly take a step away, and as expected, the creature follows. Good. I need to keep his attention off of Cal.

Behind me, the hounds sit in rapt fascination while the centaur grins maliciously. Apparently, they're perfectly content watching me die at the hands of this fucker.

"I know your father." The monster continues to prowl forward in a decidedly cat-like manner. When he smiles, tiny fangs pierce his bottom lip.

"Oh. You guys buddies?"

If the murderous glint in his eyes is any indication, that answer would be a 'hell no.'

"He killed my owner," Pussy Man hisses. "Sucked her dry."

I'm really hoping he means her blood, or else I'm going to vomit.

I chance a glance at Cal, relieved when I see the steady rise and fall of his chest. He's still alive, thank fuck, but I don't know the extent of his injuries.

Pussy Man follows the direction of my gaze, and pure satisfaction shines in his eyes.

"Is he your friend?" he taunts, crouching down and trailing a finger down Cal's cheek. "He's a handsome fellow."

"Don't you fucking touch him," I hiss, my fangs instinctively elongating at the threat. Pussy Man leans down, a cocksure grin on his face, and bares his own teeth. Instead of a cock-measuring contest, it's a teeth-measuring one. And dammit, I'm going to win.

"Did you know that I'm only part cat?" he queries. "The other half of me?" His eyes shine and contort, becoming distinctly reptilian in appearance. "The other half of me is a snake." Those two fangs I noticed earlier expand in his mouth until they're approximately the size of my own. His mouth opens wildly as he prepares to bite down on Cal's vulnerable neck. Before he can do it, though, I jump on his back, taking us both to the ground. Pussy Man takes no time in grabbing my sensitive wrist and sticking his fangs into my skin.

Immediately, pain begins to heat along my veins, my body turning sluggish. I feebly claw at his face, my fingernails leaving inch-deep gouges in his fleshy skin. I hope he needs Botox.

As my consciousness rapidly begins to wane, darkness pricking the edges of my vision, I see Cal begin to twitch and stir. He shakes his head once and then twice, moving jerkily to his feet. He blinks rapidly as he attempts to orient himself before his eyes come to rest on me.

With an enraged roar—the likes of which I never heard before—Cal lunges forward and grabs Pussy Man by a wisp of his dark hair.

"Don't touch her." Cal's voice is guttural, almost a growl, and causes my stomach to tighten into dozens of small, intricate knots. It's dark, deadly, and possessive. The cupid hurls daggers at the other monster with his eyes before slowly, hypnotically, opening his mouth.

Pussy Man's face goes slack as his eyes turn glazed. His lips part as a sigh of pure bliss escapes him. I can't help but notice his naked cock growing in size until it's poking Cal's stomach. A strange, pink mist emits from Pussy Man's open mouth and enters Cal's. With every drag, color returns to Cal's cheeks and his hair becomes glossier and fuller.

The monster's face begins to shrivel until the bones are visible through the papery, yellow skin. Panic flitters to life in Pussy Man's jaundiced yellow eyes, but when he finally tries to fight back, his movements are weak and half-hearted. In almost slow motion, his skin begins to flake off in tiny particles, collecting in a pile by his feet. Soon, he's nothing but bones.

Cal is panting, his wings fluttering behind him as he stares down at the dismembered body.

"Cal?" I whisper, uncharacteristically frightened. Of him.

He smiles, slow and seductive, as his dimples appear in both of his cheeks. "They wanted to make me a monster, so a monster they shall get."

Dammit. My stomach is totally fluttering right now, and it's no longer in a "I want to piss myself in fear" type of way. It's more of a "psycho is a sexy look on him" way.

"Are you okay?" Cal kneels beside me, surveying me with a disconcerting intensity. I feel small and delicate compared to his broad-shouldered frame.

"It's not every day that a pussy tries to poison me," I slur, still feeling the effects of said poison. I know it'll only be a few more minutes until my vampire healing kicks in and boots the toxin out of my system.

"Come on." Cal jumps to his feet and easily scoops me up, carrying me as if I'm a toddler. "I think we found what we were looking for."

"The portal?" I inquire, my eyelids drooping. Still, I force myself to follow the direction of his gaze to see room number 69 and the initials VD. Funny, Dimitri. Real fucking funny.

"What the fuck happened!" Vin appears from around the corner, Frankie and Mason on his heels. His eyes flicker from the hounds and centaur to the rapidly decaying skeleton and then to me in Cal's arms. Rage flares to life in his dark eyes as he takes a threatening step forward. "Give her to me."

Cal surprises me by growling. No lie. Actual, honest-to-fuck growling. He twists his body slightly to keep me hidden from the other men's prying gazes.

"*Mine*," he bites out in an inarticulate voice as he sets me on my feet.

Vin freezes automatically, something flashing in his hooded gaze too quickly for me to see. He raises his hands slowly, almost placatingly, as he ventures another step forward. Mason and Frankie do the same, the former appearing confused and the latter as impassive as ever.

"We're not going to hurt her," Vin says slowly, one foot extended. Cal releases a hiss of air and drags us both backwards, stopping when my back is flush against the wall. He continues to huddle his body protectively over me, almost as if he considers the other three men threats. "But we need to go through the portal."

"*Mine.*"

"Um…" I tap his shoulder impatiently, ignoring Vin's warning shake of the head. "I'm not yours. I'm not anyone's. If anything, you guys are all mine. So, ha."

Cal freezes before slowly, mechanically, turning his head to meet my eyes. "Yours?" His hand trails almost reverently down my cheek before cupping my jaw—in a completely platonic and friendly move, of course. "You're beautiful. The most beautiful girl alive."

"Look, beauty is a concept constructed completely by society, and therefore cannot be measured, because different people have different opinions," I babble. "And regardless of the definition, it cannot be quantified, so beauty can't be accurately compared."

I have a serious case of foot-in-mouth disease.

This is why my father disowned me.

"Come on," Mason says, shooting me an amused smirk. I bite down on my lip to keep from sticking my tongue out at him like a petulant five-year-old. "Let's go home."

Home.

At one point, that thought would've made warm flurries spring to life in my stomach. But now, it only makes me feel cold and empty. How can we go back to the Academy without Barret? How can we pretend that we're okay when a piece of us is dead?

I know Cal is on the same wavelength as I am when he tightens his arms almost imperceptibly around me.

Vin, dagger raised, opens the door Pussy Man was blocking. A glimmering portal—shining like the stars themselves have been plucked from the sky and tossed into a swirling vortex—takes up the entirety of the room.

"We need to wait for Hux and Jack," I say defiantly, crossing my arms over my chest and adopting a fierce scowl. I know the effect is lost on the others when Cal begins to rock me like a baby.

The guys exchange an eloquent look before, as one, they nod.

"No can do, Pinkie!" Mason says cheerfully, skipping up beside Cal and pecking me on the nose. "Hux will roast us over a fire if we allow you to stay."

"You can't make me leave," I growl, unveiling my fangs. Mason's expression only appears more amused.

"Actually, we can."

Before I can protest, Vin sidles up to my other side and plucks me out of Cal's arms. Then, he tosses me forward.

Directly into the portal.

CHAPTER 33

I'm spit out onto the Academy's grounds in an undignified heap. Of course, the portal fucking hates me and decides to drop me down face first. And since my mouth was already open in a silent scream, I end up with a mouthful of dry dirt.

Cursing Vin to hell and back, I stagger to my feet to the enthusiastic cheers of the assembled crowd. Those jovial cries abruptly fade away like a candle flame being blown out when they get their first look at who actually popped out of the portal. The silence is stifling—uncanny, almost—as I face the crowd with an imperious set to my chin. It feels as if I'm naked, their scrutiny flaying open my skin until my bones and tendons are revealed.

Dimitri Gray leans against the wall with an almost insouciant slump. When he sees me, he straightens and smooths out his crisp black suit. Stalking forward, he grabs my hand and raises it into the air, a smirk on those delectably wicked lips.

"Violet Dracula has completed Round One of The Roaring!" he declares into the stunned silence. I really should be offended. Half of the audience appears livid, as if they had hoped I would die in the games, while the other half seems genuinely confused, almost as if they can't possibly believe that someone like me would win. Fuck them all. Anger swarms in my stomach as if a thousand angry bees have been released. I take a deep, calming breath, attempting to regulate my emotions before they explode out of me.

The portal behind me sparks and fizzles, and a moment later, Vin gracefully rolls out, ending in a crouched position with his blade still clutched firmly in his hand.

This time, the audience continues to cheer when Dimitri steps up beside him, takes his hand, and declares, "Vin Van Helsing has completed Round One of The Roaring!" Vin studiously ignores me, his eyes flickering to a group of men and women alike who are chanting his name. Other Van Helsings and hunters, if their blood-thirsty eyes are any indication. With one last furtive glance in my direction, noting the rage emanating from my eyes, he stalks towards his family with a raised chin and patronizing smirk.

Asshole.

Condescending, sexy asshole.

How dare he shove me through the portal without my consent? How dare he? My anger continues to fester inside of me, thrumming through me like a wire of electricity.

Mason, Frankie, and Cal soon follow, one after the other. Mason flashes the crowd a cocky grin as Dimitri announces his name to the masses. I can't help but notice an abnormally tall woman near the front of the crowd bedecked in a gown of pure silver, snakes hissing and curling around her head. Is that…Medusa? Mason's mother? She's the only audience member who isn't smiling, her lips compressed into a grim line. When she catches me staring, her eyes turn from haughty to livid, pure malice dripping from her as venomous as the poison from her snakes. She looks at me as if I killed her puppy.

"We did it, Pinkie!" Mason cheers with a whoop, racing towards me and lifting me in his arms. He spins me around twice before reluctantly placing me back on my feet.

I try to offer him a feeble smile, but it's forced. I honestly don't know how to feel right now. My emotions are turbulent and erratic. A part of me wants to curl into a ball and sob, my grief for Barret nearly palpable. I haven't fallen apart yet, but that only means the crash is inevitable. You can't lose someone you care about without severe ramifications. And intertwined with my grief is a need for vengeance so strong and staggering that I feel physically sick. I want to find Alex and his sick, sadistic father and kill them both. I want them to feel every ounce of pain and fear Barret did as he died. I want them to scream for relief—relief only I can give them. I want to be their fucking angel of death.

Finally, I feel immense and cloying worry. I have no idea where Hux and Jack are, if they have made it back yet, if they're still coming. I pray that they heard Dimitri's ominous statement towards me before I was pushed through the portal. What if they didn't make it to the hospital in time? What if they were injured?

Panic pulses through me, and the only thing keeping me from completely succumbing to insanity is the knowledge that they're still alive. I don't know how to explain it, but I know innately that they're still alive and well. I can feel their presence like a ball of light, hovering just at the edge of my awareness. I'm certain I could reach for it if I needed to, could caress it and let them know of my presence.

Is it…?

Is it because we're mates?

Before that lone, traitorous thought can get traction,

Dimitri grabs my arm and begins to drag me towards the Academy's entrance.

"What the hell?" I gripe, craning my neck to stare back at the others. Cal is nowhere to be seen, but Mason and Frankie are staring after me with knowing expressions. I don't see Vin, but I have no doubt he's watching me, despite being hounded by his fan club. And no, I'm not salty, thank you very much. I have a fan club too. It's just a different type. Mine is more of a "death to Violet Dracula" club. Pretty sure they have matching t-shirts with my face on them and a large red X slicing through the image.

"We need to talk." His words are domineering, succinct almost. The crisp nature of them matches his immaculate appearance.

"Can't we talk around witnesses?" I babble as he drags me down the hallway and towards his office. "You know, in case you murder me and hide my body?"

I don't actually believe he's going to murder me, but a girl can never be too careful.

"If I wanted you dead, you wouldn't be standing here right now." He turns his head slightly to stare at me with those frosty blue eyes of his. I gulp at the intensity of his gaze before ducking my head in an admittedly submissive move.

When we reach his office, I'm surprised that his secretary is nowhere to be seen. At my curious expression, he states, "I gave Miss Birdy the week off to watch the games."

"Oh…that's surprisingly nice of you." I follow him into his office with only a little trepidation. Again, it's not because I think he's going to hurt me, but because everything about Dimitri confuses the shit out of me. He's the epitome of contradictions—one second, he's hot, and the next, he's ice cold. I have no idea where I stand with him and what he even wants from me.

"I'm not a monster, Ms. Dracula," he purrs, leaning against his desk with his arms crossed and legs extended.

"Technically, we're all monsters." I move to sit opposite him, the position allowing him to tower over me. I don't feel any fear, however. Just safety.

Which is ridiculous, because Dimitri is the most dangerous fucker around and can possibly kill me with his pinkie finger.

And...

Now, I'm imagining my headmaster repeatedly jabbing me with his pinkie finger until I fall to the ground covered in bloody welts.

"I see that you listened to me for once," he states in his deep, baritone voice that slides through me like whiskey. I know immediately he's talking about his advice to travel to the hospital.

"Next time you want to help, could you be a little more clear?" I raise a single eyebrow at him, and his face pinches together. "Maybe slide me a note? Send up a smoke signal?"

"That would be cheating." His frown deepens. "And I'm prohibited by magic to cheat."

"Then why did you...? Oh." Understanding causes my eyes to widen slightly. "That's why you were being all vague and shit."

"I was being as concise as possible." His nose scrunches slightly, as if he has smelled something pungent. "I'm just grateful you listened to me."

My good mood instantly sours as pain spears my chest.

"Barret didn't make it," I whisper hoarsely, the agony of that simple statement suffocating me.

"That's a shame." Despite his words, Dimitri's expression remains carefully blank and apathetic. That only exacerbates my rage, and I shoot to my feet with anger tightening my chest.

"You don't give a shit, do you?" I take a step closer, my pulse skittering at both his proximity and my own anger. "You don't care that someone died." It's not a question.

"People die all the time." He stares down his nose at me, expression unreadable. "You may not be familiar with death yet, but you'll have to learn. Death will follow you everywhere, Violet Dracula."

"Is that a threat?" I ask, my fangs lengthening in response to his words.

"It's a promise." His cold eyes ensnare my own, and I'm helpless to look away. "But I also promise to protect you. I'm..." His face twists before settling into a grimace. "I'm sorry for your loss."

"People apologize about death when they have nothing else to say." This close, his peppermint scent curls around me, warming my body. "But you're not sorry. Not really. I think...I think you're happy that he died and not me." I gauge his reaction carefully, unsurprised to see no change in his expression. Still, I know that to be the truth. Dimitri will not hesitate to let the other men die if it means keeping me safe. But what I need to know is... "Why?"

"Why does the sun rise and fall? Why is the grass green and the sky blue? Why do we all inevitably face death? Why are only some of us granted immortality? Why? That is the question, isn't it? It's the only word that encompasses every thought one may possess."

"Dimitri, don't fuck around with me." My teeth are clenched so tightly, I'm afraid I'll chip them. "I want answers."

He ducks his head until my entire vision is consumed by him. His heady, distinct scent surrounds me completely, consuming me from the inside out. It's impossible to turn away from his icy, ethereal beauty—his unattainable beauty, as if he's some god and I'm a besotted peasant.

"Emotions are fickle things, Violet Dracula," he says, his voice a decadent treat that I want to devour. "Why is your heart breaking? Why do you feel anxious? It's because you have emotions. It's because you care."

"Are you saying you care about me?" I breathe, though I shouldn't be surprised. Dimitri has proved to me over and over again that I'm different from the other students. But it all circles back to my original question, "Why?"

Why me?

Why now?

"Maybe you should focus less on what I'm saying…" His finger trails up my arm, leaving goosebumps in its wake. He softly caresses my neck and then my cheek before outlining my lips with the pad of his thumb. "And more on what I'm not saying."

"I don't like riddles, Dimitri," I hiss, just barely holding in my moan. "Use your words like a big boy."

Dimitri's eyes harden, and I fear that I pushed him too far, too fast. He leans over me, but I find that I don't cower away in fear. Instead, I hold his gaze defiantly, watching the ice in his eyes begin to crack.

He leans forward and kisses me.

Maybe "kisses" is too tame of a term. Dimitri devours me as if he's starving and I'm the only meal available. His lips claim my own ruthlessly and possessively, his teeth biting down on my bottom lip hard enough to draw blood. His hands go to my ass and cup both cheeks, pressing me against his straining erection.

Oh. My. Fuck.

I'm making out with Dimitri Gray.

He grabs my hips and lifts me clean off my feet, spinning me around until my ass is on his desk. Throughout it all, his lips don't leave mine, his tongue tangling with my own.

His hands grab the front of my shirt and rip it down the

middle. Immediately, his lips travel to the crest of my breasts revealed above my sports bra, sucking and licking at the sensitive skin.

In that moment, he's no longer made of ice. He's completely and utterly fire. Everywhere he touches, I burn.

He pulls down one of my straps, my tit springing free, and wastes no time taking the tip into his mouth. It's brutal and intense, everything I've always known Dimitri Gray to be. He releases my nipple with an audible pop before immediately giving the same treatment to the other one. His tongue circles the sensitive tip but never touches as he stares up at me from beneath his sooty lashes. When I try to reach for him, try to tangle my hands in his white blond hair, he grabs my wrists with a growl.

"No," he hisses, pushing my hands away and shoving his thumbs into my shorts and panties. He pulls them both down, the material ripping with his agitated movements. With a tenderness contradicting the feral need in his eyes, he drops to his knees between my legs.

Oh. My. Fuck.

I'm about to get oral from Dimitri Gray.

Maintaining eye contact, his tongue swipes up my slit before circling around my bundle of nerves. My eyes practically roll to the back of my head as white-hot liquid pleasure courses through me.

"Fuck, yes," I moan, throwing my head back. The move inadvertently pushes out my breasts, and he wastes no time in kneading the flesh with the hand not holding my thighs apart.

And then, he shoves his face into my dripping pussy and destroys me. I'm pretty sure I've died and gone to heaven as he sucks, licks, and kisses my aching mound. When he adds two fingers beside his tongue, scissoring them, I can't hold back the scream of pure ecstasy as I throw my head back, tears burning my eyes. My orgasm rushes through me like molten lava, and it takes all of my tenuous self-control not to proclaim Dimitri as the Oral God.

When I finally come down from my high, he has a smug smirk on his lips and his eyes are heated. My arousal drips down his chin, but he easily catches the escaped drops with his long, skilled tongue.

And, fuck, if that isn't the sexiest thing I've ever seen before.

When he stands, the outline of his cock is clearly visible through the material of his dress pants.

"Let me—" I reach forward, but he stealthily sidesteps me.

"You should get back to the others." He straightens his tie before running a hand through his meticulously brushed hair. In all the time I've known him, I've never seen it out of his customary ponytail. A part of me wants to see it loose and free, framing his face. That part of me wants to see him lose control for the first time in his life.

"What about…?" I nod once more towards his cock.

"That's my problem," he says crisply, eyes narrowing. And I know that he has once more reverted back to his glacial persona. I can't help but feel immense sadness, which is utterly insane. He's nothing but an asshole, and I'm just the idiot who fell for his charm.

"You going to find someone else to fuck?" I snap, unable to contain the jealousy that percolates in my stomach. His grin widens, revealing perfectly white teeth. The teeth of a predator…designed to lure you in and then bite your head off.

"Would that make you jealous, Violet Dracula?" he questions, taking a step closer. Something about hearing him say my full name causes lightning to burst through my veins. But I'll be damned if I let that show.

"Nope. No jealousy. None whatsoever."

I'm totally not jealous. If he wants to have sex with a different girl, I'll just...cut her into tiny pieces and then feast on her blood. And then, when she's begging for mercy, I'll chop up her pussy and feed it to the dogs. Dimitri? I'll cut his dick into perfect curds and force feed him every bite.

Totally not jealous.

"Fortunately for you, this problem can be resolved with my hand," he states curtly, eyes glinting with mischief.

My pussy immediately turns wet again at the thought of him touching himself while thinking of me. Shameless hussy.

"It wouldn't be the first time," I say, remembering the intoxicating scene at the club. I have no doubt that Dimitri ran away to rub one off while I sucked Frankie.

His hand tenderly, almost reverently, cups my cheek before lowering towards my breast. His thumb flicks over my pointed nipple before lowering to my aching pussy. He cups it harshly, his fingers lightly tracing my lips, before releasing me.

"You drive me insane." Despite his words, his tone has absolutely zero inflection. He could've been speaking about something as mundane as the weather.

"You still haven't answered why," I whisper as he brings his fingers to his lips and licks the juices from them. His tongue trails around first one finger and then the other, his eyes never leaving my own.

Those fingers better go back inside my pussy pronto, or else I fear I might spontaneously combust.

"The next game is tomorrow," he states nonchalantly as he once more captures my breast. His finger lightly trails around my aching nub, never touching me where I so desperately need him to. Finally, when I swear I'm going to die of frustration, he lightly grazes my nipple with the pad of his thumb.

"You're avoiding my question," I gasp as his other hand

lowers to my aching pussy again, circling the juices around my clit.

"Remember what I said—you should focus less on what I'm saying, and more on what I'm not saying."

"You're such an ass." My hands grip his shoulders to keep myself steady as he pinches down lightly on my bundle of nerves. This time, my orgasm is slower as it rushes to the surface, almost like lava in a volcano. It swirls and percolates before steadily rising and then exploding. I bite down on his shoulder, rumpling his pristine black suit, but he doesn't seem to care.

Dimitri steps back, once more smooths down his suit, before turning on his heel and exiting the office.

"What the…? Get the fuck back here!" I scream, stomping my foot. And then, "I have no fucking clothes, asshole! How am I supposed to get back to my dorm?"

CHAPTER 34

VIN

I sit with the other hunters on the uncomfortable steel bleachers, tension thrumming through my body as I glance repeatedly in the direction Violet disappeared to with Dimtiri Gray.

"Your parents are fighters. They'll be fine," Michelle—a fellow Van Helsing and my first cousin—states, patting my knee sympathetically. Obviously, she's misread my agitation, but I'm not going to correct her. She can believe what she wants…as long as Violet is nowhere near her radar.

"They'll be fine," I parrot mechanically, but internally, I'm wishing for the exact opposite. Is it fucked up that I don't care if my parents return to me alive? They're abusive and cruel fuckers who care nothing for their children. I'm fortunate that their ire only seems to be directed at me and not Vanessa. I wouldn't be able to handle it if my twin got stuck in the crosshairs of their incandescent rage, capable of lighting entire buildings on fire.

I wouldn't admit this to anyone—not even Violet—but

I'm also worried about Jack and Hux. Where the fuck are they? Violet will sever my balls if they don't return. And...I sort of like the ornery, two-faced bastard. Bastards? I still don't know the correct terminology.

The portal shimmers brightly before a familiar monster steps out, chin raised imperiously into the air.

Mr. Pumpkin, one of the professors, steps up to Cheryl Ness and grabs her blue-skinned hand in his.

He clears his throat awkwardly, obviously uncomfortable with giving the speech in Dimitri's absence, and screams raggedly, "Cheryl Ness has completed the first round of the Roaring!"

The audience immediately erupts into raucous cheers as Cheryl bows, a shit-eating grin on her face. When she meets my gaze, she winks flirtatiously, and I seriously try not to vomit in my mouth. What did I ever see in her? Besides, obviously, a quick and easy fuck.

Some people believe that women are the only ones who are ruthlessly and persistently pursued, but that's not true. Some women have just as much trouble hearing "no" as men do. Her behavior sickens me, especially when she makes an immediate beeline towards the bleachers and squeezes her dainty body between Michelle and me.

When she places a manicured hand on my knee, I just about explode.

"What the fuck do you think you're doing?" I hiss out of the corner of my mouth.

Her body tenses, eyes hardening, but her smile remains pasted in place. "I thought I was doing you a favor, Vinny Poo." Her nails tighten on my thigh until blood is drawn. I don't bother reacting to the brief stab of pain. After all, I'm used to it.

"A favor?" I scoff. "You're pathetic."

"Really?" She finally turns away from the portal to face

me directly. "What would your family think when they discover that you left me for Dracula's daughter?" Her tone is laced with barely disguised horror. "And—" She cuts off suddenly as my Aunt Petunia waddles towards us, her pregnant belly straining beneath her floral shirt. "Petunia, darling! It's been way too long!" Cheryl air kisses both of the woman's cheeks. "How's the little one?"

As the two begin to converse, I take the opportunity to rip Cheryl's claws off of me.

"I'm going to piss," I snap when my ex's eyes narrow into slits. Before Aunt Petunia can catch a glimpse of her hideous expression, she smooths it out and replaces it with a serene smile.

"Hurry back, Vinny Poo!" She waves her hand enthusiastically as I hurry down the bleachers and away from the portal.

"Hurry back, Vinny Poo," I mock as I press my forehead against the brick siding of the Academy. Each breath seems to be wrenched from my lungs as I struggle to regain control of my turbulent emotions. All I want is to be with Violet right now, to ensure with my own two eyes that she's safe and well. How is she coping after Barret's death? What is Dimitri saying to her?

I'll be the first to admit that I'm slightly overprotective of the tiny vampire. Okay, *slightly* is the wrong term. I'll go psychotic if anything happens to her, especially at the hands of my own family members. She's my mate, my…my love. At least, I think I love her. Is this what love is?

"I don't want to hear it," a familiar voice snaps. I lift my head just in time to see Mason charge around the corner, Medusa on his heels.

"She's going to be the death of you," his mom hisses, teeth bared. "I refuse to allow that."

"Refuse?" Mason releases a self-deprecating laugh. "Since

when have you ever cared about me? Violet is the best fucking thing that has ever happened to me." He spins to face his mother completely, rage etched into every line of his face. "So you can kindly fuck off." His hand trembling slightly, he removes a joint from his pocket and quickly shoves it between his lips. With his other hand, he grabs a lighter, and the distinct scent of Fairy Blossom permeates the air, making me sick. I've always hated that shit. Not as much as Violet, but enough for me to stay clear of it when I'm not at parties. I consider myself a social smoker, but Mason? He's addicted. Already, I can see his time in the arena has made him shaky and unhinged.

"Violet Dracula is a menace that must be stopped," Medusa continues, gracefully striding forward. She's abnormally tall for a woman, and unlike her son, dozens of snakes slither around her head. She's not ashamed or embarrassed of who she is, which is something I can admire. Her words, however, make me want to stab the bitch.

My body coils as tightly as the serpents on her head as I remain in the shadows, both of them oblivious to my presence.

"She's my mate." Mason's voice is as dark as I've ever heard it. Pure venom laces his words, more potent than any of Medusa's little beasts.

"She's predicted to murder you." She takes another step forward, but this one feels more threatening than any of the others. When her hands wrap around Mason's throat, I just barely stop myself from lunging forward and ripping her away. "The prophecy said that Dracula's daughter is fated to be your death."

"Violet would never hurt me," Mason wheezes out, clawing at her hands. After a moment, she releases him with a rather disgruntled huff.

"Either you get rid of her...or I will." With that threat, she turns on her heel and stalks away, her silver skirt cascading around her like molten starlight. Mason remains behind, panting. His eyes are wild as he tentatively touches the bruises now dotting his pasty neck.

I clear my throat once, and he jumps, startled. The joint falls from his lips, and he quickly stomps it out.

"How long have you been there?" He doesn't sound upset, only resigned. His shoulders droop ever so slightly as he scrubs a hand down his face.

"Is she going to be a problem?" I ask instead. The thought of anyone harming Violet is inconceivable. Friend's mom or not, I won't hesitate to do what needs to be done to ensure her safety.

"I'll take care of her," Mason promises, tone bleak.

"I don't like this." A chill that's not from the wind sweeps across my skin, causing goosebumps to pebble on my arms. Medusa is, for lack of better term, a goddess. If she sets her eyes on eliminating Violet...

No. That can't happen. I won't allow it to. I will set fire to Mount Olympus before anyone harms a golden strand of hair on Violet's perfect head.

"I'm worried about her," Mason admits after a moment of silence. His eyes flicker up to mine before quickly lowering again. The tick in his jaw commandeers my attention. "Barret's death destroyed her. I don't even think she's realized it yet, but she will. Soon. I'm worried what she will do."

"What if Hux and Jack don't make it back?" I query, staring in contemplation in the direction of the portal and crowd. From this angle, I can't see them, but I can hear their cheers as more and more monsters fall through the portal. So far, they've been no one I know.

Which only makes me even more anxious.

"They'll be fine," Mason assures me softly. He finally closes the distance between us to clasp my shoulder. "They're tough sons of bitches. As is Vanessa." He stares at me pointedly, easily able to read me after years of friendship.

"I haven't always been the best brother to her," I admit, staring off into the distance like I'm in some kind of cheesy romantic comedy. Fuck my life.

"Are you talking about the time you cut off the balls of that one dude who cheated on her?" Mason questions seriously, and I wince. That wasn't one of my finest moments. "Or, are you talking about that Christmas when we were ten and you stole all her presents and threw them in a fire? Or the time you tied her up and put her on the table during Thanksgiving and told everyone she was the new turkey? Or the—"

"I get it!" I snap, raking my fingers through my dark hair. "I've been a shitty brother."

"Nah, man. You've been a *brother*." Once more, Mason pats my shoulder. "I love the little turd like a sister too." He sighs, following the direction of my gaze towards the waning sunlight. It isn't quite night yet, so the sky is painted in shades of orange and dark blue. "There's still hours until the first round ends. How about we go find Violet instead of driving ourselves crazy with worry, m'kay?"

Violet...

I need to see her. Need to hold her. Need her to promise me that everything will be alright. How is it that one slip of a girl managed to upheave my entire life? She barged into my world like an out-of-control freight train and quickly became my new one. A part of me resents her for how reliant I've become, but the rest of me is only grateful she deemed me worthy enough to be called her boyfriend.

The other hunters would call our relationship horrendous. I've never felt the need to atone for my sins before, but being with her? Loving her? That's the gravest sin of all, and one I unapologetically embrace. I don't need to gain penance for caring about her. It's the one thing I'll never apologize for.

"Let's go comfort our girl," I say, slinging my arm around Mason's shoulder.

I can only pray that Violet's demons aren't too much for her to handle.

CHAPTER 35

A knock on the door startles me out of my reverie.

It took me way too fucking long to find a suitable outfit when I left Dimitri's office. Knowing my clothes were beyond saving, I ripped the curtain from the rod and wrapped it haphazardly around my body. Honestly, Dimitri Gray is such a little shit. Now, I'm back in my room, cursing him to hell and back.

When the knock sounds again, I release a growl of frustration, padding on bare feet towards the door. I have changed into my favorite light pink skirt and black tank-top, the material my armor and my sword against whatever the world throws at me.

I push open the door, my eyes immediately landing on two handsome faces. Mason is leaning against the doorframe nonchalantly, face uncharacteristically pale and shadows beneath both his eyes, while Vin is staring down at me with a tight-lipped scowl.

Or, more accurately, at the baby on my hip.

"It's been a long time," I whisper meekly.

Mason finally chances a glance up, his eyes widening in alarm when he catches sight of me and the baby.

"Oh for the love of…" Vin trails off, pinching the bridge of his nose. "Violet, it has been less than an hour."

"A lot has changed," I respond despondently. I glance at the baby's chubby face before resting my gaze on Vin. "You're not the father."

"Of course I'm not the father!" he snaps, forking his fingers through his pitch black hair. "Is this because I shoved you through the portal? Did your petty ass really kidnap a baby to prove a point?"

I turn towards Mason, who is flashing me a cocksure grin, eyes dancing with mirth.

"Mason is the father," I announce proudly, and Vin's fingers tighten even more on his nose. At this point, I'm pretty sure he's trying to break it.

And he calls *me* dramatic.

"Hell, yes!" Mason fist pumps the air. "My sperm is so badass, it doesn't even need to enter a vagina to work its magic."

"Zeus, have mercy," Vin mutters under his breath. Releasing his nose, he levels me with a penetrating glare. "Violet, love, did you kidnap a baby from the hospital?"

"Of course not!" I protest indignantly. "I stole the little guy from a supermarket. Finders keepers."

At his look of horror, I drop the act and release a heavy sigh.

"I'm just fucking with you. This is Cynthia's little brother. I'm just watching him for her as she finishes getting ready for her date."

"Do you know how long it took me to find my D-sized boobs?" Cynthia exclaims as she sidles up beside me. Despite taking the last half hour to dress and do her hair and makeup, Cynthia looks the exact fucking same as before. I honestly can't see any difference. The same sheet of black, tangled hair. The same pale face and slightly yellow eyes. The same too-sharp teeth in a too-small mouth. The same flowing white dress that swishes with every step she takes.

Without a word, Cynthia takes the baby from my arms and begins to rock him back and forth.

"I'll drop him back off to my parents," she states. "Thanks for watching him."

"Yeah…" I can't help the wistful sigh that escapes me as I watch her disappear. Honestly, I have no idea what the fuck is wrong with me. It's not that I want kids anytime soon, but I think the possibility that I might never be able to have them is really hitting me hard. If what Diedre Stevens said is true, I'm not even a vampire, let alone Dracula's daughter. So what am I? Can I even reproduce? What if I die before I get pregnant or married? Why am I having such morose thoughts today? Is it because Bar—

Nope. Not going there.

"You're the strangest creature I've ever met," Vin deadpans as he steps into my small dorm, Mason at his heel. With another sigh, I move to sit back on the bed and hug a pillow to my chest.

"What's wrong, Pinkie?" Mason moves to sit beside me while Vin remains standing, his arms folded over his chest.

"What's wrong?" I release a bark of humorless laughter, throwing my head back. "What isn't wrong is the better question. Barret's dead. I'm apparently some sort of fucked up monster. Dracula is avoiding me—and he might not even be my dad. I have a bunch of monsters who want to kill me just because I have vampire blood in my system. And I might never be able to have a fucking baby!" I'm panting by the time I finish my spiel, but fortunately, there are no tears in my eyes. I know that the second I start crying, I won't be able to stop, and I can't have that. I need to be strong, if only for a moment.

Brows cinching, Mason asks, "You want…a baby?" He looks as if he's going to be sick.

"No! I mean, not anytime soon." I'm rambling—which is never a good sign. It means I'm closer to losing my wits than I initially believed. "I just want the option, and I might not have that because apparently, I'm fucked up. Did you know that? Did you? I'm fucked up, even in the monster world. F to the U to the C to the—"

"We get it," Vin interrupts, tone scathing. Eyes heated, he lunges forward until he captures my wrists in both of his hands, slowly lifting them until they're above my head. "But why the fuck do you keep saying that about yourself? I don't like it when you refer to yourself like that." Fire blazes in his eyes as he surveys me from head to toe. My chest heaves as if he is physically undressing me, one piece of clothing at a time.

Mason lazily begins to trace my collarbone. "You're not fucked up, Violet," he whispers, and you know shit just got real when he uses my real name. His hand lowers until it's cupping my breast, his thumb twisting my nipples through both my shirt and bra. His boyish smile makes him look innocent, but his chiseled jawline, broad shoulders, and prominent cheekbones make him appear anything but.

"You're perfect," Vin growls, leaning over me until I'm forced to fall on my back. "You're a goddess, and the world's too fucking dumb to see you as one."

"You're biased," I point out as his tongue lowers to my neck, trailing upwards until it reaches the edges of my lips. I lift my chin, emulating the confident woman I've always wanted to be. And also giving him more space to worship me with those wicked lips of his.

"You don't see yourself the way we see you," he breathes, breath fanning against my parted lips.

"And how do you see me?" I'm barely breathing, my entire focus fixated on both the beautiful man in front of me and the second beautiful man beside me. My shoulders physically deflate as if a heavy rain washed away all of the tension.

"As someone to be loved and cherished," he whispers before crashing his lips to mine. I moan low in my throat as his addictive taste bombards my senses, momentarily making me lose my mind. But I don't want his sweet kisses. Not now. I want to punish him for making me leave Jack and Hux behind. For allowing me to live when Barret didn't. For breaking my heart at the Halloween party those many weeks ago, when he disappeared with Cheryl instead of protecting me.

I bite down on his lip hard enough to draw blood before immediately licking it away, his flavor exploding on my tongue. Releasing him, I turn my head to the side to kiss Mason. As always, he's an enthusiastic kisser, putting all of his passion and emotions into the heated kiss. Our tongues tangle together as he tugs my hair to the point of pain. Pulling away from him, I turn back towards Vin and resume where we left off. I know he can taste Mason on my lips, but that only heightens my arousal. My core is throbbing, desperate for what only these two men can give me.

I want to be punished.

I want to feel pain.

"Have you two ever...?" I gesture between the two of them, vivid images assaulting me. Mason pulling Vin into a fervent kiss, their lips clashing just as their personalities do. Their hands roaming each other's bodies. Their cocks rubbing against each other with each clash of their lips.

"Head out of gutter, Pinkie!" Mason says, gently whacking me on the back of the head. "Not happening."

"Not even a teeny tiny little kiss?" I ask, pushing out my bottom lip in a pout. Vin and Mason exchange a glance over my shoulder, and I swear I stop breathing. I can feel my arousal dampen my panties as a sultry grin pulls up Mason's lush lips.

"One kiss, you say…" he whispers, crawling towards Vin. He runs his hands up his muscular thighs, his chest, and then his broad shoulders. Vin lowers his hands to Mason's back… and then lowers them some more until they're inches above his rock-hard ass.

They lean towards each other, eyes closed, and I rub my thighs together to alleviate the ache. I'm panting as if I've just run a million miles.

When their lips are a hair's breadth apart, they turn towards me at the same time and begin to pepper kisses on either side of my neck, chuckling darkly.

"Not happening, Pinkie," Mason says as he suckles my skin. Vin twists my face to recapture my lips, his tongue prodding the seam before I finally relent and open my mouth to him.

"Tease," I breathe against Vin's lips.

In answer, he merely resumes his brutal kisses while his hand cups and squeezes my breast.

"But just because we won't play with each other…" Mason murmurs.

"Doesn't mean we won't both play with you," finishes Vin. And sweet merciful Zeus, I swear I cream my panties right then and there.

"What type of play are we talking about?" I pant as Mason's hand feathers underneath my shirt, across my stomach, and up to my chest. He begins to knead my tit through the lacy material of my bra, lips curved into a bewitching, sensuous smirk. "Jump rope play? Hopscotch? Uno?"

"What the fuck, Violet?" Vin murmurs as he plants kisses

up and down my neck. When he reaches my ear, he grabs the lobe between his teeth and bites down gently. "You're so strange."

"I'm only strange because you're too normal," I counter immediately. Before I can claim Vin's lips once more, a whine reverberates through the room. All three of us freeze, only our heads moving to stare at the closed door.

"Is it our baby?" Mason teases, finger idly drawing circles on my chest.

"Shut up." I elbow him as the whine sounds again, followed immediately by incessant scratching. I make a move to get up, but Vin places a hand on my chest to push me back down and strides across the room, the evidence of his arousal poking through his gym shorts. He grabs his blade that he must've put on my dresser and wrenches open the door.

"Biscuit?" Mason exclaims, sitting upright and staring at the hideous mutt outside my dorm room door. The creature tilts his furry black head to the side, rivulets of color sludging down his back. He looks as if he has been through the meat-grinder, his ears torn and riddled with holes. His amber eyes train on me as another desperate whine escapes his body.

"You named the mutt from hell Biscuit?" I query as the creature, ignoring Vin entirely, gallops into the room, jumps onto my bed, and curls into a ball near my feet. His tongue lolls out of his mouth, and I can't help but notice it's a hideous shade of gray.

"He seems to like you," Mason points out as Biscuit chirps happily.

Oh my freaking god. He is adorable.

"Can I keep him? Please? Please? Please?" I scratch him behind his tattered ears, and he leans into my touch, body vibrating with his contented purr.

"Violet…" For the millionth time that day, Vin pinches the bridge of his nose. "You can't just keep a murderous Frankenstein-created beast as your pet."

"But he's sooo cute." I press a kiss to his furry nose. To the beast, I ask, "Where are your brothers? Did they come too?"

"She said she wanted a baby," Mason points out with a wicked grin. He leans around me to pet Biscuit's rough hide.

"Why do I even bother with these children?" Vin murmurs, more to himself than to us. I'll have him know that I'm extremely mature and intelligent for my age, thank you very much. And because I'm so mature, I'm going to refrain from sticking my tongue out at him and then slicing open his throat to drink his blood dry.

Mature Violet for the win.

Abruptly, Biscuit begins to cough, eyes widening slightly in his distorted face. Mason grimaces as a slimy beetle flies from the hound's mouth and bounces off the wall.

"Ewww," he laments, nose scrunching in disgust.

"Did you eat a beetle, handsome man?" I coo to the dog. "Silly puppy."

"It's a monstrous, fifty-pound beast of mass destruction," Vin deadpans. "*Not* a silly puppy."

Before I can retort, a green mist slithers across the floor of my room like a palpable entity. Immediately, my hackles raise as Mason grabs my waist, pulling me against him.

Vin spins towards the fog with his dagger brandished, eyes spewing vitriol and something akin to fear. "Who's there?" he demands.

Because when the mist comes a'knockin, you go a'runnin.

Yes, that's actually a nursery rhyme in the monster world.

The green mist begins to swirl rapidly like a tornado, and the acid in my stomach sluices around. Slowly, it solidifies into the silhouette of a large, muscular man with broad shoulders and dark skin.

Barret's green hair is wildly mussed as he flashes me a sheepish grin.

"I would highly recommend *not* being eaten by a dog." He pauses, an unsure expression crossing his handsome face. His painfully beautiful, handsome face. His painfully beautiful and *dead* handsome face. "Why are you all looking like you've seen a ghost? Do I have blood on my cheek?"

CHAPTER 36

For as long as I can remember, I never knew what to call the man who created me. Was he my father? My creator? Something else entirely? All I know is that I went from nothing but a thought to a sentient being. In the process, I was gifted with an intelligence that surpassed those around me and an impenetrable body.

Not even a knife to the heart could kill me.

Now, I sit across from my father—my manufacturer?—in the small kitchenette I share with Mason, Vin, Jack, and Hux. He languidly sips from the porcelain teacup while his sharp eyes assess me.

Frankenstein is a sinewy man. Nothing significant about him in the slightest. His hair is beginning to gray, the wispy strands shorter on the top than the sides. A fine, pointy mustache rests above his thin lips, and his eyes are wrinkled with age—not from smiling or laughing. I don't think I've seen the man laugh once in his life. His tan shorts contrast greatly with his plum-colored button up that seems a few sizes too large. The fabric swallows him whole.

Currently, his knee is bouncing with agitation as his eyes flitter from my face to the window and then to the closed door.

As well as being the top scientist in the world, he's also a paranoid maniac. Living for centuries will do that to a person.

"You wanted to talk?" I ask curtly, glaring daggers at my own cup of tea. I have no intentions of actually drinking the liquid. Frankenstein made it himself, and anything that he creates is immensely dangerous—a tree that is being cut down, just waiting to fall and demolish everything in its pathway.

"Are we safe?" Frankenstein queries, jumping to his feet to survey first the windows and then the kitchen itself. He opens up every cupboard and places a strange, silver device on the swinging wooden doors. No doubt, it's one of his newer inventions designed to track for both spells and listening devices.

As I said before, Frankenstein is a paranoid bugger.

Instead of answering, I allow him to sweep every nook and crevice of our quaint kitchen. Only when he's satisfied that there's no one lurking in the closet does he sit back down across from me. He eyes the teacup warily—almost distrustfully—as if someone put poison in it during the few minutes he was away.

"Safe. Yes, safe," he mutters to himself as he grabs the porcelain cup, tips it over, and stares intently at the engraved initials of the artist on the bottom. Hot tea cascades over the edge of the table and hits his lap, but he doesn't even blink at what I'm sure is a blistering sting.

"What did you wish to discuss with me?" I level him with a glare capable of freezing fire. I've always been a cold, unfeeling man. For the longest time, I thought that was all I was capable of being. After all, I'm nothing but an experiment brought to life by a burst of lightning. Only Violet is capable of unthawing the ice surrounding my heart, leaving me feeling warm, and at the same time, bereft. That impassiveness has been my defense mechanism since I was first created. It feels odd to have it suddenly chipped away from me, baring the man underneath. The man I hadn't known existed.

But around my father, I'll remain cold. I'll remain the uncaring, apathetic piece of meat he created in his image. If he knew the truth, that my very genetic makeup was beginning to alter because of the mating bond, he'd lose his shit.

Experiments aren't meant to find their mates, aren't meant to fall in love. We're fated to wander this world as nothing but a machine for the monsters to use and discard. Human consciousness trapped in a body capable of withstanding time itself.

"The beasts you created for the first game were remarkable," I say at last, knowing that flattery is one of the only ways to breach his crazy mind. As expected, he sits up straighter and preens under my praise.

"I spent all year working on them. I see you met a few..." He nods towards the corner of the room where one of his creations stands sentry. For some reason, I haven't been able to shake this monster. The centaur chose to remain in the arena, but the hounds and the man with no face followed me. I have no idea where the mutts disappeared to, but the man remained with me, delegating himself as my servant and protector. I sense no ill intent from any of them, so I'll let them be. For now.

"Yes, well, I have you to thank for that," I reply, refilling his now empty cup. Without allowing it to cool, he brings it to his mouth and chugs it, brown liquid dripping down his chin. I just barely cover up my expression of disgust. "He seems quite fond of me. No doubt, he recognizes pieces of you in me."

Frankenstein waves away my words, grabbing the entire teapot and drinking straight from the nozzle. "You, my dear boy, have done great work as well. I've seen those Violet Dracula dolls and—"

"Those Violet Dracula dolls?" I interrupt, my muscles bunching. I'd thought we eliminated them all. Those sex dolls have been nothing but a nuisance, and I know they've hurt Violet as well. I can't even imagine what she has gone through with the knowledge people have used those dolls for both pain and pleasure. It makes the ice in my stomach turn to molten lava, seconds from bursting and igniting this entire fucking world on fire.

"Why, yes." His brows cinch together in confusion. "You sent one to my office just the other day."

"I did no such thing," I protest immediately, adamantly. When his brows raise even higher, I work to moderate my volume. "I believe there's been some mistake. We've chosen to…discontinue that line."

I don't bother correcting him by saying Mikey—Merlin's dead son—was the one to create those dolls.

"Ridiculous!" Once more, he waves his hand as if he's trying to eradicate my words straight from the air. "They're my top seller. So far, our company has sold over one thousand of those dolls."

Ice sludges in my stomach as his words register. My hands grip the edge of the table until my knuckles are white, nearly translucent.

"Your company decided to make more of them." Though it's not a question, Frankenstein treats it as one.

"Oh, yes. It's good business. Good business." He bobs his

head eagerly, extending a hand as if he's encouraging me to celebrate with him.

"She's innocent, Frankenstein," I manage to grind out through gritted teeth. "A child should not pay for the crimes of their parent."

"Dumb. Dumb. Dumb." With a burp, he drops the teapot back onto the table and wipes his mouth with the back of his hand. "Money is power, and Dracula is money." His shrewd eyes narrow, and I suddenly feel small again. Small and vulnerable, like a forlorn child desperately wanting to please his father. "You care for this vampire?"

"No," I spit out, and I leave it at that.

Frankenstein nods his head once more, turning the cup around and around in his hands.

"A lot is planned for the second game." His head whips up to pierce me with an unreadable look. Just as quickly, he ducks his head and begins to hum softly beneath his breath. "It's going to break you. Break your little vampire. Break the entire monster world."

"What are you talking about?" I sit up straighter, my mind processing this new information. Magically, Frankenstein is prohibited from giving me any details about the next two games. He's quite literally enchanted not to.

So why is he risking his life to tell me this? Is it another trap? Something else entirely?

"Death is coming to us all, my boy," he sings, his low, eerie voice causing goosebumps to skitter up and down my arms. "Because even when you think the games are over...they have only just begun."

JACK

"What is a panty liner?" Hux asks abruptly, and I stumble to a stop. My brother, utterly oblivious, continues walking, and I quicken my pace to catch up.

"W-What?" I stutter out, his murky silhouette nearly indistinguishable. My eyes have somewhat adjusted to the darkness, but I'm still unable to see any of his features. It somehow makes him even more eerie and malevolent—a shadow waiting for its moment to pounce.

And then he goes and says stuff like…

"Panty liner." He pauses, and I nearly plow into him until I manage to catch myself. Slowly, as if speaking to an imbecile, he repeats, "Panty. Liner."

"I heard you the first time." I'm sure my cheeks are on fire. Actually, can I even blush in this disembodied form? Do I even have a body? I suppose it's within the realm of possibilities that if I so desired, I could contort my body in whatever form I wish. Afterall, I'm quite literally nothing but a figment of my brain. "Why are you asking me about a…" I practically choke on my own spit. "Panty liner."

"It was in the pink device," Hux states, as if that explains it all.

"Hux." Honestly, that's all I can say at the moment. Just his name, over and over again.

"The…what's that word…phoney? Violet's."

"So you saw a panty liner in Violet's phone?" I squeeze my eyes shut to fight off the inevitable encroaching headache… before remembering that I don't actually have a body and I sure as frick don't have a head for it to ache. I suppose it's phantom pain from all the times before when I had to deal with Hux's nonsense.

"It was in a speech bubble," Hux continues, almost nonchalantly, as he continues walking. I don't know how long we've been trekking forward, each step taking us farther and farther away from where we saw the portal of light. All I know for certain is that panic grips my heart as I think about the unidentified person currently inhabiting our shared body. Is he with Violet right now? Has he hurt her? Hurt the others? I don't think either of us will be able to forgive ourselves if anything happened to any of them. "Jack, are you listening to me?"

I shake my head vigorously, ignoring the ominous voice in my head warning me that Violet's in imminent danger. I know it's nothing but my own subconscious and anxiety, but a niggle of doubt still remains.

"Sorry, continue, brother."

"Panty liners," he repeats, and I swear if I have to hear my brother say "panty liners" one more time, I'll go insane. Well, more insane than I already am, considering I have his psychopathic butt in my head. "She asked Cynthia to pick some up for her."

"First, why are you going through her phone? That's an

invasion of privacy, and she'll be extremely mad when she discovers that you read her text messages." I can only imagine the unrepentant eye roll that he'll be giving me. I'm not surprised, though. Violet's the only person he has ever allowed himself to care about. He still doesn't quite understand societal norms and human decency. In his mind, it's completely acceptable for him to snoop through Violet's personal belongings, because he cares for her and has no malicious intent. It's wrong, of course, but that mentality has been ingrained inside his brain for centuries.

"I wanted to make sure there was no threat," Hux states, only confirming my suspicions. "Now, what is a panty liner? And why doesn't she trust me enough to provide one for her?" A hint of vulnerability creeps into his voice, as if he's genuinely upset that she didn't contact him first and foremost. It's just another thing that has been drilled inside of him—only he can adequately provide for his mate. I'm pretty sure he doesn't even trust the other men to protect and care for her without his presence.

Clearing my throat against a knot the size of Texas, I mansplain, "A panty liner is...errr...something that females put in their underwear."

His body goes rigid, visible even in the inky blackness. "Are her other mates not providing her with satisfaction? I will have to have a talk with them on how to properly please a lady."

Horror consumes me. Now, I'm picturing Hux sitting opposite Mason, Vin, and Frankie as he gives them the birds and the bees talk.

I'm just waiting for the day when he discovers the dildo in Violet's nightstand. He might actually go insane, believing some monster left his dick behind.

"No!" I blurt, waving my hands in the air, despite the fact that he can't see the gesture. "It's not for pleasure."

"So why would she put it in her underwear?" His shadowy head cocks to the side.

"Okay, listen," I begin, desperately trying to remember what Violet told him before. "You have heard of the, um, Great Period, correct?" At his barely decipherable nod, I hurry to continue, "Well, a panty liner helps capture all the blood that is dispelled." There. Straight and simple.

But, of course...

"Wouldn't a tarp be more effective in eliminating all of the blood? You place the dead body on the tarp, roll it up, and barely any blood remains on the floor." Hux points out matter-of-factly. "Is a panty liner another name for a tarp?"

"Yes," I blurt before I can stop myself. "Yes. Yes, it is. Now, can we talk about something else? Please?"

The last thing I want to do is continue talking about my girlfriend's panty liners with my sort-of brother.

Hux resumes walking, his gait confident and determined. The tension he emanates hangs palpably in the air between us, nearly suffocating.

"Who is this fucker that dares try to take control of *my* body?" Hux hisses. When I obnoxiously clear my throat, he relents, "*Our* body."

"It could be one of Frankenstein's tricks," I point out, but Hux is already vehemently shaking his head.

"I don't think so. I think..." He trails off with an agitated grunt. "Maybe it's someone wanting revenge for *your* past transgressions."

I can't help myself; I break into raucous laughter, bending at my knee and holding my stomach. Surely, Hux hears the words he says when he speaks them, right?

"You're joking."

When he remains quiet—the silence explosive—I reel on him with tightened fists. "For all of these years, I have done nothing but cover for *you*. Every murder. Every 'accidental' death. Every mistake. Don't you dare turn this around on me."

"What the bloody hell are you rambling about?" Hux asks, exasperated.

"The massacre in the eighteen-hundreds at the governor's home," I state as I begin ticking them off on my fingers. My blood boils at the memory. I had allowed Hux one month of free rein, only to reawaken to see myself standing in a blood-bath. Body parts littered the ground, staining the tiles red with blood. Male. Female. Young. Old. No one escaped my brother's brutality.

And maybe I'm just as bad, for I immediately contacted my father, and together, we set fire to the Victorian mansion. All traces of Hux's illicit activities were covered up, never to be talked about again.

"Or the time that you hanged all of those men in London," I continue. Sure, those men had been vile, disgusting crea-tures intent on raping and murdering women, but that still didn't give Hux the right to play judge, jury, and executioner. Once more, he left me alone to deal with the aftermath.

"You don't have the right to judge me," Hux huffs. "Not that I did any of those things. *You're* the one who was given the nickname of Jack the Ripper."

His words send me staggering back a step as horror consumes me.

"What are you talking about?" I gasp, and though I can't see him, I have the distinct impression he's rolling his eyes.

Abruptly, the room around me begins to change and distort, the darkness transforming into distinct shapes. A bed. Canopy. Distressed wooden desk. A window over-looking the Thames.

I'm in a memory.

Hux's memory.

Before I can even contemplate the ramifications of this

new discovery, I'm propelled forward until I can't differentiate where he ends and I begin.

I STARE AT THE INK BLOBS DOTTING THE YELLOW PARCHMENT, THE words glaring back at me and hardening my heart.

Brother, Jack's familiar messy scrawl states, *You have one month.*

My scowl deepens as I crumple the paper into a ball and toss it across the room. It hits the bed, sliding unceremoniously onto the ground.

Jack thinks he's doing me a favor by setting me free, but he's only prolonging my torture. The darkness...the darkness, I'm used to. It's the light that scares me, the sheer brilliance of it all. I can hide in the darkness, but the light illuminates everything I wish to remain hidden.

Every time Jack pulls me to the forefront of our shared mind, I'm forced to relearn an entirely new world. Doesn't he understand that a monster like me deserves to be contained to the shadows?

I finally allow myself to survey my surroundings, noting the minuscule details, such as the canopy over the bed and chaise lounge adjacent to it.

And the body lying haphazardly on the ground, coated in blood. Her hair is orange and stringy, lying in clumps around a pretty face, and her dress is ripped down the seams, baring her breasts. A single slash wound stretches across her throat.

"What did you do, Jack?" I whisper in horror, knowing he won't be able to hear me. What did this woman do to deserve such a brutal end?

But if there's one thing that has remained consistent over time, it's that murder—especially the cold-blooded type—has consequences.

With a sigh, I make quick work of wrapping the body in an

ornately detailed rug. Then, I tentatively venture down the grand staircase, staring at the pebbled road and numerous horse-drawn carriages.

Satisfied there are no wandering eyes, I head directly towards a carriage I can only assume belongs to Jack.

"How the bloody hell do I work this thing?" I ask scathingly, circling the majestic horse. I haven't the faintest idea how to connect a carriage to it.

Releasing another heavy sigh, I plop the body over my shoulder and walk aimlessly down a side street.

I'm desperate to ask my cohabitor—there's really no other word for the man who shares my body—why he murdered the woman. But alas, the world may never know. I'm not one to shy away from death, but this murder seems senseless. Jack has never been one to murder someone in cold blood, but maybe I don't know my brother as well as I thought.

After only an hour of trekking through heavily dense forests, I come to a stop in front of a cerulean, sparkling lake. Whistling beneath my breath, I waste no time in dumping the body into the water, watching the waves lap at it until it's completely submerged.

A sharp intake of breath has me glancing over my shoulder at the man staring at me in wide-eyed horror.

"Oh bloody hell," I gripe again as I lunge forward, easily snapping his neck. I watch him fall to the ground with a thud before I pick him up and place his body in the lake as well.

Thirty years later, when Jack allows me control of the body again, I discover that the "lake" had been the river Thames and the city was London. I also discover that countless bodies—all murdered the same way as the one in Jack's home—were found throughout London, some with their internal organs removed.

I never asked Jack about the girl, and he never brought it up.

But the media quickly coined him...us...Jack the Ripper.

~

I'M WRENCHED OUT OF THE MEMORY WITH A GASP, ONCE MORE completely engulfed in darkness. I stumble forward desperately until my hand connects with Hux's shoulder.

"What the hell was that?" I breathe.

"What was what?"

"You didn't see that?" I'm beginning to believe I'm losing my mind. Ironic, considering I'm currently trapped in it.

"See what?" Now, Hux sounds annoyed, as if I'm purposefully being dense.

"What were you thinking about just then?" I demand, and something in my tone causes his own to sharpen.

"The late eighteen-hundreds, when you allowed me out to play for a month. Why?"

I swallow heavily, wringing my hands together as I attempt to articulate the thoughts running rampant through my head. "Because I think I just saw your memory."

He freezes before taking a step closer and squeezing my shoulder.

"I never blamed you for what happened," he admits after a moment, and I know he's talking about the woman's death. "I knew you had your reasons."

"But that's the thing, Hux. I didn't murder that woman. I didn't murder any of those people." The mere thought makes me sick to my stomach. I'm no saint—you can't live as long as I have and still have clean hands—but senseless murder has never been my forte. Bile churns in my gut as a shocking revelation sits in my stomach like poison.

"You claimed you didn't murder those people I accused you of. Were you telling the truth?"

Hux scoffs once, actually sounding offended. "Of course I was telling the truth. I take credit for my kills."

My breathing is erratic as I struggle to hold on to my sanity.

"M-Maybe we've had a third interloper longer than we

expected," I manage to stutter out at last. Hux's hand tightens on my shoulder to the point of pain.

"What do you mean, brother?" The ire in Hux's voice makes his accent thicker.

"It means…" I lick my unbelievably dry lips. "It means that I don't think we're the only two in here. I don't think it's *ever* been just us two."

CHAPTER 38

VIOLET

I was once slapped in the face with a flaccid dildo. Honestly, I have no idea why they even make those things. Yes, it is a thing—if you don't believe me, look it up. To make a long story short—one of my human girlfriends accused me of kissing her boyfriend. I hadn't—girl code and all—but she didn't believe me. The next thing I knew, she was whacking me across the face with said flaccid dildo. I remember being both shocked and horrified as I rubbed at my reddening cheek.

Seeing Barret alive and well, grinning shyly? It was the monster equivalent of being bitch-slapped with cock.

"Barret?" I breathe as I stare at him like he's a mirage, an illusion capable of disappearing with the next gust of wind. "How are you…? Why are you…? How?" I scrub a hand down my face as the beginning tendrils of hope bubble low in my stomach like a corrosive acid. But hope is an immensely dangerous emotion to have. What happens when the hope fades? You're left with nothing but crippling pain and loneliness.

Is this another game? Another aspect of the Roaring?

"How are you still alive, man?" Mason queries, disbelief and suspicion evident in his tone. "Cal and Violet watched you die."

My nails dig into my skin as I ball both of my hands. "You better start explaining, Barret, because I'm sort of crapping my pants right now. Figuratively. And soon to be literally if you don't start talking."

His beautiful face is pinched in confusion as he cocks his head to the side. His green-tinted hair billows in the breeze from my open window as he regards us curiously. I half expect him to dissipate into a cloud of smoke. The dead can't come back to life, can they? It's not possible. Not even Dracula can escape death by the hand of a god-blessed dagger. I saw Alex shove it into his heart. I saw him fall, blood forming around his mouth.

So how is he here? How is he standing in front of me with a confused smile?

"Didn't Alex tell you?" His large eyes blink innocently up at me, but my unease only ratchets up a dozen notches.

"That fucking asshole?" I hiss through gritted teeth. "If I saw him, I would sooner stab my blade through his chest than partake in a conversation. Unless the conversation is how to effectively remove the balls off a male while he's still alive and screaming."

Vin, beside me, winces and cups his crotch. "That's nasty, Vi."

Ignoring him, I refocus my entire attention on the dead guy. "How are you here? I saw you die." My voice breaks on that final word, and that memory will forever haunt me like a tattoo that has embedded itself on my heart. No matter what I do, I can't remove it, and I'm beginning to think that I don't

want to. A part of me wants to live with the hurt and pain—
to remind myself that I survived it once, and I can survive it
again.

"I ran into Alex when I first stepped out of the portal."
Barret still sounds confused as his dark eyes flicker from
first my face, then to the guys' on either side of me. "He told
me that he knew of a way for me to save your life." He
shrugs once, his large shoulders reaching his ears. "And I
did it."

"That doesn't make any sense," I interrupt. For a lot of
reasons, actually. The most important being that Alex hates
me and wants to wear my innards like some sort of fucked
up scarf. And I, similarly, want to use his head as a basketball.
Obviously, Alex was playing Barret, but I just can't understand why.

"He told me that his father possessed a god-blessed
dagger," Barret continues, lips pursed delicately.

"A dagger that he stabbed you with," Mason interjects.

"Wrong." With a sigh, Barret moves to sit on my desk
chair, spinning it around so he's straddling it. "The dagger
was normal. He knew it wouldn't kill me, as long as one of
my bugs was able to crawl through the portal."

"Okay, start from the beginning." Vin moves so he's
standing slightly in front of me, and I can't tell if he's
protecting me from Barret...or protecting Barret from me.
My emotions are running rampant at the moment, fear,
anxiety, and that bastard hope all fighting for dominance. All
I want to do is leap into Barret's arms like a heroine in a
romantic movie—you know the type. When the girl
discovers that her long-lost love is actually alive and well.
Honestly, I made fun of those movies when I first watched
them. What female would forgive her significant other for
faking his death? I would sooner castrate him and feed his
balls to my pigs. After I bought a bunch of pigs, of course.

Now? I can see the appeal of slow-motion running into his arms, and that pisses me off.

"As I said before, Alex found me as soon as I stepped through the portal," Barret states slowly and carefully, his brows furrowed.

"Just because you talk slower doesn't mean we understand what the fuck you're saying," Vin snaps, and a flicker of hurt crosses Barret's face.

"He told me that his dad—a real douche canoe, that guy—wanted to kill Violet. Of course, I couldn't let that happen, so when Alex came up with a solution, I accepted." He shrugs once more, as if that's the end of the story. Already, his gaze is fixed on one of my leather schoolbooks, his fingers idly tracing the patterns engraved on the spine.

"Barret, what happened next?" I whisper, my throat clogged with emotion. Seeing him alive and well…it sort of makes me want to kill him for putting me through such pain to begin with.

"I ran into you and Cal." He drops the book and gives me his full attention once more. His sooty lashes blink rapidly as he rests his chin on the back of my desk chair. "When Alex and his father came, I did what Alex told me to do—I stepped in front of the blade meant for you. I would've done it anyway, but it was a relief to know that I wasn't going to actually die. It wasn't god-blessed, despite what Alex claimed." With a pained expression, he rubs at his chest where the blade entered. "I tried to tell you guys, but there was a shit ton of blood."

"Yeah," I choke out, swallowing the sob that wishes to escape. "A lot of blood."

"Alex kept up his end of the bargain by grabbing one of my bugs and taking it with him through the portal. Unfortunately, there was a little incident that involved your dog and my beetle form, but he took me to you, so I can't complain.

And now, here I am." He extends his arms on either side of him, a happy smile on his face.

"Barret..." A choked noise squeezes past my closed lips before I can contain it. "You motherfucking asshole!" Hands trembling, I raise them and place them on his well-defined chest. "I thought you died! Cal thought you died! How could you do this to us? How could you allow us to believe..." I trail off, dropping my hands to my sides as if he's on fire.

"I did what I did to protect you," Barret says slowly, that adorable crease between his eyebrows growing even more pronounced. His confused gaze flickers to the men behind me. "Did I do something wrong?"

"Nope," Vin says simply.

"Nothing at all," Mason adds.

"Yes, he fucking did!" I protest, resisting the urge to throw him over my knee and spank the shit out of him. "He made me think he was dead. I mourned for you, asshole!"

"But I'm still alive." Barret sounds even more bemused as he stands slowly, stepping away from the chair. "Isn't that a good thing?"

"Of course it's a good thing, you beautiful fucker."

With a huff, I stalk away from him, placing my balled hands on my hips.

Barret's alive.

He's here...and he's alive.

He's safe.

With a choked sob, I spin around and throw myself at the giant man. His arms immediately clasp around my waist, holding me steady. Tears prick my eyes, but I refuse to let them fall. Nope. Not me. Badass vampires don't cry.

"You motherfucking shit-eating asshole," I sob into his neck. His arms flex as they tighten around me, his head lowering to rest on top of my own.

"I'm sorry I scared you," he whispers, quietly enough that the others can't hear.

"And I'm sorry I called you a motherfucking shit-eating asshole, you motherfucking shit-eating asshole," I manage to gasp out. After what feels like hours—but I know is only a few minutes—I get myself under control enough to step away and scrub at my wet eyes. From allergies, of course. "Did you see Cal yet? He needs to know you're okay."

Barret shakes his head. "I went to see you first. I assumed he would've been with you." His slashing eyebrows pull low over his dark eyes. "Do you think he's okay?"

"I'm sure he's fine," I say, more to myself than to him. Remember that pesky little bugger, hope? Well, I need to hold onto that with two hands, or else I'll fall apart at the seams. "We can go look for him." Turning towards Vin and Mason, I ask, "Can you guys—?"

"Sit at the portal and wait until Hux or Jack appear?" Mason finishes for me, flashing his signature crooked grin. "I would be honored to, m'lady."

"Whipped," Vin murmurs to his best friend.

"Yes, in the bedroom," Mason deadpans. He grabs Vin's shoulder and spins him towards the door. "Besides, I'm not going to be sitting by myself on the bleachers, am I? So who's the whipped one?"

"It appears to be both of you," Barret points out innocently, and I swear I could hug the big guy. Especially when Vin and Mason simultaneously glare at him.

"Please, for me?" I ask, batting my lashes. I know both Jack and Hux are strong and resilient, but I won't be able to settle down until I see with my own two eyes that they're safe. I send a silent prayer to whoever's listening that they have made it out of the arena in one piece.

"Because you asked nicely," Mason teases. "But I'm expecting a reward for good behavior."

"A sexy reward?" I lift a brow, and heat instantly enters his eyes, darkening the color.

"If it involves you on a bed with a bow on top, then yes."

"Come on, Casanova," Vin huffs, dragging him from the room. But not before I catch his expression—longing and lust so pronounced that I'm left breathless. Vin may not be willing to play with Mason…but he's more than happy to play with me while Mason's in the room.

I wonder what that will be like. Me…them…us.

Barret's words pull me out of my wistful fantasy. "Where do you think Cal will be?"

"We'll check the upper levels of the Academy first," I say immediately, shaking my head to clear my muddled thoughts. "But you know Cal better than I do. Where do you think he is?"

"Normally, when he's upset, he'd find himself a pussy to fuck," he states matter-of-factly, and I have no doubt he's quoting Cal verbatim. For reasons I don't wish to decipher, the mere prospect makes me uneasy. As if sensing the direction of my thoughts, Barret glances at me out of the corner of his eyes. "But I doubt that's what he's doing."

"So then where would he be?"

Barret scrubs at the whiskers on his chin absent-mindedly. "He's part fairy, and fairies often have certain vices they partake in." I nod once in understanding. It's why fairies rule the drug world—their own cravings and addictions make them capable of creating the perfect substance.

"And what are Cal's vices?" I question.

Barret makes a face. "Sex, as you probably know. And alcohol, particularly the fairy variety."

With a sigh, I reach for Barret's large hand and drag him out the door.

"Come on. I think I know where he is."

CHAPTER 39

VIOLET

The club I went to with Frankie is even more crowded than it was previously. Every monster who attended the Roaring seems to be waiting patiently in line.

"Come on," I say, putting Jack's car into park.

I'm severely underdressed this time around, but I can't be bothered to change. Not when I'm already worried about Cal.

Barret's hot on my heels as I bypass the line and face the familiar, bald bouncer who was so smitten with Frankie.

Yeah, not at all salty about that, thank you very much.

Forgoing formalities, I step on my tiptoes and stare the man intently in the eyes. It's taboo for a vampire to use compulsion on another monster. More than that, some would consider it an automatic death sentence.

Frankly, I don't give a damn.

"You will allow me and my friend admittance," I whisper,

my words curling around him like a tightening leash. His eyes glaze over as his tattooed arms drop to his sides.

"I will...?"

"You will allow me and my friend admittance," I repeat, pushing even more power into those words. I can see when they embed themselves into his mind, for he immediately steps back, sweeping his arm back to let us through.

"Hey, what the fuck?" someone from the line exclaims, but I don't bother turning to see who's speaking. Hopefully, he didn't see me use my compulsion. If he did, and he reported me...

Refusing to allow those thoughts to fester, I stalk into the dimly lit club. Like before, the pungent scent of sweat and alcohol barrage me, and I wrinkle my nose. Why can't clubs smell like...I don't know...Febreze or some shit. Maybe that'll be my new invention.

I scan the thrashing bodies for a familiar pair of red wings and light pink hair.

"There!" Barret points his finger across the room to where Cal is disappearing around a corner, his hand intertwined with a person I can't see.

"I thought you said he wouldn't have sex," I ask, unable to contain the sudden surge of jealousy that crashes over me. I remind myself immediately that I have no right to feel jealous. He's not my boyfriend, just a friend. Besides, I have four other men who care about me and kind of, maybe, love me, quirks and all. I don't need to add another one.

Ignoring my outburst, Barret leads us through the crowd, one of his hands gripping mine and the other shoving bodies away at random. His profile is shadowed, but even still, I can see the determined set to his jaw and the fire burning in his eyes.

When we reach the hall Cal disappeared down, I pause, tugging on Barret's hand until he stops as well.

"I think he went into one of these rooms." I nod towards the various storage closets lining the perimeter. The last thing I want or need is to walk in on Cal balls deep in some skank.

"Let's look." Barret begins to open one door at a time. The first shows a male with fur sprouting on both of his arms as he fucks a female. I awkwardly stand in the doorframe as he pounds into her.

"What the fuck?" the man bellows, and the woman screams, attempting to cover her pert breasts.

"Sorry. Continue banging," I whisper awkwardly, waiting until Barret closes the door.

The second door has two females kissing passionately, their tops off and ample breasts on display.

"Wanna join?" one of the girls asks as she circles the other female's nipple with her tongue.

"Sorry. Continue banging."

The third room is, of course, the same, but this one has three guys and four girls.

"Sorry. Continue banging."

It's the fourth room that sends icy dread skating down my spine.

"Cal?" I whisper as Barret stands in the threshold, frozen.

It's definitely my pink-haired cupid, but I've never seen such rage on his face before. It distorts his features entirely until he's barely recognizable. His eyes are a solid shade of red, madness lurking in their depths, as he stands over a familiar male.

Alex's father.

His face is mottled and bloody, one of his eyes completely swollen shut. A myriad of bruises darken his skin—some fresh and light pink, while others are a hideous shade of blue and black. His bloody lips curl in a hideous sneer as Cal towers over him, radiating fury.

"Cal?" I repeat, but he doesn't seem to hear me, too lost in his anger and rage. I desperately turn towards Barret and shove him forward, hoping he'll be able to penetrate Cal's… darkness. That's the only word capable of encapsulating what I'm seeing. He's every inch the dark and dangerous monster you read about in horror novels. When Barret remains silent, mouth agape, I say, "Cal, Barret's alive."

"He was going to hurt you," Cal manages to bite out, his tone guttural and nearly unrecognizable. "He wants to kill you."

"But he didn't." I take a tentative step closer, but before I can touch him, Barret wraps an arm around my waist and drags me behind him. "What the hell?"

"He's not sane right now, Violet," Barret whispers urgently. "He's dark."

"What the fuck do you mean?"

"Fairies can be either light or dark," he continues, forcing me backwards with each step he takes. "Cal was light…and now he's dark."

"And?" I struggle futilely, but it's like fighting with a brick wall. Barret is apparently hewn completely from stone.

"And a dark fairy is dangerous. It's a curse, Violet. He's obsessed with blood and vengeance. He's not the Cal we once knew." His voice breaks on those final words, but I'm already vehemently shaking my head in denial.

"No, you're alive. Once he sees that you're alive and well, he'll snap out of it."

Barret continues to move us until we're nearly out the door.

"It doesn't work like that, Cheese Curd." The arm around me tightens as he walks us backwards. "Maybe if he was a normal fairy, yes, but he's not. He's also part incubus."

"If he kills that man, he'll be arrested for murder." There's no graver sin than a monster killing another monster. Sure, the council will look the other way if the victim is a vampire, but a man like Alex's father? I don't need a brain to know that he holds some sway over the ruling government. His death will warrant a manhunt and execution.

Desperate, I scream, "Cal, Barret's alive. He's here. Look behind you. He's right here. With me. We're both safe."

A familiar dagger appears in Cal's hand, the blade glinting in the artificial lighting. The copper handle fits perfectly in his clasped fingers as he brandishes it back and forth.

A god-blessed dagger.

"Cal!" I beg. "Cal, don't do this. This isn't you."

When he spins around to face us, I don't see the man I care about. His teeth are elongated, more beast than human, and his glowing red eyes burn like the fires of hell themselves are trapped in those tiny orbs. A snarl distorts his mouth even further as his eyes flicker from Barret to me.

"This is what they wanted!" he hisses, the noise nothing like his usual melodic voice. "I'll do what I need to do to protect you. I'll become an even bigger monster than the one they thought they created."

Fear creeps down my spine and roots my feet to the ground. Not even Barret can pull me away, though he for sure tries.

Cal turns once more towards his victim and raises the dagger. And then, with one fatal swoop, he plunges it into the necromancer's heart.

Black lines erupt from around his eyes like dark, gossamer spider webs. His lips part in a silent cry as blood forms around the corners of his mouth. Those dark, dark eyes—spinning with the secrets of the universe—fixate on me with pure hatred and venom. A sinister smile curls up his lips as more and more blood drips down his chin.

Despite dying at Cal's hand, his words are addressed to

me and me alone. "This isn't over, vampire slut." With that, his eyes close and his body goes limp.

Dead.

Dead.

Dead.

He's dead.

That one thought plays on repeat in my head as I stare at his fallen body and then at Cal's crouched form. His chest heaves with each breath he takes. As I watch, horrified, black lines—similar to the ones I saw on Alex's father's face—clamor up and down Cal's wings, bleeding into the enticing red.

Barret freezes, similarly stunned, as he stares at his best friend.

"What did you do?" he whispers.

Slowly, Cal unfolds himself from his crouched position and rises to his feet. With one foot on the body, he removes the dagger from the man's chest and caresses the silver blade.

"I did what had to be done," he whispers, those pure red eyes training on me behind Barret's shoulder. At his attention, Barret continues to move us out the door, his body a shield against the avenging angel.

"I would never hurt her," Cal hisses.

"But you're scaring her," Barret counters immediately.

Ignoring them both, I glance anxiously in both directions. At the moment, the hall appears to be empty, but I know it won't remain as such. Especially if this is a hotspot for orgies, as the closets displayed.

"We need to go. Now." Ignoring Barret's cry of protest, I brush past him and grab Cal's hand. Immediately, the red in his eyes begins to recede and his fangs shrink back into his mouth. Confusion dances in his eyes as he stares from me to Barret and then to the body we left behind. "Barret?" he whispers, sounding young and small, like a forlorn child. "You're alive?"

"We need to go," I repeat, extending my other hand towards Barret, which he accepts. I tug them forward until both men stand on either side of me, a protective wall of muscle that no one will be able to breach.

"What happened?" Cal whispers. "What did I do? How are you alive?" He addresses the last question at Barret. "Am I dead?"

"You're not dead," I huff as I storm through the crowd of sweaty dancers. Fortunately, no one gets near enough to touch me with Cupid and the Boogeyman at my sides. The monsters might not know who they are, but the power they emanate is almost palpable. No doubt, they recognize an apex predator when they see one. "At least, not yet. But we're all going to be if we don't get the hell out of here."

Cal appears momentarily struck speechless, but he allows me to drag him through the club and to Jack's car parked illegally on the curb.

"You're alive," Cal repeats as he climbs into the backseat. Barret, surprisingly, takes the passenger one. "Violet..." I finish buckling my seatbelt and glance at him through the rearview mirror. "Did I hurt you?"

"No," I say immediately, ignoring Barret's huff of disgust. "Cal, do you not remember what happened?"

I pull onto the road and hightail it out of there, no doubt leaving track marks on the asphalt.

"I remember...Barret dying." He glances at his best friend, as if the sight of Barret physically pains him. "And then I remember crossing through the portal. I was so pissed and upset." He rakes his fingers through his tousled pink hair. "I was walking back to the academic building when Alex and his fucking father stepped through the portal. I remember that I was furious that they somehow survived when Barret

didn't, and then I recalled how they tried to kill you. I just…
snapped, I suppose. I don't remember anything after that."

"You fucking killed him," Barret snaps, and I've never heard my gentle giant sound so furious before. His body thrums with pure, undiluted energy, the wispy green strands of his hair standing on end. "You murdered the necromancer."

"No…" Cal whispers, clutching at his head. "I wouldn't have killed anyone."

"You did, asshole. And you didn't even do it in the games, when it would've been legal." Barret's hand tightens on the armrest of his chair as his face twists. "And now, you just made Violet an accessory to the murder of a high-profile monster. Which, as you know, is punishable by death." Barret's lips compress into a thin line as he faces straight ahead. "You just killed us all."

CHAPTER 40

O nly seventy-eight competitors survived the first round of the Roaring.

Seventy-eight.

According to Vin, Hux and Jack made it out of the arena with plenty of time to spare. But when I went to go visit them, they were nowhere to be seen.

I slept restlessly that night, consumed with worry for Hux, Jack, and Cal. My mutt slept at my feet—yes, I claimed the ugly, adorable creature—pitiful cries escaping his fanged mouth, as if he sensed my agitation. He began to cry in earnest when I left him this morning.

Now, I stand once more in the center of steel bleachers as I prepare myself for the next round of the Roaring. Like before, Frankie and Mason stand on either side of me while Vin waits beside his family. I'm grateful to see that Vanessa has survived the first round. As my designated best friend, I sort of have to cheer for her, though I would anyway. I can see how much Vin loves his sister.

I'll be the first to admit my disappointment that Asshole One and Asshole Two—read as, Vin's parents—survived as well.

The second game of the Roaring is supposed to test our intelligence, though none of us have any idea what to expect. Last year, they placed the competitors in rooms that were on fire and forced them to find a way to escape. The year before that, they buried each competitor alive and gave them three hours to find a way out.

I scan the throng of competitors anxiously, but I don't see Hux or Jack anywhere. That only amplifies my tension as I bounce from foot to foot. Are they okay? Did something happen in the arena? I'm desperate to hear Hux's thick accent whisper, "Precious Treasure." But, like, not in a creepy way. In a totally romantic and sexy way.

"What happened last night?" Mason whispers conversationally as we wait for Dimitri to once more take his spot on the stage. "When you found Cal?"

Oh, nothing much. Just a little murder and mayhem.

Automatically, my eyes flicker to where Alex stands by himself opposite us. His dark eyes narrow accusingly, and I can't help but wonder if he knows about what happened to his father. Barret's confession flitters through my brain like a pair of incessantly flapping butterfly wings, and I stare at the giant in a new light. Why did he help me? Or was that just a ploy? Was he trying to gain Barret's trust?

Fuck, I'm getting paranoid. Dealing with so many cocks will do that to a lady.

"Welcome!" Dimitri's cold voice slithers over the assembled crowd. "You are here because you survived the first round of the Roaring." The audience cheers, pumping their fists and whistling enthusiastically. It's kind of demented, if you think about it. Half of these monsters lost a family member or a loved one, yet they're still laughing as if nothing bad had just transpired. As if we hadn't lost hundreds of lives.

Then again, that's the monster world. Only the strongest survive, and the weak aren't even mourned.

"For this round, each competitor will enter a door designed specifically for them." As if on cue, a door materializes in front of each competitor. All of them are insignificant in appearance, though their colors and shapes vary. Mine has intricate trim around the sides and a hanging flower plant overhead. "Your goal is to exit your room in exactly one hour." His cold blue eyes train on me, and his devilishly wicked lips quirk to the side. I'm suddenly bombarded with memories of me in his office as he expertly eats me out, his fingers tweaking my nipple.

Totally appropriate thoughts to have when you're potentially facing imminent death. Way to go, Violet.

"Each room is different," Dimitri continues, maintaining eye contact. "Nothing you see in your room is a trick. But be warned," his voice lowers ominously, "you might not like what you hear."

I know his statement is directed at me, but I can't quite understand what he means. Is this a hint?

"Be careful, Pinkie," Mason says seriously, his expression grave. I can tell he doesn't like the fact that he won't be able to protect me during this challenge. Honestly? I don't like that either. Sure, I'm not the most athletic monster, but I can break balls and take names with the best of them. I want to—no, I *need* to—protect my men, no matter the cost. I'm going insane with worry.

"You may now enter," Dimitri states, and one by one, the doors fly open.

My heart hammers in my chest as I step through the glittery, silver portal.

"You're a survivor, Violet," I whisper fiercely to myself.

"You'll kick the ass of any monster who dares try to harm you. Badass Violet for the win. Your men will be safe. Have faith."

"Are you talking to yourself again?" a familiar voice drawls, and I blink rapidly to orient myself to my new surroundings. I appear to be in a sparsely furnished room with a single couch against the far wall opposite a coffee table and recliner. There are no windows or doors, and the portal has already dissipated. Sitting lazily, almost languidly, on the couch is none other than Dracula himself.

Opposite him, Dimitri leans against the wall with his arms folded over his chest and his frosty stare freezing me in place.

"Is this real?" I whisper, my back flush against the wall.

"I can assure you that it is." My father rolls his eyes as he takes a drag of his cigarette. He's dressed in a black trench coat pulled open over a suit and tie. His dark hair is slicked away from his aristocratic, almost elegant features. In private, my dad can be a little…eccentric, but around other people, he has a tendency to act like a massive douche. His mannerisms change entirely around people. Instead of behaving like the "cool dad," he turns stoic and cold. I have long since accepted Dracula, no matter the face he wears.

"What is this about? Is this the competition?" I glance desperately between my father and Dimitri, but both men are impassive.

"Have a seat." Dracula nods towards the chair opposite him, and I daintily perch on the edge. My body thrums with excess energy as my eyes dart anxiously in every direction. "This was the only way I could speak to you without others knowing."

"Wait." I hold up both hands. "Did you hijack the Roaring?"

"As soon as Dracula finishes speaking to you, we'll bring

you back to the arena," Dimitri states simply. "As I said before, each room is designed specifically for the contestant." His lips quirk marginally, and I realize that the sly bastard has somehow found a way to cheat the system. Not that I'm complaining. If this gets me answers, then I'm willing to do just about anything.

"I've been needing to talk to you," Dracula begins, leaning backwards on the sofa and extending his legs. He crosses them at his ankles and places his clasped hands on his stomach. "You have questions."

"Of course I have fucking questions!" I jump to my feet, my agitation demanding physical movement. Pacing, I scrub a hand through my disheveled blonde curls. "Why didn't you tell me that Diedre was my sister?"

"Because I have a lot of children," he answers simply. "Thousands, more or less." He shrugs his shoulders nonchalantly, as if he didn't just drop a bomb the size of Alaska in my lap. I have over a thousand siblings?

Someone needs to give Dracula a condom.

But not me, because, ew.

"Was she telling the truth?" I continue, my stomach twisting into dozens of tight, intricate knots. "Am I not your biological daughter?"

Dracula releases a heavy sigh, the tick in his jaw commandeering my attention. His reaction only reinforces what I have already suspected.

"It *is* true," I whisper in numb horror. "I'm not your daughter."

And if Diedre was telling the truth about that, then was she also telling the truth when she said one of my men helped frame me for murder? No, I can't think like that. I refuse. The second trust is broken, it's impossible to mend.

"No, you're not." He presses his lips together. "At least, not through blood. You're my daughter in every other sense of the word." The sincerity in his eyes is impossible to doubt. He hasn't once claimed Diedre as his own, but me? He claimed me for the entire world to see. In his own sick, demented way, the asshole loves me.

"What am I?" I stare down at my hands as if I've never seen them before. For my entire life, I've thought these were hands that belonged to a vampire—and not just any vampire, but Dracula's daughter. Who am I? *What* am I?

"I don't know." He leans forward and rests his elbows on his knees, forking his fingers together.

"You don't know," I repeat dubiously. My eyes flicker to Dimitri, still standing silently in the corner. Why is he here? What part does he play in all of this?

"You can trust him," Dracula says, misreading my expression. "He's loyal to me."

Dimitri's eyes flare at his words, face tightening in distaste, but he doesn't contradict my father. I have the distinct feeling that Dimitri is loyal to no one but himself... and to me, though I don't speak that thought out loud. Everything about the assassin-slash-headmaster is confusing. He's nothing but a sexy contradiction—a beautifully wrapped package that carries nothing but spikes.

I want to demand they tell me how they know each other, if Dracula hired Dimitri from the start to protect me, but I don't want to know those answers. I wouldn't be able to survive if Dimitri was only protecting me because of a deal he made with my father.

"Tell me what you know," I demand at last, and Dracula's face tightens at my tone. He never liked when I talked back to him.

"Nineteen years ago, I received a call from a close confidant of mine...Dorian Gray." I release a startled gasp as I once more stare intently at Dimitri, but his expression is neutral as we discuss his estranged father. "Dorian Gray had discovered something peculiar, and of course, he contacted me first and foremost." Dracula nervously licks his upper lip, the only indication that he's distressed by this conversation.

"Nineteen years ago…when I was born. Let me guess? He found me?"

Dracula releases a bark of dry laughter. "Don't be so vain, my sweet daughter. He actually found your rather pregnant mother."

"My mother?" I stop pacing and whip my head around to face him. The only thing I remember about her is that she died when I was younger from an accidental overdose.

"She was lying in the middle of the forest, sobbing. Dorian was there, as well as his son." He nods towards Dimitri, who has gone rigid, lines of tension evident in his beautiful face. "She was dying, and she begged for me to look after her unborn baby. I accepted, of course, because I knew your mother."

"You…knew her?" The more he talks, the more confused I become.

"We were lovers many years ago," Dracula admits with a dismissive wave of his hand. Obviously, that disgusting snippet of information isn't relevant to the story.

"Who was she?"

My stomach tightens to unbearable levels until I fear I'm going to expel the meager contents currently residing in my stomach.

"Your mother fell in love with a very evil man," Dracula continues, ignoring my question. "And when she tried to leave him—taking you with her—he attempted to murder both of you. I vowed to keep you safe and love you like you were my own. I even had a witch place a spell on you to dampen your powers while keeping the ones that were decidedly vampiric strong. As you got older and more insistent that you know your birth mother, I had that same witch implant fake memories to keep you satisfied."

"Who are my parents?" I demand, dropping myself into the chair opposite him. My legs feel wobbly and leaden, and I have no doubt that if I were to attempt to stand a second longer, I would collapse. Dimitri moves to stand beside me, face expressionless sans the slightest hardening of his eyes.

"Your mother is Hera, Queen of all the Gods, and your father is none other than Lucifer himself, the original monster. Your lineage encompasses two mythologies, two very different types of monsters, but both have their own set of enemies. If the world discovers who you truly are, you won't have only a few monsters attempting to kill you. Every species in every world will be gunning for your ass."

CHAPTER 41

VIOLET

"Hera," I repeat numbly as I stare at my hands. Hands that belong to the daughter of a goddess and the devil. Only minutes ago, I was desperate to know my identity—who I am, who my parents are, what my species is. Now, I'm desperate for Dracula to break into laughter and assure me that this is nothing but a sick, demented joke. I'll do anything to remain in my tiny, oblivious bubble for a few more minutes. Just a few. I'm not ready to face the world and the implications of his words.

"Even before we were lovers, we were close friends," Dracula continues, eyes effectively keeping me silent. "When she asked for me to look after her daughter, I couldn't refuse. That very night, you were born. A healthy, beautiful little girl." He speaks with a reverence that I've never heard before, and I have to wonder if that respect is for me...or the power I apparently wield.

"Is she...dead?" My heart begins to thump erratically as I move my hands to the armrests of my seat. I squeeze until I fear I'm going to break my fingers. Pain like I've never felt before consumes me as completely as a tidal wave. I fear I'll become lost in it. Drown in it.

"Hera?" He reclines back in his chair. The only indication he's anything other than aloof is the tightening of his eyes. My father is a master of illusions, a master of perfecting his blank mask. To the untrained eye, he appears almost bored with this conversation. Only someone who knows him as well as I do can see the jittery way he holds himself, the way his fingers tap a staccato against the couch's armrest. "Fortunately, your mother is alive and well."

"And she hasn't come for me?" I can't hide the hurt that creeps into my voice.

"You know it's not safe," he answers curtly.

"Because of Lucifer?" I stick my thumb into my mouth and bite down, the blast of pain almost welcoming. It penetrates the numbness that settles heavily in my head like a depressive fog.

"Lucifer is the original monster," Dimitri interjects, startling me. For a while, I had forgotten he was here, lurking beside me like a sexy shadow. "He *created* all of the monsters we know today."

"And he fucked my mom." I scrub a hand down my face, wishing I could just as easily wipe away the pain and betrayal trapping me six feet underground. Because, yeah, I'm pissed. Fucking furious. For years, my father led me to believe I was nothing but a vampire, his favorite daughter. That latter statement may be true—and I know that blood doesn't always equal family—but he still lied about my identity. He still made me believe that my mother was dead. I carried the pain of her death like battle armor. It made me stronger, while at the same time, it weighed me down. My mother is *alive.* Should I be ecstatic? Over the moon?

But the fact that she can't see me? Can't talk to me?

It only exacerbates my rage.

Dracula lightly brushes a strand of his meticulously groomed hair out of his eyes. The onyx strands contrast greatly with his pasty, almost sickly, skin. Why did I ever think we were related? Looking at him through a new lens, I realize we look positively nothing alike. While his hair is as black as pitch, mine is sunlit blonde, the strands interwoven with shades of white and a light brown. While his skin reminds me vaguely of alabaster, mine is as smooth as porcelain with a slight tan most vampires could only dream of acquiring. His nose is long and thick, the tip slightly crooked, as if it had been broken one too many times, while mine is tiny and pert. His lips are thin, while mine are lush.

"At the moment, Lucifer believes you to be dead," Dimitri continues, once more commandeering my attention. His hands are clasped primly behind his back as he tilts his chin up. "He knows that he didn't kill Hera, but he truly believes that he killed his demon spawn."

I raise my hand in the air. "As his demon spawn, I very much protest to being called 'demon spawn.'"

Ignoring me, Dimitri continues. "The world can never know the truth about your heritage. When Dracula agreed to take you in as his own, relations between vampires and the other monsters were not nearly as tense."

"Tense." I snort once at the absurdity of that word. "They're butchering us."

"And what will they do if they discover the truth about you?" Dracula cocks one dark eyebrow as his shrewd eyes narrow imperceptibly. "They won't kill you, Violet. At least, not right away. Some will wish to use your powers for their own purposes. Others will hope to get favors from Lucifer and Hera, unknowing that the former wishes that you were dead and the latter is unable to confess to being your mother."

Shifting on the uncomfortable seat, I drill my dad with a penetrating glare. "This doesn't make any sense. I'm a vampire. I drink blood."

Once more, it's Dimitri that answers. "You do." He nods, moving from his spot in the corner to stand beside my father, who still reclines on the couch. He's every inch the graceful, elegant predator with his frosty ice-blue stare and his pure white hair pulled back into a severe ponytail. "Your birth father, Lucifer, is the creator of all monsters, including vampires."

"Are you saying that Lucifer is a vampire?" I gape, struggling to understand their words. This entire thing sounds insane. Half of me wants to believe that Dracula's pulling one over on me. Any second now, he'll break into peals of laughter, point a finger at me, and say, "Gotcha." Maybe this is part of the Roaring. Maybe this is how they'll finally break me.

"Lucifer is a demon. Not just any demon, but the devil himself," Dimitri corrects. "But, yes, he does drink blood."

"You'll come to discover that you're stronger than the average vampire," Dracula adds. "Faster. Smarter." Okay, yeah, that one gets a snort out of me, but Dracula continues on as if I hadn't interrupted. "You'll discover, over time, that you have more powers as well."

"Like what?" I whisper. I don't even want the powers I have now, let alone new ones. Both humans and monsters alike fear those that are different. And frankly, I like my heart in my body and my head on my shoulders just as much as the next person. I don't want to die because of who my parents are.

But unfortunately, life isn't always fair.

"Your mother is Hera," Dimitri says. "She's the Goddess of Marriage and Birth."

I groan low in my throat, dropping my face into my hands. "Please don't tell me that my superpower is popping out babies left and right. I don't think my vagina can handle that."

Dracula looks slightly queasy, but Dimitri rolls his eyes. "No, of course not. But it could explain why you have more than one mate."

"Mate?" My father sits up abruptly, glancing between the two of us with narrowed eyes. "What the hell is he talking about? When did you get a mate? Or mates? I'll rip his balls straight from his body! Or their balls!"

"Dad," I warn, "stop it."

"You do realize I've been called Vlad the Impaler for a reason, right? And it's not because of my sex skills."

"Oh my god, Dad, seriously?" I cover my mouth to keep from vomiting, especially when he exchanges a conspiratorial wink with Dimitri.

"A little murder has never hurt anyone before," he says lightly, eyes already gleaming at the thought. I wonder what he'd do if he discovered Dimitri Gray had just face fucked me the day before in the headmaster's office. I'm pretty sure they wouldn't be so "buddy buddy" after that.

"We're not murdering my…errr…mates."

"So you admit you have them."

"Nope! We're not doing this! Fuck, Dad, you're so embarrassing."

"Embarrassing." Dracula pouts and reclines back on the sofa. "I'm a pretty damn cool dad."

"You give me emotional whiplash," I counter immediately. "Sometimes, you're saying stuff like 'cool dad,' and other times, you're snapping my neck."

"It's called tough love," he responds petulantly. "Have you heard of it?"

"Enough of this," Dimitri interrupts, taking another step forward until he's between us. "We need to get Violet back to the arena before her hour is up."

"Does this mean I beat the second round?" I can't help but ask, and when Dimitri nods once, I release a deafening squeal. "Fuck, yes! Violet for the win!"

Dracula pinches the bridge of his nose—the gesture reminding me eerily of Vin—and shakes his head sadly. "What am I going to do with you?"

"Nothing, because you chose me and you can't return me now." I stick my tongue out at him.

"I wouldn't want to," Dracula says, surprising me with his earnestness. "You're my daughter, and I love you."

My heart stutters to an abrupt halt at his words before taking off once more with a vengeance.

"I don't know what the third game is," Dimitri cuts in, lips tightening into a thin line. "They haven't told me any details about it, which only makes me more suspicious. You need to keep an eye out, Violet. A lot of the people here—including the monsters in charge of the Roaring—would like nothing more than to see you dead and Dracula punished."

"What's new?" I ask dryly. "They—"

I never get to finish my sentence.

The room around me begins to rattle, pictures flying off the walls.

"What the hell?" I squeal as my chair topples to the side, propelling me to the ground. Immediately, Dimitri is crouched protectively over my body just as the room explodes in flames.

Red and orange consume the entire room, spouting like errant fireworks. They hiss and stutter as the room begins to vibrate. Smoke enters my nostrils, and I bring my shirt up to cover my mouth and nose. Dimitri remains on top of me, his body protecting me from wayward objects. Each grunt and hiss of pain destroys a fundamental piece of me.

And when he goes silent, my entire heart shrivels into a messy ball of emotion.

"Dimitri?" I whisper, my throat burning from the smoke. The ceiling above shows nothing but a myriad of flames, each one creeping closer to where I'm lying.

With Dimitri's body over mine, I can only move my head, and I can't help but turn to where I last saw my father.

Dracula's eyes are wide with terror, his lips slightly parted. In the center of his chest, protruding from his heart, is a god-blessed dagger.

My sob gets lodged in my throat as I begin to tremble all over.

"Dad?" I whisper, tears cascading down my face. "Daddy?"

The flames are getting closer and closer, and I know with painful certainty that I'm going to die. Very few things can kill a vampire. God-blessed items, for one. Beheading. A wooden stake through the heart. And…fire.

Hands trembling, I cup Dimitri's pale face, noting the blood on his forehead from where a wooden beam has hit him.

"You stupid asshole," I say softly as I brush away the flyaway strands of his white hair. For the first time in his life, he doesn't look perfect. He looks dirty and disheveled and broken. "Why did you protect me?"

I press a chaste kiss to his forehead as I wait for death to claim us all. Unbidden, my eyes travel back to my immobile father, and the tears begin to fall faster. A gripping, consuming pain wraps around my heart like a coil of barbed wire. With each consecutive squeeze of the organ, the points dig into the flesh until I'm weeping blood.

I vaguely see men in black entering the room from a shimmery portal, but sleep is threatening to drag me under. It's impossible for me to resist the seductive pull.

One woman stands out from the rest, her features so familiar that I can't help but blink repeatedly up at her. Her tall, slender frame pauses above me as her snakes slither and hiss.

"Medusa," I murmur sleepily, and her smile grows.

"Child." She crouches so she's at level with me, her eyes spewing pure malice. "We need to talk."

EPILOGUE

MASON

The walls continue to close in on me as I rapidly spin the dial on the combination lock.

"Come on, come on, come on," I murmur to myself. Blood drips from an open wound on my arm, and my face is littered with nasty scratches. One of the walls reaches my side, its sharp prongs digging into my ribs, and I release a pained yelp, stumbling away. Of course, that only makes my back hit a wall made entirely of burning red embers.

Time is running out. I know that as surely as I know that if I don't get the combination right, I'm going to die in this fucking room.

I refuse to leave Violet—after all, I'm nothing if not a stubborn asshole.

Finally, I place the last number in the lock, and the walls immediately stop moving. To my left is a wall made up entirely of keen nails. To my right is one laden with knives. Behind me is my favorite—the burning one—and in front of me is one dripping in poison.

The air around me begins to spin rapidly, like a silver tornado has plowed through the room, and I release a breath of relief when I'm deposited back onto the stage.

"Fucking hell," I murmur dazedly as the audience chants my name. I'm not gonna lie, hearing their cries does wonders for my ego. With a cocksure grin, I raise a fist into the air, and the crowd practically creams their pants.

Mr. Pumpkin shuffles to stand beside me, his face red and blotchy and dripping with sweat. I'm surprised it's not Dimitri here to greet me, but I can only assume that he is with Violet.

Which means my girl has finished the second challenge.

Relief like no other washes away the tension from my shoulders.

I need to find my Pinkie pronto and finish what we started yesterday. If that means I have to see Vin's cock, then so be it. Hell, I'd even be willing to stare at Frankie's garden hose if that's what she desires.

Speaking of the devil…

Frankie waves me over from the side of the stage. After Mr. Pumpkin announces my victory, I saunter after him with my hands shoved into my pockets. Vin is already leaning against the Academy wall, covered in soot and looking worse for wear, but otherwise fine.

"You were cutting it close, Mason," Frankie says, shifting uncomfortably on the grass. Unlike me and Vin, Frankie doesn't have any cuts on him that I can see. A part of me is sort of jealous that the bastard is basically impenetrable.

"How much more time did I have?" I glance towards the audience who is cheering as another competitor—this one the Bog Monster—materializes on the stage.

"Less than two minutes," Vin snaps. He repeatedly runs his fingers through his dark hair as his eyes glare at a spot on the wall.

"What's your problem?" I finally ask, his agitation causing *me* to become jittery. I don't even know what's the matter, and already, I'm thrumming with excess energy. The tension that had previously dissipated has returned with a vengeance.

"Violet hasn't returned," Frankie murmurs, and I swear all of the blood drains from my face, leaving me cold and empty.

"What?"

"She hasn't fucking returned yet," Vin snaps. "Most of the competitors did ages ago, including Vanessa, but Violet hasn't arrived yet. Even Cal and Barret made it out a few minutes ago, but I have no idea where they disappeared to."

The area above the stage glimmers brightly, and a body gracefully rolls from the portal. Jack—or is that Hux?—smiles brightly at the crowd, his dark hair brushed back into a man bun. When has either of them ever worn a man bun?

As the audience dies down and Hux/Jack makes a beeline towards the Academy, Frankie waves his hands to capture the man's attention. Hux or Jack glances once at our group and smirks before stalking away, whistling an unfamiliar tune.

"What the fuck?" Vin glares daggers at his retreating back. "That was weird, right?"

"Very fucking weird," I agree, staring after our friend suspiciously. "Did something happen between Violet and them?"

"Not that I know of." Vin rubs at his chin in consideration. "But even if they had a fight, Hux would be buying out grocery stores of chocolate right now while Jack would write her some stupid-ass poem. Neither of them would ignore her —or us."

"Fuck, where is she?" I tear my gaze away from Hux/Jack and focus once more on the stage. Above, the final countdown begins.

Ten.

Nine.

Eight.

"Come on, baby," Vin murmurs, eyes clouding with pain. "Come on."

Seven.

Six.

Five.

"Pinkie…" I whisper.

Four.

Three.

Two.

One.

The audience roars once more as a loud buzzer resonates through the open clearing.

"And that concludes Round Two of the competition!" Mr. Pumpkin screams, his voice lost in the jubilant noise of the crowd.

"She's not dead," Vin whispers hoarsely, shaking his head rapidly. "She's not dead. I can feel that."

"Then where the fuck is she?" I ask. "Are you fucking positive she didn't make it?"

"I was the first one out." Vin's face is deathly pale, and his hands shake by his sides. "I've been standing here. Waiting. And waiting. And waiting."

"Enough!" Frankie steps forward until he's between us. "She's still alive, okay? We know that much through the mating bond." It's the first time any of us has talked so candidly about it in front of the others.

"We'll find her," I whisper resolutely. Because if some fucker decided to take my girl…he'll pay. They'll all pay. "No matter what."

"No matter what," the other men echo, steely determination etched across each of their faces.

We may be men, but we're monsters first and foremost. And us monsters? We kill those who dare to hurt what belongs to us.

We're going to get Violet back.

Or we'll die trying.

ACKNOWLEDGMENTS

This is always so tough to write! Each book takes a team, and I have the best one.

First, I would like to thank my family and author friends. This is probably getting a little redundant, but I seriously have no words to express my gratitude towards you guys. You guys are amazing.

My alphas and betas...thank you. From the bottom of my heart, thank you for all the time and effort you put into my stories. Ellen, Ash, Kelly, Rachel, Katie, Kerry, Dara, Haley, Angie, and Nina. You guys are rockstars.

Thank you to Meghan for your amazing proofreading skills and for being able to get me in last minute.

Thank you to Logan Keys for creating this amazing cover and being so incredible to work with.

Finally, I would like to thank you, the reader, for continuing to stick with me. I hope you love Violet and her mates as much as I do.

ABOUT THE AUTHOR

Katie May is a reverse harem author, a KDP All-Star winner, and an internal bestselling author. She lives in West Michigan with her family and cat. When not writing, she could be found reading a good book, listening to broadway musicals, or playing games. Join Katie's Gang to stay updated on all her releases!

2. First Dates

CO-WRITES

Afterworld Academy with Loxley Savage (Academy Fantasy Reverse Harem)

1. Dearly Departed

2. Darkness Deceives

Her Immortal Legacy with Elena Lawson (Time Travel Paranormal Reverse Harem)

1. Chasing Time

STAND-ALONES

Toxicity (Contemporary Reverse Harem)

Blindly Indicted (Prison Reverse Harem)

Not All Heroes Wear Capes (Just Dresses) (Short Comedic Reverse Harem)

Charming Devils (Bully/Revenge Reverse Harem)